MW01094958

A Lord of Snow and Greed

Greed

THE WINTER COURT SERIES

A CROWNS OF MAGIC UNIVERSE SERIES

ASHLEY MCLEO

Editing by Emily Lawrence & Owl Eye Edits

Cover art by Sanja Gombar

Interior art by Joey Kao @queen_joey on IG

Chapter art by Anna Spies of Altra Luna Art

Map by Cartographybird Maps

Ebook ISBN: 978-1-947245-90-7

Paperback ISBN: 978-1-947245-93-8

To the readers who held their breath for the answer.

MAJOR SETTLEMENTS ◎
MINOR SETTLEMENTS ◎
NOTABLE LOCATIONS ◊

MORIAL
HOUSE
ARMENIL

VIRTORIS
ISLAND

NORTH LANDS

LEIRE
HOUSE
VIRTORIS

FARVERG

THE

SHIVERING

SEA

AVALDENN

KETHOR

AALBORG
HOUSE AABERG'S
ANCESTRAL SEAT

BITRA
HOUSE RIIS

EASTERN LANDS

VANTALIA

STORMY
BAY

SOUTHLANDS

GRINDAVIK
HOUSE
ITHAMAI

ICE TOOTH
MOUNTAIN RANGE

FOREWORD

Dear reader,

At the back of the book there are two reference pages.

One details the nine kingdoms of Isila.

The other dives into the greater noble houses of Winter's Realm. If, while you're reading, you want to know more about the Sacred Eight families, that's where you will find the information.

Welcome back to Winter's Realm,

Ashley

CHAPTER 1
NEVE

The question hung in the cold night air, freezing time.

"Neve, will you marry me?"

My heart skipped a beat before taking up an unnatural staccato rhythm. Was he serious?

I stared down into Prince Vale's deep brown eyes, pools of warmth that were locked on me. He waited for my answer, one knee bent, snow falling languidly around us—a stoic picture of a prince trying to do the right thing. Trying to help one of his own. Help *me*.

I took a step back and blew out a long stream of white breath that the wind sweeping down the alley quickly whisked away. "There has to be another way."

The famed Warrior Bear of Winter's Realm didn't look crestfallen. He didn't even appear surprised. The wrongness of the moment made my stomach churn.

But Prince Vale Aaberg hadn't proposed to me for

love. We didn't have that. Just a fragile trust and simmering attraction stretched between us.

It was not enough to marry for.

The prince wished to marry his soulmate. Not for politics or wealth or status, as was usual in the royal courts. No, this male I'd underestimated in so many ways wanted only the singular fae who could match him. He wanted a love that could rip open the sky and tear the stars from the night. His mate.

As someone robbed of her dreams for so long, how could I rob him of his? Even if denying him meant my death?

From behind Vale, Lord Riis, the king's spymaster, cleared his throat. "There are no other options." Unlike Clemencia, Anna, and Sir Caelo, all of whom had also witnessed the proposal and waited for my answer, the spymaster appeared self-assured, not astonished.

"I can run." I gestured to the horses waiting at the far end of the dark, narrow alley.

Above us, murmurs clouded the air. My throat tightened, and I swallowed to clear it. How long had they been there? How many were up there, watching us? Despite my questions, I didn't look up for answers. I took heart in knowing they were at least two floors up and likely could not hear this conversation. Though they surely couldn't miss the prince down on one knee . . .

"I'll ride like the wind from Avaldenn," I added. "The king won't learn that I'm gone. Not for hours."

Though I sounded confident, a little more doubt

crept in with each word. Minutes prior, I'd staked a vampire prince. My gaze strayed to where Prince Gervais's head had rolled after Prince Vale decapitated him. The skull was disintegrating, turning to ash. His body too, leaving behind his clothing and the cloak he'd worn over his finery. Only an ancient, powerful vampire would turn to ash that fast.

Burning moon. I'd killed a royal of the Blood Court.

And that was *after* I'd escaped Frostveil Castle, where the King of Winter had publicly claimed me. So I'd killed a royal of one court and defied another, all in one night. Worst of all, I'd allowed the king's son to help me.

My confidence crumbled, and I began to tremble.

Lord Riis came to stand next to Prince Vale. His long, red mane blew in the wind, reminding me of yet another redhead who had turned my life upside down. Warden of the West, Roar Lisika. My hand slid down to my pant pocket, and I exhaled as I felt what I sought.

Against all odds, the vials containing Roar's and my blood were still there. Whole and unshattered.

Roar had betrayed me. And in a move of sheer stupidity—or perhaps terror, I wasn't sure which—he'd fled Frostveil Castle without the vial of blood that sealed our magically binding deal. The blood was his insurance, and mine, against betrayal from the other.

I was not about to let either vial out of my sight.

"Lady Neve, you might make it a respectable distance, but in the end, running is futile," Lord Riis spoke softly as he came to a stop beside Vale and me. "The news of the vampire's death is spreading." He looked up at the apartments, where people whispered about the happenings in the alley. "Take it from one who knows how fast gossip can percolate. This will move faster than you can flee."

A lump rose in my throat, and vaguely, I heard the others shuffle. I'd brought Anna, Clemencia, and Sir Caelo here tonight. My foolish plea to run and my insistence that Clemencia and Anna escape Avaldenn with me had put us all in danger. Somehow, I had to protect them.

"The king won't kill me anyway?" The words tried to freeze on my tongue, but I forced them out. Maybe if I did this, my friends could flee. But I wouldn't do so if it spelled certain death. At the very least, I wanted a chance at life. "Even if we wed?"

Lord Riis shook his head, and snowflakes drifted down from his long, red hair. "Once you and Vale are bound, you become family. King Magnus is many things, but a kinslayer is not one of them. He didn't even kill his birth father, Prince Calder Falk, and he despised that fae more than any other. Nor did he kill King Harald, Queen Revna, or any of their children during the rebellion. I believe he'd have to be desperate to be labeled as a kinslayer." The spymaster's dark brown eyes traveled between me and Vale. "Take the Aaberg name. Use Vale's reputation. His sword. That is your best chance. I promise you."

The Lord of Tongues's tone was soft but firm. And

as much as I wanted to deny the idea once more, I could see he believed what he said. Him, a male who had likely spun plots for the crown, seen many betrayals, and watched plans hatch. He believed what he said. How could someone like me dare to think I knew better?

"Neve." Prince Vale found his words.

I turned to him, trying hard to keep the tears swimming in my eyes from falling. What a mess I'd made.

"It's not ideal, not what either of us would have dreamed, but I know my father very well. You'll never leave this city alone and live for more than two days. This plan"—he took my hand, his own inked with the bear claw tattoos that signified his house—"it's the best way."

"You don't deserve this," I whispered. "You deserve what your heart wants. We barely know one another."

"What I know of you, I like and admire. My family has failed you so many times. I want to right those wrongs." A small smile curled his lips. "Plus, if I'm being honest, I could do worse." He winked.

My laugh surprised me and lifted a bit of the heaviness pressing down on my heart. Two figures joined me on each side.

Clemencia and Anna, my friends, watched me carefully. I met Anna's gaze first. Her normally upturned eyes were blue and round rather than their usual dark brown hue. All thanks to Sir Caelo's glamour. With the knight's magic, my human friend looked fae, pointy ears and all. Still, in the way she regarded me, I recognized my oldest and dearest friend.

"Do it," she said. "You have to."

"I agree with her," Clemencia whispered. She, too, was still in disguise. Blonde with yellow wings and a large nose, rather than dark brown hair, blue wings, and pert nose she'd been born with. "You won't be safe anywhere else, my lady. Not from King Magnus. Nor the Blood Court."

And nor would they. Unless I wanted my friends to die with me, I had only one choice.

I swallowed and turned back to the prince. "I will."

He arched an eyebrow. "Will what? You took so long deciding that I've already forgotten what I asked."

I rolled my eyes. "I'll marry you, Prince Vale."

"Lucky for you, Vale," Sir Caelo said, his tone light and teasing. His violet eyes, courtesy of the knight's own glamour, twinkled. "Otherwise, I would have never let you hear the end of it that a commoner denied your proposal."

The prince smirked at his friend as he rose from where he'd gone down on one knee. "We'll need to find a staret."

"Not any old staret," Lord Riis said. "You will require the *Grand Staret*. He'll be in the Tower of the Living and the Dead. That is where you'll wed— standing before the Heart Drassil. There is no greater sign of legitimacy than being wed by the most revered holy fae. Before the great northern tree."

I inhaled a sharp breath of frigid air. A Drassil tree.

6

No one else knew what had happened moments before. How the whispers of the Faetia, the souls of our fae ancestors who could live in Drassil trees, spoke to me.

Nor did anyone know I'd made a deal with those departed souls. One that had saved Anna's life—*for a price*.

What that price was, I had no idea. Nor did I regret my choice. Not even when faced with circumstances such as these.

I wanted freedom, had risked my life multiple times for it. Instead, I'd soon wed a prince and live in a castle, in proximity to King Magnus, a powerful fae who hated me.

But maybe all I had to do was stay alive long enough for Prince Vale and me to plan a better escape. Inside, hope rose like a spring well.

Yes, that was what I'd do. I'd take more time and concoct the perfect plan that would win me freedom *and* free the prince to find his soulmate. The lingering heaviness in my chest lifted. There was a way forward. But it wouldn't be done tonight.

"We should go," Prince Vale said. "Minutes lost might mean the difference between life and death. I—"

Racing hooves sounded down the street, around the corner. The prince tensed, surely thinking the same as me. We were too late. Somehow word had already gotten to the king, and he'd sent knights after me.

But then three horses appeared, all bearing riders. One with pink hair and wide blue eyes.

"There you are!" Princess Saga, the youngest Aaberg, cried out.

"Sister," the prince's voice came out strangled. "What are you doing here?"

"I saw what happened with the vampire, and Neve, and the proposal," she explained, forcing a shiver down my spine.

Princess Saga had not been present. Nor had she been among those watching from the rooftops. No, she was a seer—one of the rarest and most eerie powers a fae could have.

"And you thought you'd do what?" her brother asked.

Lord Riis answered with an approving nod to the princess. "That she'd wake Lady Sayyida and Lady Marit, and in doing so, provide valuable witnesses from greater houses. Ladies who the king wouldn't dare to kill to hide his son's marriage to a murderous commoner."

"The spider's right," Sayyida piped up from behind Saga, her inky curls blowing about wildly. Lady Marit Armenil, from the great house of the far north, nodded as if to emphasize Sayyida's words. "Now, which of you is Neve?"

Saga must have known from her vision, but she didn't tell the other two, and none of them could see through glamours. I raised my hand.

Saga dismounted her horse and her pure white fur cloak billowed behind her as she spun to rummage in her saddlebag. "Sorry we're not dressed appropriately for a wedding, Neve and Vale. But at least the bride will be."

I blinked. "Excuse me?"

Saga pulled out a gown. *My* amethyst gown. The first thing I'd made for myself. "You can't marry in that getup, now, can you? Even from here, you reek of blood." Her nose wrinkled as she gestured to my blood-spattered pants and boots. "This is still dirty from the ball, but . . . I figured it was better than nothing."

"I-I guess so," I said.

Saga placed the dress back in the saddlebag. "I'll keep it until we get there. You might get blood on it."

"Right," I replied, half amused, half nervous about what I was about to do. "So it seems we should be on our way?"

The prince, still looking thunderstruck at all that had happened as he went to his destrier, brought it over and helped me mount. The others climbed onto their own horses and when Prince Vale swung up to join me, I tensed. Then I laughed dryly at the reaction.

Back when I thought I'd be leaving Avaldenn and figuring it could do no harm, I'd given into temptation and kissed the handsome prince. Now we were about to be wed. And yet I worried about him touching me while I rode? How silly.

There were far more important matters to fret over.

As we set off through the streets, falling in line between Lord Riis at the front and Sir Caelo riding behind us, I twisted to the prince. We were close enough that if I whispered, no one else would hear over the plodding of hooves on cobblestones.

"Promise me something, Prince Vale."

He arched an eyebrow.

"If there is ever a real chance for me to escape, let me run and start a life I would have chosen. Then you can find your soulmate and marry her. That way we'll both be free."

"Are you sure?" He leaned closer, filling my nose with his tempting scent of sandalwood and the first snow of winter. "Even if you run in the distant future, you may never be truly safe without my name to protect you."

"Only time will tell that. Please, Prince Vale, promise me. I need to believe I'm not robbing you of your one true love."

A stiff nod. My request was, no doubt, going against his noble nature. "I promise."

We hadn't gone far, only three or four blocks, when Lord Riis paused and turned to take in the rest of the line. He was such a large, barrel-chested male that he commanded the attention of all. "Sir Caelo. Lady Clemencia, I have an idea and need a word."

"Anything, my lord." Sir Caelo urged his horse forward. Clemencia did the same, and the rest of us waited in a deserted street.

I didn't hear the request as the Lord of Tongues spoke to the pair in private, but once they were done, the knight and my lady-in-waiting peeled off in two different directions and disappeared.

"What was that about?" I asked warily.

"They'll return soon," Lord Riis replied and continued to ride, sure the rest of us would follow, which we did. "With additional reinforcements. And I will send someone I trust to pick up the vampire's clothing, spread his ashes to the wind, and clean up this scene. We'll leave as little trace as possible."

More people? For a moment, I was about to ask why, but as Saga rode up next to us, the question fell away. The princess looked pale.

"So it looks like you'll be sticking around?"

"Seems so."

For now, anyway.

"You'd better be good to her, Vale."

A low chuckle left the prince's lips, his body vibrating against my back with laughter. "You need not worry about me."

"No . . ." Saga replied, eyes on me. "I suppose not."

The hairs on my arms rose. She was holding something back. Had she seen more than what she reported? Or more than what the others had seen?

In her vision, had she seen me make my deal?

I swallowed, hoping that wasn't the case. I wasn't ready to talk about that. Not yet.

Perhaps never.

CHAPTER 2
NEVE

The Tower of the Living and the Dead rose above the other buildings of Avaldenn. Only Frostveil Castle loomed larger, its white-hawk-topped spires reaching for the waxing moon.

Though the name of the holy building mentioned one tower, that was inaccurate. A series of circular pillars spun out from the largest, tallest central one, like a giant spider web of interconnected buildings. It left me no question from where the complex took its name. A ten-story masterpiece of black stonework, the central tower was as dark as Frostveil Castle was white. And up close, the black stone came to life, as though the masons had splashed the smooth stones with glittering mica. A night and the stars—the very objects the starets and staretesses living inside studied and worshipped.

According to Vale, the Heart Drassil grew at the center of that imposing tower, and that was where we would wed. As we approached the gate, I leaned back so that only Vale could hear me. "Are there rules?"

"Rules?" Prince Vale echoed, his breath grazing my ear and making my neck tingle.

"For going inside."

I believed, as most did, that our magic was from the stars, gifted by angels who used celestial power to create all magical orders. Some fae, however, believed something far deeper than me. The most religious among us thought gods had been the ones to create all magical orders. That they had lived amongst the stars before dying.

A smaller faction among the religious decried that belief. The most religious fae claimed the gods weren't dead. That they were resting. And one day, they'd awaken.

No one knew for sure what would happen if they woke up, and I'd never thought too much about it. Until recently, vampires had dictated my life. Now fae lords did. I didn't need revived gods adding their opinions too.

"Just be respectful," the prince replied. "Oh, and when we stand before the Drassil, it will be barefoot. An old custom."

Considering we were in Winter's Realm, I deemed that particular old custom a silly one but said nothing as Lord Riis spoke with the guards. A moment later, the gate squealed open, allowing us access to the Tower grounds.

"Prince Vale, prepare to speak with the Grand

Staret," Lord Riis called over his shoulder as we passed through the gate.

No one spoke as we stopped at a hitching post, tied up the horses, and strode through the outermost smaller towers down a little path made of that same sparkling black stone. The snow-dusted path led to the central tower. Double doors rose before us, spanning at least two stories. On the doors, a painted moon glimmered like the heavenly body itself.

Lord Riis's massive fist came down on the wood three times, and the right-side door cracked open to reveal a wide-eyed female faerie wearing a black smock dress with gold stars circling the high neckline.

"My lord?" She stared up at the Lord of Tongues, questions in her eyes. She couldn't have been over sixteen turns and appeared to have been roused from sleep.

"I'm Lord Riis, here with Prince Vale and Princess Saga. We wish to see the Grand Staret."

The youngling blinked at the mention of Lord Riis's name, but when he mentioned the prince and princess, her eyes snapped past the Lord of Tongues and widened. Belatedly, she opened the door fully. She curtsied and as she did so, her wings rose a touch. They were shriveled, reminding me of Roar's wings. Was she another victim of the blight that Roar had told me about? She was certainly young enough to have been affected.

"Apologies, Prince Vale, Princess Saga, and Lord Riis," said the youngling. "I didn't recognize you. Only beggars come in the night. And of course, as a novice, I don't leave the Tower often, so I'm not so familiar with your faces."

Even if she frequented court daily, her confusion was understandable. Blood had frozen on Prince Vale's clothing and Saga was far paler than I'd ever seen her. I doubted I looked any better.

"I take no offense," the prince replied. His sister echoed his sentiment, and the girl's shoulders loosened before Lord Riis pressed the matter, making her tense once more.

"The Grand Staret. Where is he?"

"He's asleep, my lord."

"Wake him."

For a moment, the novice looked like she might argue, but she opened the door and allowed us inside. I spied a single chair across from the double doors. Her post for the night. A book lay atop her chair. Judging by how she had looked when she'd opened the Tower's doors to us, the book had not been exciting enough to keep her awake.

"Please, wait here while I fetch him." The novice shut the doors, latched them, and scurried off, her fast footsteps echoing as she rounded the curve of the main tower and disappeared from sight.

In here, the scent of smoke—incense—hung heavy. Like the outside, the inside of the Tower of the Living and the Dead glimmered. Artists had etched constellations into the stone hallways. Torches affixed to the walls made the constellations shimmer. I took a moment to study the one right across from the door but could not name it. Heat flushed my face. Though my lack of knowledge about the dead gods had never bothered me before, standing in such a place of grandeur and reverence, I felt like I should know such a thing.

"What if he says no?" Sayyida whispered, gray-blue eyes wide. She exchanged a look with Marit, who chewed on her bottom lip and twirled a lock of fire-red hair between her fingers. "What then?"

"He won't," Prince Vale shot back, his tone defensive.

Sayyida snorted, but as a knock came at the main door, she opted to stay quiet and open it. Powerful floral scents wafted inside, preceding three females, two faeries and one nymph, who scurried inside with Clemencia at their heels.

"The rest were, um, occupied," Clemencia said, catching Lord Riis's eye.

"These three will do. Lella, Dagny, and Minthe, how would you like to leave the hustle and bustle of the city? You could move to a smaller brothel in a nicer town?"

My confusion cleared. These were whores in Lord Riis's employ.

"With better pay," the faerie with cascading red curls and a large bosom stepped forward, speaking for the lot.

"How does triple your earnings sound?" Lord Riis offered.

"I want a madame position and pay, my lord."

Lord Riis let out an amused chuckle. "I should have seen that coming. Yes, Lella, I can make that happen. With one condition."

"What's that, my lord?" Lella asked, full eyebrows arched and eyes glinting.

"Tell as many people as you can what you're about to witness. Do it as fast as you can. While you travel, and after you settle into your new home."

"All we need to do is gossip?" Lella's lips tilted up until she looked like a particularly satisfied cat. "I guess it's good that pretty young thing"—she nodded to Clemencia—"pulled the three of us from the Warm-snap Tavern, isn't it, my lord?"

Lord Riis's lips curled up in amusement. "I have to say, she chose well. Minthe? Dagny? Are you amenable to moving your contracts, spreading the word, and, of course, earning more coin?"

Minthe and Dagny agreed, and by the time those short-winded negotiations finished, Sir Caelo had arrived with two other figures in tow.

In the time since we'd last seen him, the knight had removed his glamour. His hair was short and black once again, and his bright blue eyes were alert as he brought the newcomers inside.

One, a reedy youngling of sixteen or seventeen, looked familiar. I was studying him, trying to place those warm gold eyes, when Prince Vale went to the boy.

"Filip, this is dangerous. I'm not sure Lord Balik would want you here."

Filip puffed out his chest. "My father would be honored for me to attend your wedding."

"You won't convince him, Vale," Sir Caelo countered. "He overheard me speaking with Sir Qildor." Caelo inclined his head toward the other newcomer, a strapping knight with violet eyes and donning the heavy gold cloak of the Clawsguard. I'd seen him before too. He was the knight guarding Prince Vale's door the evening I'd stumbled into the prince's room through a hidden door. He'd seen me leave and remained quiet on Prince Vale's orders.

"I tried to warn Filip off already," Caelo continued, "but he claimed that as your squire, he should be here."

The prince's squire.

That struck a chord, and a memory of the day I'd met Prince Vale resurfaced. The squire had trailed the prince, a sword in hand. And he looked even more familiar because I'd met this boy's sisters.

Filip was a Balik, from the noble house of the southlands, brother to Eireann and Baenna. I'd played nuchi with those ladies my first night in Avaldenn. Their brother looked much like them: the same honey-colored eyes and golden-brown hair, the same rich, terra-cotta skin tone.

"I don't *need* to convince him." Prince Vale's voice took on a harder tone, to which the boy's eyes widened.

"You wouldn't order me away, my prince. I'm your squire, meant to be with you when you're in danger." The youngling paused, wisdom in his honey-gold eyes. "And surely, you are now. From what I heard Sir Caelo say, you will need as many reputable witnesses as possible."

"And some less fine reputations too." Lella sniggered.

Prince Vale looked like he was about to argue, but before he could get a word out, heavy, rushed footsteps sounded. Others were coming. Lord Riis placed his hand on the prince.

"They're here. It's done, and the lad is right, anyhow. He should stay and bear witness." The prince glowered at the high lord but didn't argue, for at that moment, a tall and girthy figure rounded the curve of the building.

Despite the late hour, the Grand Staret wore robes spangled with starlight that seemed to shift colors from dark purple, to navy, to black, and even to silver as he moved. Though I was an expert on fabrics, I couldn't say why the robes looked the way they did, but I was sure of one thing. They were meant to impress, to intimidate, to show power.

And they did. They also gave the ancient, wrinkled faerie an air of confidence that many didn't have when faced with a stone-faced Prince Vale. This holy fae, however, marched right up to the prince and scowled.

"Highness, why in all the nine kingdoms are you storming into my tower so late?" His teal eyes dipped to the blood on the prince's jacket before straying to the three whores. "And with such mixed company?"

So a bloodied prince was fine, but three whores was pushing it. I wasn't sure I liked this holy fae.

"Staret Arkyn, I apologize for my state. However, I have need of you."

The Grand Staret arched an eyebrow.

"This is Lady Neve." Prince Vale took my hand.

He eyed me, my true visage still beneath the glamour. "Ah, Lord Roar's"—he cleared his throat—"*acquaintance.*"

My neck warmed. Had the high lords and ladies and holy fae of the city ever taken me seriously?

"Yes, well, that engagement is over," Prince Vale replied. "And Lady Neve and I have decided to marry. You will perform the ceremony in front of the Heart Drassil. And you will do it right now."

Grand Staret Arkyn paled. "You wish to marry her. Here." He craned his neck to peer around Prince Vale. "Without the king and queen present?"

"Correct."

"I see." Grand Staret Arkyn let out a long, disapproving hum. "Quite unusual circumstances, my prince. I must say, very, very unusual. Might I ask why you are so rushed? Surely, it's not because this, *ahem*, lady, has been defiled?"

I scoffed. Defiled my round rear end. This fae was behind the times if he thought anyone in this room was concerned about me, or *anyone*, being a virgin when they wed.

"My reasons for wishing to wed Lady Neve are none of your concern, Staret Arkyn." Prince Vale's hand strayed to his sheathed sword. "And I'll have you know that should you choose not to oblige my request; you will meet a rather quick and dire end by *Skelda*." He patted the hilt.

I nearly choked.

"I'd regret it," the prince continued, "but not as much as not getting what I want. Her. Bound to me on this night. So make your choice, your holiness."

Staret Arkyn's chin lifted in defiance. "This tower is one of the three pillars of the Kingdom of Winter. Among the people, I am as influential as your king father. You wouldn't dare."

The prince leaned closer, blade glinting in the torchlight. "Wouldn't I, Arkyn?"

Like a flash of lightning in a storm, his sword was out. I shuffled back, as did most of the others. Only Sir Caelo and Filip Balik remained where they'd been, unsurprised by the prince's move. The prince pressed the tip of his sword against the thin skin of the Grand Staret's wrinkled neck.

"Should you perish," the prince continued, "your successor would automatically elevate to your position, would she not? I'm sure that, so soon after coming into power, she would be more than willing to perform the ceremony tonight."

My heart was thundering. Would we spill more blood tonight? If Prince Vale made good on his threat, what would the repercussions be? Was it worth it to pile them onto the charges we'd soon face?

Stars, he was doing this for me. Because I'd made him promise to see me to safety, and Prince Vale didn't break his promises. If he killed the Grand Staret, that holy blood would be on my hands.

My throat tightened as if the blade were pressed to my own skin. I couldn't handle that. On a night of impossible and dangerous events, it was too much.

I was about to step forward, to tell the prince that we'd find another, that it wasn't worth risking, when Grand Staret Arkyn spoke.

"I'll do it." The old faerie scowled. "But should the king ask what took place this night, he *will* be told all."

Prince Vale sheathed his sword. "I'd expect no less, Staret Arkyn. Now, let us proceed to the Heart Drassil."

The Grand Staret spun, his robes twirling out around him with the motion, and stomped down the hall. We followed, everyone silent, in shock at what the prince had done.

As I walked along the curve of the tower, I tried to shake the lingering fear from my body. In moments, I'd be getting married, binding myself to the House of Aaberg for as long as it took for the prince to get me out of this kingdom. Where I'd go after, where I could really find safety from the royal hands of Winter, I had no idea.

All that mattered was this night and the days after. That was when we'd learn if this insane plan would truly work. If we had a real chance.

The Grand Staret stopped before a set of double doors. "Touch nothing in this room."

Was he taking us through his private chambers? No, surely the holiest of fae would have a bedroom at the top of the tower. What, then, was he so concerned about?

My answer came as I stepped through the shining black double doors and found myself in a library. My fingers itched, always unable to resist books, and in this grand, mysterious place, so many shelves waited to be plundered.

As we walked deeper into the library, the ceiling opened. Because it followed the curve of the tower, the room was in the shape of a crescent moon, like the scar over my right temple. Half of the space was open air and above models of constellations glittered, suspended in the air by magic. Against the wall we'd entered by, however, were stairs leading up to other floors. Ten in total.

I squinted, trying to count the shelves on each floor. There had to be at least a hundred shelves on each floor. Moon above, how many books did this place hold?

"There are more underground." Lord Riis came up next to me, and I snapped my mouth shut. "Aside from the House of Wisdom and the Royal Library, there is none larger in all the kingdom."

My lips parted as a sense of wonder spread through me. "It's lovely."

"Most of these books are dedicated to the stars and the history of our kind." Lord Riis peered down at me. "I wonder what you might learn here, Lady Neve?"

The question was so odd that it ripped me from my wonder, but only for a moment because we'd reached a door at the far end of the library and the Grand Staret turned.

"The Heart Drassil is outside. Should anyone feel unworthy, I would suggest they remain here." His eyes grazed over the whores, who glowered at the old judgmental fae.

"Neve, you still need to change." Saga shuffled closer, past Anna and Clemencia, who had been following close behind me the whole way. "Can she change in the stacks, Grand Staret? No one is here, right?"

The holy fae frowned. "Be quick. We shall prepare." He waved the others outside, but I stopped Sir Caelo.

"Before I do this, can you remove my glamour?"

He arched an eyebrow. "Sure. Would you like for me to do yours too?" The knight looked at Anna and Clemencia, but I answered for them.

"Only me. They might need the glamour still."

I did not say that when this was done, when I was under Prince Vale's protection, I planned to ask Lord Riis for a rather large favor.

No one disagreed, and Sir Caelo got to work, removing the layers of magic on my face and body, stripping it off until his hands dropped, and he took a step back. "Done."

"Perfect," Saga piped up. "Now she needs to clean up and change, so shoo."

He opened the door, allowing in a stiff winter breeze before he slipped outside. Only Saga, Anna, and Clemencia remained with me.

Anna's eyes shone with tears.

"What's wrong?" I asked, all too aware I'd brought her back from the dead not even an hour ago. Was she in pain?

"I'm fine. Never imagined I'd see this day for you."

I hadn't either. Not really.

Back in the Blood Court, I never imagined that I'd marry. I hadn't wanted to. There, slaves only remained married for as long as their masters kept both partners. Though I had to admit that, in my dreams, I sometimes imagined marrying someone, my soulmate, but that's all it was. A dream.

And while I was attracted to Prince Vale, and my body definitely wanted him, I couldn't say with certainty that I'd choose him under less dire circumstances. I barely knew the male, though admittedly, I liked what I knew about him.

"It's not an ideal wedding," I exhaled and looked to the princess. "No offense."

"None taken. I love my brother but . . . No, this isn't ideal. I think, though, that it's right." She paused; her lips pursed as if she wanted to say something more but she did not.

Stars, I wanted to ask her what she'd seen in that vision. But before I could, the princess extended my dress to me.

"What do you say we get you cleaned up and ready for your wedding, Neve?"

CHAPTER 3

VALE

I'd never imagined that my wedding day would turn out like this.

Since I was young, I'd been told that my marriage would be for an alliance, but I'd always hoped that one day, I'd wed my soulmate. While Lady Neve was the most attractive female I'd ever laid eyes upon, I found it impossible to believe that we were soulmates.

Wouldn't I have felt our bond already?

It doesn't matter, I told myself and rolled my shoulders back. I stood in a courtyard, barefoot, upon the roots of the Heart Drassil, the living, breathing soul of the Tower.

Lady Neve might not be my soulmate, if such a person even existed for me, but she was a fae of Winter's Realm. A lady in need. A person I'd promised to protect, and one who had been through far too much in her life. She was one of my people, and I'd shield her from my father's rage.

29

If a prince didn't have honor, he had nothing.

I did not regret my choice.

"You should lose the sword." Caelo approached and held out his hand, gloved to keep out the biting wind and lightly falling snow. "I'll watch over *Skelda*."

I unbuckled my belt and passed him the lot, belt, sheath, and blade. My best friend took it before meeting my eyes again.

"You're sure?"

"I am," I said.

Caelo patted the blade. "I know you inherited this blade, but the name always fit you, you know?"

In Old High Fae, *Skelda* meant protector. Centuries ago, back when my sword had been named, more fae would have recognized the translation. The fae of Winter's Realm rarely spoke Old High Fae. And when they did, it was usually in the House of Wisdom or the very tower I stood inside.

"Thank you." I clapped my friend on the shoulder. "You'll stand with me?"

"We all will." He referred to my closest friends, soldiers who were of the same mind when it came to the fate of Winter's Realm. The cabal, as my sister liked to call us.

I gazed beyond Caelo and found Lady Sayyida and Marit Armenil speaking with Sir Qildor. He, along with Caelo, myself, and four others, was part of the cabal. Filip Balik, my squire and the second youngest son and heir to the Balik great house, watched me earnestly, set apart from the group. He would join the cabal in an instant if I'd let him. But at sixteen turns, Filip was too young. The age of adulthood in my kingdom was seventeen, but the cabal only allowed members who had reached twenty turns.

After all, the cabal wasn't a rebel organization, but we did things that my father might not approve of. Like now, my fellow members would surely do anything to protect me from the choice I'd made. One that would send my father into a rage.

The door leading into the Tower's library opened and all those in the circular courtyard turned. When I followed suit, my breath caught.

Neve hovered on the threshold of the courtyard, unglamoured and as stunning as ever.

No vampire blood streaked her face. Her long, silvery white tresses were pulled back and styled in an elegant bun, with wisps of hair falling around her face. Saga had traded cloaks with Neve so that the bride's was clean. Beneath the white fur cloak, Neve wore the same gown she'd worn to the Courting Festival's opening ball.

The amethyst gown showed off her ample curves to perfection. It was the same dress she'd worn when we'd danced. When we'd almost kissed—right in front of my father and Warden Roar.

Heat raked through my body. The dance we'd shared at the ball, the potential simmering between us had been so hot that the rest of the fae, the music, the dancing, *everything*, had faded away. That night, despite its disastrous end, would be forever imprinted into me.

"Are you sure about this, Prince Vale?" Grand Staret Arkyn asked. He'd been standing alone on the other side of the courtyard, a silent act of rebellion against the rites I forced him to perform.

"I'm certain. Perform the noble ceremony."

The staret lifted a brow. "Not the love match?"

From his point of view, it was an odd choice. I was forcing him to wed us. Surely, he believed it was because we were in love.

The staret could keep thinking that.

"They're more traditional for my house," I said, which was true. My parents had taken noble vows, as had my grandparents on both sides and their parents before them. When one could not lie, arranged marriages required different vows than a marriage born of love.

"Very well, my prince."

Neve approached, and my nostrils flared as I caught her scent, one I couldn't quite describe, but it reminded me of waking deep in the forest on a crisp morning but with a hint of something warmer and more complex. What was that?

Vanilla. Smokey vanilla—from the campfire. I landed on the warm note as she stopped to stand before me.

"You had the glamour removed," I said, trying to compose the primal part of myself that wanted to scoop Neve up into my arms and kiss her. To claim her, even if this was all for show. She wasn't mine, no matter how my body reacted to her. We barely knew one another.

"I wouldn't want to marry looking like someone

else." She cleared her throat and unease crossed her delicate features. "Do you mind?"

Mind? Stars and Fates no.

"I prefer you like this," I admitted.

Her shoulders loosened. "Ready?"

"As ever." I took her hand and guided her so that we stood facing one another at the base of the Drassil tree. I turned to take in our witnesses and finally landed on the staret. "Begin."

Grand Staret Arkyn needed no book. He had memorized every ritual his profession performed in this kingdom, and some from other fae kingdoms too. The only item he required, he pulled from his robe.

Neve blinked but said nothing as the Royal Staret laid the soft sash patterned with silver and gold stars across our left wrists. He left the ends hanging.

"We gather this night, beneath the stars and the moon and in Winter's cold embrace, to witness the binding of two houses," the staret began, his tone as cool as the snow falling on my cheeks.

I looked at Neve, searching for hesitation in her eyes, but there was none. Not even a flicker. Instead, a quiet strength radiated from the female.

"A union such as this is sacred," Staret Arkyn continued, "so I ask, do you two enter this union intending to protect and honor one another?"

"That is my intention," I said without hesitation, handing her the words.

"That is my intention," she echoed, violet eyes still locked with mine.

The Grand Staret wound the cloth around our hands once. My tattoos, the bear claws I'd gotten inked on my hands when I reached adulthood, disappeared beneath the starry fabric. "And do you promise to put the well-being of your union and whatever family you might create first?"

"I promise," I said.

The staret looked at Neve.

"I promise," she said, not a drop of tremor in her voice.

"Do you, Prince Vale, give your name to this female?"

"I do," I said.

"And do you, Lady Neve, accept the name Aaberg as your own?"

"I do," she replied without hesitation.

The Grand Staret wrapped the sash once more. He then tucked the ends in, binding us. "Place your free hands on the Heart Drassil."

Neve blinked but recovered her composure quickly, and together we shifted to face the tree and settled our palms on the bark.

Above, the eggplant-hued leaves danced. It wasn't unusual. I was of royal blood and from time to time had been called to siphon magic into Drassil trees. Every royal, and most nobles of a certain magical level, did this. It stabilized the magic of the kingdom.

Or it had, for a while.

I scrubbed that thought from my mind, not about to go down that path during such a poignant moment in my life. No sooner had I focused than a light glowed from beneath Neve's palm, and she seemed to be . . . listening?

I shot her a sidelong glance, wanting to know what she heard. In answer, she shifted her hand toward mine and touched me.

Whispers filled my ears, indiscernible at first, but slowly they became clearer. Insistent even.

We bless this union.

I sucked in a breath. This moment in the ceremony was symbolic, a second given to the Faetia to approve or deny a marriage, though it had been many turns since anyone reported them speaking up in one way or another. Not since King Harald Falk and Queen Revna Falk wed.

Not until now anyway.

Neve's fingers trembled, and I could tell she was about to pull back, to take her hand off the tree. I wrapped my smallest finger around hers, hoping that would halt her. Hoping to hear more. Long seconds passed that felt like a full turn, and finally, she exhaled. She stayed.

"By the power vested in me by the Crown and the Tower of the Living and Dead, and with the witnesses of the Faetia, the stars, the Fates, and the dead gods above, I pronounce you husband and wife," Staret Arkyn rolled into the finish. "You may kiss the bride."

We removed our hands, and she looked up at me, shock gleaming in those brilliant gem-toned eyes.

Slowly, my free hand cupped her face, and I vanquished the distance between us.

We'd kissed before, but this was different. Symbolic.

And yet, my lips still burned when they touched hers, as she accepted the kiss and met me. If we'd been alone, I'd have pulled her in more tightly; I'd have tasted her with my tongue.

Instead, I mastered myself, and we broke apart.

The Grand Staret turned to the witnesses. "Prince Vale Aaberg and his wife, Lady Neve Aaberg. May you live long and—"

A flash of light came from behind, halting the staret before he could finish. He spun and his eyes widened.

The Heart Drassil was glowing a brilliant silver.

"By the dead gods," Grand Staret Arkyn whispered. "I've never seen . . ." he trailed off as the glow faded to nothing, leaving behind a regular Drassil tree. Then, without another word, without so much as looking at us even, the staret stormed out of the courtyard.

Neve swallowed. "What did that mean?"

"I-I'm not sure," I replied. "I think it might have had something to do with what we heard." I paused. "You did hear the whispers?"

"I did," she replied softly, confusion in her tone.

At the edge of the courtyard, someone shuffled. I tore my gaze from her to find that our witnesses stared at us, open-mouthed. Waiting.

"Come, let us join the others," I said. "Perhaps one of them will enlighten us." Lord Riis, the eldest and most worldly of all of us, most likely.

"Welcome to the family." Among our witnesses, Saga recovered first and engulfed my new wife in a hug. "Prepare for madness."

"I'm ready." Neve smiled as she hugged my sister back.

Once they broke apart, Saga met my gaze. "So? What was that flash about?"

"We were hoping one of you might answer that," I ventured.

Blank faces stared back at us. Not even Lord Riis appeared to have an idea.

"Well, the Grand Staret knew," I said. "I'll request he explain. Tomorrow."

Our group looked exhausted, and I had little doubt that the Grand Staret was already deep in the maze of the Tower.

"Sounds good to me." Saga stretched her arms wide as if already envisioning her bed. "Back home?"

Neve held up a finger. "I need to speak with Lord Riis. And I believe Prince Vale and I will need to sneak in without an entourage around us, anyway?" She eyed me.

"We'll make an official appearance tomorrow," I agreed.

Yet another thing to plan. We'd try to break the news in a way that meant as few people were around my father as possible.

My sister nodded. "We'll go back now. It'll draw less attention."

Everyone offered their congratulations and the high

ladies left, then the whores of the Warmsnap Tavern shuffled to the side of the courtyard to wait for Lord Riis. The knights and Filip stood a fair distance away too, huddled against the wind with Anna and Clemencia, awaiting my instructions.

Neve turned to the high lord and waved him over. "Lord Riis, I have a favor to ask."

He gave a knowing smile. "Might it have to do with your lady-in-waiting and your friend?"

"Observant as ever," Neve said, unsurprised. "I ask that you take them away from the city. Hide them. I have the prince's name, but they do not."

The pain that rippled across her face at the admission was undeniable. Surely, she'd rather the ladies remain here. For her sake, because she would need friends. I would too. But my new wife was cunning and had seen my father's cruelty firsthand.

Clemencia and the human, Anna, needed to leave. To hide.

"I know where they'll be safe," Lord Riis replied and turned an eye to me. "Normally, I'd have one of my sons escort such important figures, but unfortunately, they must stay in Avaldenn."

"The bleeding Courting Festival," I muttered.

The whole thing was a ruse my father and brother had devised. One that was not panning out as any of us expected.

"Precisely," Lord Riis replied. "And I'm already spreading my own guard thin by sending escorts with my employees for their safety." He waved toward the whores. "Might I ask to borrow a Clawsguard to escort Lady Neve's friends?"

As a member of the royal family, I was qualified to dispatch any of the elite knights of the Clawsguard. And while I didn't like the idea of either of them leaving my side right now, Neve wouldn't rest unless her friends were safe.

"Caelo, come here, please." I motioned my dearest friend forward.

He joined us, a question in his eyes.

"I need you to escort Lady Clemencia and Lady Anna—"

"I'm not a lady," Anna piped up. The human was eavesdropping. She had better hearing than I expected too. "Just Anna."

I smirked. "Anna, then. To safety. Wherever Lord Riis tells you to go." I arched an eyebrow at my friend, hoping he'd read into it correctly.

Escort them. Make sure they're safe. Do not leave them if you sense even the slightest hint of danger.

"Of course, Vale." Caelo bowed his head. "I'll confer with Lord Riis, and we'll set out tonight."

I turned to my new wife. "Say your goodbyes. Then we return to Frostveil."

She broke away, leaving me with Lord Riis and Caelo.

"A piece of advice, my prince?" Lord Riis whispered.

"You seem to be full of it tonight, Lord Riis."

"This night?" His eyes twinkled. "Who taught you to hold your sword?"

I snorted out a laugh. "The toy?"

He'd given me a wooden sword when I was three turns of age, taught me to hold it. Caelo had been so jealous that a moon later Lord Riis had gifted him one too.

"The idea is the same."

The sword master I'd trained with as a youngling had said as much too.

"You have your moments of wisdom, Uncle." I offered the familial term I hadn't used since I was younger as a sign of gratitude.

"Learn what that flash was. If not by Staret Arkyn, then seek the House of Wisdom." He exhaled and his breath turned white in the cold. "I believe you have a close contact there?"

"I do," I said, not at all surprised that he knew.

Riis's eldest son, Luccan, was part of my cabal. As was the scholar the high lord was hinting about.

"I'll figure it out," I said.

"And keep her safe," he added.

I sensed that he wished to say more, but Lord Riis merely bowed and left me alone, standing in the snow and waiting for my new wife.

CHAPTER 4
NEVE

As we approached the palace, Prince Vale leaned forward, pressing his chest into my back. Tingles erupted along my arms, but as I wore Saga's borrowed cloak, he didn't notice.

Thank the stars he didn't. It was confusing being married to someone I was attracted to but possessed no true claim to. Better to keep my reactions to myself.

"Pull that hood down as far as it will go to cover your face," he said, his deep voice barely above a whisper. "Face down too."

I pulled the large hood over my brow to obscure my face. Frost had formed on the white fur, but it melted as it touched my forehead and cheeks. I wiped the moisture away and made sure each strand of my hair remained tucked inside the hood.

Upon leaving the Tower of the Living and the Dead, we'd discussed how we'd enter the palace. The prince, thanks to a youth spent with the mischievous

Sir Caelo, knew of at least two weaknesses in the castle's defenses. Weaknesses the pair had used to sneak out at night and indulge at seedy taverns. One had to be strong and stealthy to access them, which we both were, but in the end, we decided on another route.

We would not sneak onto Frostveil's grounds. No, we'd simply ride right in.

Guards had seen Prince Vale leaving the castle, so there was no point in him hiding who he was, and I would pose as a high-end whore. Apparently, it wasn't unheard of for the fae of the night to visit the castle. And though my new husband claimed he'd never brought one home, we supposed that there was a first time for everything. Even when others believed I was waiting in his bed, little more than a strumpet moving between the Warden of the West and the Prince of Winter's Realm like the shifting tides in the harbor.

Not that I cared what others thought. What mattered was that with the prince escorting me, the guards wouldn't question our entry. The Warrior Bear was trusted, and it was unlikely that word of the evening's events had already reached the ears of the gate guards. And certainly not those who mattered most in the palace. We hoped that we had a few hours before the king heard of our marriage.

"Lo!" one of two guards at the gate yelled as we approached the portcullis. Not only could he not see my face, but a thick blanket of snow spun around us now. Since I'd killed the vampire prince, it had only fallen thicker and faster. The winds off the Shivering Sea had only grown more biting too.

"Who's that?" the guard called out.

"Prince Vale and a friend," the prince replied, voice booming.

The guards didn't reply, not until we stood close enough to smell the tea they kept on hand to warm their bones and keep them awake through the night watch. I imagined them peering through the snow, wishing they were inside. Even the heartiest fae of winter could catch a chill in gales such as these.

"Ah, so it is you, my prince." The guard who had spoken raised his brows and exchanged an impressed look with the other. No doubt they would while away the hours until the sun rose, gossiping about the lucky prince, feasting on two females in one night. "Let me lift the gate."

The gate rose and ice cracked off and fell to the ground. Once we passed through, the prince behind me urged the horse forward. "Try to stay warm tonight."

"We're doing our best. Have *fun* tonight, my prince." There was a definite suggestion to his tone, and the other guard sniggered.

Prince Vale said nothing as we rode to the stables and stopped. "Stay on Carpus's back. Head down."

He dismounted, then disappeared inside.

I leaned closer to the horse and patted his neck. The creature was the largest I'd ever ridden, and from what I could tell, perfectly trained. The way Vale said the horse's name hinted that it might be his personal steed.

"Carpus, huh?" I whispered, my hand running down his velvet mane. "I'm Neve. Thanks for the lift."

Vale reappeared suddenly, making me jump and straighten. His eyebrow arched in amusement. "Having a nice chat?"

"Making sure he knows his service is appreciated."

"It always is. This destrier has gotten me out of more scraps than I can count." Vale held out a hand to help me dismount. "No one is there."

"Not a surprise, really. It has to be the hour of the aura owl," I muttered, suddenly aware of the exhaustion seeping into my bones. I hadn't allowed myself to feel it earlier, but now it roared forth, unwilling to be dismissed for a moment longer.

A brief reprieve from the frigid wind was all too short as we stabled the prince's enormous horse.

"Stay close." Prince Vale took me by the hand.

He led me into the frigid night air once again. My hood was still up, my face to the ground, so I trusted him as we raced closer to the castle. When we stopped, I peeked.

"No door?" Our discussion had been about getting onto the palace grounds, not inside. I'd assumed we'd use a servants' entrance or the like to avoid running into the king, queen, or Prince Rhistel, my new family members.

The queen I was undecided on, but the heir and the king . . . Burning moon, one couldn't ask for worse family members. Thank the stars for Saga.

"We're going in the way you came out." The prince

wrapped his powerful arms around me. Again, those chills enveloped me, but I hid the pleasure from my face. "I'll fly us up."

"Are you su—*aaahh!*" The wind stole my words as we launched into the air.

"Quiet," he murmured as his sheer black wings beat, taking us higher and higher.

I marveled at his strength, his control. I could fly and had needed to do so to sneak out of the palace, but it hadn't been seamless. Far from it.

He lifted us upward, never straying from the shadow of the palace, and when we reached his suite, hovering before his floor-to-ceiling windows, he shifted my weight into one arm, as if my strong, curvy body weighed practically nothing. With his other hand, Prince Vale pushed open the window I'd left unlatched when I escaped, and we soared inside.

Gently, he set me down, lifted my hood, and allowed it to fall down my back. "We made it without incident."

"Thank goodness." I began unclasping the fur cloak.

I'd assumed that once he deposited me inside, he'd go back and enter the way he'd left—through the door. Instead, the prince turned and shut the large window behind him.

"Won't your guard wonder where you are?" I asked. "You left out the door so I could pretend to bathe, remember?"

He shrugged. "There's no reason to put on a show for my guard. Tomorrow, my father will hear what happened . . ." he trailed off, his tone brittle. "I only wanted to get us inside so that we might sleep peacefully for one night."

Right. Sleep.

My eyes wandered to the bed, to the messy sheets, where hours ago the prince and I had kissed. I could still see places where I'd gripped the sheets.

At the memory of our passionate kiss, my breath shortened. It had been nothing like the one we'd shared at our wedding. No, when I'd leapt at Prince Vale, it had been under the assumption that after this night, I'd never see him again. That one kiss couldn't hurt.

One kiss that felt like fire burning in my veins. At the memory, my neck warmed.

He seemed to sense my unease because the prince took a step away. "Speaking of bathing. Did you get all the vampire blood off you?"

I shuddered. Saga, Anna, and Clemencia had done their best to clean me up for the wedding, but the sensation of vampire blood on my skin clung to me.

"A bath would be welcome."

He ventured out of his bedchambers, down the short entry hall that exited into the wider castle and disappeared into his private bath. A squeaking of knobs met my ears. A few plops of something being tossed into the tub, and moments later, Prince Vale appeared. He had taken off his sword belt while he was back there and undoubtedly thrown it in that miniature armory he kept so close.

"I put the plug in, adjusted the temperature, and

tossed in oil balls. They're meant to relax you and it's still hot. The water elementals are working overtime with so many nobles staying at the castle. They've had to heat ungodly amounts of water daily."

"Thank you, my prince."

He cleared his throat. "About my title. Between us, that should only be used in the most formal situations. Most of the time, you can call me Vale. We are married, after all."

I swallowed. Roar had made a similar request and that had gone over *so well*.

But the prince had a point, just like Roar. It would look odd for me to be so formal with my husband all the time.

"I can do that," I said finally.

He nodded, pleased, and then walked to the bed and sat on it. The creaking of the wood beneath the mattress was too much for me. Brought back too many visions. I had to be out with it.

"What about the bed?" I blurted.

"What about it?" The corners of Vale's lips twitched as he patted the mattress in a way that told me he knew exactly what he was doing.

My hands landed on my hips. "*Hilarious.* Do you relish seeing me squirm?"

"Only when I believe you're thinking of us." Vale licked his lips. "In my bed."

Stars alive!

"Well, I wasn't," I lied. "I plan to sleep on the settee." I gestured to the furniture in front of his hearth as if a wild gesticulation could hide the discomfort in my tone.

"And what would we say tomorrow if my father, or anyone, for that matter, bursts in to find my new wife asleep on the settee?" Vale shook his head. "Oh, no, we'll be sharing my bed tonight, Neve. We'll be sharing it every night that you're here."

At my name, his voice took on a growlier tone. I didn't even think he realized he was doing it, but my body responded, sending a shot of heat through me.

"We're not having sex tonight," I said, then realized that while the fae were not known to be prudish, Vale was royal. This might be the kind of court where the bedsheets were checked to see that a royal marriage was consummated. "No one will know, right?"

Vale let out a full belly laugh, the first in hours, and it loosened his entire stance. Mine too, somehow. I exhaled, a tiny amount of tension seeping from my shoulders.

"Do you mean are they going to come looking for virgin blood?" He snorted. "If they did, they wouldn't find it for half of the newlyweds in this kingdom. Plus, everyone thinks you were with Warden Roar and that I was bedding you after the feast, anyway. They won't question it."

In all my concern over the hours to come, I'd forgotten about our little cover story. Maybe I should have been concerned about my reputation, but at Vale's words, only relief flooded me. Let the court think what they would about my appetite in the bedchambers.

"However." He leaned forward, placing his elbows on his knees. "Before you bathe, I have one question for you."

I cocked my head.

"About the whispers when we touched the tree . . . did you hear it bless our union?"

My spine straightened. "I did."

"It was odd enough to hear something, let alone that." He let out a low hum.

"Why? They don't speak to people?"

"I've touched Drassil trees, even that one, many times. It's part of our royal duties, but that has never happened."

My lips parted. "Not to you? Or anyone?"

"If it's happened to anyone in my family, they've never mentioned it." He paused. "But you've heard something before today. Haven't you?"

My throat tightened, and I was tempted to lie. But why? Vale and I were in this together, our situation was even more perilous than the one Roar and I had devised. I needed to be open with him.

"I have. In a little city called Traliska, Roar blessed the tree. I wanted to touch it too, almost felt called to do so. I heard whispers almost the moment my palm grazed the bark. Do you know what that means?"

Perhaps it had something to do with my magic? I didn't know what sort of power ran through my veins and would not still for days to come.

"I don't. Were they distinct? Like when we heard the tree say the Faetia blessed our union?"

Him saying the words made my heart race. And not from attraction.

"Not distinct," I admitted. "The ones that spoke to us in the Heart Drassil sounded serious."

"They did." He exhaled. "I suppose that'll be another thing to research at the House of Wisdom."

"And where is that?"

"Close to the castle. Have you heard much about it?"

"No."

"I think you'll like it. It's a place where the best scholars in the kingdom live and learn," Vale replied, surprising me with how he could deduce such a thing about me after so little time together. "I have a close friend who studies there. He can help us."

"Is he part of your *cabal*?" I teased.

Vale gave a playful smirk. "He is. In time, you'll meet them all."

The faint tinkling of a bell came from the bathroom.

"But for now, you'd better get in the tub before it overflows," Vale added. "It's close."

I pulled my borrowed cloak tight around my body. Before the ceremony, the princess had gathered up the pants and tunic I'd been wearing during my failed escape. Seeing as the clothing wasn't mine, I didn't care that she'd brought them back with her. But I had made sure to grab the vials of blood out of my trouser pocket before they left my sight. They were now tucked in the cloak, safe and sound. Where would I keep them? Vale didn't know about them, and I had no intention of telling him. Of telling anyone.

"Would you mind giving me a place to store my dress?" When another issue presented itself, I added, "and supplying a sleep shirt? Or something?"

"The top drawer is yours." Vale patted his dresser, a wide wooden thing that was large enough to hold all the clothing I'd ever owned. "And while you bathe, I'll send a servant to find your sleeping gowns and a few dresses to choose from for tomorrow. Servants can deliver the rest of your things later."

"Thank you, Vale." I paused, marveling at how well he thought things through. He had a militant mind. One trained to expect any and all sorts of issues or attacks. "For everything."

My gratitude seemed so insufficient for what he'd done—defied his father's orders. Married a commoner and one who had killed a vampire royal, at that.

"You're welcome. We're in this together now, Neve."

I nodded and when he said nothing more, I went to soak in his copper tub. To cleanse the horrors of the night from my body. To try to relax.

Because tomorrow would bring another day, and with it, the wrath of the King of Winter.

CHAPTER 5

VALE

The sun had risen. Out my window, snow drifted to the ground. Down in the castle yard, I heard wheels rolling, horses neighing, and distant shouts—all signs of fae starting their day. And at my side, Neve slept, her long, white hair cascading around her, and her silver wings tucked close to her back.

My wife.

Moon above, I couldn't get over it.

Not even after I'd watched her sleep for hours.

I hadn't slept a wink, but I was relieved that she had managed to find rest. My wife would need her strength today. For when my father called, his fury would be great.

This wasn't the first time I'd gone against the king's wishes. What youngling did *everything* their parents wished?

Though this time was my most severe transgression. Not only had Father claimed Neve for his own, and he'd done it in front of other lords and ladies, but I had wed without his knowledge or blessing. Without concern about how it would make our family look. And, most importantly, without an alliance in mind because with royals, that's what a marriage was.

The female in my bed, the one with her silvery-white hair splayed out around her face so prettily, could offer me no alliance. Quite the opposite.

Once the Blood Kingdom heard what had happened, they'd demand retribution. As she had taken our name, my family would have to protect Neve, or the vampires might believe our house, our kingdom, fractured. A risky proposition. At the first whiff of weakness in our realm, the Blood might attack to gain territory—to take fae slaves. They had before, many centuries ago.

The threat of them doing so again remained alive and well. It was why we had no vampire representative in our court, nor a fae in theirs, though housing diplomats from other kingdoms was a practice in most kingdoms. Whenever a fae had to deal with vampires or went to the Blood Court, they did so heavily armed. If not, their lives were in their hands.

So my family would have to appease the vampires. How, I wasn't certain, but Neve should not have to pay for what had happened. She'd been through too much in her short life for me to allow it. She should have never been a blood slave to begin with.

She is a fae of Winter's Realm. We should have protected her, but we'd failed. No more.

Neve stirred, pulling me from my musings. I turned, facing forward so she wouldn't see me watching her when she woke, though the sharp intake of breath told me that my presence had still shocked her.

"You're awake," she whispered, voice raspy with sleep. Stars, her voice made me want to reach out and touch her. "Has anything happened?"

"Not yet. Any minute now, though, I expect it will."

She rubbed her eyes and sat up. Last night, servants delivered her nightgown and a few items of clothing from Warden Roar's old suite. The night gown, though it was hers, was a touch too small, and the top of her full breasts was on full display. As though I were a youngling, my cock twitched.

"I should get dressed." She pulled aside the covers, releasing a scent that was quintessentially hers from where the covers had trapped it.

I inhaled, savoring her scent. "The bathroom is all yours."

"I don't need to bathe, so I'll be fast." She chose a dress and disappeared down the hall, shutting the door behind her. My shoulders slumped.

Our marriage wasn't one born of love, but honor. Yet, the day after we wed, despite all the danger coming our way, I felt even more attracted to Neve than before. The taste of her few kisses had not been enough, but I wasn't sure she'd ever want more.

To take my mind off things, I dropped to the floor.

Exercise always helped me find my center, so I lay on the ground, placed my hands flat, and worked through one hundred pushups. I reached number ninety-one when a knock came at the door. Mid plank, I froze.

The summons. Quick as the gales that often rolled off the Shivering Sea, I rose and went to the door, expecting to find a messenger waiting.

Instead, my mother stood there, her blue eyes wide, her body trembling. Behind her, the Clawsguard on duty wore an expression of terror. No one, not even the strongest knights of the realm, liked to be around Queen Inga when she was in a fit. She was too power- ful, her magic too strong.

"Vale." Mother's voice was dry, raspy, *desperate*. "Tell me it isn't true. You did not wed her."

So it began.

"I did, Mother. If you—"

"How could you be so foolish!" Her hand snapped out, and I stiffened, knowing what was coming. The moment her fingers touched my jaw, a pressure built in my skull as my mother ripped through my memories of the night before.

I winced as pain shot through me. Burning moon, she had never taken so little care when examining my memories.

She jerked back as if I'd slapped her. "Your sister. Lord Riis . . . When he learns . . ."

"Father will do nothing to Saga," I said, not needing her to specify who 'he' was. Out of all his children, my father doted on my sister the most. She was his pride and joy. "And Riis should be protected by his status. As will Lady Sayyida, Lady Marit, and Filip."

I did not mention Neve's friends, the whores, and certainly not Caelo or Qildor, both commonborn fae who had risen to knighthood. Their lack of a noble birth house put them at risk.

My mother shook her head. "Vale, he's furious. I'm not sure noble standing will dull his—"

The bathroom door opened, and Neve stepped out, only to freeze in the hallway. Though many of her dresses the servants retrieved were the Lisika colors of crimson and gold, she hadn't chosen one of those. Today, she wore a green dress, something simple and elegant. Normally, Mother would have complimented Neve on how lovely she looked. Today, however, the queen's face grew red.

"*You!* How dare you entrap my son!"

A snarl burst from my lips. "She did no such thing, Mother. She—"

"I saw what happened, Vale. *Saw it all.* If she hadn't run, none of this would have happened."

"You're right, Majesty." Neve stomped closer, fury in her violet eyes. "Had I stayed, had I not killed a vampire prince, and had your son not offered his protection, things would be different. For one, it would be someone else coming here this morning. Retrieving me to throw me in the king's harem!" Her face had turned a livid shade of red. "So excuse me for running, but I was in a situation that you, with all your privilege and protection, could never comprehend."

"You think I've never had to make a difficult choice?" The queen's voice dipped to a growl.

Though many would have cowered, my new wife did not back down. "I won't say that, but I will not apologize for my other choices. Not to you, Majesty. Not to *anyone*. I did what I needed to survive."

The air crackled with unseen lightning, and for a moment, I was certain Mother was about to order the Clawsguard standing outside my door to drag Neve to the dungeon. That, for the first time, I'd have to defend my wife from my own blood.

But then Mother's shoulders fell. She swallowed thickly. "You would do well to smother that attitude when you meet my lord husband. Come. He has called for you both."

"And he sent you?" I asked.

"To confirm what we'd been told."

My jaw tightened. Would Father allow us to defend ourselves? Or would he hear last night's events only from my mother's lips?

"Fine," I spat. "Neve?"

"Let me get my boots." She dashed deeper into my suite, emerging again a moment later, ready.

Mother sneered. "I hope you're both truly ready for what's coming. Follow me."

I extended my hand to Neve. She took it without so much as blinking. We fell into step behind my mother, united.

I'd been a part of many teams in the past. Like when I'd played various sports as a youngling and trained my magic alongside other young males and females born into the Sacred Eight. My time in the royal army came later, and those armed brothers and sisters were second in my heart only to those in my cabal.

But this partnership felt different. No one I'd sided with had ever elicited the bodily reactions that Neve did. Never had I needed to go against my family to protect those on my other teams.

We twisted and turned through Frostveil Palace, my home for as long as I could remember, and it didn't take long until I figured out where we were going. The throne room. Father didn't use the throne room often. Only when he wanted to impress. To awe.

I'd counted on this interrogation being fairly private, but perhaps I'd been a fool. Nearly every great lord and lady in the kingdom were in Avaldenn for the Courting Festival. Would they all be there?

It didn't take long for me to learn that it was far worse than I had imagined. Not only was my entire family present in the magnificent white room, but like the night of the Courting Festival's opening ball, the throne room was filled with members of the Sacred Eight. Even more surprising, lesser jarls and their lady wives were present too, along with far more members of the Clawsguard than usual, and the Grand Staret.

I swallowed and shot Neve a sidelong glance. But she wasn't watching me. Nor had she seemed to notice others watching *us*. Rather, her eyes stared resolutely ahead at the thrones.

When I turned to face my father, I spotted yet another person I hadn't expected to be present.

Sir Qildor stood off to the side, at the base of the steps to the throne. He was not in uniform, but rather, he looked as though he'd been pulled from his bed. My stomach twisted. Not on active duty, so why was he so close to the thrones? And why were other Clawsguards behind him, hands on the hilts of their swords?

"*Here.*" Father's voice boomed through the cavernous throne room. The few people who had not noticed our entrance were paying attention now. It wasn't lost on me that today Father wore the Crown of Winter. He didn't wear it often and usually only in the most official of capacities. Some believed that was because Father was not pretentious, but I knew the truth. The crown he *really* wanted, the Frør Crown, had been lost since the Falk reign.

With Mother three paces ahead, we walked through the center of the crowd. Upon reaching the thrones, Mother climbed the steps, joining my family. I stopped and stared up into my father's bright blue eyes.

"What happened?" Father asked my mother as she sat on her high-backed golden throne. The royal blue cushions took her weight, and she leaned back, seemingly unbothered.

"They have wed. In the eyes and by the hands of the Grand Staret, with many witnesses present."

"Who?"

Mother's gaze shifted to Saga. "Our daughter, the ladies Sayyida Virtoris and Marit Armenil. Sir Caelo,

Sir Qildor, and Squire Filip Balik. I believe that is more than enough?"

My lips parted. She had not mentioned Lord Riis. Nor Clemencia and Anna.

Then again, Clemencia had remained glamoured. Anna had too, but Mother had never known the human in the first place—just like she did not know the whores from the Warmsnap Tavern.

But Lord Riis . . . was Mother omitting him because they were childhood friends?

Against my better judgment, I twisted and took in the room. Though my scan was quick, I saw no sign of the Lord of Tongues's giant stature or dark red hair that glinted copper in the right light. The other Sacred Eight families were present. Where was he?

"Look at me, Vale," Father growled.

I snapped back to the moment to face him, and Neve squeezed my hand.

"And before?" the king asked. "The vampire?"

Mother's chin lifted. "Lady Neve killed the prince. Our daughter must have foreseen it before it happened and gone to help. Then she got pulled into the wedding."

"And our son and his friends were trying to help the devious Lady Neve," Father growled. "Against *my command*." Frost crept along the arms of his throne.

Though I couldn't see them, I felt the crowd pull back. Rhistel and Saga mirrored the motion, leaning away from our father. Only Mother remained unfazed.

"Then you married the whore," Father continued,

as the frost climbed the high back of the throne, turning the gold to white. "Have you got anything to add, Vale?"

My shoulders rolled back. "Only that she's no whore, but my lady wife. A female who now bears your name, Father. A Princess of House Aaberg and family."

"Bleeding skies!" Father shot up. "If you think I'll allow this marriage to stand, Vale, you're mistaken. You—"

"It *must* stand." The Grand Staret stepped forward, stopping at my side but with a good three paces between us.

"What in the stars?" Neve whispered.

Indeed. Why was the very fae who had not wished to perform our ceremony sticking up for us? And interrupting the king at that?

"What did you say, Grand Staret?" Father's pale face had turned red, and snow of his own creation swirled at his feet. He didn't use his winter magic often, but sometimes, when he was angry, Father couldn't control the magic born of this very land. That never boded well for those around him.

"As I've already told you," Grand Staret Arkyn's replied, voice level as he was a fae of power in his own right, "I did not want to perform the ceremony, my king. However, there is something else I did not mention before. A sign."

Father's moon-pale fingers curled around the frost-covered arms of his throne. "Of what, pray tell?"

"At the end, there was a sign from the Faetia.

Perhaps a message from the stars and the dead gods themselves."

"Which was?" Father growled.

"That their marriage was approved. Fated. Holy." The staret paused. "Even a king should not be able to undo the will of the Faetia—perhaps even that of the dead gods."

Blood pounded in my ears. Had that been what the bright light meant? An outward symbol to others of what the Faetia whispered to us? The staret above all others would be able to tell us.

"As I am the highest staret in this kingdom," Staret Arkyn continued, "I will not allow any under me to go against the will of the dead gods, either."

"Under you?" Father pushed up from the throne.

"In holy matters—yes."

A collective sharp intake of breath filled the silence the staret's words left. For a moment, I thought Father would scream, would roar, would threaten the staret.

Instead, he stomped down the stairs to stand face-to-face with the holy fae.

"*You dare defy me?*" Each word hissed out of the king as if it pained him.

"I will not go against the will of the stars."

"I can replace you, Staret Arkyn."

"Might I remind you, my king, that my position is held until death."

"Easily arranged."

The old fae lifted his chin. "Not without great issue to the Crown. The Tower of the Living and the Dead holds great sway, and the nobles are not the only ones capable of enacting change in a kingdom."

Change.

What a polite way to phrase what he really meant: *rebellion*. Should my father go against what Grand Staret Arkyn deemed the will of the dead gods, the holy faction of our kingdom would start an uprising.

The Grand Staret could manage it too. The Crown ruled, and most cowered before it, but in the hearts of the commonfae, the Tower of the Living and the Dead and the House of Wisdom held significant sway. A king might not survive going up against the Tower. Especially if any of the more devoted houses like House Balik or House Armenil and their people sided with the Tower.

It would not be the first time the greater houses were split. They'd divided during my father's rebellion too, and that had only been decades ago. We were already dealing with the Falk loyalists. Not very successfully, at that.

If the way the air grew colder and ice particles formed around us was any sign, my father knew that too. He was weighing his options.

Finally, he regained control of his magic and the air warmed again. He twisted and pinned his icy gaze on me.

"Keep your whore wife, but do not think your actions will go unpunished. There's a death to answer for. The Laurents will *demand* blood. And they are not the only ones."

My hand slid up Neve's arm to her shoulder, and I shifted her behind me. "Remember my promise at the feast, Father."

Touch her and lose your hands.

"I will make good on that," I added, my voice dipping low.

Father's lips spread in a cold smile that promised malice. "Whore and prince killer aside, you're right. She is family now, bears our name, perhaps will even bear my future line. Might already, for we all know that she spread her legs for you last night."

Gasps flew from the crowd, but I kept watching him. He had something up his sleeve.

"I wouldn't risk harming my blood, son." He twisted, snapping his long, white fingers. "Bring Sir Qildor here. And find Sir Caelo."

My stomach fell as soldiers pushed my friend forward, still in his sleep clothes, and shoved him onto all fours. His violet eyes met mine for a moment before he gave a cry of pain. Ice manacles formed around his wrists and ankles, so thick that even a male as strong as Qildor could not break them.

"The whip," Father commanded and held out a hand.

The weapon appeared too fast, and the king's fist closed around it, his knuckles white with the pressure. Frost formed on the weapon, which then turned to sharp ice shards at consistent intervals.

"Father, no!"

He glowered at me. "The price for your actions."

"I will take the lashings."

"You will not."

Before I could speak another word, an icy grip formed around my leather boots. Ice shackles froze them, *and me*, to the ground. Neve gave a little whine, and I twisted to see her smaller boots were also blue with frost and circles of ice ringed her ankles.

"But *he* will, my son." Father raised the weapon, then brought it down.

The whip cracked, and a moan rang through the hall as Sir Qildor gripped the ground. At the first strike, a tear had formed in his sheer violet wings, making my throat tighten.

I called air magic, my strongest power, and circulated air, as warm as a son of Winter could make it, around my feet. But it did nothing. No surprise there. Father wasn't only the king in title. He possessed the strongest winter magic in the realm. Switching tack, I bent at the waist, hoping to force my feet out of my rigid boots, but Neve's grip tightened on me.

"He'll freeze you up to your knees," she whispered. "Then he'll go longer on Sir Qildor." The column of her elegant neck bobbed as she swallowed. "Harder."

How was it she knew my father so well already? Or did she just know the cruelty of kings that well?

I had no idea, but my wife was right. One wrong move, and I'd be stopped, either by ice or by one of the many guards at the king's command. My father might even kill my friend. I stood still as the whip cracked twice, three times, four. I stopped counting at ten.

The iron tang of blood hung heavy in the air and my friend's moans, which had started out as loud and gut-wrenching, grew faint. Weak. Still, Neve gripped me tight, and I tried to cling to the belief that he'd stop, that he'd see sense. But when the skin of Qildor's back was little more than ribbons punctured by ice spikes and multiple tears riddled his wings, my refrain vanished.

I'd opened my mouth to speak when Mother rose from her throne. "I believe that is enough, my king."

Father froze and turned slowly, his glacial gaze so intense that anyone else would have run.

Not Mother. Full of grace, she descended the steps and placed a hand on her husband's shoulders. "He's a Clawsguard—an elite soldier. They take so long to train. Don't waste that talent."

"You're right. I will move on to Sir Caelo," Father growled. "Where is he?"

Silence hung in the air, heavy and thick and suffocating.

"We cannot find him, my king," said Lars, an older Clawsguard. He was among my father's most trusted. "No one has seen him since last night. He was supposed to report to rounds this morning but did not show. He's not in his room either."

Snow swirled viciously around the king again. "When he's found, bring him to me. He, too, will pay for bearing witness to my son's idiocy. For not stopping it and protecting Vale from following the whims of his cock."

I began to protest when Father turned his ice-blue

gaze on me. "As for you, go to the docks. Tell the vampire's ship what happened and to leave my port. We will send diplomats to their court later." Father released the magic holding my feet in place and stormed out of the throne room.

CHAPTER 6
NEVE

S taring down at Sir Qildor, at the shredded skin on his back, the tears in his wings, and the blood sprayed across the white stone ground, I wanted to die.

He'd endured this because of *me*.

The worst thing was, neither Vale nor I could have stopped it. My ankles still stung from the king's cold ice shackles, and that was indication enough. But even if we'd been free to move, it would have been fruitless to try to stop King Magnus.

Down to my marrow, I recognized mad power. I had seen that same glint in many masters' eyes.

Had either Vale or I tried to stop the king, things would have only gotten worse.

"Qildor." Vale went to his friend the moment the king disappeared from the throne room, dropped to one knee, and placed a gentle hand on his friend's arm. "I am so sorry. Let me help you."

Qildor didn't reply. Perhaps he couldn't. As Prince Rhistel appeared in front of me a moment later, I lost that train of thought.

The heir to Winter's Realm sneered down at me, as tall as his brother, and with the dark hair, wings, and eyes, though that was where the similarities ended. "I suppose congratulations are in order. You almost snared a warden, only to entrap a far larger, albeit dumber, prize."

My jaw tightened as the heir continued.

"Father might not have killed you, dear sister, but I'd watch my back if I were you." His voice dipped into a whisper as he pressed his black wings down against his back. "Vampire assassins will find their way into Avaldenn. Perhaps even inside the white walls of Frostveil."

My throat tightened. Stars. I hadn't even thought of that.

"A pity. I had hoped to sample you for myself once you were in the harem." Apparently unable to help himself, Rhistel's dark brown eyes dipped to my lips. "Enjoy your time in our family, Princess Neve. Enjoy all that the royal house can offer you, *while you still can.*"

He marched through the crowds of nobles, all pointedly not looking at Qildor. Behind the heir, the queen followed, waving a hand to dismiss people along the way. Like a fast-moving tide, footsteps rushed out of the throne room.

My fists clenched. Why had none of them helped? Where was the outrage?

My narrowed eyes scanned the exiting crowd, looking for the reaction I sought. I found it, but only in a few faces.

I took heart that many of them were familiar. Sayyida and her older brother Vidar stood in place, their tanned faces pale. Marit was exiting the throne room, an older male's arm wrapped around her shoulder to guide her, but she was also wiping her eyes, as though she'd been crying for Sir Qildor's fate. Filip Balik, Vale's young squire, had, in fact, vomited. The many members of House Balik, all with that golden-brown Balik complexion, helped the younger member of their house, though one, a male who appeared to be around thirty turns, watched us with hawk-like intensity.

"Neve," a familiar voice came from behind, soft and shaky. "Are you all right?"

I twisted to find Saga descending the steps that led up to the thrones, unshed tears in her eyes. I swallowed.

"My father . . . he . . . stars, I'm so sorry." The princess's teeth bit into her bottom lip as her gaze drifted to Qildor, then back to me. "I anticipated his anger, but I didn't think this would happen."

Like Vale, Saga saw her father differently than I did. They claimed he hadn't always been so hard, so cold, so cruel. Though both understood the king was far from perfect, I'd gathered they remembered and clung to a kinder version of him.

"He chose Qildor because he knows Vale is his friend." I understood the machinations of the king because I'd spent so long trying not to garner the attention of those in power, like him. "It hurt Vale more this way."

"True," Saga breathed. "We need to get Sir Qildor to the healers." She waved over a male fae wearing a gold cloak clasped with a bear claw. "Sir Yaggril, help my brother transport Sir Qildor." Her dainty hands clapped for attention, not that she needed to do so. Everyone who remained in the throne room was watching us. "Someone else, get a stretcher! Now!"

Two guards who'd been by the doors raced out of the room.

"We'll need more help." The moment the words left Vale's lips; four others appeared: Vidar and Sayyida Virtoris, and Filip Balik, along with the older Balik male I'd noticed standing with the family. He was brown of skin and gold of eye, with lustrous honey-brown hair and wings. A cloak of rich, shimmering gold cascaded from his shoulders and if that wasn't enough gold, the male wore a gold hoop nose ring, three gold rings on each hand, and two impressive gold cuffs over each of his ears that resembled a ram's horns.

Rams. The animal of House Balik. And so much gold—a primary house color of the same family, alongside hunter green and black.

"Filip," Vale started, "you shouldn't be here."

It was true. The young faerie appeared to be barely holding it together. But at his prince's words, Filip's chin lifted. "I'm staying and helping."

The gilded lord shifted his attention to me. "I'm

Sian of House Balik. I suspect you and I will become more familiar over the next few days."

I had no idea what that meant, but it didn't matter. "Lady Neve."

"*Princess* Neve of *House Aaberg*," Sian corrected. "Use what powers you've been given. If you are to survive this, you will need to squeeze every drop of life from that fruit."

I nodded, somewhat stunned by his forwardness. Once the stretcher arrived, Saga's Clawsguard, Sian, Filip, and Vale helped raise Sir Qildor off the floor.

It wasn't easy. Even the tiniest of motions sent Sir Qildor into great pain, but once he was on the stretcher, his guttural moans lessened.

"We'll be at the healer's sanctuary soon, my friend," Vale murmured and then met my eyes, his own filled with anguish. "Clear the way for us, ladies."

I shivered at the command in his voice, honed from many turns of leading fae on battlefields. Despite being distraught, Vale fell back on his training. Though the circumstances were dire, I would be lying if that didn't heat my blood.

"On it." Sayyida positioned herself in front of the stretcher. Intending to use my body to protect the stretcher, I took the right side next to Vale, and Saga took the left.

In the corridors, we passed hundreds of fae, but none met our eyes. None dared to look down at the brutalized knight.

Anger burned inside me. This was how powerful,

horrible people got away with things. No one looked, no one dared, because deep in their hearts, they knew Sir Qildor's fate might have been their own.

After what felt like an age, we reached the healers' wing, a quiet part of the palace. Or at least, it was today.

Bursts of sage and vinegar filled my nose as I held the door open so that the males could shuffle the stretcher inside. A step into the sanctuary, Vale called for a Master Healer. Before I crossed the threshold, however, Saga caught my arm.

"Can I speak with you?"

I stopped and cocked my head. "Sure. What's wrong? Other than the obvious." I gestured into the sanctuary, noticing for the first time the insignia by the door. An eight-spoked wheel with four stars laid atop in the shape of the goddess of healing's constellation. I wondered what that meant.

"I haven't gotten to talk to you yet." She cleared her throat. "About what I saw."

My spine straightened. I'd not expected this, but if anything was a welcome distraction from what had happened to Sir Qildor, this was it.

I shut the door, leaving us alone. "I'm yours."

The princess swallowed. "Well, keep in mind that I don't have full control over my seer powers yet. I'm better with winter magic, particularly using wind. But my seeing powers come and go as they please, and I'm not great at deciphering what I see. Sometimes it's symbolic, not real truth, and I—"

"Saga." I laid a hand on her shoulder. "Whatever you saw worried you. Please, tell me."

"Obviously, I saw a vision of your fight with the vampire and everything that happened there, but I heard what he said to you too." She swallowed loudly. "About *owning you*."

My hand dropped from her shoulder. I'd been so worried about what I'd done, the deal I'd made with the Faetia to save Anna's life, and how others would react to the killing of a vampire prince, that I hadn't stopped to consider my past.

"Is it true?" the princess murmured. "You were a blood slave?"

A pregnant pause filled the air, tinged with the lingering copper scent from Sir Qildor's blood. I could lie to her, but why would I? In the short time I'd known her, Saga had shown me great kindness. I considered her a friend and felt we could become even closer. But not if I continued to lie to her, not if I told her that part of what she saw was incorrect.

So I exhaled and explained. "I was a blood slave, have been for most of my life. I escaped, but not before killing a vampire. One connected to the royal house. Roar took me in, and we made a deal so he could avoid your father matching him."

Saga's eyes widened. "It wasn't real?"

She meant my relationship with Roar.

"No. I thought we had a friendship, but I was wrong."

Saga's eyes dropped to the ground. "I'm so sorry,

Neve. You must think us all so silly. So flippant and wasteful and—"

"I don't think that about you, Saga," I assured her. "Since the moment I arrived here, you've been so kind to me. But please, don't tell anyone about my past?"

I did not add the part about the deal I'd made with the Faetia. Had she heard that too?

"I won't. And I haven't told Sayyida and Marit. I only told them enough to get them out of bed and on to horses so we could find you and make sure everyone was alive." She swallowed. "That I hadn't seen it all wrong. That's happened before, and I . . . I had to be sure."

"Thank you. And I must know," I prodded. "What else did you see?"

Saga looked like she wanted to apologize again, but instead, she cleared her throat and rolled her shoulders back. "Nothing more from last night. But there *was* a flash of another time too. In a place I've never seen. It confused me at first because it didn't fit and then I worked out that I was seeing a different vision on the back of the first." Her gaze shifted into the sanctuary again before she continued; her usually bright blue eyes somehow darker than normal. "It was of you and Vale. Both of you were covered in blood and somewhere dark. So dark, Neve."

Probably not the port then. Vale hadn't asked me to go to the vampire ship with him, but I planned to. He was in this mess because of me.

"Roar was there," Saga added. "He looked like he'd

struck you verbally, but I don't know what he said. All I know is that you looked shocked. And furious." She let out a long breath, squeezing her eyes shut for a moment as if to push out the memory of what she'd seen. "I'm telling you so that you can do your best to stay out of that situation. There was so much blood and my brother was there and I-I can't lose him."

My throat tightened, but somehow, I nodded reassuringly. "I'll be on the lookout for signs that might indicate your vision is coming true."

"Thank you," Saga replied, her tone a little stronger, as though she felt better by telling me what she had seen. "I think I'm going to go speak with Mother. Try to calm her, if that's even possible. Perhaps I can win you her alliance."

The memory of the queen's face and her accusation in Vale's room rang through my mind loud and clear. I doubted Saga could perform such magic, but it was worth a shot. "I'd appreciate that."

She went on her way, leaving me alone to ponder the vision. A dark place where we were covered in blood?

My hand drifted to my dress pocket, where I sometimes kept the vial containing Roar's blood, only to find it empty. Right. After servants had delivered my personal effects last night, I'd hidden both vials in a drawer that Vale cleaned out. I hadn't thought to grab them when the queen arrived and pulled us from Vale's suite. The blood vials, my insurance against any deceit on Roar's part, were safe in the prince's rooms.

Safe. What a novel concept.

The door to the healer's sanctuary opened. Out came Vale and the others, all pale and damp-faced from the dash through the palace.

"What did they say?" I asked. "Will he heal quickly?"

Or at all? That possibility made my stomach swoop.

"He's in the best hands," Vale replied, his voice low and drenched with pain. "But it will be at least two weeks before he can resume any sort of normal life. A couple more for his wings to heal all the way."

I shuddered, knowing what it was like to have mutilated wings. At least the rods that had been in my wings were uniform, the surrounding membrane not torn. Poor Sir Qildor's injuries were far, far worse.

Vale noticed my reaction and gave a sad nod. "My father drove the whip in hard and deep and it was coated in his magic, which the healers will have a hard time extracting." Vale shook his head, eyebrows knitting together. "He's nearly as powerful as he is unreasonable."

"Careful with your words." Sian came closer, rustling his honey-brown wings as he moved. "You never know who's listening."

"Especially now that you're a pariah," Sayyida added, tucking in wings that matched her eyes to better fit into the circle. "Or at least as much of one as a prince can be." She looked around. "Where'd Saga go?"

"To help her mother," I replied.

Though she tried to hide it, Sayyida looked a little disappointed. "When are you going to the ports, Vale? I can go put people in place to make sure you're as safe as possible. Your father won't offer help."

Vidar's eyes widened. "You'll not be going alone, sister. I'll join you. Who knows what might break out once Vale delivers the news?"

"Neither of you has to do that," Vale replied.

"I don't let my friends run into peril like that without aid," Vidar shot back.

"Neither do I." Sayyida nodded at me.

Vale shook his head at her gesture. "Neve isn't coming. She—"

"I am," I cut him off. "You're in this because of me. I won't let you run off alone to tell a ship full of vampires that their prince is dead."

"Because you'll protect me?" He smirked, and though the implication was obnoxious, my stomach gave a little flutter.

"I'll do my best."

"You're not trained." He paused and then added, "Which we will be remedying soon."

Sayyida gave a chuckle. "Maybe not formally trained, but Saga said that she saw *Neve* kill the vampire. She's not defenseless, oh great Warrior Bear." She pumped her eyebrows to goad him.

"Thank you." I winked at her. "And there's nothing you can do to change my mind, Vale. I understand how dangerous vampires can be."

The others wrinkled their brows at that. Among

those who remained, only Vale knew my secret, but I didn't elaborate. "I'm coming. You won't be stopping me."

For a moment, he looked like he'd argue further, but when no one came to his aid, when no one tried to convince me it was a bad idea, he sighed. "Fine. Vidar and Sayyida, ready sailors at the docks in case things turn sour."

"We're heading to the docks now," Vidar said and strode off, his sister a half step behind him.

Vale turned to Sian and Filip. Both Balik males had been watching the conversation with quiet thoughtfulness.

"I'm coming," Filip said before Vale had a chance to deny the youngling. "I'm your squire. That's what I'm here for."

"And another warrior would not be amiss," Sian added.

"I was going to ask if you'd help scour the castle for Clawsguards." Vale rolled his eyes at his squire. "And if you insist on coming, wear something more appropriate to a fight. You too, old friend." He inclined his head at Sian's flamboyant attire.

"Too much?" Sian grinned, and it transformed him from stoically handsome to devastatingly charming.

"Gold won't protect you from fangs like steel and fighting leathers." Vale chuckled dryly. "Not even that much of it."

"House colors, my friend. I can't help it if the royal house doesn't embrace theirs as we Baliks do." He wiggled his fingers, each sporting a shiny gold ring that gleamed against his skin.

Vale shook his head in amusement. "Meet at the gates in an hour?"

"We'll see you then." Sian clapped a hand over Filip's shoulder and the pair left.

Alone with my husband, Vale turned to me. I expected him to be upset that I'd forced my way into this dangerous outing. Instead, he met my gaze with a steely one of his own.

"And you will need trousers and as many stakes as I can strap onto your body."

CHAPTER 7
VALE

I strode down the bustling streets of Avaldenn, Neve to my right. At each of our sides were Sian and Filip, dressed in fighting leathers embellished with impractical but impressive gold-plated steel on the chest, back, and shoulders. Their wings, both honey-brown, were vanished, though I wasn't sure if that was because they wished to keep them secret from the vampire sailors or to better protect their wings. As added protection, a contingent of twelve armed Clawsguards surrounded us.

Sayyida and Vidar would have had plenty of time to rouse sailors to be on the lookout for trouble. And yet, I worried.

Not for me. Nor Sian or the Virtoris siblings, or even for lanky Filip, who had been undergoing magical growth spurts more often lately. No, my concerns were with Neve. I'd urged her to wear leathers for protection. That protection was hidden beneath a thick royal blue cloak. She was also armed with two daggers and six stakes, two of them ash. Though I doubted there was another royal vampire in the kingdom to use the ash wood stakes on, but one couldn't be too careful.

I shot my wife a sidelong glance. Was it enough? If she was among the fallen, it would mean that all we'd done was for nothing. I wished for her to stay safe within the castle walls, but she'd been so bleeding insistent on coming, and truly, I couldn't deny her. Prince Gervais Laurent was dead at her hands. Her wish to be present when we told Gervais's ship to leave was well within her rights.

Perhaps the ship would adhere to the code for diplomatic vessels and leave peacefully. Perhaps I would have nothing to worry about.

I wasn't holding my breath.

"It snowed more last night." A hint of a wobble touched Neve's tone, the first indication that she might be nervous. "After we slept, I mean."

I didn't bother telling her that I hadn't slept a wink. The city of Avaldenn was used to snow and great frigid gales of wind coming in off the Shivering Sea, but she was right. It had snowed quite a lot.

In the narrower side streets, fae were still either shoveling or using their magic to move the snow to the sides. Fae had been likely working on it since the small hours.

"It only stopped right before the king called everyone to the throne room," Sian said, an unimpressed expression on his face. "It was an odd storm.

Only lasted about five hours but some are saying this is the most snowfall the city has received in that short a time."

"Are there storm clouds on the horizon?" I asked, intrigued.

"None," one of the Clawsguards replied. Two others echoed his words.

We were nine days from the tenth moon. Early for the most intense winter storms to begin. Usually, I paid little attention to the weather. However, with Caelo on the run and the distinct possibility that my wife might need to escape the city in the coming weeks, that had changed.

I didn't trust my father when he said he wouldn't harm Neve. Perhaps he wouldn't today, or tomorrow, or even a turn from now. But one day, he would unleash his wrath. King Magnus did not allow slights to go unpunished.

My father hadn't always been cold and cruel and unpredictable. Growing up, I'd idolized him. He'd always loved his children and treated us well, but as I turned from a youngling to a grown fae, I began seeing his flaws. Like how he flaunted his harem and whores around Mother. And then there was his insatiable lust for power.

In the weeks since I'd returned from fighting orc tribes and given him vital information on the Hallow of our kingdom, he'd been a fae possessed. He desired the Ice Scepter. The item had the power to turn the tides of winter and possibly stop the blight, a mysterious illness that had plagued our lands for two decades, from continuing to affect fae lives. For Father though, the Hallow had another meaning: it gave him the legitimacy he craved. Unfortunately, so far, we had no leads.

"Look alive, Vale," Sian said gruffly as we turned onto the street that funneled down to the harbor.

I straightened as the muscles of my face fell into a cold expression that I knew struck fear in the hearts of my opponents.

Minutes later, salt filled my nostrils, along with the reek of docks and sweat. For the moment, the winds were down, though that might change in an instant.

Amidst the bobbing *karves*, fishing boats, and the largest ships belonging to the Royal Nava or House Virtoris, the vampire vessel was easy to find. It gleamed against the gray sky, large and ostentatious, with a black sail bearing a crimson serpent poised to strike. I spotted a chandelier glittering on the top deck.

Fae loved luxury, no one could deny that, but vampires took decadence and indulgence to a whole new level.

"Are Sayyida and her brother ready?" Neve whispered.

I cast a glance about and caught sailors watching us. Each armed with their typical rust-covered daggers, and, more atypical for sailors, a sword. One female caught my eye and touched her heart. Yes, they were watching. Waiting for trouble.

I nodded back, pleased the Virtoris siblings had

prepared the sailors and armed them, likely with weapons from one of House Virtoris's many ships.

"They are," I said. "Sayyida and Vidar will be near the Laurent vessel. Are you ready?"

"I-I am," she exhaled. "Stay by me?"

She turned her large eyes up to me, and despite myself and the danger we were walking into, I found myself momentarily captivated.

Blinking, I shook the clouds from my mind. They had no place here. Not when so much was on the line. "Don't leave my side."

I swore a little of the tension in her shoulders loosened. I didn't know how she trusted me when most of my family despised her, but she did. Saga must have spoken well of me.

Wood creaked beneath our feet as our entourage strode down the long dock leading out to where the Laurent ship bobbed in deeper waters. Awaiting our arrival were two vampires, dressed in Laurent crimson and black.

"Sian, you do the introductions," I murmured.

The eldest of High Lord Balik's many children swaggered forward, breaking through the front line of Clawsguards as we reached the ship.

"Prince Vale and Princess Neve are here to speak with your captain," Sian announced.

The vampires bowed, though every line in their taut bodies hinted that they did not wish to do so. When they rose, the taller and paler of the pair wrinkled his nose. "Why the visit, Prince of Winter?"

"That is for your captain to hear," Sian shot back. "This is a diplomatic ship, no? Therefore, a prince, or any high lord or lady for that matter, has the right to step aboard and speak with those in charge."

"*Our* prince is at your castle, though," the vampire replied. "Why not speak with him?"

My jaw tightened. I'd wondered if the vampires had already heard of Prince Gervais's death. But no, the gossip had not yet reached his ship. I supposed it wasn't a surprise. What commonfae would want to tell a vampire that their prince was dead? Only one with a violent death wish.

Sian glared. "Again, you speak above your station. Now, are you going to allow us up?"

The pair exchanged a long, pointed glance until the one who had remained silent shrugged. "Go on then."

I took Neve's hand as our company strode up the gangplank two-by-two. At the top, a dozen interested faces stared back at us. Most of them were stone-cold and eerily still, vampiric faces, but there were the humans present too, and I recognized the moment Neve noticed them because she stiffened.

She hadn't thought about the blood slaves aboard. For that matter, neither had I. My focus had been on her. Keeping her safe. Despite all my precautions to arm Neve and warn her of the violence we might find aboard, I'd failed to consider the basics of vampire culture.

Like any ship bound for a long journey, they brought their food with them.

"Come," I whispered, and she fell back into step, back into her performance of someone who had never been a blood slave.

The Winter Court had slaves too, though far fewer than vampires because we no longer actively sought humans to serve us. Those at Frostveil Palace had either been there since the Cruel King's reign or been born to a mother who was also a slave.

The only other way for a human to become a slave was for them to slip through a portal into the Realm of Isila and eat fae food. Once our food passed their lips, the human was forever bound to our realm. A potion could be given to the human *before* they ate, allowing them to leave later. However, humans who slipped through a portal on accident didn't know that and they usually ate before someone found them.

If they were found in Winter's Realm, by law, one of three places had to take in the trapped humans: a noble house, the House of Wisdom, or the Tower of the Living and the Dead. In short, a place that could feed, shelter, and protect them from others who might use them for more nefarious purposes.

Sometimes those humans became paid servants rather than slaves. However, that was incredibly rare. In Winter's Realm, power was everything, and humans had none. That fact had always made me uncomfortable, and even more so now that I was married to Neve.

Neve had been a slave in the Blood Court. Did she recognize those on board? My attention strayed to the scar on her right temple. Had a cruel vampire given her that scar? I still wasn't sure why she hadn't used the balm I'd gifted her to erase it. She'd done so with her other scars. But to bring it up felt too familiar.

"To what do we owe the pleasure, Prince Vale?" A vampire with long blond hair and a jagged scar across his right cheek cut through the crowd to stand in front of them all. He bowed. Belatedly, the others bowed too, but I focused on the vampire who had addressed me.

He was better dressed than the other sailors and the badges on his red uniform told me he was an officer.

"I'm here to speak with the captain."

The vampire cocked a sandy blond eyebrow. "That'd be me. Captain Barvo, at your service. To my cabin, then?"

The captain waved for us to follow through the crowd of sailors and humans to the upper deck. I took in the area. There were fewer vampires milling about up here—only five.

Five, plus the captain, we can handle. But if the whole crew attacks . . .

Many of us were trained soldiers, but vampires were formidable foes. Their incredible speed alone made me wary of fighting them. I swallowed, hoping that the Clawsguard, Sian, and Filip were ready for anything. And that the sailors Vidar and Sayyida put on alert were close enough to hear if something went amiss.

"I'm afraid the cabin I use for work is small, like most spaces on ships. Only two of your soldiers can fit inside, along with the gentlefae, of course." The captain gestured to Sian and Filip.

I chose my best fighters and directed the other ten to remain outside. They fell into a line before the door. If the captain found that suspicious, he didn't let on, only opened the door and waved us inside.

Captain Barvo's cabin was sparse, decorated in the colors of the royals he served, but with a distinct flare I assumed was all his own. The captain seemed to have a bit of an obsession with warmer climates. Images of a lush and green jungle that were more suitable to the farthest flung Southern Isles of the Summer Court than the Blood Kingdom hung on the walls. He'd even managed to squeeze a hammock into the corner of the crowded office.

His desk took up the most space, a vast expanse of honey-colored wood littered with maps and papers. One map caught my eye.

It was an old one, depicting the Islands of the Shadow Fae. Those islands no longer existed. They'd disappeared, along with the Shadow Fae, during Queen Sassa Falk's reign. Of all things, why would he have that on his desk?

"A personal obsession," Captain Barvo said when he spotted me eyeing the map of the Shadow Fae Isles. "They had so much gold, some of it might still be in the sea. When I'm not sailing for the royals, I do love the rush of a treasure hunt." His eyes twinkled. "Have a seat." The captain offered me the better of the two chairs opposite him.

I ushered Neve into one chair, taking the more worn seat, which earned me an arched eyebrow from the captain. But he said nothing as Sian and Filip flanked us, and the two Clawsguards permitted into his office stood behind.

"I'm intrigued as to why the Warrior Bear himself would be visiting us." Captain Barvo, now seated, leaned forward to place his elbows on the desk and tented his fingers. "Rumor has it you don't much like ships, Prince Vale."

Internally, I cringed at the embarrassing truth. Though I was in the army, and sometimes had to sail with the Royal Nava to help fight off pirates, I did not relish life on a ship. My fear of being submerged in water was one of my weaknesses.

"I prefer the back of a horse," I admitted. "Though it's not unknown for me to grace a ship's decks."

"Of course not." The captain gave a small smirk. "So what brought you to mine?"

"This ship is under diplomatic protection, correct?" I asked. "No blood or blade will be drawn when docked in other kingdoms?"

"This isn't starting off well." Captain Barvo leaned back, and his arm dipped closer to the dagger he wore before he caught himself.

"Answer the question," Sian barked.

The captain glared at my friend. "Correct. This is a diplomatic vessel. We shall draw no blade. Nor blood—save for the purposes of nourishment, of course. A necessary caveat for those of my order."

At my side, Neve stiffened, but Barvo didn't notice,

wasn't as attuned to her as I was. No, his eyes drifted back to me.

"Of course." I cleared my throat. "Now that we're clear on that, I regret to inform you that your prince has died."

The captain's eyes widened. "What did you say?"

"Prince Gervais met his death last night," I said without hesitation. Weakness could not be shown here.

"How?" The captain's voice took on a dangerous growl. "Under royal guest rights, he was supposed to be safe."

"That's true," I allowed. "However, the prince attacked and forcibly drank from our people. Which, as everyone aboard this ship knows, is against our laws. We provided your prince with fae blood and offered him volunteers to drink from. He took liberties with our people."

"With whom?" The captain stood; anger restrained but visible in the tight lines of his neck. "A merchant? A peddler? A whore?"

"It matters not what they did for a profess—"

The captain lunged. Neve screamed, and I acted on instinct, leaping up, throwing my arm out, and with all my might, flinging the vampire to the side and into the wall.

"Sian, protect her!" I drew my sword. At my side was young Filip, stake in hand.

"What happened to not drawing blood?" the captain rasped as he stood. "Or did you just mean yours?"

"You wouldn't dare attack a royal," I replied.

"You're right. I can't draw *your* blood, Prince Vale, not if I wish to keep my head back home, but that doesn't mean I can't take theirs." He flew to the door, darting past the guards in the room with ease, little more than a blur with his great vampiric speed.

"Behind you!" I roared, hoping I wasn't too late to save the outside Clawsguards from an attack.

"They killed our prince!" Captain Barvo bellowed. "Prince Gervais is dead!"

I didn't need to see the Clawsguards to know they'd fallen into a fighting position. Or that the closest vampires were already upon them. Metal struck metal. Preternatural growls rang from the lips of vampires.

I darted out the door, desperate to help my escort. "Sian, keep Neve safe!"

"You heard him—burning moon, get back here!" Sian yelled as someone barreled into me from behind, then another person. I twisted. Neve was squished between me and Sian.

She gasped, wriggled her way out, and I grasped her wrist. "Get back in the cabin. Sian and Filip will—"

"Vale, watch out!" Sian growled, drawing a blade and pushing Neve into the arms of his younger brother.

The captain was upon us again, his dagger flying.

"Your guards will die. One by one," Captain Barvo grunted as I pulled my sword and met his metal with my own. The news had sent him into a rage. He could no more honor the diplomatic treaty than keep the fury from his eyes. "And you will see their blood spill on the decks of my ship."

He wasn't wrong. Though I focused on the captain, I didn't miss when one of my guards fell to his knees. Thankfully, he had backup. Another fae took the head of the vampire looming over his comrade. Vampire blood sprayed as two more opponents went down.

The vampires on the top deck had attacked, but we had the numbers, at least until those below arrived.

"I did it!" Neve shrieked from behind. "I killed your prince because he was trying to kill me!"

I prepared for Captain Barvo to swing around me, to go for her, but then she added, "however, I'd think before you take another step, Captain. I'm Prince Vale's wife, a member of the royal family of Winter's Realm."

The captain froze, his eyes wide, dagger still aloft. I halted my attack, waiting. For a moment, neither of us moved, though the fighting continued behind us. Another vampire head flew, another fae soldier took a dagger in his leg.

"Prince Laurent attacked *your wife?*" the captain breathed as he met my eye. "She killed him? In defense?"

"Yes!" Neve screamed. "I killed him in self-defense. Or he would have murdered a member of the Royal House of Aaberg! That cannot stand!"

The captain sucked in a breath and spun. "Stop! All who fight for the banner of Laurent, stop!"

"And those who fight for House Aaberg!" I added,

not wishing to draw more blood if we were, in fact, at a standstill.

The skirmish came to an abrupt halt as twenty more vampires appeared from below decks. Not far behind, the sailors from the docks soared our way with Vidar and Sayyida. So many were covered in blood.

I sucked in a breath. Had others from our side died below? Was the captain going to continue now that he had backup? But then the captain gave the signal for them to hang back. To stop. The vampires didn't look pleased about it, but they did as ordered. As a result, the fae sailors, Vidar, and Sayyida lowered their weapons.

He twisted to face us again. "Your name, my lady?"

"Princess Neve of House Aaberg," my wife replied, her chin tilted up. "And I believe that, as he attacked me first, your prince was in the wrong. I had every right to defend myself. And I may be new to the royal house, but I believe that attacking a royal is grounds for war. Much like this might be considered?"

Captain Barvo looked unsure if he believed her, but possibly because the fae couldn't lie, he didn't lash out again. "You're correct, Princess Neve. Royals adhere to codes and if Prince Gervais . . ." he trailed off, collecting himself. "I cannot spill more blood here today, in your kingdom, knowing this. I cannot bring war to my kingdom."

"Precisely," I said, understanding he didn't do so out of a sense of righteousness.

Neve was right. The Crowns of the nine kingdoms of Isila did not strike one another. And if we did, it was an act of war. Should Captain Barvo proceed with the fight and his own king and queen hadn't approved of him starting a war with the Winter Court, he'd be executed.

The fact that Neve hadn't technically been a princess but a common fae when Gervais struck at her didn't need to come up.

I glared at the captain. "We came to tell you the truth and to ask you to leave. *Today.* If you do, I will omit news of this skirmish to the diplomat we send to your homeland to discuss the aftermath of your prince's death." I gestured to the blood on the decks, the dead vampires and downed fae.

Captain Barvo cast his dead crew members a pained glance. A male like him would understand that, among the courts, their lives were less than that of a princess.

The captain sheathed his dagger. "We will leave. No harm will befall you from me or my crew."

"Good," Neve replied. "Now, can we go?"

"I think that's for the best." The captain stepped aside. I motioned for Neve to take my hand. She did, and I found her skin clammy, shaking.

"I'll send a scout by last light to make sure you are gone." I glared at the captain.

"We will be, Prince Vale," Barvo replied. "After all, I have news to relay to my king and queen."

CHAPTER 8
NEVE

The reek of vampire blood remained lodged in my nostrils as we walked away from the Laurent ship, down the series of docks, and finally stepped foot onto the cobblestone streets of Avaldenn. I blew out forcibly and inhaled deeply, desperate to free myself of the stink, and succeeded with mixed results. Though the salt and seaweed of the air blowing in off the Shivering Sea was strong, not even that could fully drive the stench of blood out.

My lower lip trembled. Stars, that had been awful. And the vampires, the way they moved and seeing their flashing fangs. I shuddered.

At least no one from our side died . . .

Two Clawsguards had sustained wounds, but they were still with us, carried back to the palace by their fellow soldiers.

I wasn't sure how I'd decided to tell the captain I'd killed their prince, putting an immediate target on my back. I only knew I'd felt the need to because I suspected it would stop the bloodshed.

A royal attacking a royal wasn't a matter for common sailors to undertake. No matter that I hadn't been a royal during the attack.

But they didn't know that.

It was a technicality. One that had stopped the spill of blood. One that would get rid of the ship. One that would buy us time.

"That was quick thinking." Sian came up beside me. Filip fell in line next to his brother, a thoughtful expression on his youthful face. Sayyida and Vidar had stayed at the docks to watch the vampires, just in case.

"Indeed." Vale looked down at me. "Exactly what weapon training have you had, Neve?"

The question caught me off guard and my mouth opened and shut twice before I answered. "None. I was never given the opportunity."

What vampire master in their right mind would train their slaves with weapons? And during my time with Roar, I'd been far too busy learning about the most influential members and ways of the Winter Court to worry about physical training.

"I can slash with a dagger and . . ." I nearly said *use a stake*, which was obvious. If I wasn't capable of sending a stake into a vampire's heart, we wouldn't be in this predicament. "But give me a sword or mace or anything larger, and I'd probably hurt myself more than an opponent."

Vale nodded as though he'd expected nothing less.

"We'll remedy that. You begin training with weapons today."

A thrill ran through me at the idea. I'd never thought much about being able to wield a sword. Training with Vale was expert training, and I was lucky to be offered such a thing.

The prince let out a long, tension-filled breath. "As my brother said in the throne room, hired blades will come for you."

I blinked. I hadn't even known he'd overheard that.

"The Blood will most likely send those who train in the valleys of the Red Mist Mountains. Red Assassins, they call themselves," Sian agreed. "They're the best their kind has."

"I know." During my time in the Blood Court, I'd heard tales of the Red Assassins. They were stealthy, discreet, and absolutely lethal.

"Well"—Sian eyed me up and down—"you look strong and have a good foundation. Are you quick?"

Good foundation. I bit back a laugh. My thighs had always been thick, and I'd always liked them that way, but it still sounded like such a diplomatic phrasing.

"Not as quick as you," I replied as we rounded a corner. The Clawsguards ensured that citizens of Avaldenn parted for us as we went. The ability to walk in a city and not have to take care to notice where you were going was odd. In Sangrael, I'd always been on alert. Thanks to the orc attack in Guldtown, I'd remained observant there too, though to a lesser degree. "I'm fast, though."

Sian looked at Vale. "I think Luccan's place would be best to start. The palace will still be talking about the pair of you, and you don't want an audience."

"Agreed." Vale halted and the guards around us stopped too. He pointed at two guards. "You and you will come with me, my wife, Sian, and Filip. The rest will help the injured to the castle and take up the posts you were assigned before I requested your presence. If anyone from my house asks, my wife and I are going to visit friends. If anyone *else* asks, they are not privy to knowing the details of our married life."

"Are you sure, my prince?" one guard asked, his gold cloak billowing behind him.

"Where we're going we do not require more than two Clawsguards. Now, don't delay. They need to get to the healers." Vale gestured to the injured.

The sworn soldiers didn't argue a second time. Those Vale had dismissed trudged onward, through the city, bound for Frostveil Palace. The remaining two waited.

"Come," Vale said. "We're going to Lordling Lane."

Lordling Lane wasn't the real name of the street, only a more accurate one. And it appeared exactly as one would imagine it. That was, if they imagined the most luxurious and decadent street in Avaldenn complete with sprawling homes, chic taverns, high-end restaurants, one very nice-looking public sauna, and shops that catered to the ultra-wealthy of the city.

I gaped as we passed by one shop that had a russet-red fur cloak, likely from a fox, in the window. The price tag was astronomical for such an item of clothing. I knew good and well how much labor it would take to make such a garment, and the materials couldn't be worth that much.

"Ice spider silk is woven into it," Sian said.

I tilted my head. "What?"

"You were staring at that red cloak. It's only so expensive because ice spider silk is used in it."

"And that's valuable?" I'd never heard of such a material.

"The spiders live in the Ice Tooth Mountains," Sian explained. "Their silk is the strongest material we have. It also protects from magical attacks and keeps magic restrained."

"Some are as big as a troll! And they're so *vicious*." Filip shuddered. "Only an insane fae would harvest that silk for a cloak."

"Yes, vicious indeed." Sian grinned at his little brother before meeting my eyes again. "Our home abuts the Ice Tooth Mountain Range. We're familiar with the spiders and how to keep them deep within the mountains."

I tried not to think of a spider the size of a troll, most of whom stood fifteen heads tall, double Vale's height. "When you say that silk keeps magic restrained, what do you mean?"

"If one wanted to bind magic and didn't have the power to do it themselves, that's what they'd use," Sian replied.

I pondered that as we walked down the lane. Tavern owners tried to lure us inside. All of them recognized Sian and Vale and bowed as we passed. The lord and the prince waved the eager tavern owners off, promising they'd be by soon.

We were nearing the end of the street when Vale and Sian came to a stop in front of a gate. A fae stood guard, but he opened the doors when he saw the pair.

"Lord Luccan is in. As are his lord brothers."

Vale nodded. "Thank you."

I eyed Vale sidelong. "I've heard many say Lord Luccan, but I thought he was a bastard? Is that common?"

"He was a bastard," Vale replied, eyebrows raised. "My father legitimized him before the Courting Festival. Have you spoken to Luccan before?"

"No, though I've seen him and heard stories of him from others," I answered. "He's interested in Clemencia, my lady-in-waiting. And Roar was the one who mentioned him—as a bastard. Roar seemed obsessed with it."

"Some nobles are obsessed with such things." Vale shook his head. "Though I will say it's entirely possible that Roar didn't know of the legitimizing until he got to court. The western territory is far away."

"Even if he did, I think he would still look down on Luccan." The way he'd said it led me to believe that.

Now that I had some distance, Roar's beliefs struck me as inconsistent. He'd pretend to be engaged to me, a blood slave, but dislike a person who was born out of wedlock? There had to be a history I was unaware of.

"Perhaps. Sometimes nobles are willing to overlook a slight of blood. Though they rarely forget."

I got the sense he was speaking of his father, a known Falk bastard.

We climbed the steps to the manor house. At the top, Vale instructed the two Clawsguards we'd brought with us to wait outside.

"There will be no need for you to hover in my friend's home," Vale said when one looked ready to protest. "He has protection too." He gestured to the gate, and the guards fell back to stand on either side of the door.

Luccan Riis's home rose before me, three stories high, an unassuming off-white color trimmed with the red shade of House Riis. The only unusual thing about it was a spiderweb painted over the front door. Another nod to Luccan's noble house.

The door opened before we could knock, and to my surprise, Luccan stood before us. "Saw you out the window. What have I done to earn the pleasure of a visit from Vale and his stunning wife?" Luccan winked and in spite of myself, heat rose in my cheeks. I knew little of this tall, broad male, save that his father was the king's spymaster and Clemencia liked him. But with his long red hair and dark brown eyes, Luccan was very handsome. He also had the most stunning pair of wings

I'd ever seen; red veined with orange and yellow so that they almost looked to be made of flame.

"What are Filip and me? Gryphon dung?" Sian arched a playful eyebrow.

"Compared to the new princess, I'd say so." Luccan opened the door wider. "Thank the stars you don't smell like it, or I wouldn't be letting you in."

"I'd like to see you try to stop me from coming inside, you prick. Some *cabal brother* you are," Sian muttered.

"I do love that term that Princess Saga cooked up. It's clandestine and mysterious! She has such a way with words, your sister." Luccan shot Vale an amused glance.

The prince rolled his eyes, like he did when Saga used the term, but I suspected that was simply to irritate his sibling because the smile on Vale's lips told me he was warming to the term too.

Despite Luccan's ribbing, he exchanged playful shoulder punches with Sian as we entered the home. Filip watched the exchange with longing in his golden eyes. I suspected that the younger son of House Balik didn't have as close a circle of friends.

"How did you know about Neve and me? You weren't at the gathering this morning at the palace, or were you?"

"It's the talk of the city." Luccan grinned.

As Luccan's father, Lord Riis, had intended.

"Right." Vale seemed momentarily astonished before collecting himself. "Might we use your sparring facilities?"

The eldest Riis son's eyebrows rose. "Of course. We're having a bit of fun now." He cut me an amused glance. "Did you bring your wife to show off, or . . ." His nostrils flared. "Is that blood?"

My brow furrowed. None of us had been injured, only the two Clawsguards and they were on their way to the castle. How was Luccan smelling that?

"Luccan has a powerful sense of smell," Vale explained. "Nearly as strong as a vampire's."

"And you still loved Clemencia's perfume?" My hands slapped over my mouth. Burning moon! I couldn't believe I'd said that!

Luccan's eyes brightened. "You and your lady-in-waiting spoke of me, did you? Where is she?"

"I'm not sure. She had to take leave."

Technically, the truth. I didn't know where Clemencia was at this exact moment. And if Lord Leyv Riis hadn't told his son about what had happened last night, then I shouldn't either. I'd let Vale handle that.

"Oh." Luccan's face fell a touch. "Pity. She was such a light at court."

"Yes, she is," I agreed.

He turned back to Vale. "Now, the blood?"

"First, why weren't you at the castle this morning?" Vale replied. "All the other Sacred Eight were."

He, too, wondered what the Lord of Tongues had told his sons.

"After Vale threatened to cut off the king's hands at the feast, I wanted a bit of distance from the palace," Luccan continued. "Arie and Thantrel wanted some as well. As we live in the city, Frostveil guards had no objections to letting us slip out. We plan to return soon though, unless there's a reason we shouldn't do so?"

"You'll have to, but you should know of the latest news." Vale told Luccan an abbreviated version of last night's events. He then proceeded to the events of the morning when the king had whipped Sir Qildor and then our skirmish on the vampire ship. When Vale was done, Luccan's mouth was hanging open.

"It seems I have some things to cover with my father," he said after Vale ran out of story.

"That would be wise, and now you understand why we need your training facilities."

"Your wife will need to learn to protect herself."

"I can't be with her at all times. So yes. And we'd rather spend as little time at the palace as possible today."

"Then let's go." Luccan waved for us to follow. "Thantrel, Arie, and Father are down there now."

"Your father is here too?" Vale asked.

"He arrived a few hours ago. Why?"

"The guards didn't mention him," Vale replied.

Luccan shrugged and turned around. "He requests not to be spoken about."

Vale shot me a look.

I was no mind reader, like the queen, but I felt certain that I knew what he was thinking about. Vale was recalling that his mother had neglected to mention Lord Riis when she told the tale of how I'd killed the vampire prince and our wedding.

Of course, she'd also left out the fact that I had been a blood slave. And the whores, Clem, and Anna, being present at the scene of the crime. Had she not seen those memories? Or maybe just because she hadn't recognized the ladies, she had not seen fit to mention them? Or had there been so much going on in Vale's head that some things slipped by her?

I wasn't sure but omitting Lord Riis had felt pointed. I wanted to know why, and I suspected Vale did too.

We descended two floors, revealing that the manor house was five floors, not three, as it appeared from the outside. At the bottom, there was only one door. Luccan paused, pressed an ear closer to the door, and let out a soft chuckle. "Father convinced Arie to join in this time. Sounds like he's enjoying himself!"

Vale laughed too, and Sian and Filip bore twin smiles. I wondered what was so funny but didn't get the chance to ask as Luccan Riis opened the door.

The scent of sweat and metal billowed out. I wrinkled my nose and peeked inside, only to find a stocky male fae with curly red hair and the same lovely shade of wings as Luccan stumbling backward, straight for us.

"Bleeding moon, Arie!" Luccan held out a hand before the male collided with him. "Watch where you're going!"

The male spun and narrow copper eyes blazed through Luccan. "I'd love to, but our ogre of a brother doesn't fight fair!"

"Like that would matter," another male voice, this

one deeper than the other two, rang through the room. When I caught sight of him striding across the vast room empty of furniture but with many assorted weapons hanging from the walls, I sucked in a breath.

With deep red hair that trailed down his back and those wings seemingly made of fire, this had to be another Riis, though this male was the most stunning. He was tall but lithe, unlike Luccan and Lord Riis, who were both barrel-chested, and rivaled Vale in size and stature. This male, on the other hand, struck me as ethereal with olive green eyes framed with the longest lashes I'd ever seen and . . . Was he wearing eyeliner?

"Even if I fought clean," the stunning male jeered, "you wouldn't stand a chance. Fates, Arie, you need to train more."

Arie scowled. "Those in the House of Wisdom don't need to fight with blades. Or savage maces."

The other male swung the mace that Arie was looking so pointedly at, a huge smirk on his face.

"We fight with knowledge and words. Far more civilized," Arie muttered. "I don't need to have my arse handed to me to be of use."

"Both knowledge and physical strength are important," another voice boomed, and Lord Riis appeared from an alcove he'd been doing stars only knew what in.

I blinked. For the first time, the spymaster's wings were not vanished or hidden beneath a cloak, and they looked exactly like his sons' wings. Or rather, theirs looked like his. If I had such lovely wings, I'd never hide them. I wondered why he did.

Perhaps they draw too much attention. A spymaster might not like that.

"Welcome, Prince Vale. Princess Neve." Lord Riis inclined his head, and his sons did the same, Luccan rolling his eyes as he did so.

We showed Lord Riis the respect due to a lord of the Sacred Eight. Once the niceties were observed, Lord Riis arched an eyebrow.

"I must admit, I'm surprised to see you here. Has there been a problem?"

His sons exchanged confused glances, but the question confirmed my suspicions. Luccan wasn't playing coy. Rather, Lord Riis was being careful around his sons. He hadn't told them about last night.

"Perhaps Neve and I could speak to you privately?" my husband offered and gestured to a corner of the room.

"As you wish." Lord Riis nodded, and our trio separated from the others, who promptly began joking around, mostly at Arie's expense. I watched, amused and feeling a little bad for Arie as he stormed into an attached room. What else was down here? My answer came a moment later when Arie emerged with a sword. Though there were weapons hanging on the walls, there also appeared to be an armory attached to the sparring space.

"Should we be concerned?" I asked as Arie ran at

Thantrel, sword raised, face red, and eyes burning with a desire to pummel his brother.

The Lord of Tongues spared his sons a glance. "They're brothers. They love one another, but Thantrel knows what to say to get under Arie's skin."

"He lives for those moments." Vale snorted as Thantrel sidestepped Arie's attack with ease and grace and a huge smile on his face.

"That he does. Now, is everything all right?" Lord Riis asked once we were out of earshot.

"Fine," Vale replied. "We took care of the vampire's ship. They're leaving."

Riis's eyes widened.

"You didn't hear that my father requested I do that myself?"

"I have been absent from the castle all morning."

That wasn't an answer. After all, he was the king's spymaster. Lord Leyv Riis had many small spiders crawling around, listening, gathering information.

"The king sent the queen to retrieve us this morning." I took control of the conversation, desperate for answers to the questions swimming in my mind. "She used her magic on Vale and saw what happened last night." I paused, watching the Lord of Tongues's face closely. "But when she recounted the night to the king, she failed to mention that you, Clemencia, Anna, and your employees were present. I understand why she omitted those who were glamoured and the whores, but not you. Any idea why she did not share that information?"

Not even the barest flicker of surprise showed on his face. "The queen possesses powerful magic, but sometimes she misses things. As we grew up together, I was her test subject many times."

He said it almost fondly, though I couldn't see why. I wouldn't want to be a test subject on someone rifling through my mind.

"So you think she missed it?" I asked.

"It's true that Mother can miss things," Vale conceded. "I think she moves too fast, especially when angered. But she said your name."

My eyes widened. That must have been when I was in the bathroom. Vale and I had some serious catching up to do.

Lord Riis shrugged. "I cannot say. I haven't seen the queen since yesterday."

Vale eyed him. "I suppose it's possible that she was more focused on the wedding when she told my father. You could have slipped her mind."

Leyv let out a dry chuckle. "Yes, I'm sure the queen was not at all happy to hear of your nuptials."

"No," Vale agreed. "House Aaberg, save for my sister, is not accepting of my choice."

"Right, well." Lord Riis glanced at his sons. "I would appreciate it if you two didn't mention my involvement last night to the king. As I have assured the safety of loved ones, I believe it is not too big an ask."

He was right. He'd done a lot for us.

"We can't control what the queen says, though," I ventured.

Lord Riis exhaled. "I might convince her not to speak about it. In any case, I'd better try, or she might turn her anger to me."

"Good luck with that," Vale said. "And by the way, I need to make sure Caelo stays away from court. Father whipped Sir Qildor and threatened to do the same to Caelo. He can't return. Not until the king's fury cools."

"That could be a good long while, Vale," Lord Riis said. "And Caelo is a sworn Clawsguard. He will not like staying away."

"It's an order. How can I get him the message?" Vale leveled Riis with his stare.

The spymaster sighed. "I'll send the message."

"Thank you." The prince's attention shifted to me. "Now, we need to train."

CHAPTER 9

NEVE

S weat dripped down my brow, but I didn't dare wipe it away or even take my eyes off Filip.

We'd been sparring in Luccan Riis's training room for hours. Although I was starving and muscles I hadn't even known I possessed were aching, I wasn't about to give up. Not when I'd finally lasted a full five minutes against an opponent.

Sure, he was the smallest and youngest opponent Vale had pitted me against, and I hadn't technically beaten Filip, but I'd take what I could get.

He was, after all, not without his skills. The squire had been training for many turns. He wielded this wooden sword with power. He didn't tire as quickly as me. However, Filip lacked in one department.

His coordination was off—an odd predicament for a fae.

One I was determined to use to my benefit. I'd maneuvered us to the edge of the room, where I could use other means to defeat him. I inhaled slowly, taking in how he'd dropped his right shoulder. He was preparing for an attack.

When he lunged, I was ready for him. I twirled out of the way and used all my strength to shove the youngling into the stone. He slammed into the wall, groaned, and I whipped my wooden sword up so that the point grazed his neck.

"I did it!" I squealed. "You're dead!"

"Don't sound too happy about it." Filip glowered, dropping his sword and rubbing his shoulder, which had taken the brunt of his weight when he hit the wall. "I'm going to go get water."

Sian, who'd been judging his little brother's every move, snorted. "The strong don't run from a fight. Even if the fight is a female who, only today, learned how to use a sword."

Vale did his best to hide his smirk. He didn't succeed.

Filip growled, and, without saying another word, stomped from the room. Once his footsteps disappeared up the stairs, the males broke out into laughter.

I shook my head. I was missing something. "What's going on?"

"Filip is going through a growth spurt—with his magic," Lord Riis explained. "He's already powerful enough to be named heir to House Balik, but he isn't out of the woods yet. As younglings grow more into their powers, they sometimes become discombobulated. Filip has a turn or so left to experience that pleasure."

"Clumsy." I felt a little bad for the male I'd been trying to skewer with my practice sword for the past hours. "He's better than that, isn't he?"

"He is," Vale assured me. "But not today."

"Well, I'd like to try sparring with someone whose body isn't warring with them." I crossed my arms over my chest.

"He was still a challenge, no?" Thantrel asked, batting his long eyelashes. "Because, respectfully, Princess, you can't handle any of us." A smirk grew across his face. "Well, perhaps you could take on Arie."

"Lay off Arie," Luccan snorted. "It's only fun teasing him when we get to witness how red he gets."

But Arie Riis was long gone, returned to Frostveil to get away from his brothers, so that wasn't an option, anyway.

"Vale, spar with me," I insisted.

My husband took up a sword, one made of real metal. "Fine. You grab a real sword too. It'll be good for you to feel the difference, even if you don't practice with it often."

"Then why practice with it at all?"

He smirked. "Because I don't expect you'll be getting in a single hit."

I scoffed.

"Don't worry, Neve," his smirk widened at my indignation, "I'll go easy on you."

"I can't say the same."

His eyebrows shot up, and, from the sidelines, Sian snorted. "You married a fiery one."

"It seems I did," the prince said as we fell into position.

Over the hours, I'd learned the basics, footwork, and how to hold a wooden, then a real sword. Those weren't too difficult. However, maneuvering the long wooden blade through the air posed more of an issue. To transition to a real sword so quickly would be even more challenging, but I took heart. In the short time we'd trained, I'd already improved, and I intended to continue to do so. And if I could, I'd wipe that smug expression off Vale's face too.

"Call it," Vale instructed.

Luccan counted us down, and it didn't surprise me at all when Vale hesitated, handed me the first move.

I darted forward, sword slashing down. Vale deflected the attack, spun, and smacked me on the arse with the broad side of his sword.

"Oh-ho!" Luccan jeered. "That sounded like it hurt!"

"Rather pleasant," I announced, playing it off because it hadn't hurt. Only my pride stung.

"She enjoys rough play, Vale," Thantrel teased. "I like your wife more and more by the minute."

"Careful, Than," Vale growled, probably pretending to be territorial over the female he supposedly loved. He acted so well that he almost made me believe it too.

Metal clanged and whined in the basement as we continued to spar. Round two, three, and four passed, all of which Vale ended with efficiency. As he'd said, I'd not managed a single strike and what was worse, the weight of the metal sword was already becoming too much. On the fifth turn, he allowed me to wear myself out a bit more, circling, darting forward, and then back.

He was toying with me, and it was infuriating.

The prince knew it too because a smile sprawled across his handsome face. "Shall we end this?"

I snarled, and a growl rose out of my throat, the sound far more ferocious than I intended.

A small chuckle left his lips. "I've awoken the beast inside. Very well, then. I suppose I should cage it."

He lunged, long black braid flying behind him as he neared. I ran backward, parrying two upper strikes in rapid succession. Pride rose within me, and a grin spread across my face. I was warding off the famed Warrior Bear! I—

My back slammed into a wall. My breath left me and before I slipped to either side, Vale was there, so close that I could smell his heady scent of falling snow and sandalwood. Slowly, he brought his sword tip to hover above the skin of my neck as his free arm rose, so that he leaned into the wall.

Blazing moon! I was trapped, and this time not by my own machinations!

"A cage for a very pretty little beast," he whispered, his lips so close to mine that I shivered. "Admit defeat, Neve."

I sucked in a breath. The scent of his sweat and the sharing of our breaths made my head spin. I wanted little more than to run my hands through his hair, feeling at the shaved under portions at the sides that were only visible when he wore the longer parts pulled back like he did now. Feeling for the hidden parts of him that others rarely saw.

"You've done well, wife, but today is not the day you beat me."

I blinked. Something in his cocky tone made me more aware of the sword hanging at my side. Forgotten in the moment of being trapped by him.

We'll see about that. I took a deep breath so that my bosom rose and fluttered my lashes to distract him.

Desire clouded his eyes and his shoulders loosened, and that's when I struck, quickly drawing my blade against the outside of his thigh, hard enough to draw blood, but not so hard that he wouldn't heal within the hour.

Vale winced and his eyes widened at the realization of what I'd done.

"Strike for me. Looks like I beat you, husband," I cooed as he groaned, and his friends erupted with laughter. "Perhaps you should finish the job next time before you begin gloating."

"Such a dirty little fighter." Vale shook his head and pressed off the wall, amusement in his eyes alongside the lingering desire.

"I do what I must." I winked.

"I'll keep that in mind. I—"

Footsteps thundered down the staircase, and Filip appeared, a letter in hand.

"My prince, Lord Arie sent a message. They have announced the next Courting Festival event. It's this afternoon."

I groaned, which did not fail to catch anyone's notice.

"I agree," Sian muttered. "This farce of a festival has gone on for too long."

"It just started." Luccan took the paper.

"Too long," Sian said emphatically.

"I suppose that means we need to return to the palace," Vale said. "You'll need to prepare for whatever my father has in mind."

"It says a gathering. With wine, so at least there's that." Luccan waved the paper. "It's a few hours from now, in the middle of the afternoon. Odd time for it."

"Then he has something planned," Vale muttered.

"Well, at least I got in one win," I sang as though the idea of the king calling a gathering didn't make my blood run cold.

My jest lightened the mood a bit, and we began to put away the sparring swords and weapons. Vale told Sian and Filip that he wanted to walk the city alone with his new wife. The brothers shared twin grins as they left, Thantrel following close behind, while Luccan rummaged deeper into the armory for something. Vale and I were about to leave as well when Lord Riis approached.

He hadn't sparred much. Rather, he watched the younger males and gave me advice. During the hours spent training, I'd learned that Lord Riis had been quite the fighter in the Aaberg Rebellion, and he had much to offer. Was he about to share one last tidbit?

Maybe he's about to tell Vale not to get distracted by a pretty face. I smirked, loving that I'd get to tease the prince about that.

"Prince Vale, Princess Neve, I have something I'd like to share with you," Lord Riis said before twisting toward the armory. "Luccan! A word."

Riis's eldest son poked his head out of the training armory, his eyebrows drawn together in confusion. "Yes, Father?"

"Come here."

Luccan wiped his hands on his trousers as he ran over. When he came to a stop, Lord Riis pinned his gaze on his son.

"I'm going to show them our family secret. You need to tweak the magic on it to accept their blood."

Luccan sucked in a breath. "Are you sure?"

"They might need a fast escape."

Luccan still appeared dumbstruck. I shot Vale a sidelong glance, but he looked as confused as me. What were they about to show us?

My bewilderment only grew when we approached a wall and Luccan took out a dagger and cut his hand. Blood welled, spilling over on to his palm as he placed it on the wall.

Light flashed, ripping a gasp from my lips.

"Is that *a gateway*?" Vale murmured. "But how do you have one here? Does my father know?"

My eyebrows furrowed, which Lord Riis caught.

"Gateways are also known as portals, some to places within this kingdom, some to other realms, such as the human world, or sometimes, parts of other kingdoms. This one was made in secret."

Vale shook his head. "Leyv, having a new gateway made within the kingdom is a capital offense."

"I'm aware," Lord Riis murmured.

A muscle in Vale's jaw tightened. "Their mere existence was a great matter of contention between him and the previous Warden of the West."

"Roar's father?" I asked, unable to help myself.

"Yes," Vale answered. "The previous Warden of the West was the last known gateway maker in the kingdom. Father forced him to close nearly every gateway in the kingdom, most of them within the western territory. He only allowed him to keep one open outside Guldtown—and an additional portal to the human world not far from Avaldenn. Those only exist should we require supplies. The warden was *furious* that his gateways were taken away."

"True," Lord Riis acknowledged. "Which is why I did not tell the king about Luccan's magic, though I saw a blessing from the stars."

"Blessing?"

"Being the king's spymaster can be dangerous, Princess Neve. There are many fae whose lives I have ruined." Lord Riis placed a hand on his son's shoulders. "Luccan trained, in secret, so that our family might make them as an escape route, in case the worst happened."

"You mean if the rebels attacked the city?" Vale asked. "That seems far-fetched."

"As your father's spymaster, rebels and other powerful fae target me. I would not allow my sons to be unprotected. Nor did I wish for your father to use Luccan for his own purposes. Or worse."

Vale looked stunned but didn't argue.

"I don't want to work for the king. Or be killed for magic he doesn't like," Luccan added. "Besides, Vale, in the city, we only have this one."

My husband sucked in a breath. "But elsewhere?"

Red stained Luccan's cheeks as he realized his misstep. "There are more."

Vale stiffened. "To other kingdoms? Or worse, *worlds?*"

"No, I'm not that advanced. My gateways only extend within Winter's Realm."

Vale let out a long breath and ran a hand through his hair, clearly disturbed by the information.

"As your friend, I ask that you hide my secret," Luccan whispered. "My father wanted to share this to keep you and Neve safe. Surely, that's worth not telling the king? Adversaries *will* come for her."

Vale's eyes drifted to me and lingered there for what felt like an age. This had to be hard for him. Luccan was his close friend and part of Vale's cabal. And yet, Luccan had hidden his secret from Vale. To keep himself out from under the king's thumb, sure, but that indicated Luccan believed Vale might go to his father.

Deep in his heart, did the eldest Riis son still worry about that?

"I won't say a word about this to my father."

"Good. Now"—Luccan gestured to the daggers Vale and I had worn for our visit with the vampires—"draw blood. I'll need it so the portal will accept you."

Vale pulled aside the tear in his pant leg, but the blood there was dried, the wound so minor that it was already closing. So instead, he drew a dagger across his palm and then handed the blade to me. I hissed as my skin parted and blood welled.

Luccan pointed to the spot on the wall where his own blood still soaked into the stone. "Touch the wall. I've already primed it."

I placed my palm on the wall and another flash of light nearly blinded me. Vale flinched back, but a moment later, the light was gone.

For a moment, I was tempted to walk through. To disappear. Start a new life and taste true freedom. Vale had said he wouldn't keep me here and that would give him a chance to get what he wanted—to find his soulmate.

But no. Too many witnesses had seen us arrive at Lordling Lane and enter Luccan's home. Plus, I couldn't do that to the prince. Not after all he'd done for me.

I side-eyed Vale, shivering as I took in his handsome features. It would be far smarter to stay awhile, to learn the sword and how to wield other weapons from him. That way, I wouldn't be so helpless when I traveled to another kingdom—hopefully with Anna in tow. Then, one day, after the prince and I had planned meticulously for my departure, I'd go.

The thought made me sad, even though it was inevitable. The plan all along.

"There you have it," Lord Riis said. "The gateway needs only blood to open. Additionally, our protections are linked, so your blood now works on the wards on the gates and the front door of this house."

"Where will the portal take us?" Vale asked.

Lord Riis smirked. "I will leave that matter a secret for now, my prince. Know that should you need to flee and use this gateway; you will be safe and far away from Avaldenn."

CHAPTER 10
NEVE

The sun was peeking out from the clouds when we left Luccan Riis's home. Vale's Clawsguards lagged a respectable distance behind us as we made our way down Lordling Lane, bound for the castle hand in hand, putting on a show for the city.

I wished we didn't have to return to the palace. Today had been surprisingly fun. Sure, I'd be sore for a few days, but it had been empowering learning to use a sword.

And beating Vale hadn't hurt either. My lips curled into a self-satisfied smile.

"What's going on in that head of yours?" Vale asked, his tone light, teasing. "You look far too pleased with yourself."

"Can you blame me? It's not every day you best the Warrior Bear at swords." Through the slits in my cloak, I fluttered my wings playfully.

He scoffed and shook his head. "We'll see if you can do it again tomorrow."

"Tomorrow?"

"You'll train daily. Early in the morning too," Vale replied in that commanding tone that made my stomach flutter. "That way, we'll be less of a spectacle. In the early hours, the castle training facilities are usually empty."

I groaned but didn't argue. There was wisdom in his decision. The days and nights were sure to be filled with Courting Festival events and when danger came, I had to be ready. Though I was sure Vale would give his all to protect me, I needed to do so myself too.

"No more sparring at Luccan's home?" I asked.

"No," Vale murmured. "We were already outside Frostveil walls today, but it would look too odd, us leaving at the crack of dawn each morning. Plus, who knows what my father has in store for the festival? Best to use the castle facilities."

I wished we could spend more time outside the castle but understood his reasoning.

Down the snow-lined street, a square opened before us, stalls up and open for business. From them, fae hawked wares, food, and services.

"What's this?" I had lived in Sangrael and walked the streets of Guldtown but I'd never seen a place quite like this.

"A roving market. They sell in all areas of the city. The best hand pies in the city are from that stall over there—Ragnor's." He pointed to a very elaborate stall with three dwarves working away inside. The line was so long it wended through tables closer to the center of the square. One faerie left with her order, a hand pie, her eyes wide with glee. She came our way and passed by us without so much looking at the prince strolling the streets.

And when I smelled the pie, I understood why. It smelled so good that my stomach released a loud growl.

Vale's eyebrows popped up. "Sounds like you have a white bear in your belly. You're hungry, I take it?"

"Very," I said. "But I can wait until we get to the castle."

Vale shook his head. "It's been far too long since I visited Ragnor's. Let's go there."

Not about to argue, we approached the stall and got in line. We stood there for no more than ten seconds when the oldest dwarf with a long, blond beard bound with leather ribbons in intervals to keep it out of the food, spied Vale.

The dwarf waved. "My prince! Please, there's no wait for you. Come up here!"

"We're in no hurry and fine back here, Ragnor." Vale waved back.

"You might be fine." A sly grin spread across Ragnor's bearded face. "But I'm not so concerned about you, my prince. Your new princess, however, I'm quite interested in. Bring her up here!"

Over the course of their exchange, those in line had turned to stare at us, most looking pointedly at me. The young fae right in front of us waved us forward. She was a tall dryad with bark-like skin and four arms that resembled branches more than arms. During my time in Winter's Realm, I'd seen few dryads and wondered if having four arms was common, or if this was yet another result of the blight hitting this land hard.

"My prince, you saved my sister's village. Please, go ahead."

Vale allowed the dryad to usher him forward, but it didn't stop there. Fae of all races gave up their place in line. All of them had a reason to thank Vale—most having to do with fighting orcs and ogres around smaller villages in towns where their loved ones lived.

When we reached the front of the line, Ragnor smirked. "Why even fight it, Prince Vale? A brief wait for a sumptuous pie over the sword that protects us all? Even the lowest born of Avaldenn knows how to be proper."

The prince smiled. "Of course they do. I would never assume otherwise."

"What can I get you two?" Ragnor pinned his steely gray gaze on me. "You have not been here, my lady. Perhaps I can tempt you with my bestseller." He grabbed a pie from the top of a pile and tore it open.

A savory scent filled my nostrils and drew saliva into my mouth. Meat, onions, and even small green peas filled the pie wrapped in a flaky golden crust.

"I'd love to try that," I said, not even caring what kind of meat was inside the pie. "Thank you."

Ragnor beamed as he handed me a fresh one and took Vale's order. The prince was partial to pheasant.

Vale also purchased pies for our guard and when we'd attempted to pay—which Ragnor declined with great gusto—we left to take a seat at one of the many tables in the square. The Clawsguard sat at one of the tables next to us and wasted no time digging into their pies.

I took my first bite, and the perfect blend of savory and spicy flavors exploded across my tongue. I moaned, which didn't fail to coax a grin out of Vale.

"Good?"

"Why doesn't the castle serve these at dinner?"

Not that the castle food was bad. I thought it splendid, but this was a new level of exquisiteness.

And to think it came from a stall on the side of the road.

"My mother loves that flavor too," Vale said and for a moment, his eyes went hard. I suspected because he was thinking of the morning, when his mother had been furious to learn what he'd done. "You didn't ask, but it's wild boar."

"Boar? Are they found around here?" The only time I'd seen a wild boar, a goblin had been riding on its back, retreating into the forests of the midlands.

"No, but the meat is transported quickly into the city. The beasts mostly stick to the midlands where the temperatures are milder. You'll rarely find them in the mountains or even too close to the sea."

"Your mother is from there, correct?"

"Yes. The Vagle seat is in the heart of the midlands. She grew up and lived there until she came to court. She married Father not too long after. For a brief period, she moved east and lived in his family's castle until the rebellion ended."

King Magnus's rebellion had lasted two turns, and I would have been around two when the rebellion ended. I looked around the square, wondering if the people here had been present for the fighting. Or maybe they'd fought too.

Had my family? Not for the first time, I wondered where my family was from. If some of them were still alive. Clemencia had told me that the rebellion had shattered many lives. I suspected my family had been among the affected. Why else would my mother be fleeing to the west, where she'd perished from exposure and left me to be scooped up by vampires?

"How old were you when the rebellion ended?" I asked Vale. "Actually, how old *are* you right now?" I couldn't believe I hadn't thought to ask.

"When we moved here, I was seven, about to turn eight. I'm twenty-nine."

I'd known that Vale and Roar were about the same age, but not that they were exactly the same. I'd heard many nobles had pitted them against each other as younglings. Now that made much more sense. Roar and Vale were the same age, almost the same height. They'd both been born into great houses and were well matched in many physical feats. It would have been hard not to compare the two.

Stars, I wished I understood why Roar left. Wished I could give him a piece of my mind too. Even if he had the best reason in the nine kingdoms, I had that right to know why.

I took another bite of the pie, hoping it would distract me. It did, and for a few precious moments, I lost myself in its deliciousness again.

"You?" he asked and then lowered his voice. "Do you know?"

"Twenty-three." My master had been fairly certain that I'd been around two turns when he found me. Younglings changed drastically turn to turn, so it was easier to estimate their ages.

"So," Vale ventured and shifted in his seat. "Now that I've realized I didn't even know your age, I feel like I should know more about you. We are married, after all."

I glanced at the guards. Vale knew my past, so he wouldn't talk about the fact that I'd been a blood slave. But what then? "What do you want to know?"

"What's your favorite color?"

I snorted. "Oh, you're going deep on that one."

"I'm starting easy." He laughed. "Humor me."

"Amethyst," I said. "Like the gown I made. You?"

"I've always favored blue. Maybe subconsciously, since it's a house color." His gaze met mine. "Though now I'm beginning to like violet."

Warmth crept into my cheeks. What a flirt.

"What do you like to do for fun?" I asked.

Vale leaned back. His hand pie was already gone.

"Fun? Sparring with Caelo, I suppose."

"You sound so convincing," I teased. "Do you not know how to have fun, my prince?"

He fell silent for a moment before he shook his head. "Not lately. Before the Courting Festival, I was preoccupied with fighting orcs and . . ." he trailed off, swallowed. "Doing something for my father."

His neck tightened, but I didn't press and ask what that *something* was. I had a secret too. So I didn't feel as though he had to tell me everything.

"I think we need to get you some hobbies."

He laughed dryly. "What about you?"

"I read and sew."

His brown eyes searched for something more. "Because that's all you could do for a long time. But now you have an entire kingdom at your fingertips. Is there something you've been dying to try?"

I mulled that over for a moment, letting my attention drift to a crowd of faerie younglings, all with shredded wings. All likely victims of the mysterious blight. I hoped it didn't affect their magic too, but all the same, my heart went out to them. I understood the sense of helplessness that could come with such an issue.

"Learning the sword will be my new hobby," I replied, never wanting to settle into that helplessness again. "It's difficult and I'm sore, but I can't deny that it's useful, and I had a bit of fun. Especially when I beat you."

He elbowed me gently. "This will never stop, will it?"

"Unlikely." I winked at him. "Perhaps I'd like to sail too."

His jaw tightened. "Sail? I'm afraid I'm not one for the water. Though I'm better on larger vessels."

That's right, Captain Barvo had said as much. "Did something happen?"

"As a youngling, I nearly drowned." Vale shuddered. "Since then, I've disliked being dunked in water. Or worse, diving into the depths of colossal bodies of water."

"Showering?"

"That's fine. Feet on the ground and all that."

"Thank the stars. For a moment there, I worried you'd start to stink and as we're sharing a room . . ." I wrinkled my nose. "I don't even want to imagine!"

A laugh burst from the prince, the sound so full of life and warmth that it set frostflies fluttering in my belly.

Lunch, regretfully, came to an end, and Vale and I returned to the palace grounds. The entire way back, even as we strode through the castle gates, I'd dreaded walking through the corridors of Frostveil. Of seeing the king, queen, or Rhistel.

"We'll go this way," Vale said after dismissing his Clawsguards and leading me not through the front door of the palace, but to the side. He'd claimed to want privacy with his wife and seeing as the prince was on the castle grounds, the Clawsguards were happy to oblige. "There's a side door, one closer to my rooms. You should know about it. Just in case."

In case we needed to run. That thought was being drilled into my head. The scary part was that it was valid. It wasn't so much a matter of 'if' I'd be attacked, but 'when.'

I paid close attention to how Vale swung us around the outside of the palace, through a small garden of winter hedges and pruned trees brimming with red winterberries. Benches completed the look, making the garden a place suitable for quiet contemplation.

"Saga's garden," Vale said, noting how I took in the area. "She likes outdoor places to think, so Father had it planted a few turns back."

"How thoughtful." I despised the king and hearing about times when he'd been kind shocked me.

"Like I said, he wasn't always so intense. Nor so cruel." Vale sighed. "And he's always had a soft spot for Saga. His only daughter. He's harder on Rhistel and me."

I didn't reply as we exited the garden and he turned onto a path that led right up to a part of the exterior castle wall covered in ivy. Through the green, I spied wood.

"Camouflaged," I said. "Why?"

"It's a servants' door," Vale replied. "Mother wanted to minimize its appearance."

Vale brushed aside the ivy tumbling down a trellis. It had to be spelled to stay warm because, though the plant was hearty, few plants thrived in such cold conditions. Not naturally, anyway. I'd learned from Roar that most winter fae used greenhouses, and though I hadn't seen them on the palace grounds, I suspected they were around. Somewhere on the royal grounds and likely in the city too. There were too many fae to feed in Avaldenn for them to rely solely on imports from the warmer kingdoms.

We entered the castle into a plain stone corridor. If Vale hadn't already told me that this was a servants' area, I would have known. The parts of the palace that the royals inhabited were sparkling white and immaculate. With walls of plain gray stone, this area was clean but not as stunning.

"Come on." Vale took my hand and pulled me down a hallway.

I peered into an open doorway as we passed by. Most looked like common spaces for servants. One was a kitchen.

"How many kitchens are in the castle?" I asked Vale as we climbed the stairs.

"What?"

"Kitchens? How many?" Frostveil was enormous and one kitchen wasn't enough for the royals and the courtiers. Perhaps the servants had dedicated kitchens too?

"A dozen? I'm not sure."

"Have you stepped foot in a single one?"

He eyed me. "Most recently, during the night of the Courting Festival's opening ball."

Oh. Right. The night Prince Gervais appeared, and I'd lost it. Lord Riis had pulled me into the kitchens off the throne room, and I'd been confronted with the harsh truth that the winter fae didn't only rely on paid servants for their labor, but slaves. Human slaves, from what I'd seen.

One had even pointed to my scar—mistaking me for someone at court. That had to have been the case because the haunted look in her eyes didn't make sense otherwise.

"Are you all right?" Vale asked.

"What?"

"You fell quiet." We reached the top of the staircase and were in the more opulent part of the palace. He turned left, and we climbed a wider white stairwell.

Shockingly, no one was around. I wondered if that was because they were preparing for the event being held in a couple of hours. Or if Sir Qildor's whipping scared them into their rooms.

"Oh, nothing," I said.

I could tell he didn't believe me, but he also didn't press. We continued in silence, finally arriving in the hallway where his suite was located.

"Does anyone else in your family live in this part of the palace?" The king didn't. I knew this because, unfortunately, a pair of Clawsguards had shown me to his room. Saga was not nearby either. From her room, she had a sea view, and Vale, for whatever reason, looked down into the palace yard. But perhaps Rhistel or the queen were nearby?

"No, they all chose rooms facing the Shivering Sea. Though Mother and Father are in different towers." His lips tightened. "A view of the sea would be nice, but I kind of like looking out into the yard."

I would have chosen a view of the sea, but to each their own.

As we approached the door, my eyebrows knitted together. "Why is no one at your door?"

"I took the Clawsguard stationed at my door with us to the port. He was one of the injured. I suppose no one replaced him after. Seeing as I wasn't there and the door is locked, it's not a big deal."

"I always thought they followed the royals everywhere." I gestured to the empty space behind us. "But Saga ditched her Clawsguard too. Once."

When she'd pulled me from the Lisika suite and forced me to gamble the night away with her friends. The memory brought a small smile to my lips.

"Once?" Vale laughed. "Saga ditches her shadows as often as she can."

"Seems to run in the family."

"I've been known to dismiss them," he admitted sheepishly. "And no, we're not supposed to, but it's nice to have time alone."

I didn't know how Saga managed it, but I supposed that since Vale was a warrior, the knights saw no harm in following the prince's orders. For now, that was fine. But in a few days, once the vampire royals had the time to send assassins, I would feel a lot better if guards surrounded us at all times.

"That might have to change," I said as we reached the door, and Vale brought out his key. "At least for a little while."

He nodded and stuck it in the lock. "I won't put you at unnecessary risk. Now, to our room, wife." A soft but strong hand pressed into my back, urging me to go in first.

I repressed a delighted shiver at his touch and instead pursed my lips. "A polite gesture, *husband*. Though you might want to stop staring at my rear."

Color filled his cheeks. "Can you blame a male?"

I crossed the threshold, a laugh spilling from my lips. But when I caught sight of the inside of Vale's suite, that laugh died.

From the door, I could see into the bathroom. My eyebrows pinched together. It was a mess with towels on the ground, along with the soap and other bottles filled with personal care potions, balms, elixirs and the like. I'd been the last one in there and most certainly had not thrown anything on the ground . . .

"Vale," I whispered as the hair on the back of my neck stood on end. "Someone has been inside your rooms."

"What? That's impossible."

But it wasn't. Heart hammering, I dashed down the short hallway leading into his open bedchamber, and when I reached the bedroom and laid eyes on the floor, I gasped.

Broken glass glinted on the floor, shimmering in two pools of blood.

CHAPTER 11
NEVE

"**N**o." The strangled word burst from my lips. "No, no, *no*!"

I rushed forward, not even bothering to be careful about the glass or the pooled blood on the ground and flung open the drawer I'd hidden the vials inside.

Someone had tossed it. A few others too, judging by how clothing littered the floor or hung partially out of the drawers. And whoever had done so had been looking for the vials filled with Roar's and my blood.

They'd found them too. Destroyed them.

"Bleeding skies!" I slammed the drawer shut and my fists formed into tight, furious balls.

"Neve? What's going on? Did they take something?" Vale rushed after me. "How—" He stopped at the edge of the room; his eyes caught on the ground. "Is that your blood?"

I didn't reply. Couldn't. I couldn't even think

straight. I was so furious that even my wings burned with anger.

Someone had been in here, someone, no doubt, sent by Roar. He'd known that in his escape from the city, he left behind the vial of my blood. He'd also correctly assumed that I'd taken it. And he'd hired someone to destroy them, thus destroying our deal—or what had been left of it, anyway.

More importantly, if it turned out to be true that he left for no good reason, there was no way I could ever demand he pay for what he'd done. The danger *he'd* put me in. I could no longer drink the blood that sealed our magical deal.

Not that I'd ever *wanted* to drink it. Given my past as a blood slave, the idea disgusted me. However, knowing that it had been an option *was* comforting in a messed-up sort of way.

He'd taken that from me. Roar turned his back on me and broke our deal.

On the nightstand lay my stack of books that the servants had brought from the Lisika suite, along with my clothing and other meager belongings. I grabbed the top one from the pile, spun on my heel, and hurled it at the opposite wall.

"Neve! What's going on?"

A snarl burst out of me as I hurled another book at the wall, but before I grabbed for a third, the prince's powerful arms wrapped around me.

"Tell me," he whispered, pulling me close to his chest. "Tell me what happened here. Besides the obvious . . . why are you so upset? You're not bleeding, are you?"

"No," I murmured, my heart still thundering, my limbs trembling. "No, I'm . . . I—Stars, it's awful!"

I fell apart, tears cascading down my cheeks.

Vale scooped me up in his arms and strode across the room, glass crunching beneath his boots. Gently, he set me on the bed and sat next to me.

"Please"—he took my hand in his and the warmth of his skin comforted me—"tell me what happened. I can help."

"Y-y-you can't," I whispered. "There's no way."

"Maybe I can surprise you."

He already had. So many times. And yet, I had no doubt that in this matter, Prince Vale would be as helpless as me.

Still, the way he stared at me with those bottomless brown eyes softened my resolve. What was the point of keeping my deal with Roar a secret now? Vale knew so much else, and I was certain he hadn't been the one to break the vials. He knew of my fake relationship with the Warden of the West, and now it was time that I told him all that had transpired between Roar and me.

"Roar and I weren't just playing at being engaged so he could avoid being matched. We made a deal. I was to play the role of his fake fiancée while at court, and when we returned to Guldtown, he'd give me safe passage to the Kingdom of Summer. That way, I'd be as far from the vampires as possible."

He nodded, perhaps already intuiting that if I'd

gotten myself into the mess I'd made that I'd also agreed to some sort of deal regarding the vampires. "Go on."

"We sealed the deal in blood and magic." I gestured to the pools of blood. "If one was betrayed by the other, they had to drink the betrayer's blood."

"Ah." Vale sucked in a breath. "And what would happen to the person who broke the deal?"

"Crippling pain."

"I see." Vale's nose wrinkled. "Warden Roar still has help in the castle. It wouldn't be difficult for him to buy a favor, as he's the richest fae in the kingdom."

"But breaking into *your* suite!" I sniffed. "That's beyond brave."

"True, but many people heard my father order me to the docks. It wouldn't have been illogical for them to think I was taking the knight guarding my room too. This might have happened hours ago."

I gazed down at the blood spilled on the ground. It looked dry.

"I'm sorry that I wasn't careful enough with my security," Vale said. "That this happened to you. Had I known, I would have helped you take greater precautions. I will from now on." His face twisted. "The warden is a snake, Neve. Put nothing past him."

My teeth dug into my bottom lip. This was so reminiscent of when Roar warned me about Vale. Of course, now I had enough information of my own to make a judgment, but I still had questions.

"Why do you hate him?" I asked. "What exactly happened?"

Vale blinked. "Excuse me?"

I exhaled a long, shaky breath, trying to calm my nerves. "Roar told me why he dislikes you, and Saga mentioned something happened between you two that made you despise him as well. I'm curious to hear your side of the story."

Vale's eyebrows shot up. "What did the warden tell you?"

I swallowed. Before I came to court, this story had colored so much of my perception of Vale. Now that I knew him better, I suspected he'd be ashamed of his past actions. I didn't want to make him feel bad for abandoning his soldiers, but I desperately wanted to know his side.

"You and Roar were fighting against orc tribes, somewhere in the Ice Tooth Range. He did say that you weren't friends, even then"—I paused—"but he also said that you left his forces to fight and die in a valley. They were losing, and you looked down from a peak and didn't help them. Why?"

Vale's lips parted. "I remember that. We were twenty turns."

"That's what he said."

The prince's face hardened. "And did he tell you the reason I left his forces in the valley?"

What had Roar said? I was certain I'd asked why Vale had done that and . . . The memory clicked, like a match struck in a darkened room.

"He said he wasn't sure," I replied.

One corner of Vale's lips lifted in annoyance. "Oh, he did. Just not at that moment. He found out later that there was an even larger host climbing the mountainside. My soldiers and I returned down the slope to hold them at bay and finish them off."

My throat tightened. Roar had, once again, omitted information. My fists clenched. When I'd asked him about that day, I'd been too new to the fae way of skirting the truth to realize. Later, I'd learned, though. After I found out that Roar neglected to mention he'd been secretly feeding me a potion to protect me from the queen's mind-reading abilities. Had he asked, I would have accepted the potion, but he hadn't asked. He'd acted like the vampires who'd owned me, assuming he knew what was best for my body. Since that day, I'd become more wary around the Warden of the West.

"I take it Roar left that out?" Vale prompted me out of my rising anger, back to the moment.

"He did."

Vale's eyes sought mine. "I may dislike the Warden of the West, Neve, but I'd never leave Fae of Winter in a bind on the battlefield. Not as long as I can swing my sword."

"I believe that. So you fought down the mountain, fought oncoming forces and won, and that was it?"

"By then, there were smaller orc tribes coming from all directions. My army branched off. And Roar managed to claim victory and survive."

Yes, Roar had said, *"Soon after the army dispersed to take on smaller tribes."*

The snake!

He'd done so well and manipulated my opinion of Vale before we met. All because Roar despised the prince—envied him. And though the two males were, in many aspects, evenly matched, perhaps he even feared Vale?

"I'm sorry," I whispered. "When I got here, I thought so poorly of you, and it was all because of what Roar had told me. It's why I wasn't the warmest of fae when we first met."

Vale's lips twitched. "Not to sound cocky, but I am pretty unused to females being so standoffish. Though . . . I have to admit, your reaction intrigued me." He exhaled. "It's why I was lurking around your corridor the night you arrived. You'd *flummoxed me*. I'd been half hoping you'd emerge from the Lisika suite—without Roar, of course—so I could get a better read on you."

"Then I ran right into you!" I shook my head, recalling how I'd flattened myself against his hard chest. "Stars, that was mortifying."

"Not to mention, tense."

"You were so grumpy! Probably because you'd been caught!"

"And if you were any colder"—he poked my shoulder—"I would have thought you were made of ice."

Together, we laughed. The sound of it melted a

little of my worry. Yes, Roar had betrayed me yet again, but I'd also learned Vale's side of the story.

A story that resonated in my heart as the actual truth and made far more sense.

Still, I didn't plan on letting Roar get away with what he'd done. Neither leaving me here nor twisting his words and preying on my naiveté.

No, the next time I laid eyes on the Warden of the West, I intended to make him pay for all he'd put me through.

Though castle servants would clean it up without argument, we both thought the blood would garner more questions than we were ready to answer. Together, we wiped the blood from the ground and disposed of the glass. We'd finished when I caught sight of the books I'd thrown on the ground, spines up and pages splayed.

I cringed. It was so unlike me to manhandle a precious story.

One by one, I picked up the books, noting one of them was the one Roar suggested to me. The one his older brother, Brogan, loved.

I patted both tomes. "So sorry," I murmured, wiping dirt off the covers. "Won't happen again."

No matter their connection to the conniving warden, I felt bad for treating them poorly. For many turns, books had been one of the few bright spots in my world.

"I'm sorry, but are you talking to a book?" Vale teased.

I turned to find that he'd shed his shirt. My mouth went dry as my gaze scanned his tattoos and the rippling muscles beneath. We needed to wash up for the Courting Festival event soon. Still, couldn't he warn a lady that he'd stripped?

"I am," I said haughtily. "Books are my friends."

He pressed his lips together, clearly trying not to laugh. "I see."

"I expect that you've spoken to your sword."

That smug amusement vanished as pink tinged his cheeks. "Well . . ."

"Ha! Caught!"

"*Skelda* and I are long-time friends."

My lips curled. I'd heard that term before but hadn't put two and two together. "That's her name, isn't it?"

"It is."

"High Fae, if I'm not mistaken?" Yvette, my human mother figure in the Blood Court, had taught me High Fae, as well as Vitralic, the vampire language, and English. Though I was not as fluent in the language of fae as I was the other two.

"Yes. It means—"

"Protector." The word I'd been searching for materialized. "Fitting."

"Yes, well, I supposed it helped inspire me to do

good." Vale shrugged, and my gaze caught on how his shoulder muscles moved like water.

Bleeding skies. It should be against the law to look so enticing.

"Don't you need to wash?" I might not be able to keep my promise about not jumping him if he didn't leave.

"You're right. I'll be quick." He walked down the short corridor that led to his bathroom.

Once I was alone, I turned to the books again. I had yet to start the one Roar had mentioned. His brother, Brogan's, favorite. Perhaps the story would be so good it could take my mind off things?

I picked up the book and turned to the title page. But before I could read a word, my gaze caught on something. The book was a fabric-bound hardcover, well-loved over the turns if the rounded, softened edges of the front cover were any sign. Opposite the title page, a black fabric had come apart at the top corner.

I didn't recall it looking like that before. Had it happened when I'd thrown the book?

And, more importantly, what was poking out of the fabric? I squinted and picked at the fabric.

Paper. There was a piece of paper tucked inside.

Carefully, I shook the book and the paper moved. It was loose, not part of the book at all.

Roar had said he and his brother hid notes in their books. The warden had searched this book in particular for a message after his family died on their journey to the southlands. Had I found one of Brogan's last messages to his younger brother?

My stomach clenched, and I shut the book. No matter how furious I was with Roar, reading such a note felt wrong. Too personal.

And yet, I reached for the book again, but before my fingers grazed the cover, a knock came at Vale's door.

"Vale? Neve? Are you decent?"

I snorted, recognizing the voice. Saga had come calling.

As Vale was washing, I answered the door and found the pink-haired princess standing before a Clawsguard, a small flask in her dainty hands.

"Come in," I said. "Vale's bathing."

"Seems you might need to as well," Saga teased and wrinkled her nose. "Did you go running or something?"

I waved her inside and shut the door behind her. "Vale was training me in the way of the sword. I still need to bathe."

We strolled into the suite. I was glad Vale and I cleaned up the blood and shattered glass. I did not need more questions.

Saga's eyes widened at the mention of sword-work. "Not a bad idea."

"You say that like you're surprised."

Saga chuckled. "I'm not. Vale's the least erudite person in our family, but he is still very intelligent. And sensible. I'm more surprised that I didn't think about him training you."

"Stars, you're humble," I teased and gestured to the flask. "What's that? Not Dragon Fire, I hope?"

Saga shivered. "The next time I see a bottle of Dragon Fire will be too soon." She held the flask out to me. "You need protection. More than just physical."

"And? What is it?"

"The potion that helps keep my mother from your thoughts. It's called a Mind Rönd. It came from the White Tower today, so it's fresh. It shields your mind from attacks."

The same one Roar gave me without my knowledge. I almost wanted to deny the Mind Rönd potion on that fact alone, but too much was on the line.

Plus, Saga was offering it to me. Not forcing it upon me.

I took the flask. "How much do I drink?"

"At this dose, a mouthful a day," Saga said. "And truthfully, that isn't a complete guarantee. Rhistel, Vale, and I take a much stronger Mind Rönd potion twice a moon, but if she wants to, Mother can still read our thoughts."

I recalled that day the queen broke into her sons' heads. They'd appeared pained.

"It's easier for her to do it to us, though," Saga added. "We're her blood, of her own flesh, so we have a deep connection. She'd have to try hard to do it to you —after you take this, that is."

"Then I best not give her the chance."

"Limit contact, no touching, and you should be fine."

I uncorked the flask and took a swig.

"The flask should last a week, if not a couple of days more," Saga said.

"What happens when I need more?"

"I'll make sure you have it. It's in everyone's best interest that your true past stays hidden."

"And you think your mother knows nothing of it?"

"After we took Sir Qildor to the healers' wing, I spent hours with Mother. We talked about you. Not once did I get the impression that she knew you were a slave."

"But I'm sure your mother can keep a secret." After all, she was a mind-reading queen. I could only imagine the things she'd learned with each turn of the sun.

"Yes, but Mother and I are close." Saga shrugged. "I did my best to feel her out. I'm pretty sure she has no idea."

It would have to do.

"Thank you, Saga." I set the flask on the dresser. "I appreciate you looking out for me. For being a friend."

"I meant it when I said I'd like you as a family member. Never expected it would actually happen. Or quite in the manner that it did, but"—she lifted a delicate shoulder and gave a half smile—"here we are. And I'll do what I can to protect you from Father's ire." She looked away, uncomfortable about bringing up her kin.

I hated that the king was related to Vale and Saga. Both were good and kind, and the king was despicable. That he had ever been different was difficult for me to believe.

Saga cleared her throat. "Well, I guess I'll see you at the Courting Festival gathering." She brushed a hand down my arm in farewell and winked slyly. "Do try not to incite more gossip, sister."

CHAPTER 12
VALE

H and in hand, Neve and I walked to where the Courting Festival event of the day would take place. With each step, my shoulders grew tighter.

Though my sister had protected Neve against our mother's magic—something I was disappointed in myself for not having thought of—so much could still go wrong. And that was only considering the fae.

I wasn't worried about the vampires. Not yet anyway.

It would take days for Captain Barvo's ship to land upon the shores of the Vampire Kingdom and hours still for him to reach Sangrael, the heart of the Blood Court. Then the royals would have to hire assassins. Or worse.

Will the King and Queen of the Blood Court come?

Before the thought could take root, I vanquished it.

No reason to worry about that when threats lived

inside the castle. Threats to my new wife, a fae of Winter's Realm I had sworn to protect. Threats who shared my blood.

Father and Rhistel remained my primary concerns, and I wasn't sure which one posed a greater risk.

No one outside our family knew the full truth of Rhistel's magic. My father had seen to that. With the use of my twin's gloves, spun from the strongest ice spider silk, his dark power was easy enough to hide. He also possessed winter magic, though that was far less concerning and not as powerful as Father's winter-based magic.

Nor was mine.

It vexed the king that his sons could only manipulate portions of winter magic. I wielded my winter magic as frigid gales and frost pulled from the moisture in the air. Rhistel favored his winter magic in the form of water, which he turned into weapons of ice.

Of the three Aaberg children, only Saga possessed the full magic of winter, able to make snow fall, create a cage of ice, and gusts that would freeze a fae solid. But even her powers were weaker than Father's by quite a lot. Her visions were the stronger of her magic, though far less predictable.

Music up ahead snapped me into protector mode.

Neve glanced up at me. "Everything all right?"

Since seeing the blood vials, her assurance against Warden Roar's wrongdoings, smashed on the floor, she'd pulled herself together. I needed to do the same.

"Fine," I assured her. "We should stick together."

"I have no desire to be caught alone with your father."

"Or my brother."

She laughed dryly. "Definitely not."

Although I was certain she was curious about him, my new wife had not asked about Rhistel. An oddity. Most people wanted to know more about the heir—even if they disliked Rhistel as a person.

Unfortunately for the public, with few exceptions, my twin was a very private male. Once, I'd have been counted among those he confided in, but not for many turns. I couldn't stomach some things he did, and that tore us apart.

We approached the solarium where Father was hosting the afternoon's event. His choice of the bright, plant-filled space told me that this festival event would be smaller than the others.

I was proven right when we reached the door to the sun parlor and two Clawsguards waved us inside.

I inhaled the scent of vegetation and humidity. This room had been designed differently from others in the castle—always kept warmer and smelling fresh.

"It's lovely." Neve's wings fluttered slightly and stretched as if they, too, were taking in the fresh air. "Not at all what I expected."

"Mother's doing," I said. "She brought in plants far more suited to the Summer Court to give the solarium an *exotic* look. The decor requires many earth fae to keep alive. A tremendous drain of resources for the beautification of one room."

"Maybe so, but I appreciate the effort." Neve's lips curled up in a small smile, and my stuffiness evaporated a touch.

After all, resource suck or not, the solarium looked nice. And those flitting about inside appeared to appreciate the efforts. Many Winterborn and bred fae had never seen so much green in one place.

At first glance, one hundred fae milled about, most of them members of the Sacred Eight or the wealthiest jarls in the kingdom. My father and brother huddled in a group of three such jarls. I frowned when one smiled with glee.

Jarl Triam was young for a faerie of his elevated position. At forty turns, he lived in a small city in the midlands and enacted law right beneath House Vagle. His land was known for being infested by ogres, but that wasn't the most disgusting thing about the place.

Since Triam came into power ten turns back, he'd taken three wives, all of whom had died under mysterious circumstances. Had the wives not been lowborn and Triam not been such a close friend to Fival Vagle, my mother's brother and acting lord of the Staghorn Castle, there would have been an investigation. But there hadn't been.

Was Triam in the running for a new wife? My nose wrinkled, hating the idea.

"A smaller gathering than the ball," Neve said, squeezing my hand. "I think that's a relief?"

She didn't sound so sure. Understandable. A smaller

event meant fewer eyes on us, but it could still be dangerous.

"Always keep your defenses up," I murmured back as, from across the room, Sian caught my eye and waved. "Let's begin over there."

Together, we wended through the room, moving closer to the vast windows spanning the far wall and curving up to form a large part of the ceiling. Outside, the Shivering Sea stretched into the horizon. Whitecaps tipped the waves, hinting that the wind was up. Flurries of snow fell too, and dark clouds stretched across the sky like a bruise. A storm was rolling in. Again. Of late, we'd had many more than normal.

Inside, though, Frostveil Castle was as warm as ever. At least in temperature.

The experience of walking through a crowd of fae and no one stopping me to speak was decidedly frigid. As I was a newlywed fae, congratulations should spew from the lips of every courtier.

That did not happen. Most stared, but if I caught their eyes, they looked away. I suspected that, at the moment, few wanted to be associated with us—the pair who had earned a trusted Clawsguard a whipping.

I cringed. Before we retired for the evening, I needed to stop by the healers' sanctuary to see if Sir Qildor was awake and how he fared. The knight was a dear friend, part of my inner circle. A cabal member. I huffed out a laugh, unable to deny that I was warming to the term, though I had yet to let my sister know. Some things an older brother needed to keep to himself.

"Vale." Sian patted my shoulder when we joined his small group, consisting of Vidar Virtoris, Thantrel Riis, and two of Sian's many siblings, his sisters, Baenna and Eireann. "I take it the journey back to the castle was uneventful?"

"The vampires have already sailed west for the Blood Kingdom," Vidar interjected, brushing aside a large leaf caressing his shoulder.

Neve let out a low breath. She hadn't seemed worried about the vampires. Apparently, she'd been hiding her worry well. Not a surprise considering how well she'd been playing a part at court.

"We stopped for lunch at Ragnor's," I replied as a servant appeared with a tray of sparkling fae wine and small toasts topped with a fermented fish and winter-berry. Not wishing to have bad breath, I opted for the wine, then handed a glass to Neve. She took it and sipped, her lovely eyes going wide at the taste.

"It's good, isn't it?" Vidar asked, bestowing the same smile on my wife that I'd seen steal the hearts of many courtiers. Unfortunately, he was already taken.

Father had betrothed Saga to Vidar a few turns back. Their union had not yet come to pass because Vidar had, until recently, been sailing the seas for the majority of the last three turns. It was a voyage every heir to House Virtoris took. For her part, Saga didn't seem to mind his absence, but I suspected that soon they'd be wed, and I'd be able to call my dear friend brother.

"Did anything out of turn happen?" Vidar asked. "In the city?"

The question surprised me, but it shouldn't have. The Virtoris heir was always one to expect trouble. I supposed that was only natural when you would inherit an armada that often had to deal with pirates in the northern seas around our kingdom.

I shook my head. "Nothing happened."

"Except that I ate *far* too large a lunch." Neve's hand landed on her belly. Her gowns were limited to those that Warden Roar gave her, but she'd found a navy blue one in the lot of House Lisika colors. So much bleeding crimson and gold.

I made a mental note to have Saga's seamstress come by my suite and measure Neve for new gowns. Ones in my house colors. Even if our relationship was a sham, she needed to look the part for as long as it lasted.

"Ragnor's is so good!" Eireann's wine sloshed close to the top of her glass as she gesticulated. "I haven't been since we arrived in the city for the festival, but Father always takes the family."

"Says it costs him a fortune because Ragnor's is expensive, but it's worth it," Baenna added.

"More like it costs him a fortune because your parents have so many bleeding children." Thantrel laughed, his cheeks flushed pink from the drink.

My outgoing friend had changed from sparring attire into an outfit I could only describe as a half dress. The back flowing long, the front ending in a normal tunic. Thantrel had eccentric tastes, and I suspected he liked the attention those tastes earned him.

"Only one way to stop that." One red eyebrow, trimmed and darkened slightly, probably to emphasize the gold shimmer Thantrel wore on his eyelids, arched. He pretended to toast the Baliks.

Eireann scowled. "Perhaps give your own father that advice? He has too many children to count!"

They were both right. Lord and Lady Balik of the great house of the southlands, had nine children, quite a lot for a faerie family. Our kind often had trouble reproducing, but as we also lived for thousands of turns, larger families could still be created. The Baliks, however, did not seem to have any problem birthing heirs as once they began, many were born in rapid succession.

Lord Riis had never wed. And yet, the Lord of Tongues sired as many children as House Balik and House Armenil, the great house of the north that boasted six heirs, combined. The only difference was Lord Riis's children were all illegitimate.

Many expressed their surprise when Father allowed Luccan, Arie, and Thantrel to attend the Courting Festival. Or summoned them, more like.

Then again, the king hadn't done so out of the kindness of his heart. He possessed a reason for wanting the nobles here, and Lord Riis had to be included in the lot. Hence, Father legitimized Lord Riis's eldest sons, and they received invitations.

The ladies set to discussing other matters, and Neve

fell right in with them. That surprised me for a moment, but then I recalled that the day Neve arrived at court, and Saga invited her to a game of nuchi. Baenna and Eireann had probably been playing too.

Happy to let Neve relax a little, I turned to Sian and Vidar, the latter of whom was nodding excitedly.

"You and Sayyida would make a great match." Vidar plucked a small hand pie off a tray as another servant came around. "If you wish, I can bring it up to the king?"

"Appreciated," Sian said. "And I agree that we're well suited. If anything, we're aligned in personal matters."

Vidar nodded. "She'll need a husband who is understanding. One who expects little in the, uh, bedchambers, and who doesn't mind if she takes to the sea."

My lips curled. It wasn't well-known at court, but Vidar was close to his sister and two turns back, she'd confided in him that she preferred female company. Since then, Vidar had been fretting over the day Lady Virtoris set a marriage for her daughter.

The proposed match between Sayyida and Sian worked out well, as he preferred male companionship.

That and the fact that, although Sian was the eldest son of Balik, he was not the heir to their house. That honor went to my squire, Filip, for House Balik, and Vidar for House Virtoris—both the magically strongest of their lines.

Of course, Sayyida and Sian would still be required

to expand their noble houses, but once that duty was done, I expected the pair could pursue their own desires. A clever match, indeed. Normally, I would offer to broach the topic with Father, but after my actions, that would not go over well, a fact that I was sure Sian had considered already.

"It's odd that the king has not set any matches yet," Vidar mused.

"The Festival has only been on for a few days," Sian countered. "I'd rather the king take his time. Observe us and set matches that benefit those in them. Not just House Aaberg."

At that, my cheeks warmed. A Courting Festival had not been called for a long time. And everyone recognized it for what it was: a way for the king to curate matches, power structures, and the futures of noble houses that benefitted the king and his lineage.

Not that matches benefiting House Aaberg were the *only* reason for the Courting Festival. Far from it.

"I see nothing wrong with you and Sayyida marrying," I replied, not about to bring up the Ice Scepter.

My friends, nor anyone else, knew of how Father, Mother, Rhistel, and I suspected one noble house held the Hallow of Winter's Realm. And, though I disagreed with Father and my brother in many respects, in this, we were of one mind. The search for the Hallow of Winter would stay a family secret.

Sian waved over the closest brownie bearing a tray of wine and switched his out for a fresh glass. All the while, he watched the circle around my father. "I wish those jarls would shove off. Then I'd go speak with the king about a union between my house and the Virtoris family right now."

"One is Jarl Salizier," Vidar said, taking in the group of lesser nobles with interest. "He tried to court Sayyida just last turn."

Neve twisted, apparently having been listening in despite appearing engrossed in her own conversation. The sly fox. "She told me that! We ran into him on the way to the tourney and Sayyida mentioned how she didn't like him at all." My wife smiled at Sian. "No competition."

To my shock, Sian, an elite warrior of the south-lands, blushed at Neve's attention. Had I not known him so well, I'd almost have thought he was taken with her romantically, but that wasn't it. No, it was that Neve was so sincere and bright, it took Sian by surprise.

"Thank you, Princess Neve," Sian replied. "I—"

Horns blared, making me start slightly. Perhaps it was the bubbly drink, or perhaps being among my closest friends, but I'd lulled myself into a sense of calm.

My father waved for attention and the crowds fell silent. "My wife, Queen Inga, and I would like to thank you all for coming today. I realize we sent invitations to the Courting Festival on short notice." Father lifted his glass. His pale cheeks had already taken on a ruddy sheen.

"Invite?" Sian whispered with a snort. "A summons, more like."

"Shh," his sister, Baenna, hushed him.

"I've called you here to announce that I have settled on two more matches during this Courting Festival," Father continued. "As you know, my first blessing did not go as planned." His ice-blue eyes sought Neve and, taking the king's gaze as an open invitation to gawk, others stared too.

She slunk back, but I would have none of that. I took my wife's hand and squeezed it. Remembering herself, and I hoped that she was stronger than nearly all the fae in this room, Neve's shoulders rolled back, and her chin lifted.

The king scowled but continued on. "The matches I'm about to announce, however, I believe will be quite beneficial to both houses involved. And the kingdom at large." Father turned to a gathering of faeries, most of them with red hair and wings in various shades of green —House Armenil. "Marit Armenil, come forward."

Neve sucked in a breath, but I waited, wondering what Father had decided. Marit was the eldest child of House Armenil, the great house of the northern terri- tory. She was not the most magically powerful and hence not the heir, but to hear Saga tell it, Lord Sten Armenil, Warden of the North and his wife, Lady Orla Armenil née Balik, valued Marit's opinions on many matters. Their daughter was well-educated and kind and knew how to relate to the people of the northern territory.

The Armenils would expect an excellent match for such a prized jewel.

With grace born from many turns of etiquette

classes, Marit glided over to stand next to Father. Though she appeared pulled together and was quite far away, I caught the slight trembling of her light green wings. The king nodded at her, a smile growing on his face—one that made my blood grow cold. That was the smile Father used when he was about to deal a blow.

What was he thinking?

The Courting Festival was a means for the king to exert power and dominance over other houses, but if Father was about to set a poor match for Marit . . . No, that was a horrible idea. He wouldn't be so foolish.

"You, Marit of House Armenil, will wed a male I have chosen for you. One with great wealth and influence. Together, you'll bring the midlands to prosperous times."

I blinked. Midlands? That left only a handful of lords.

"Jarl Triam, please come forward and greet your bride," Father said, loud and clear.

I stiffened as murmurs rippled through the crowd. Father was matching Marit with a jarl who had been thrice wed already? One who had likely murdered his wives?

He's insane.

Two males stepped out of the crowd to face the king. One, Jarl Triam. The other, a mountain of a male, bearing the white wolf insignia over his breast—Lord Sten Armenil.

"I won't allow it," Lord Armenil shouted. "Not my daughter. Not with him. I—"

"I thought we might hit this hitch, Sten," Father cut the great lord off as Clawsguards closed in around Lord Armenil. "Thought you might wish for more say over which house your eldest landed in? So I'll give you a compromise. The only one I will allow."

Lord Armenil's eyes narrowed. "You must've realized this was a poor match if you premeditated a compromise, Magnus."

"*King* Magnus," Father growled. "And yes, it is my job to foresee outcomes. Now, would you like the chance to hear your option? Or shall I bring in a staret to perform your daughter's ceremony right now?"

Sten Armenil's freckle-strewn face paled. "What is the compromise?"

"I have yet to send a diplomat to the Blood Court. If you wish for a say in your daughter's marriage, you will go. Explain what happened to their prince, and I might allow you to sway my choice." Father held up a single finger. "Until then, she will stay with Jarl Triam."

Lord Armenil appeared shocked and for good reason. Usually, the Crown tasked Warden Roar to deal with the vampires. In his absence, Father sent my uncle Captain Vagle. But the Warden of the North? We had never sent him into vampire territory.

He had no past with them. No rapport. No ties. It very well could be a suicide mission.

And I suspected Father knew that. My fists clenched, but as Lord Armenil spoke next, I knew the future was set.

"I'll go," the Warden of the North said. "But she

will not stay with him. Marit is pure, and she remains with my family until they are wed."

"During the nights only," Father shot back. "During the day, your daughter will be with her fiancé. She may have a chaperone if you wish. Upon your return, we will speak about a different match."

The words he didn't say, '*if you return,*' hung in the air.

Marit's chest heaved as silent sobs wracked her, but her father only gave a stout nod and went to collect her.

With the matter settled; Father captured the crowd's attention once more with that conniving grin of his. "Now, for the second match of the day . . ."

CHAPTER 13

NEVE

The room held its breath.

I didn't know who Jarl Triam was, but I recognized the fear riddling Marit's face. She reminded me of how terrified I'd felt when Prince Gervais first threatened me in Sangrael.

Back before I'd tasted freedom. Back when the only thing I had to lose was my life.

I would bet the ruby ring Roar had given me—the same one discarded in a drawer at the moment—that Jarl Triam was a threat.

Socially. Financially. On her status?

Her life? At the thought, my mouth went parchment dry.

The king prattled on about how the second match was one fated in the stars. One in which a jarl had made plain his desires for the female.

"Who am I to stand in the way of true love?" King Magnus crowed, high on his own power. To my disgust, those in the crowd clapped. Did they think the king was so charismatic? Or did they want to appease him to keep themselves safe?

"On with it," Vale growled low enough so that no one else, save perhaps Sian standing at my husband's other side, could hear.

Yes, hurry, you pompous windbag.

"Jarl Salizier, come forward." The king motioned at the crowd of lesser lords hovering around him since we arrived. Though I'd seen him only once, I recognized the thin jarl with the thick blond beard and rosy cheeks who joined the king.

"And Lady Sayyida Virtoris, come forth and greet your match." King Magnus's tone hardened as he turned to face Sayyida, next to Saga and Lady Virtoris.

Saga blanched, and even from far away, the veins popping in Lady Virtoris's temples stood out.

Sayyida merely shook her head.

"Is something wrong with my choice?" King Magnus growled.

Lady Virtoris stepped forward and spoke for her daughter. "We've already spoken with the jarl and refused his offer. He is from the midlands."

"*And?*"

"We are seafaring people, Majesty," the Lady of Ships continued, her voice stronger after the initial shock. "Sayyida is a captain in the Royal Nava. That is where she wishes to stay. She can't very well command ships from a castle in the landlocked midlands now, can she?" Lady Virtoris's chin lifted. "Not to mention that I believe my daughter to be too good for the jarl."

Whispers abounded, but my attention had strayed back to Sayyida. She, too, had pulled on a brave face and crossed her arms over her chest as though they were armor. But would it work?

"That is where you are wrong, Lady Virtoris," King Magnus spat. "Your daughter has proven that she is nothing special. Dare I say, I should have punished her for attending recent events and not bringing them to my attention. Not even trying to stop them."

The Lady of Ships's lips parted in shock that had to be similar to the jolt running through me.

Recent events . . .

The king had matched Sayyida and Marit, both high ladies who had attended my wedding to Vale! They were nobles with power and armies of their own. The king could not punish them in the same manner as Sir Qildor—not if he wished to keep the Sacred Eight on his side.

However, he could, by rights and tradition, match them and give them horrible husbands—ones he knew they did not want.

Which was what he was doing.

My fists clenched at my sides as a mix of fury and guilt rolled through me. I hated the king for doing this, for hurting innocents.

Worse, I was responsible. Had I not said yes to Vale, none of this would have happened.

But then again, I'd most likely already be dead if I had said no.

I swallowed the lump rising in my throat. At least Anna, Clemencia, Sir Caelo, and the whores who had witnessed our wedding were far away and safe.

Thank the stars Lord Riis had known to send them away. That he'd had a place to keep them.

But what of Filip? I found the young squire in the crowd, standing by a male I assumed to be his father. My jaw tightened. Would the king match Filip too? And cruelly so?

"He's too young to be matched," Vale whispered. "Filip is safe, for now."

So he'd come to the truth of the matter too. That we were responsible for this misery. And yet, he'd said nothing either. That led me to believe that staying quiet was the smart thing to do for now. Perhaps if we fought it, the king would force my friends to wed at this very moment, ripping them from their families. In Marit's case, he'd already insinuated as much. At least this way, if we played our cards right, there was a chance to fix this.

I would ask Vale to bring it up with his father.

"Now"—the king's voice boomed, quelling the murmuring running through the crowd—"that the matter of the matches is settled, we shall celebrate." He lifted his glass of wine. "To the new betrothals! New alliances!"

Those in the crowd raised their glasses, even those of the House Armenil and House Virtoris. Even

Sayyida and Marit, though Marit's arm was shaking and Sayyida only did so at her mother's insistence. If Sayyida had it her way, she'd probably hurl her goblet to the ground.

With the toast finished; the king turned back to speaking with the newly betrothed jarls. The newly matched ladies, however, bolted from the solarium. Marit did so with grace, but Sayyida with so much fury that she knocked over two potted trees and bulldozed through a group of ladies on her way out.

Saga wasn't far behind Sayyida.

"Vale," I whispered. I had to be there for the ladies who had taken me in and who were now hurting because of me.

"Let's go," he said. "Don't run, though. Don't draw more attention to them."

I parted through the crowd. Sayyida, Marit, and Saga had already disappeared through the door. A few Armenils left too—though Lady Virtoris remained with two of her children, one male, one female, both in their mid to late teens, whom I had not met. They followed close behind their mother, who seemed to be doing her best to steal the king away from the jarls. Not having much luck by the looks of it.

Vale strode behind me, fending off the few people who tried to get his attention. Apparently, we were no longer the main gossip of the court, so speaking with the prince wasn't as much of a risk.

We were nearly at the door, the Clawsguards we'd

arrived with waiting to escort us, when Prince Rhistel stepped into my path.

I ran right into him, and though I pulled away, I couldn't help but notice how different he felt from his brother. Softer, leaner, more delicate. And where my new husband smelled of sandalwood and freshly fallen snow, Rhistel's scent was that of libraries—old parchment and wax dripping from candles. Not repulsive, though the way he wrapped his hand around my wrist, soft and forcibly sensual, was.

I ripped my arm away.

"So *testy*, sister," Rhistel drawled. "I came to speak with you. I figured I'd better get to know you while I still can."

The potent scent of wine filled the air between us. The heir was drunk. And from the way his eyes caught on my chest, I suspected he was horny too.

"Don't touch me," I hissed. "And get out of my way."

Rhistel's face hardened. "Just because you're no longer a whore doesn't mean you can speak to me that way." He lifted his hands and began tugging one of his gloves off.

I blinked, realizing as his pale hand emerged that this was the first time I'd seen the heir without his gloves. What was going on here? And where was Vale?

I twisted to find three large males standing in front of my husband. He caught my eye, then his widened. As if I were in danger.

I turned back to Rhistel, prepared to fend off a

blow, but the prince grinned at me, one hand bare, one gloved.

"Now, Neve, what do you say we leave this place and speak?" He reached for me with his ungloved hand.

I recoiled and was ready to tell him to keep his paws to himself when a roar rang through the room, followed by two moans and what sounded like a crack of bone on marble. I spun on my heel to find the males who'd surrounded Vale on the floor and my husband lunging at me.

He grabbed me, pulled me close, and shoved his brother backward into an approaching guard.

"Don't touch her," Vale hissed. A pause filled the air between them as every head turned to take in the fight between brothers. "She's *mine*."

A shudder ran down my spine. *Mine.*

I despised the territorial term—the sign of ownership. I'd had enough of people owning me for an entire lifetime. And yet, nothing in me revolted when Vale said it. Rather, my insides warmed.

Rhistel's rebounding, however, doused that heat, closing the distance between us again and pointing a bare finger at his brother.

Vale dodged it and maneuvered me behind him.

What in the stars?

People were shouting—my name. Vale's. Rhistel's.

I cringed. We'd attracted attention again, so much. *Too much.* I was about to tell Vale to let it be, that we had to go, when the queen swept into the scene right up to her eldest son.

Queen Inga's brilliant blue eyes blazed. "*Rhistel*. Do not force my hand."

She spoke softly, quietly, but fire filled her words. The haze of drunkenness cleared from Rhistel's eyes and fear rippled across his face. Without a word, he pulled his glove on.

"Go, Vale," Queen Inga growled. "Leave. Take her with you. Keep her out of our sight."

Vale said nothing, just wound my fingers through his and we left the solarium.

I perched on Saga's bed, patting Sayyida's back. The princess sat on the other side of Sayyida, holding her friend's hand, providing comfort as Sayyida wept.

Wept.

I never thought I'd see the day.

"This won't happen," Saga whispered for the tenth time. "I won't allow it. I'll speak with my father."

"And say *what*?" Sayyida shot back. "If my mother with her armada and all the might of our House can't sway him, how can you, Saga? He's furious! With me! With Marit! We should have never . . ."

She trailed off, but the unsaid words hung in the air.

They should have never helped us. They never should have attended my wedding. I swallowed.

"I'm so sorry that Vale and I put you in this situation," I murmured. "It's all my fault."

"No, Neve, it's not," Saga interjected. "Perhaps it

was hasty for us to stay, to stand against my father and wound his pride in that way, but he is making these choices." Her face grew stony. "It's a punishment, but it cannot happen. I won't let it, Sayyida. I won't."

The princess took Sayyida by the chin and turned her friend's head to her own. Their eyes locked. Sayyida licked her lips and Saga's gaze softened noticeably.

Not for the first time, I lingered in the middle of a very intimate moment. There was something between them. Did the king see that? The queen? Saga's brothers?

Vale had known that Sayyida preferred females, but did he know about Saga? That I was certain she preferred the same—and Sayyida in particular?

"Sian and I had a plan," Sayyida said. "We were going to wed and then I could sail and do as I wished." She stared at Saga, the faerie betrothed to Sayyida's own brother. "And he could do as he wished too."

"We'll make it right," Saga insisted. "Father has allowed me to push back my marriage to Vidar for many turns. He said nothing about you wedding Jarl Salizier soon. We can buy time, then dissolve it."

My heart clenched at the triangle—or perhaps a square?—that my friends were in. Though Vidar seemed very kind and the type of male many females would love to marry, he wasn't what Saga wanted. Did *he* know the truth? Perhaps they, too, had made a pact?

For her sake, I hoped so.

Actually, no. I hoped the king would stop being such a giant pile of gryphon dung! That he'd see sense and call this stupid Courting Festival off. Stop harassing his people.

Then the smiles of the jarls came back to me. Well, some of his people were happy about the results. But not those I cared for.

"He threatened Marit." Sayyida wiped tears from her face. Then, shockingly, she stood for the first time since I'd arrived half an hour ago. "What makes you think he won't do the same to me?"

The princess looked away. She could give no guarantee.

But that didn't mean hope could not live on. "Saga is the king's jewel, Sayyida. He'll listen to her."

Sayyida laughed, and for once it wasn't bawdy or full of joy, but cold and skeptical. "We'll see. I need to find my mother."

"I'll come with," Saga said and made to stand.

But Sayyida held up a hand. "No. I need time with Mother. Alone."

"Oh, all right then." Saga sat again, face carefully blank.

"Thanks for everything," Sayyida added, more of an afterthought than anything. "I'll see you two later."

She left. I heard her exchange a few words outside, probably with Vale. Since we'd arrived at Saga's room, after a brief stop at the Virtoris wing where we were redirected, he'd been out there—waiting for me.

He hadn't said a word about my run-in with his brother. And while I'd been curious, I hadn't asked either. Since leaving the solarium, my priority had been to find Sayyida. To help her.

Now she was gone and the question of what had happened with Rhistel was back. Maybe Saga would know?

I found Saga staring at her hands, clearly holding back tears. I swallowed my question.

The news of Sayyida's betrothal had hit Saga hard too. I couldn't bring her more pain, not after all that I'd already put her through. Even if her father wouldn't harm his own blood directly, I'd put her brother at risk, brought ill fortune to those females who had shown me grace at court—Saga's best friends. One of them, the person I believed she loved.

"Do you need anything?" I whispered. "Want me to stay?"

Saga looked up at me, unshed tears in her blue eyes, the fingers of her right hand clenching the skirt of her dress, as if the fine fabric was the only thing keeping her in one piece. "I think I'd like to be alone too. I'll see you later, Neve. Tomorrow."

"Very well. But *please* call if you need anything." A part of me felt silly for making such an offer to the princess, a faerie with an entire kingdom at her fingertips. But I'd do anything for Saga. After all, this was my fault. I swallowed. "I'm serious, Saga. Call and I'll come. "

"I know," she replied, already moving to lie down on the bed.

I saw myself to the door, guilt twisting my insides with each step.

CHAPTER 14

VALE

Tension riddled my neck, tightening the muscles and quickening my gait as I sought an audience with my father.

I'd left Neve in my suite, guarded by Sir Arvid. Again, I wished Caelo or Qildor were present and able. Their watch over Neve would have been far preferable, but it wasn't to be. Sir Arvid was what I had.

Him and an inquisitive new wife.

Upon leaving Saga's rooms, Neve had questioned me not once, not twice, but three times about my brother. Not about why I'd batted his ungloved hand away, but rather why my mother had intervened.

I swallowed. The debate over whether to tell Neve the truth about Rhistel warred inside me.

On one hand, my brother's secret held the power to destroy him, destroy *our family*—and no matter how furious I was with half of my family at the moment, I loved them, even my mercurial twin and increasingly

197

cruel father. Perhaps that was foolish, but to say I didn't care would be a lie.

At the same time, my desire to keep Neve safe grew by the day. If she knew about Rhistel's magic, surely, she'd take more care to avoid him.

But no one outside my family knew. Only Father, my grandfather, and, of course, Mother knew. Mother hadn't even thought it was prudent to tell her brother, Captain Eirwen, and he was around the palace often. The information was too dangerous.

And yet, I wanted to tell Neve.

I trusted her. Possibly because she had trusted me with her secret. Perhaps it wasn't one that would break apart a kingdom, but if my father learned of her past, he *would* send her back to the Blood Court. It would destroy her life, just when she'd achieved some semblance of freedom.

Though my past was nothing like hers, I understood her fierce desire to run and build a new life. To be free. Royals were never completely free to do as they wished, either.

But one day, Neve would be. I'd see to it.

I rounded a corner, and the door to Father's personal library came into view. Before I could stop them, my fists clenched. I loosened them.

Though I wished to rail and storm against the king, I'd try to fix this mess without angering him and save Neve from more pain. A long, heated exhale parted my lips as I approached the door.

"My prince," said Sir Lars, the Clawsguard standing

in front of the dark wood door with a golden bear's claw inlaid in the center. He bowed and his long black hair fell in a curtain around his face.

I waited until Sir Lars rose and looked me in the eye. "Is he in there?"

"He is."

Father was never much one for lingering in crowded social events. He did so only because, as the king, it was expected of him. But on my way here, I'd noticed others from the gathering walking the halls, rushing from the chaos of the event. If they had left the solarium, then the king had as well. He'd come to one of his favorite places, his personal library. He enjoyed only the harem wing and his bedchambers more.

"Who else?" I asked.

"Prince Rhistel."

My throat tightened. No wonder the guard hadn't already moved aside, let alone opened the door and allowed me entry. He was assessing me. Because while I might be royal, I was not the king nor the heir to Winter's Realm, the two fae who outranked me in the kingdom.

"If I let you pass, there will be no violence?" Sir Lars asked, black eyebrows knitted together. He was one of my father's oldest and most trusted guards.

I paused long enough for the knight's hand to land on the hilt of his sword, pushing his golden cloak aside as he moved.

"Yes," I replied after weighing my desire to punch my brother against my desire to speak with my father and perhaps gain mercy for Neve, Sayyida, and Marit. Even with Rhistel present, I might convince our father to see sense. "No violence. We'll talk out our differences."

"As family should." Sir Lars's scarred hand lifted from the sword, drifted to the door, and opened it. "Prince Vale is here to see you, Majesty."

"Let him in," Father answered. The gruffness in his tone hinted that he'd had one too many glasses of wine. Would that help or hinder my cause?

Either way, I'd committed, so I stepped past the Clawsguard and into the small space filled with books and warmth from an ever-burning hearth.

Father lounged in a large chair, a tafl board before him. The pieces, made from the bones of a particularly violent frost giant, ranged across the squares. He seemed to be playing himself, and not particularly well either. My gaze flicked upward to find that his lips were purple. Yes, too much wine.

Rhistel, on the other hand, appeared to have sobered. His dark brown eyes glowered at me, and, in my twin's hand, he held a phoenix feather quill. On a table was a piece of parchment, glistening with ink in the candlelight.

When he noticed I eyed the parchment, Rhistel turned the page over. "What are you doing here, Vale? Thought you'd be with that wife of yours, acting like the beast you are."

My feet moved before my mind caught up, and I was across the room in a second, shoving Rhistel against a wall, pinning him down by the shoulders. He growled and snarled back.

"*Enough!*" Father bellowed. "Vale, step away from him!"

But I couldn't. Wouldn't. I suspected that even if I'd wanted to, I could not force myself to release my brother.

Beneath my hold, Rhistel jerked, trying to free himself. Unfortunately for him, Rhistel knew much of manipulation but little of physical strength. He would not be moving until I'd said my piece.

"Release him, or I'll send for your wife right now."

Rhistel's lips curled up. "Please do, Father. I'm dying to see those luscious curves again. Perhaps touch—"

I took him by the chin and wrenched his head to the side. "You will not speak of her. Or think of her. You *will* stay away from her, and I'll do my best to forget what you did in the solarium."

My twin snarled. "Have the dead gods risen or does she already have your balls in a vise, Vale? Big brute that you are, felled by that whore?"

I lifted my fist.

"Vale! Enough!" Father bellowed behind me. At his tone, the door opened.

"Majesty?" Lars's eyes landed on me and narrowed.

Bleeding skies. What was I doing? Defending Neve was important, but had I followed through with my plan —spoken with my father and not Rhistel—I could have avoided this. Rhistel might be the heir, but even he had to listen to the king.

"Outside, Sir Lars," Father growled. The door snicked closed, and the king stood next to us, his ice-blue eyes burning with fury. "Vale, release Rhistel."

"Not until he promises." The words rumbled out of me, nonsensical, given my situation. "I will not have my wife harmed by his magic."

Father's eyes narrowed and shifted to his heir. "As much as I despise the female, you will adhere to the rules your mother and I have put in place, Rhistel. The consequences are too dire."

Despise the female? That was laughable. Under other circumstances, Father would have *loved* having Neve around him. In his bed. In his harem. No matter if he had bargained her hand to another, a jarl most likely, I was certain he would have tried to take advantage of her before she wed. Perhaps after too.

But she'd defied him, and the king wanted revenge.

He hated her as much as he wanted her. Only the fact that she was married to me, and I was not only his son, but physically a match for my father, gave him pause.

Had I possessed the king's same prowess with magic, he wouldn't dare look at her.

My twin still hadn't spoken, and Father's ice-blue gaze hardened. "I believe that Vale very much means every word he is saying, Rhistel, and it will look quite bad for the family—for you—if the spare beats the heir to a pulp."

Rhistel's eyes darkened. He hated being reminded that he, with his birthright and powerful magic, could still be bloodied. All I needed to do was catch him unawares.

"You will not touch her." I reiterated, my nose a hairsbreadth from his. "Nor speak with her. You will cease calling her names. And you will not use your magic on her. If you do not agree, I won't just *beat you to a pulp*. I will tell the entire kingdom what you can do."

For the first time, fear flashed in my brother's eyes. The threat of being beaten was bad enough, but for the kingdom, likely all of Isila, to hear of his magic? It would be disastrous. Perhaps even sparking another revolution.

He held magic that would allow no other kingdom to trust us. Or, in the case of some, trust us even less than they already did. By the law of Isila, Father and Mother should have killed Rhistel the moment his proclivity to such forbidden magic arose.

Instead, they'd made me promise to never speak of Rhistel's magic, not even to Saga. And they forced the heir to wear ice spider silk gloves. The material was so powerful, it prevented Rhistel from using the taboo magic coursing through him, for unlike his winter magic, his outlawed power required touch.

"You'd be cast out." Rhistel snarled. "Our family would never forgive you. Not even Saga."

He had a point, though he should have known it wouldn't sway me. Even the loss of my sister's love, which would hit me the hardest. I'd never threaten something so dire if I didn't mean it.

"You have one choice." I pressed him harder into the wall.

Father sipped his wine but said nothing.

After another fruitless round of struggle beneath my hold, Rhistel let out a furious hiss and loosened.

"Fine. I won't approach your wife or speak with her."

"You will not use your powers on her."

"I won't."

"Nor spread tales."

He snorted. "Are they tales, though? I find them to be quite the truth."

One of my hands strayed to his neck, wrapped around it, and pressed hard against his tender throat. Beneath my grip, his pulse flared, pounding wildly. "She's no whore. I wanted her, and now she is mine. A princess of the realm that bears the name Aaberg. Your name. My name. *The royal name.*"

"And as much as I hate that Vale gave the commoner our name," our father piped up, "that demands respect, Rhistel. If you cannot respect your new sister-in-law, then who will? And with that outward disrespect, our family name tarnishes." His lips curled. If there was one thing Father could not abide, it was his name being run through the muck.

Rhistel narrowed his eyes. "My magic will stay bound."

"Release him, Vale," Father commanded. "He gave his word."

But I didn't let go. Even with his word, could I trust

him? Rhistel was clever and slippery, and his particular magic rendered him far more like Neve than he knew.

"Vale," Father's tone dipped. "I've entertained this *absurdity* long enough. Release Rhistel."

My arms fell to my sides, and, not trusting me, Rhistel took three paces to the side, his hand lifting to rub at his neck as he did so.

Father twisted toward him. "Leave us."

"Father, we were speaking before this brute"— Rhistel gestured to me—"interrupted."

Father's eyes closed, a sign of his thinning patience. "I've already told you my thoughts on matters regarding the Festival. If you have more to say, Rhistel, find me tomorrow. For now, go lick your wounds." He gave my brother a look of disgust.

Though Rhistel was the heir, and a clever, cunning fae, Father hated that my twin didn't possess physical strength.

"I need to speak with Vale." Father turned his attention to me.

Rhistel's cheeks grew red, and he looked like he wanted to argue, but instead, he spun on his heel and left the library, the door slamming behind him.

Once we were alone, Father shook his head. "Your brother will always remember that."

"It's not so different from our other fights," I said. We'd had many over the turns. Many in which Rhistel had obliterated me with his words, and I'd returned in kind with a well-placed punch to the gut.

"Don't fool yourself." Father swept to the table upon

which bottles of wine from the Summer Isles, Dragon Fire, and specialty liqueurs from the Mage Court sat. "You've chosen that commonborn female over your blood. Your twin."

"We haven't been close for a long time, Father. And a female tore us apart before."

"This is different." The king poured a small glass of Dragon Fire and downed it. "The female has stirred up more trouble than she's worth, Vale. If you hadn't given her our name, I would have killed her already."

I swallowed at the way he said it. So matter-of-factly. As if she were a boar we were hunting and not a fae of our kingdom. A subject that we had sworn to protect. Then again, Father didn't always take that promise to heart.

Thank the stars for Lord Riis. He'd been the one to see that my name, more so than my strength, would save Neve. The king might have killed many during his rebellion, but no one of his direct bloodline met his axe. He was no kinslayer. And in his eyes, marriage was as binding as blood. More so even. After all, his own blood had failed him when he was a youngling, but the ties of his mother's marriage to the male who had raised him, those had stayed true.

"You love her?" Father asked as he poured himself a glass of wine.

My mouth fell open.

His eyebrows arched, and he went to a seat in front of the ever-burning hearth. "Foolish as that may be, and as much as I hoped you only lusted and loved what was between her legs, I cannot help but think you do. Irritating myself and the Warden of the West would be an added bonus, I suppose."

I risked so much for Neve. I cared for her. Of course, she was beautiful and there'd been an attraction between us since the first day we'd met. At least on my part. There was an undeniable pull between us. I thought of my wife—her smile, her laugh and my stomach tightened.

"I have my answer," Father muttered, apparently coming to a conclusion when I was still reeling from the question. "Come sit."

He was acting so casual, like I hadn't defied him, like I hadn't attacked his heir. Like he hadn't whipped Sir Qildor for my actions. Or schemed to marry Marit and Sayyida off.

What was he up to?

I sat across from him, the heat of the flame warming my left cheek as I studied my father.

"You expect me to rage?" the king drawled out as though he were bored. "I see that you won't be parted from the female, so it is time to move on to more important things. She is family, and hence, I will treat her as such." Another sip of wine. "I'd much rather discuss issues pertaining to the kingdom."

I didn't believe him. He might move on for a night, a day, even a few weeks, but not forever. Eventually, Father would want to make Neve pay for what she'd done. At the very least, he would not protect her when vampire assassins came to call. They would be a perfect out for him. A solution to a problem that, despite his cool exterior, I suspected gnawed at him every waking second.

"As you wish, Father."

"At last, some deference." He smirked again, playful this time, though no warmth reached his cold eyes. Another hint that he was twisting the truth—moving on, for now—but the grudge would fester inside him.

Most races of fae were long-lived. Faeries included. We didn't need to rush to even the score.

My father proved that during his rebellion. When he'd plotted his revenge on the blood family who'd ignored him, particularly Calder Falk, Father had long been an adult. He had plotted and schemed with the most influential houses, all displeased with the Cruel King's reign. He'd even wooed my mother, a younger noble fae, and once a lady-in-waiting for Queen Revna. With her insider knowledge, Mother proved a pivotal figure in bringing down the royal house.

It took many turns to put things in place, and even more to win the rebellion. I'd been young, but I still remembered the day we came to Frostveil. The day the Crown of Winter's Realm was set atop Father's head.

So much had changed since then. The White Bear's Rebellion exterminated two great houses. Many others were killed. Turn after turn, the magic in the kingdom dwindled. And, most recently, Father became colder, harder, more cruel—much like his uncle, the late King Harald.

"We need to stick together, Vale," Father said. "If

there is anything my own issues with my birth father taught me, it is that."

I blinked. Mother was the mind reader, but it was almost like he'd glimpsed my thoughts, speaking of his birth father like that.

"Had he acknowledged me, had he treated my mother with respect, he would still be a prince of the realm." Father swirled the wine in his glass. "I do not want our family to fall in the same way my biological father allowed his to crumble."

This, I understood. I'd have felt similarly had I experienced the neglect Father endured. Had Father brushed me aside, claimed I was nothing, when my mother brought me to court. Or if I lived in Lordling Lane, right beneath his nose, was the spitting image of him, and he didn't even look my way. That had happened to my father, not me, but I understood his pain.

Father had been angry with me many times, had taken it out on others and treated me cruelly, but he *always* reminded me we were family. We were Aabergs and our bloodline, the dynasty we were building in the name of the faerie who'd given Father his own noble name, mattered.

"Rhistel might not forget what you did," Father added, bringing our conversation back around to my assault on my twin, "but you must try to repair things with him."

"I'll do my best." It was all he'd get out of me. All

that I could promise until I was certain Rhistel would keep his word.

"Good. Now, I'd like to speak with you about things I've noticed about the Festival."

I leaned forward. Despite coming here to advocate for Neve, I decided that, for now, she was likely safe. Father seemed prepared to move on. I'd have to be on alert for vampires coming at the behest of their monarchs for vengeance.

Plus, though it felt a bit like a betrayal to Neve, I couldn't help but be interested in what Father had to say. I knew why the Courting Festival had been called. I'd been the one to bring to light information that had prompted its conception. This matter was even larger than Neve and me. Bigger than any single fae and could benefit all those who called Winter's Realm home.

"You have an idea of who holds the Ice Scepter?" I asked.

"I've seen no sign of magical growth in any of the lords or ladies at court," Father mused. "However, I have noticed high lords acting strangely."

"Who?"

"Lord Roar, obviously." Father scowled. "Both Lord Riis and I have sent emissaries to find him, to bring him back. We have heard no word yet. Then there's the matter of Lord Riis himself."

For a moment, I gripped the chair tighter but loosened my grip before he noticed.

Lord Riis? A traitor?

Before I delved into that matter, Father continued. "And Lord Balik has been acting quite odd."

I tilted my head. I had noticed no odd behavior from the ruling lord of the southlands. "How so?"

"Hiding away in his suite. Socializing only with the Armenils, who, truth be told, after your petty act of rebellion, I have doubts about too."

I scowled. "Because Marit was present at my wedding? That's absurd."

Father glared at me.

"She was only there because she's friends with Saga and my sister insisted she come. The same with Sayyida. I'm sure you've already asked Saga about it."

And I was more than sure that Saga had told Father the truth, up to a point. He clearly didn't know that Neve had been a blood slave. Or about Lord Riis's involvement in our wedding, likely out of loyalty to me, more than the spymaster.

"I have."

"Speaking of Marit, did you *have to* pair her with Lord Triam? And why marry off Sayyida at all? Their house already has a wedding coming up, and she *is* important to the Royal Nava."

"Do you dare question me?" Father's gaze hardened over his goblet.

"You only did it because they were at my wedding. And perhaps because you learned that Sayyida and Marit favored Neve."

The king snorted. "I care nothing for the opinions of young ladies. I saw good matches, and I set them."

"Jarl Triam is a monster."

"And I have given Lord Armenil an option to change the course of his daughter's fate."

I frowned. "And what of Lady Sayyida?"

"What of her?"

"Vidar is marrying Saga. Isn't that—"

"This Festival might be a front so that we can discover who has the Hallow of Winter's Realm," Father cut me off, "but *I* am still king. It is my right to create unions that will benefit our House. A right that you'd do well to remember will benefit you, Vale."

I wasn't so sure about that but understood he would not be swayed. Not tonight anyhow, so I dropped the matter. It wasn't like Sayyida would be pushed to the Drassil tree tomorrow or next week. Probably not even within a moon's time. Perhaps with a little more time and planning Saga or I might find a way for Sayyida to make a deal like the one Father made with Lord Armenil. Find a way to spare her a fate she didn't want. We had to make it worth Father's time.

CHAPTER 15
NEVE

Thumbs rubbing together, I perched on the edge of the prince's bed and stared down the short hallway that exited to the rest of the palace. I was determined to wait until Vale returned from speaking with his father. Determined to pry out the reason he'd been so scared to see his brother touch me without a glove.

Because after much thought, after replaying the scene over and over, I was certain that was what had happened. And it made no sense.

I glanced at the door again, willing Vale to come back. Wanting to satisfy my curiosity. When he didn't appear, I heaved a sigh.

I might as well get comfortable.

Hauling myself off the bed, I went to the dresser, opened a drawer, and pulled out a simple gray cotton dress. One that Roar had given me, but not one in his house colors. I'd never wear crimson and gold in combination again, not if I could help it.

I slipped off the clothing I'd worn to the Courting Festival event and pulled the dress over my head, slipping my wings through the slits at the back. Though it was plain, the cotton was soft on my skin, decadent even. A quiet sort of luxury I wouldn't expect by looking at the dress. Completing the look, I tied my hair back with a pink ribbon. The color hinted it might have been from Saga's stash.

Vale had said servants would take our laundry daily, so I tossed the other dress in the hamper and debated over how best to fill the time. Since he'd left to speak with his father, a bell had already tolled outside. Would he be gone for two hours? Or even three? What was the king saying to him?

Stars, I had so many questions and no one to answer them! I needed to occupy my mind. I was just wondering how to do so when I heard voices outside Vale's suite.

"I wish to speak with Princess Neve. Is she in his room?"

I stiffened. I'd know that voice anywhere. Why was Prince Rhistel here?

"She is, but I'm afraid I can't do that, my prince," a deep, gruff tone spoke. "Prince Vale said no one goes in or out except him."

"I'm the heir to Winter's Realm, Sir Arvid. I demand to be let in."

I rose and tiptoed down to the door.

"I understand, Prince Rhistel, but Prince Vale—"

"Is the spare," Rhistel cut him off. "I will be your king. And right now, if I wish, I can have your title stripped. Or even your head removed from your shoulders." A pause. "Should you wish to keep both, you will let me inside."

The knight didn't respond, but I imagined what was happening. Sir Arvid was working for Vale right now, but Rhistel held more power. Rhistel could make good on his threats. If I were the knight, I'd open the door.

That put me in danger.

I froze, and my heart began thrumming. Rhistel was a mystery to me, a terrifying one. After the solarium, I wasn't eager to face him again.

I spun, ready to fly from the windows as I'd done the night of my failed escape, when something caught my eye. A rectangular patch on the wall glowed.

A sharp intake of breath passed my lips as I recognized the spot. It was the very door I'd come through the night I'd been fleeing Calpurnia and her friends. The door that had spat me into Vale's chambers and then sealed itself behind me.

Like last time, the castle lent me aid.

"You *will* let me in, Sir Arvid. *Now,*" Prince Rhistel gave his order again, his voice softer this time, more soothing and . . . Somehow also convincing?

I almost wanted to open the door for him, but I shook off that lunacy and instead rushed to the glowing rectangle. A doorknob appeared out of thin air as the main door to the suite *snicked* open.

"Princess Neve," Sir Arvid called out.

I paused. His voice sounded strange too. Somehow dimmed from before. As if he stood farther away than he was. "I have Prince Rhistel here to see you, Princess Neve. Are you decent?"

In response, I flung the glowing door open and passed over the threshold, into the hidden part of the castle. I pulled the door shut behind me.

"Princess Neve?" Sir Arvid called again. "Are you there?"

"Of course she is. You didn't see her leave, did you?" Rhistel barked. "Let me through!"

Footsteps stomped down the short entry hallway that led deeper into Vale's chambers. They stopped suddenly, likely when the heir reached the edge of the bedchamber.

"Neve, where are you?" he crowed. "We need to talk."

I scoffed. I wanted to speak with him as much as I wished to meet a horde of orcs in the woods.

"I know you're in here," Rhistel added, his tone once again lower and softer. Perhaps he thought it made him sound more approachable?

My fingers drifted to the door handles before I caught myself. What was going on? It was like I subconsciously wanted to obey him.

"Prince Rhistel," Sir Arvid said, his voice still far away and monotone. "I do not believe she is here."

"Did you see her leave?"

"No, my prince."

"She might be hiding. Search the room."

Heavy footsteps walked past where I hid, and items shifted as the knight followed directions. After a few minutes, Sir Arvid spoke, "She's not here."

"How can you be sure?" Rhistel growled.

"Well, she is not *so* small that you couldn't find her."

I would have laughed had the consequences not been so dire. The knight spoke true. I was no slip of a faerie, especially not now that I'd been eating the rich food of the noble class for weeks. I'd gone from a blood slave who received only enough food to be deemed healthy, and *never* as much as I wanted to eat, to fully blossomed curves.

"Fine," Rhistel barked. More heavy-footed stomping, this time back toward the door. "To your post. And don't tell my brother I was here, or I'll make good on my promise of removing you from your position."

"I understand, my prince." The knight lumbered by.

The door to Vale's room shut, and I leaned against the wall inside the hidden part of the castle. I had no idea why Rhistel would seek me out, but I knew one thing; he didn't have a noble reason. That had been close, far too close.

As my heart rate slowed, I allowed myself to take in the hallway. I'd been here before, though I hadn't noticed too much surrounding this door. That day, I'd been convinced that someone had been singing inside the part of Frostveil Castle hidden from the Aaberg family and had wished to find them. Really, though, I'd heard Vale singing and stumbled out of the secret parts of the castle, right into his chambers. Stars, that had been a mortifying and scary night.

But it had also allowed me to see Vale in a new light. He hadn't harmed me. Never even turned me in for appearing in his suite. He'd *believed me* when I said I'd come in through a hidden door. So much so that he'd acquired the old castle blueprints and found the very door I'd slipped through.

The door I'd passed through again when I had nothing to do but wait for Vale to return. The skin on my arms pebbled.

Time to explore.

I scanned the hallway, recognizing the direction I'd come from before and deciding to amble in the opposite direction. Before I ventured forth, however, I pulled the pink ribbon from my hair and tied it to the doorknob. It wouldn't do to get lost in here and have to find a different way out. With my luck, I'd exit right into Rhistel's bedchambers. Or worse, the king's rooms. My stomach roiled at that terrifying thought.

Certain I'd be able to find the door to Vale's suite again, I set off, taking in the art that lined the corridor.

This part of the palace had been frozen in time. In here, Falk imagery reigned and there was not a single tapestry or painting of a white bear in sight. Everything looked the same as last time.

Except . . .

I stopped in my tracks and examined one portrait. Clean. Spotless, even. As was the next and the next.

Last time I'd been back here, there had been a fair bit of dust. Did that mean someone came here and cleaned?

I gasped. It was the only thing that made sense.

But what would be the point? They couldn't have been in the lost part of the palace the entire time. They'd have starved. Which meant they had access to the Aaberg portion of Frostveil, as I did.

Were they a servant? The moment I questioned it, I laughed. It would have to be a servant. I'd never seen a single noble fae clean.

What would they say if they saw me back here?

The thought both intrigued and terrified me. I stood on thin ice with the king and queen. What if someone saw me and assumed I was a rebel and that was why I could access this part of the castle?

Wouldn't that mean they weren't pro-Aaberg either? And where did I stand in that? I was, after all, technically of House Aaberg now.

Not that the castle cared.

It was all so confusing, and, in truth, my curiosity proved far too strong to be hindered by fear. I continued on, strolling the hallways and pausing at paintings and works of art. All the while, I half hoped I'd run into another person.

One statue of the eldest son of King Harald and Queen Revna, Aksel Falk, was so artfully done in white marble accented with purple gems on the sword he held that it took my breath away. I knew nothing of the prince, but I was glad the palace had hidden the statue.

King Magnus would destroy it if given half a chance, and it was too beautiful for that.

I left the statue and was taking a left turn to delve deeper into the castle when a sound caught my ear. I stopped. Listened.

For a moment, I thought I'd imagined it, but then it came again.

This way.

I gasped and twisted in the direction of the disembodied voice. Had I imagined that?

No . . . I'd heard voices before. First, when I touched the Drassil tree in Traliska, and most recently during my wedding. It had happened again when I'd saved Anna's life. I cocked my head. Was it the same voice? It was feminine and did sound like the one I'd just heard.

As if realizing I needed a bigger push, the voice spoke up once more.

Come this way.

Yes, definitely the same voice.

My nerves mounted. Did I dare? What if this was when I'd pay the price for Anna's life? I couldn't see how, but equally so, I knew better than to ignore the voice. I'd made a deal, and if this was my moment to pay up, well, I might be scared, but I'd do so willingly.

So I padded down the hallway in the voice's direction, sure that when I got to where it wanted me to go, the person, or maybe the *thing*, would let me know.

I reached the end of the hallway, or what appeared to be the end. Perhaps it extended elsewhere in the

Aaberg part of the palace, but in the hidden section, there was nowhere else to go. Nowhere but to the right or the left.

One of the doors was ajar, so I took that as a sign and peeked inside.

A vast bedroom spread out before me. I'd only seen one as large and grand inside the palace. It didn't take a genius to determine whose room I stood in.

Not with the crown of white gold, diamonds, and snowflakes displayed on a pedestal, sitting on a cushion. Nor with the armor that had been laid on a settee, as if someone had just taken it off. But what gave me the most insight was the painting of a male and female embracing. I'd seen them before, in a family portrait. It had to be the old king, Harald Falk, and Queen Revna. Judging by the size of it and the shape of the armor, this was the old king's room.

I stepped inside and scanned it, my eyes stopping on a sword glinting in a case. It glimmered prettily; the handle ending in a hawk's head. An ornate sheath complete with a leather strap to allow the wearer to sling it over their shoulder was also in the case. The whole setup was lovely and impressive but shockingly not very large. Perhaps King Harald had been a smaller fae? I studied the blade and the sheath. It wasn't even as decorated as some of the swords in Vale's personal armory. I was at a loss. Nothing in here screamed, *look at me.*

"Is this the place?"

Turn around.

"All right then." I padded out of the king's room and across the hall.

I placed my hand on the door in front of me and paused. The other door had been open, making me certain it wouldn't lead me to the public part of the palace. But what if this door did? As quietly as I could, I leaned closer to the wood and listened. No sound came from the other side so I pushed the door open.

The room I entered was lush and spectacular, at least three times the size of Vale's quarters, which were quite large indeed. Larger than the other room I'd seen, larger than King Magnus's chambers.

I lingered in the antechamber, a sitting area of sorts, taking a moment to look around. A library sprawled to my right, while a seating area complete with six armchairs and two settees, all in shades of glittering silver, sprawled across the central part of the room. To my left were three doors. I veered that way, opening the first to find a bathroom as opulent as the rest of the room, but still, only a bathroom. I shut the door and moved on to the next one. Behind it stretched a closet half the size of the main room.

Marvel clouding any hesitancy I'd been clinging to, I ventured deeper into the closet, eyeing the lovely gowns hanging from silver rods and the jewelry glittering on a pure amethyst table that dominated the center of the room.

Stars alive! The jewels in here were beyond stunning, larger than any I'd seen at court too. I picked up a circular brooch that featured a white stone in the center.

It was veined with red and gold lines that danced as I stared at them.

I sucked in a breath, remembering the night of the Courting Festival's opening ball. Recalling speaking to Lord Riis. He'd mentioned a gem that would fit this name.

A phoenix opal.

I studied the stone more closely. Yes, it looked like an opal. And the red and gold veins brought to mind fire, especially as they appeared to move, like a flame would in the wind.

Queen Revna had possessed one. Lord Riis had told me he'd sold it to her. That they were very, very rare.

Was this the old queen's chambers? It would make sense with this suite being right across from what I was sure was the old king's rooms.

Slowly, I set the gemstone down. Then, reconsidering, I picked it back up and put it in my pocket. No one would miss it, and I wanted to compare the stone to images to see if I was right.

My gaze drifted to the gowns hanging from silver rods. Moon above, what I wouldn't give to take one of those too. Though I was no longer unfamiliar with wearing finery, I'd rarely gotten to wear something so fine that was to my taste. These, though outdated, were exquisite.

The color palette of amethyst and a blueish silver. The silver struck me as perfect, like the craftsmanship of the gowns. Lovely beading. Fine lace. Sparkling gems dotting necklines and wrists. Queen Revna must have been a fashion icon in her day.

If this is even really her room. I peered around for more hints and found none that would identify the queen. Not even a single crown or tiara. Where would she keep those?

Perhaps behind the third door, which I assumed was her bedroom?

I left the grand closet and opened the last door to find that I was right. The queen's bedroom spread out before me, at least twice as large as the bathroom and closet combined. A bed dominated the far wall, and on either side of the bed hung individual portraits of the queen's family members.

Their sons appeared much more animated in these portraits, more fun. But the portraits also showed two children I had yet to find a clear image of, largely because they'd been portrayed as swaddled babes in all the other family portraits.

In this one, however, they were girls, very small, nearly bald girls. The last born to the king and queen, if my memory of Clemencia's lessons served me. In this painting, they had to be around one turn of age. They wore the cutest dresses and held hands as they toddled away from the viewer. My heart warmed at the image.

What were their names again? Clemencia had taught me, but that felt like an age ago. And even when I'd been learning them, Clem agreed that the names of the dead princes and princesses were less important than those of the living nobles I'd be interacting with. I wished I could recall and made a note to look that up too when I searched for images of phoenix opals.

I decided to move on, to take in the rest of the room, when a sound of wood scraping against wood caught my ear. I searched for it, found a small desk on the far side of the room, and watched the middle drawer move open of its own accord.

I tried to draw a full, long breath and failed. My chest was simply too tight, my heart rate higher than normal. As intriguing as I found this part of the castle, there was no denying that it was also creepy. What allowed it to act—at least somewhat—sentient?

The question died as something glowed.

"I can take a hint!" I muttered.

As if I hadn't been taking them all along from a disembodied voice, no less. The same voice who made me promise to pay a debt to save Anna's life. I squashed the flutter of rising resentment. If this was all I had to do to pay the debt, that wasn't so bad.

Of course, I had no idea if this *was* repayment. But I went along with it. For now.

On light feet, I trod over to the desk. Behind the expanse of wood loomed a case of crowns and tiaras. Interesting placement behind a desk and not in her closet full of finery. As if the queen wanted a reminder that her crowns were linked to the work of running a kingdom, rather than fashion. Or perhaps she liked to look at them as she fell asleep? It would forever be a mystery.

When I stood before the desk, I peered inside the

open drawer to find that the glowing object was a book. It lay there, amidst the jumble of quills—phoenix feather, if I wasn't mistaken—three rouge tubes, and a bracelet of glittering white diamonds each as large as a copper claw. My fingers itched to take the bracelet too, but I refrained. The sentient force in this part of the castle hadn't balked at my taking the opal, but it was best not to test my luck.

Instead, I picked up the book and delighted in the fine, buttery leather that met my fingertips. A clasp held the book shut, but with a press of a button, it unlatched. I opened the book and my eyebrows arched.

This was no book, no story, but a diary.

The *queen's* diary.

CHAPTER 16
NEVE

*S*hould *I read it?*

It felt so wrong to read a person's diary, even one from a long-dead queen. A book of thoughts and admissions and perhaps even ramblings that, against all odds, still clung to a regal scent: amber with floral notes. As if the queen had just set it down.

And yet, the voice led me here. The diary had glowed, for stars' sake!

It wanted me to read it. Or, at the very least, *something* wanted me to read it.

Swallowing thickly, I shut the drawer and took a seat at the desk. Not having supported a person for two decades, the chair protested beneath my weight, but it held.

I stared down at the first page of the diary, wondering where to start. Then an idea struck. I tilted my chin up, feeling ridiculous but determined to try, anyway.

"Is there something in particular that you want me to read?" I asked. "Or should I start at the beginning?"

The pages flipped, sending another burst of flowers and amber into my nose. Despite my unease over the sentient nature of this part of the palace moments before, my heart lifted. We were learning to work together, the creepy castle and me.

When the pages stopped, I pulled the book closer and spoke to the ceiling again. "Thanks."

The queen's handwriting was elegant and flowing, so unlike my own, which I'd always thought messy but never attempted to improve. Slaves, or even courtiers, didn't need nice handwriting.

Inhaling deeply, I dove in.

I wish I had better news to relay. Alas, my mother taught me to be a record-keeper queen, not one who shoved her head in the snow and enjoyed balls and the frivolity of court. As a result, I see much, far too much, for my own liking.

Things are not going well.

Unrest chokes Winter's Realm, and what's worse, I cannot blame the commonfae. For many turns now, Harald has been acting odd, harder and crueler. It is unlike him. Even he knows it . . . Even he wishes to change. Begs for me to find a cure for what ails him.

Often, I can bring him back to himself, healing a poison that seems to spread insidious desires inside him. But my ministrations never remain for long. Never take fully.

I cannot help but think that had I finished my training at the White Tower, had I gone against sweet Harald's wishes and become a Master Healer, he would already be better. Not that our Master Healers know what is wrong with him—or even that he is ailing. Harald will not allow that weakness to be shown to others. It's infuriating, yet unsurprising. He is acting as his own father taught him . . . Fates rest his troubled soul.

And then there's the matter of those closest to me. One has been acting strangely in ways that put her in great jeopardy.

But Inga has always been stubborn and independent. If she wishes to flirt with Leyv Riis, she will do so. Truth be told, I can hardly blame her. Leyv is not only my favorite merchant of rare goods—you should see the phoenix opal he brought me not long ago—he is also quite handsome.

I paused, fingered the brooch I'd taken, and wondered if it was the same one. And if so, would Leyv Riis say as much when I asked? Pushing aside my questions, I continued reading.

But Inga is married to Lord Magnus Aaberg, and if he finds out about his wife and Leyv, he will not stand for it.

I wish she'd be more careful. In these troubled times, I would like to keep my most favored lady, and friend, at court, but if Magnus discovers what she's doing, he'll remove her. With so much unrest in the realm, who knows when I'll see her again?

There are bright spots in my world, though. Isolde and Thyra are walking now. The twins are beams of joy during a tumultuous time. Though it may seem frivolous, I so look forward to celebrating their nameday on Winter Solstice.

The diary went on, but I leaned back, unable to proceed after what I'd read.

Lord Riis, once a merchant before King Magnus titled and elevated him to the ranks of Sacred Eight, and Lady Inga, now the queen, had been . . . what? Lovers?

Or was Queen Revna misinterpreting things?

Surely, if Lord Riis rose to Sacred Eight status, it

was because he'd helped King Magnus in his rebellion in some great way? And since then, Lord Riis had been close to the family. Saga had called him an uncle, of sorts.

Perhaps Lord Riis passed information on to the White Bear's Rebellion under the guise of an affair? He was the spymaster, after all. I glanced down at the page again, unable to believe what I'd read, what the castle had wanted me to see.

Queen Revna lost so much. Had dealt with so much. She'd known that something was corrupting her husband and tried to heal him.

But it hadn't worked. The Cruel King had only become more cruel. Perhaps mad? And eventually, the lords and ladies of the realm banded together to unseat him. Even the commonborn helped.

How horrible it must have been for the queen. From this reading, I got the sense that she was good—kind and wanting peace.

Instead, her family had been torn apart, murdered, and even those in her extended family killed for their family name. For the actions of one cruel male.

A lump rose in my throat and I leaned back, not ready to read more. Did I have to?

I tilted my chin to the ceiling. "Anything else you'd like me to read?"

In answer, the book slammed shut. I was done. Thank the stars.

"Then I'll be going."

Vale might have already returned to his rooms and

was wondering where I'd gone. I hoped he remembered the hidden door and kept quiet. But would he? Within days, vampire assassins would show up to kill me. Perhaps hoping he'd be calm was asking a bit much.

That in mind, I left the queen's chambers, the phoenix opal heavy in my pocket, and rushed through the corridors. Finally, I spotted the knob on which I'd tied the pink ribbon.

I grasped the knob and turned, hoping I'd find Vale's rooms empty. That he wouldn't have been worried or looking for me. Instead, as I entered the prince's suite, I found him at the door to his rooms too, just entering. Quickly, he shut the door behind him, his eyes wide.

"It opened for you again." He rushed to my side. "How?"

Excitement glinted in Prince Vale's eyes, and despite the information I'd learned, I smiled. It was sweet to see such excited innocence in him. I suspected that as a youngling, he'd tried many times to get into the hidden parts of the palace. What little one could refrain from that pull?

"I needed refuge. Again," I admitted.

The wonder fell from his face. "What? How so? My quarters are secure and there's no way they could have already sent assassins. The vampires only left this morning."

"Not vampires. Your brother stopped by." I shuddered. "I know you don't want to talk about what he can do, but I figured if you were worried about him touching me, I should be too. The door opened for me right before he came into your suite."

Vale spun toward the door, face set in hard lines. "Sir Arvid let him in?"

"He's the heir," I whispered lamely. "It didn't sound like Sir Arvid had much choice. I heard it all." I pounded on the wall. "From inside."

"Of course he didn't have a choice! Rhistel . . ." The prince trailed off; his lips sealing shut as if he had been about to reveal information about his twin.

For a second time, he'd protected Rhistel. Even though he was furious with him. Why? What could Rhistel do that was so bad?

"He didn't see me. Or do anything," I continued, wanting to calm Vale down.

"He shouldn't have been here. I made him promise not to speak to you or touch you. He broke that promise right away."

To make Vale feel better, I wanted to say that his twin intended to honor his word when he made the promise or else he wouldn't have been able to do so. Fae, me aside, and only for nine more days at that, couldn't lie.

But that gave the heir too much credit. I didn't trust Rhistel and wouldn't defend him.

Instead, I sought to change the subject. "Vale, there might be people living back here." I touched the wall where the door had been again.

I wouldn't tell him everything. Certainly not about Queen Revna's diary. Inga was his mother, and I needed to consider what I'd read before I shared. But some of my observations were harmless.

The change of subject worked like a charm, and the anger lifted from his handsome features a touch. "What makes you say that?"

"It's cleaner than the last time I was there. I bet someone who lives in the palace goes back there and tidies."

Vale looked thoughtful. "I could see that. It's one reason I let you go that night you slipped into my suite. Over time, two slaves have gone missing. No one looked into that much, but concubines have escaped Father's harem too. There was a search for the concubines, but they were never found. It's rumored that they must have used the hidden passages. Perhaps they stayed back there a while." He swallowed. "Healed. Rested. I don't know. Whatever they used it for, I hope it helped."

I took his hand, so much larger than mine. And warm, so warm.

As much as I hated that the king kept a harem, it gave me comfort that Vale despised the practice too. Not a surprise, considering the prince was romantic enough to have wanted to marry his soulmate.

And I'd taken that from him.

No. Not taken. I'll leave at my first chance, and he'll be able to remarry. They'll assume me dead. He'll get to find her. To love her.

Though the idea should have made me happy, my stomach churned. I squashed the ridiculous reaction as quickly as it appeared.

Yes, I was attracted to Vale, admired and respected him too, but I had no true hold on his heart. We played at a marriage. Nothing more.

"How did talks with your father go?" I asked.

He frowned. "Better than expected. Still, I'm not sure I trust him."

"How so?"

"He told me he won't take action against you."

"That's good."

"Yes, but he didn't say that he'd stop others from doing so. He might pretend to embrace you, but he's waiting for the vampires to do his dirty work. It's a sneaky way of making amends. Of not alienating me further."

"But he doesn't seem to have an issue with making a scene and punishing those who'd witnessed our marriage."

"Father has . . . other aims regarding the Courting Festival. He needs me on board for those. Perhaps his anger thawed, and he needed me more than he wished for revenge. For now, at least."

The way he said it made me think it was yet another secret the prince was holding. I leaned closer.

"Want to share?"

He exhaled. "Let's sit. This will be a long night."

I went to bed and waited as Vale changed into something more comfortable. I tried not to watch or notice the muscles rippling in his back. Instead, I stared at where the hidden door had been, where now only a smooth wall remained. When Vale was done, he turned

239

to me, face set in serious lines.

"What I'm about to tell you cannot be repeated. I'm only telling you because it involves someone we've allied ourselves with, so you have the right to know."

"Who would I tell? Saga?"

He eyed me. "Saga doesn't know. And she can't. Only Rhistel, Father, Mother, and I know."

"Fine. I won't say a thing."

He slid onto the other side of the bed, and, for a moment, I marveled at how comfortable I felt sharing this space with him. Roar and I had slept in different rooms, and I'd wanted to keep it that way. Not that that was an option here, but it didn't need to be. Vale might have secrets, but for what mattered, I trusted him as I'd trusted few in my life. Deep down in my soul, I knew he wouldn't hurt me or betray me. I just knew it.

"Given your past, you might not know about the Ice Scepter, but—"

I gasped. "I do, though! Roar told me about it!"

During my time at court, the Hallow of Winter's Realm drifted from my mind, but now the conversation in that tavern in Traliska came rushing back. "It was lost during the rebellion, and Roar told me it has affected the magic of the realm since. Possibly that it was responsible for the blight affecting the health of the fae too."

"He told you the truth," Vale said. "No one knows where it is. My family doesn't speak of it, and I'm sure the great houses have deduced that we don't have it. Perhaps the lesser houses and commonfae suspect that it's missing too, though I doubt that the latter think of the troubles of the noble houses often."

I let out a dry laugh. "No, I don't think they would care if a noble house was missing a bauble. *But* commoners are perceptive."

In my experience, slaves were even more perceptive, I wanted to add but didn't. Vale was compassionate, but he might never fully understand how I grew up. How all the slaves I'd known did. I suspected many common-born fae in this realm, especially the poorest among them, lived similarly in some regards—on a knife's edge of survival, day to day. And if the Scepter was key to their survival, someone would eventually question why the king hadn't brought it out in so long. Why he wasn't using it now.

"Many fae have been born sick or deformed, and Winter's Realm is growing more harsh." I paused. "If the temperature continues to plunge and the storms worsen, we'll die, won't we?"

"Even the most stouthearted fae of Winter's Realm won't be able to live here. We'd have to flee south to the Autumn Court or die. But if we can find the Ice Scepter, things could change. That's why my father called the Courting Festival."

A festival to suss out the Ice Scepter? "I don't follow."

"I'll explain."

And he did. Vale told me of his most recent battles with the orc tribes in the midlands, how he'd found an elder orc, and she'd given him information on the Ice

Scepter. The orc believed a noble lord of the land had taken it.

The king believed they might still have it, hence why he'd called every noble family to Avaldenn under the guise of an ancient practice, a Courting Festival.

"What if the houses had no one to marry off?" I asked. "Or what if the Heads of House, the most likely to possess the Hallow, didn't come?"

"The Heads of House were required to attend, and as for family members of marriageable age, almost all of them had at least one person fitting that criterion," Vale said. "We made sure of it. The few who didn't were jarls, old and not very well-off ones, at that. Their houses were crumbling, and they weren't at all powerful. Why take a magical object with the magic to change the realm if you have no hope of controlling it?"

"Does your father? Can he control it?"

He was Falk by blood, and it was said that the Falk line could wield it best.

"He should be able to do so, but he's never had the opportunity. By the time he took Frostveil, the Scepter was missing."

My hand pressed into the bed, and my fingers fiddled with the blanket, teasing the fur between them as I listened.

"Father believed that if the lord or lady in possession of the Ice Scepter was invited, they were likely to bring it with them—if only to take it before our Drassil tree."

I blinked. "What does that mean?"

"We have a Drassil tree at the palace, a twin to the Heart Drassil in the Tower of the Living and the Dead. It's called the Crown Tree. It's said they were planted at the same time and are intertwined even more deeply than the usual Drassil connection. Every Falk who took the crown has stood before the Crown Tree and asked the Faetia to bless them with the ability to wield the magic of this realm."

Roar hadn't mentioned that. Surprise, surprise.

"What does that do?"

"If the Faetia accepts, it binds the ruler to the land in a way no one else can claim. They become the undisputed king or queen."

"And no one questioned that your father didn't do that?"

"Some did." Vale looked away. "They disappeared."

My stomach tightened. No, the king had killed them.

"He is the blood of Prince Calder Falk, though." Vale turned his eyes on me. "The king's own brother. No one disputes that, and so most accepted his rule. In time, no one spoke of it again."

No one was foolish enough to want to lose their heads for speaking up about something that didn't affect them.

Except now it did. Things were getting worse. The storms raged more viciously. Goblins, orcs, and other brutal races of fae attacked villages or travelers for food and other supplies. I'd been part of a party attacked by goblins, and the one I'd caught in my sleigh had said as much. They starved because Winter's Realm was squeezing them at the necks.

"I see," I drew the words out. "And you said this involves someone we allied with? Who?" I had an idea but wanted the truth out in the open.

"Lord Riis." Vale confirmed my thoughts. "Though I don't see it, Father has reasons to suspect him. And he's not the only one. My father suspects Lord Balik and Roar as well."

Roar, well, I understood that line of thought. He'd fled the castle in the middle of an obligatory festival. In doing so, he'd defied the king's orders.

"Lord Balik? I haven't met him, only some of his children."

"Many regard him as the most honorable of the lords and ladies of the Sacred Eight. I can't say I agree with my father's call on this one."

"But you can with Roar and Lord Riis?"

Vale paused before nodding. "Roar, certainly. Lord Riis, well, he is the spymaster. He's cunning and adept at hiding things. And while he wasn't a lord at the time of the rebellion, he was a wealthy merchant. Those who didn't know better could have perceived him as a lord. Someone like an orc." He blew out a breath. "I think we should trust him, and I'd like to tell him that the king suspects he is acting oddly. But at the same time, I want to keep an eye on Lord Riis."

With the words in Queen Revna's diary fresh in my mind, I couldn't help but agree.

CHAPTER 17

VALE

I woke to the tantalizing scent of smoked vanilla and the weight of a delicate hand on my chest. My heart gave a hard thump as I twisted to find Neve cuddled up against me. I blinked. We'd fallen asleep on our sides of the bed, which was large enough to fit five people.

Not that I minded her being so close, but I wasn't sure she'd like waking up as such.

I shifted and became painfully aware of how *little* I minded. My cock stood at attention. Blazing moon.

We'd said no physical intimacy, and considering the odd circumstances we were in, I still thought that was wise. My body, however, was calling me a prized idiot.

Neve was all luscious curves that begged to be stroked, cupped, gripped. Her sensual lips and enchanting eyes never failed to steal my attention from whatever I was supposed to be paying attention to.

Then there was her personality, which I found warm, kind, and charming. Most of the time anyway.

I chuckled at the memory of her "beating" me in training. She'd been so pleased at winning by technicality. And the way she'd looked at me before she whacked me with her practice sword . . .

My cock twitched at the memory of that sultry violet gaze and her heaving bosom. By the Fates and stars above, maybe I was an idiot for not pursuing something physical. I was sure we both wanted to, but I couldn't break my promise.

Slowly, I slipped out from under her hand, hoping not to wake her, even as I missed the feel of her soft curves pressed up against me. We had plans to train again this morning, but at the very least I'd take care of my *needs* before I woke her.

Unfortunately, the moment I rose to sit and shifted to put my feet on the ground, the bed creaked.

Neve's eyes flew open, and her lips curled up. "Morning. Is it late?"

I cleared my throat, relieved that the tent in my sleeping pants was hidden.

"Still early," I said, guessing by how the sunlight filtered in through the window. "You can continue resting."

"I feel great!" She rose to sit, her breasts bouncing with the movement.

I placed a hand over my groin and stifled a groan.

"I'm ready to beat your arse again today." Neve stretched luxuriously. "What do you—"

A knock came at the door. "Prince Vale! A message!"

Bleeding skies! This had to be a joke.

"From whom?" I knew it had to be someone important and persuasive if the Clawsguard on duty was knocking at this hour.

"Sian Balik," the knight called. "He claimed you'd be up for training. Shall I come in and deliver it?"

The idea of the guard seeing Neve in her nightclothes was enough to make me get to my feet. In doing so, I shifted my body, hoping to hide my erection.

Her soft gasp and subsequent giggle told me I'd failed.

I shook my head. At least the door was near the bathroom. I went to the door, opened it, and poked my head outside. "Give it here."

The knight handed over the missive, and I shut the door again and ripped open the letter.

I've secured the training hall. We're all waiting.

We're all waiting? I'd figured that Sian would be there, but who were the others?

Neve came padding down the hallway, her eyes twinkling with mischief. "What does it say?"

She was trying not to look at my cock, which only made things worse.

I cleared my throat. "Sian is in the training room. He says to hurry."

"Then we should." Her top teeth dug into her bottom lip. "You should . . . ummm . . . Get working on things." She laughed at her own awkwardness, her gaze panning to the tent in my pants. An irresistible shade of pink flushed her cheeks. "I'll get ready out here and use the bathroom after you."

"Perfect." I lost no time in shutting myself into the bathroom.

I'd never been so happy to go to the palace training facilities. That said a lot considering that when I was a youngling nearing adulthood, I'd loved little more than practicing with swords. Today, though, sparring and training meant I'd no longer be in my rooms. Nor alone with Neve—the far too attractive female who wouldn't stop throwing me coy sidelong glances and amused smiles.

Since we'd left my suite, she hadn't said a word about the events of the morning but was clearly still thinking about it. That made *me* think about it and wonder what she'd have done if I'd pulled her into me and kissed her.

Our first and only proper kiss, the one not witnessed by friends and family at our wedding, played in my mind for what had to be the hundredth time. It had been a surprise, but perfect. Despite the deal we'd made, I wanted that again.

"I hear swords," Neve said as a feral grin slipped across her face. "Are you ready to lose?"

I laughed. She was far too pleased with her win. "We'll see if you get the chance to be sneaky again."

"Sneaky or not, I still won. In a fight for my life, that would be all that mattered, right?"

"What of honor?" I couldn't help but ask. My own sword master had proclaimed loud and clear that honor was of the utmost importance. He'd drilled it into me.

She turned to me; her expression thoughtful. "Worries of survival dominated my life—still do. I suppose if I were you, honor would consume me more. But me? I want to defend myself and live to tell the tale."

Again, I was reminded that though she looked every bit the princess; we came from two different worlds. Both deadly in their own ways, nevertheless very different.

Not for the first time I wondered how well I would have fared in her position. Probably not as well as I'd like to think.

"Do what you must." The corners of my lips lifted in amusement. "Though don't expect me to fall for those violet eyes again."

She smirked. "After this morning, I'm not sure I even have to work that hard."

Heat crept into my cheeks. Bleeding skies, I'd walked right into that one.

Thankfully, we'd reached the double doors of the training facilities, so I pushed one open, pretending like I hadn't heard her, which elicited a snigger from my wife.

"There you are!" Sian called out while parrying an

attack from his younger brother. The clang of steel rang through the vast, empty room. "About time!"

"They're married, Sian! Give them a break," Sayyida shouted, not far from the Balik males. Wooden practice sword in hand, she faced off with none other than Marit Armenil, who appeared red-faced and out of her depth.

Neve sucked in a breath. "We—"

I grasped her wrist and my voice dropped to a whisper. "Let them believe."

Her lips pursed, but she nodded. Friends or not, and I counted Sian as one of my dearest friends, it was best that they thought Neve and me were like any other newly married couple.

"I've warmed Filip up for you, Princess Neve," Sian continued as he rendered his brother useless by pointing the tip of his blade at his neck. "And his magic seems in check today."

"Can we not talk about that?" Filip rustled his wings. "I can't help when the growth spurt comes and goes!"

"Nor would I want you to." Sian chuckled. "You'll need that magic when you take our father's seat. And I do love watching your growth spurts as it gives me something to hold over your head when that day comes."

Filip scowled, but instead of responding to his older brother, he turned to us. "I need to trade steel for wood, and I'm ready when you are, Princess Neve."

"Actually," I said, inspiration striking, "I have an idea."

The squire stood up straighter. The youngling nearing adulthood was my squire and always very respectful, reverent even. Though he was the most magically powerful of the newest generation of Baliks, one would think Filip was actually training for knighthood, rather than to be the heir to the southlands. The lad took his training so seriously. I appreciated that commitment and had been much the same.

"My plucky wife is feeling lucky today. I'd like both of you to take me on. Working *together*."

Filip's dark eyebrows knitted together as questions swam in his honey-colored eyes. "But, no offense, Princess Neve, I'm much better than you. I'll be doing most of the work in protecting and offense."

He was, even while going through a growth spurt. But Filip hadn't trained much with another, specifically a fae who was weaker than him. It would be good for him, and as he was my squire, it was my job to provide him with challenges. Neve, too, could learn something new by working with someone, rather than going at them like a beast.

Her feral expression from her last training session came back to me, and my arousal stirred. She had been a pretty beast indeed, and as much as I'd like to see that in her again, this was valid training too.

"If Filip doesn't want to, I'll do it," Sayyida announced. "Marit needs a break."

"What are you doing here, anyway?" Neve asked.

"Marit needs to learn how to defend herself," Sayyida replied. "And I wanted to make sure my skills were up to par in case my soon-to-be husband gets any ideas." When she spoke of Jarl Salizier, her tone took on a low growl.

Father might believe that this pairing was solving his problems and putting Sayyida in her place. I wasn't so sure. If Jarl Salizier lived to see a single turn after they wed, I'd be shocked.

"Right," Neve replied, discomfort flickering across her face.

She blamed herself for the fates of Sayyida and Marit. I couldn't help but bear some of that burden as well.

"Don't act like that." Sayyida pointed her practice sword at Neve. "The king will do what he wants. But that doesn't mean we can't be prepared." She paused. "Or change our fates."

"You're right," I interrupted. We were the only ones in the training facility, but in Frostveil Castle, the walls had eyes. Perhaps literally, knowing what I knew of Neve walking around the hidden parts of the palace. "So, instead of two, I'll fight three. I'll take on you, Sayyida, Filip, *and* my dainty wife."

Her eyes narrowed as she glared at me, as if being called dainty was an insult. I smothered my laugh because that reaction was what I'd hoped for.

Neve didn't want to be small and powerless, but able to take care of herself. Fierce.

And I wanted her to come at me with *more*.

I wanted to rile the beast and for Neve to harness that strength inside her.

"If you get Vale out, I rush in," Sian added eagerly. He, too, liked a challenge.

Sayyida snorted, not at all intimidated by Sian. I had to admire that about her, for Sian intimidated many. "You're on. Marit, take a breather. Filip, Neve, get over here. I have a plan."

I blocked an attack by Filip, only for Neve to rush me, wooden blade swinging. A grin spread across my face as Sian deflected her attack and she snarled.

We'd been practicing for three hours, and over that time, we'd attempted many formations. This one was Filip, Neve, and Sayyida against me, Sian, and Marit. Two skilled against one new fighter.

Neve was far better than Marit. Not because she'd had a few hours more of training, either. No, my wife had a fire in her that Marit did not possess, though the Armenil female *was* trying.

She'll have to keep at it.

Marit darted behind Sian, who swiped at both Filip and Sayyida and pushed the latter to the ground. Sayyida snarled as, cat-like, she leapt back up and came at him again. If Lord Armenil failed in the Blood Court, and Marit wanted to survive her marriage to Jarl Triam, she couldn't hide behind others. No, she would need to be far stronger, far fiercer. It was good that Sayyida brought her here.

"Head in the game, husband!" Neve rasped, crouching while arching her practice sword to the side and down.

I leapt over the attack that would have struck my ankles. Sian had pulled off that move, knocking his brother off his feet ten minutes ago. Neve was an adept mimic.

"But my daydreams are so pretty. Like you, my *docile* snow lily," I taunted.

Her face turned red, and a laugh burst out of me but only for a moment because at that second, Sayyida landed a strike on Sian's chest, as Filip did the same to his brother's head. The older Balik dropped to the ground and the opposing team wasted no time in taking Marit out too.

In the time that the dissolution of my team rendered me distracted, Neve closed in. I parried, but she came at me again, this time striking like a viper for the gut.

She missed, but Sayyida didn't when she came behind me and placed the wooden sword's blade against my neck.

"We win, Vale. Give up!"

There was far too much joy in the young Lady Virtoris's voice. I wanted to fight it, but, unfortunately, she was right. I'd allowed distraction to get the better of me. Again.

Though at least this time, Neve's breasts had not distracted me. Everyone improved today.

"You win," I added. "About time."

"Oh, shut it, Vale," Sayyida growled. "We kicked butt in that round, and you know it."

"You did well," I conceded.

Even with Marit weighing down my side, it said a lot that the other three fought and, mostly, held off Sian and me. They'd worked well as a team, protecting one another and striking as one when possible.

Neve was still a beginner, but after two days of training, I could tell she moved quickly and learned quicker. Not that I was surprised. My wife had needed both skills to survive where she grew up. Using them here, and being on guard, was natural to her.

We only needed to hone those skills further. Give her a few moons and she'd be a sight to behold.

If we had that long.

With each passing day, the threat of vampire assassins grew. No matter how Lord Armenil tied up this diplomatic disaster, Neve wouldn't skate by without someone trying to kill her. The vampire way of blood for blood would ensure that.

"Any tips for Marit?" Sayyida prompted. "I know Vale will give Neve *personalized* feedback later, so I'm not worried about her."

I chuckled as my wife blushed. Sayyida's crassness never failed to make someone uncomfortable at court.

"You favor your right side," I said to Lady Marit to take some of the heat off Neve. "Try to be more equal or a skilled opponent will realize that quickly. And when you tire, you keep your blade too low." I held my blade like she did. "You're doing this." I repositioned the weapon. "Try holding it like this when fighting."

She mimicked me, and I nodded. "Practice will help."

"We're coming back every morning." Sayyida came to Marit's side and gave her friend a long, pointed look. "Every night if we have to—as long as there's not an event, we'll train. You won't go defenseless."

"Maybe not at all," Neve added, though more quietly. "How quickly can Lord Armenil get to the Blood Court and back?"

"By sea, with favorable winds and currents, it takes five or so days. The way back is longer," Sayyida said. "So he'll be gone for a couple of weeks."

If a foul temper took him, my father could change his mind and force Marit to marry before then, but I didn't dare point that out. The young lady looked hopeful.

"Lots of time to train," Marit spoke up. "Thanks, everyone. I—"

The doors to the training room flew open and a booming voice cut Marit off. "No one invited us to the party!"

Luccan and Thantrel swaggered inside, their wings spread out behind them like the famous peacocks of the Summer Court.

Thantrel grinned from ear to ear as he spoke. "Perhaps you couldn't handle the handsome and powerful Riis brothers?"

"With *that* eyeshadow, I'm surprised anyone can handle even looking at you," Sayyida shot back playfully.

"Don't be envious, Sayyida. Not everyone can be as stunning as me." Thantrel batted his lashes, showing off the shimmering gold shadow he favored as of late. "Right, Vale?"

I rolled my eyes and set to halting the flirting and verbal jousting before it really got started. Thantrel flirted with anything that breathed and Sayyida loved trying to get the best of Thantrel. Or anyone.

I gestured to Neve. "We're done for the day. My wife needs to rest before training further. But perhaps Sian still has a few rounds in him?"

"I do. Filip too."

The youngest Balik looked alarmed.

"You need it, Filip. Father sent you here to train with Vale, so you'd develop your skills overnight." Sian's eyes twinkled. "The Warrior Bear seems to be slacking in teaching his squire."

"He has a pretty new wife." Luccan shrugged. "Who can blame Vale?"

We had to leave before this got out of hand, as it too often did when Sian, Luccan, and I were together. I missed Caelo. My best friend would only torment me further, but he rounded out the group in a way no other could.

I held out my arm for Neve, who took it. "We're going. Is your lord father in the castle?"

Luccan ran a hand through his hair. "We all stayed here last night. He's in the suite. Why?"

"I wish to speak with him."

Luccan gave me a long look, perhaps thinking I'd wish to speak with the Lord of Tongues about the gateway or some matter pertaining to the vampire assassins. Better that he thought that than the truth—that the king suspected Lord Riis of something. Once Lord Riis knew the king suspected him of acting in a manner opposing the crown, I hoped he would relay that information to his sons, my friends, who I did not wish to see harmed either.

"All right," Luccan drew out the words, "well, he's there."

"Let's go." Neve tugged at my arm.

"She's *ready*, Vale." Sayyida sniggered.

Neve huffed. "Can you please stop?"

Sayyida shrugged but didn't commit.

I took that moment to wave to the others and gently guided my wife from the room. Once we were alone in the hall, I turned to her. "Sayyida is famous for getting under others' skin. She's only saying those things to get a rise out of you. And to keep her mind off her situation."

My wife's face fell. "I can understand that."

"If you want her to shut up, complain around Saga." I smirked. "My sister is the only one who can rein Sayyida in. I've seen her do it many times."

"I understand that too," Neve said. "You're going to tell Lord Riis to watch himself?"

"He's helped us. It's only right."

"And what if your father is correct?"

"Then I don't know."

I didn't believe Lord Riis had the Ice Scepter. The most important piece of evidence was the fact that Lord Riis had no winter magic. Why would he take the Hallow if he'd never be able to use it? I was sure Father had caught on to Lord Riis acting strangely because he was protecting Neve and me. Not because he held the Ice Scepter.

We strode through the palace, up stairs and down corridors packed with fae. No one stopped us. Still, no one, save for our close friends, wanted to be associated with us. I didn't mind that but wondered how long this would last.

Because no one stopped us, we reached the wing where Lord Riis was staying in record time.

"I forgot he was staying down here," Neve murmured, glancing at a door as we approached. "So close to me the whole time."

I blinked and then understood. Lord Roar had been staying in this wing too.

"Do you need anything from that suite while we're here? I—"

The door down the hallway opened, and a feminine voice and clicking of heels echoed in the corridors. "Take better care Leyv. Please."

My mother appeared in the hall, her back to us as

she spoke to Lord Riis, who had to be standing inside his room.

"Stars! You've got to be kidding—Vale, I have something to tell you," Neve breathed and pulled me forward. "In here!"

She opened the door to Lord Roar's old suite and yanked me inside, then shut the door softly behind us.

I glanced at the door, then at her, confused. "What's going on?"

"I-I didn't tell you everything I saw in the hidden palace last night." Neve's teeth dug into her bottom lip. "But I should. Before you go talk to Lord Riis."

"What is it?"

"I found Queen Revna's diary back there. She wrote about your mother and Lord Riis."

"That's hardly surprising, Neve. They grew up in the midlands together and have been friends since they were younglings."

"No," Neve exhaled, "she wrote that they looked *romantic*."

I sucked in a breath. But that would have been when Mother was already married to Father. I'd have been around five turns.

"I wasn't sure if telling you was smart. Or appropriate," Neve admitted. "But seeing her come out of his rooms, and she didn't mention him when she told your father about our wedding and—I don't know. I realize that in her own home, the queen has a right to be wherever she wants, but you should know before you say anything to him. What if something is going on between them?"

This might have nothing to do with the Ice Scepter, but it threw a sword into the plans. Was there something between my mother and Lord Riis? Something more than friendship?

Father was not loyal to Mother. In fact, save for official functions or matters in which he needed her council, he barely spoke to her.

My stomach twisted, and I found myself in a position of not knowing how to proceed.

CHAPTER 18

NEVE

Two days of quiet had passed since we'd seen the queen leave Lord Riis's rooms.

No Courting Festival events had taken place. No one had sought me out. Nor Vale.

We spent each morning practicing with weapons and then spent the afternoons either together or in a private lounge with Saga, Sayyida, and Vale's friends, laughing, playing nuchi, getting to know one another, and lying low. I loved those hours. In that time, I felt free, like nothing bad was coming for me.

What a joke.

We'd recently finished our morning training session. I'd already showered and dressed, and now Vale was showering while I lounged on the bed.

On the nightstand next to my stack of books was the Mind Rönd potion. Remembering that I hadn't taken my daily dose yet, I lifted the flask to my lips and took a swallow. Every time I drank the potion, it reminded me of another brew flowing through me. One that continually weakened and put me and Vale in jeopardy.

In six days, I'd be able to feel my magic, but at a cost. I'd no longer be able to lie—a quality that had saved my life many times since being at court. Would I be able to twist truths in a way that other fae did naturally? If not, and I said the wrong thing, I was dead.

As it had every time I'd considered such a terrible outcome, my heart raced. Though it was the last thing I wanted to do, I'd considered asking Vale if he could procure the same potion for me. That meant I wouldn't know what magic ran through my veins for yet another moon cycle, which would be devastating, *but* I'd feel more secure. More safe.

The door to the bathroom opened, and Vale stepped out, a fluffy towel wrapped around his hips and his bare chest glistening from his shower. Steam followed him, bringing a fresh scent into the suite.

I swallowed. For the three days, we'd remained platonic, but it was growing more difficult. In stolen glances and moments of flirting that seemed to just happen when we spoke, it had never been more obvious that we *wanted* one another.

"Should I request a painting be commissioned?" He ran a finger down his tattooed chest. "That way you can gawk whenever you'd like."

I hurled a pillow at him. "I was not gawking."

"Could have fooled me." He caught the pillow one-handed, and I silently cursed him for being so effortlessly handsome. His long black hair was still wet, and he looked delicious. When I stepped out of the bathroom, I looked like a drowned bandicota.

"I was daydreaming. About this," I lied as I held up the book on the top of my pile, the one that had been Roar's brother's favorite. I had *intended* to read it while he showered, but I'd become lost in my thoughts instead and hadn't even cracked open the storybook.

"Oh? How far into it are you?"

I sensed a trap. "I've read about five chapters."

"Has a troll shown up yet? I always loved reading about trolls."

"You've read it?"

"As a youngling." He came closer, but as he passed the spot on the wall that led to the hidden parts of the palace, he paused. Glanced at it with longing.

Besides spending time with friends during our free days, we'd tried to get into the hidden part of the palace. Four times we'd made the attempt. None of them with any luck. Apparently, when Vale was with me, the palace decided I wasn't in danger.

It was difficult to be upset at that, even if we were both dying to delve deeper into Queen Revna's diary.

After spying his mother leaving the Lord of Tongues's chambers, Vale had not told Lord Riis about the king's suspicions. That choice was eating him up inside.

Vale wanted to do the right thing, but he also wanted to understand Lord Riis better. Obviously, everyone had a past and the new information we had, combined with Lord Riis's past, made Vale question quite a lot.

In the past, the Lord of Tongues had taken many lovers. I had been stunned to learn that Luccan, Arie, and Thantrel were far from his only children. They were simply the only ones at court. The only ones *legitimized* by King Magnus and hence, able to take part in the Courting Festival.

Had the queen been one of Lord Riis's lovers once?

If so, how would that change Vale's opinion of him? If at all?

I didn't think even Vale knew the answer to that.

"Any glowing?" Vale nodded to the door, perhaps sensing that my thoughts, like his own, had wandered.

"None."

"Pity." Vale came closer and perched on the edge of the bed. "So what is your favorite part of that book so far?"

"What?"

He smirked. "I should put a shirt on if you're going to be so distractible."

"You're so full of yourself." I rolled my eyes, and desperate to get off the subject of my ogling him, I pressed the book to my chest. "Like I said, I haven't read much, but I also like the bits about the troll. I can see why you did too. You don't read about them often in stories."

Vale's lips curled up into a smirk. "No. Not even in the pages of that book." He winked. "I guess I am that distracting."

I gaped. "Stars, I hate the way fae can twist truths!"

Vale burst out laughing. "Well, you'd better get used to it. Soon you'll have to do the same."

My stomach clenched.

"About that." I set the book on the side table. "I was thinking, maybe I should take the potion again? I don't know what it's called, but it's the same one the vampires force-fed me every full moon?" The words burned leaving my throat, but if continuing to smother my magic for a while longer would save my life, then I'd do it. "It is possible to get here, right?"

"We call it the Liar's Salvation," Vale said. "It's illegal."

I swallowed. "Well, what do you think I should do, then?"

He shook his head. "I've been wondering that too. We've been lucky these past days, with no events, but tomorrow we'll have to go to the theater."

We'd received the summons this morning that our peace would soon be ending. Normally, the idea of going to the theater would fill my heart with joy. I'd always wanted to experience such a spectacle. But after two days with no drama from the Courting Festival, I wasn't ready for it to start up again.

"And it's likely that events will take place more often," Vale said. "Father might have needed time to cool down after our wedding and everything else that happened with Lord Armenil and Lady Virtoris."

"Or he was planning something to make a scene again."

"Or that." The prince turned my way. Pointedly, I didn't look at his chest, no matter how beautifully it gleamed in the midday sun coming in through the window.

Stars, the male needs a shirt!

"How do you feel about an outing?"

I blinked, not expecting that, but up for it after spending three days in the castle. "Sure. Where to?"

"You need the Liar's Salvation. There are only two places we can get that."

"And they are?"

"The Black Market"—he paused—"which would be difficult as I'm recognizable. No one would sell it to me because that's an admission that they brew it, and they can be tossed in prison. The other option is better —especially seeing as I have a friend on the inside."

"Are you ever going to tell me? Or continue to listen to yourself talk?" I jabbed him in the shoulder with my finger.

He snorted and gave me a light, playful shove in return. "We'll take a trip to the House of Wisdom."

"Where the scholars study?" I sat up straighter. "Can we see their library?"

"Maybe. I'll ask my friend."

I shifted off the bed, excitement trilling through me at the thought of a library as large as the royal one. "Get a shirt on and let's go!"

Two Clawsguards followed as we approached the House of Wisdom.

It had surprised me to learn the House of Wisdom was incredibly close to the palace, only a ten-minute walk, but in a direction I had not yet ventured.

Unlike the Tower, it was closer to the less fortunate parts of the city, where the homes were smaller and the clothing thinner, more ragged. The soldiers guiding us had offhandedly called the fae who lived here dregs, and I could see why. They were the unwanted. The lowly. The poor. At the sight of those fae, pity rose in my chest.

In the last days, the winds raged, and the temperatures had dropped even further. We hadn't noticed the cold, cozied up in Vale's chambers that morning, but these people would have felt Winter's bite. I fingered the fur lining my cloak and contemplated giving it to a far too thin female of around my height before she turned down an alley and disappeared.

I exhaled, painting the air white and wishing I'd acted sooner. A few minutes of being cold wouldn't kill me, and I could get as many cloaks as I wished when I returned to the castle.

Vale caught me eyeing one home that was little more than a shack as we walked up to the gates of the House of Wisdom. "Not everywhere in Avaldenn prospers like those in Lordling Lane."

I had known hunger and cold myself. And of course, since I'd been in Winter's Realm, I'd met a starving goblin and seen beggars on the streets of

Avaldenn, but this was so much more. And somehow, it stunned me as I took it all in.

How, in a few days of living at the palace, had I almost forgotten that these types of places, people in these circumstances, existed everywhere? How had I put where I'd come from out of mind?

I scanned the area again, trying to commit it to memory, to make sure I never forgot again, when my attention snagged on a boarded-up building. It was larger than the rest, at least double in size. Someone had painted a red symbol on the door: a horizontal line with a tipped over V drawn bisecting it.

"Is that building condemned?" I pointed to it. "Is that what that symbol means?"

Vale cleared his throat. "It's not in use, but that's not what that means."

The way he spoke, so solemn, made the hair on the back of my neck lift.

"What is it then?"

"That's a sign of the loyalist rebellion. The soaring white hawk of House Falk."

My lips parted in recognition. The V represented the wings, and the line was the body of the bird.

"I'm surprised the crown lets that stand."

"I suspect the building was recently discovered. They'll burn it soon enough."

Burn it? When it looked larger and far sturdier than half the surrounding homes? What a waste.

"What's this area called?" I asked as we reached the gate separating the House of Wisdom from the seedy neighborhood, and one of our Clawsguards began speaking to the attendant at the entrance.

"Rall Row."

"They called the people who lived here dregs." I gestured to the Clawsguards, who were too busy speaking with the attendant and being on watch to notice.

Vale cringed. "That's a slur for those who live in this part of the city. I'll speak with the guards about that later."

"A good idea," I said, glad that Vale didn't use the same terms. "And the House of Wisdom is here among the poorest fae. That seems odd to me." I gestured to the great black gate separating the row from the elaborate building that resembled a small castle.

"The Row grew around the House of Wisdom. Healers train here and many in the Row seek their services for free." Vale watched a youngling kicking a ball down the street.

The child had long white hair, and despite that being a common enough color among the fae, I caught myself wondering if he was one of my blood relatives. If so, this could have been where I'd grown up.

"This area wasn't always like this." Regret laced his voice. "The Row began developing about ten turns ago."

A decade after the rebellion. I understood what he was cryptically saying. These fae were among the first to be affected by the slow decline of Winter's Realm.

The poor and downtrodden were always the first to feel the downfall of society.

"Prince Vale, Princess Neve, this way." The Clawsguards ushered us inside the gate. "The attendant has informed a vishku of your arrival and will see to you now."

Vale winced. "I'd rather speak to Lärling Duran."

The attendant at the gate shrugged. "I'm sure the vishku will take excellent care of you."

Vale scowled but didn't argue as we passed through the gates, down a long path lined with tall evergreen trees, to the vast double doors that looked more intimidating than welcoming.

From the outside, the House of Wisdom reminded me of a smallish, rectangular, sandy-brown castle with towers in every corner.

One tower appeared to be newer, whiter, and brighter than the rest of the building.

"What's that?" I pointed to the tower.

"The White Tower," Vale answered. "Healers train and live there. Though there is a small portion that the rest of the scholars use—mostly for potions." He arched his eyebrows.

So if all went well, we'd be going there.

"They separated healers from other scholars?"

"To a certain degree, every sect of study is separate, though healers are an extreme. The Masters and the teachers live at the top of the White Tower."

"Hmm," I mused. "Have you been here often?"

"A few times."

"For what?" He read but not like I did. Then again, few read *that* voraciously. I wondered what he was interested in reading or studying.

"Rhistel is a klär, a level below the vishku, the highest honor one can achieve in the House of Wisdom. He's studied here since we were young—a perk for the heir. Most have to wait until they're adults to study in the House of Wisdom. I used to visit him."

"Oh." That Prince Rhistel did anything besides antagonize others and spout lewd comments astonished me.

The double doors opened, and Vale directed all his attention to the older, plump female dwarf sweeping toward us. She wore white flowing trousers and a top to match. A white cloak atop kept her warm.

"Prince Vale, welcome to the House of Wisdom," the female said, her deep-set black eyes blinking with interest.

"Vishku Sindri. It's an honor to be here."

"And what, might I ask, brings you here today, Prince Vale?"

"I came to speak with a friend and introduce him to my wife," Vale replied. "Princess Neve."

"Yes, I've heard that congratulations are in order." The vishku curtsied. "A pleasure, Princess Neve. And who are you here to see?"

"Lärling Duran Urgi."

The vishku's face fell. "Ah. I see."

"Is he here?" Vale pressed, which only made the vishku's frown lines deepen.

"He is. Though, I wonder if now is a good time."

"For us, it is," Vale replied. "Is he busy?"

"He is being disciplined."

I swallowed. That didn't bode well, considering we were about to ask Vale's friend to break the law for us.

"I'd rather not reward him with a visit from the prince," the vishku continued. "So—"

"I'm *dying* to meet him," I interrupted, hoping to push on through. "And we won't be able to get away from the palace for a very long time. Not with the Courting Festival going on." I gave the vishku a winning smile, and her shoulders softened as her resolve crumbled.

"Only a quick visit." Vishku Sindri waved us through the double doors.

We stepped out of the biting cold and wind. The foyer was void of anything save for a few spherical faelights to illuminate the space and mark the closed doors leading deeper into the House of Wisdom. It was spotless, but smelled like parchment and old home, as if no matter how much one scrubbed, they'd never quite rid the building of every speck of dirt.

Vishku Sindri rubbed her hands together. "It's wicked out there today."

"The cold is setting in early," Vale replied. "I cannot imagine how cold it will be around Winter Solstice."

"One of our vishkus trained in following weather patterns claims that the end of this turn will be one of the worst in a long while. They say it will seep into the next turn."

"Hopefully, the wind will be calm, though. It adds to the bite." I rubbed my arms beneath my fur-lined cloak.

Before arriving in this kingdom, I'd rarely been cold, but the Kingdom of Winter was a different beast entirely. I could still tolerate quite a lot, but the gales flying off the Shivering Sea pushed me over the edge into discomfort.

"Indeed," Sindri said. "There will be a hearth blazing where you're going. You may warm yourself there, Princess Neve. Your Clawsguards, however, will have to stay in the foyer."

Vale didn't press for the Clawsguards to follow, not that the vishku waited to see if he would. No, the moment she'd laid down the boundary, Sindri motioned for us to follow her through a door on the right. Vale told his guards to remain, and we trailed her through the door, then down an unadorned, windowless, gray corridor lit with faelights that hovered near the ceiling, casting an eerie glow upon the stone. Like in the foyer, each door we passed was closed, cut off from the rest of the world.

Why in all the nine kingdoms would a place brimming with knowledge be so plain? So boring? The only reason I could fathom was that austerity did not distract the apprentices and scholars from their studies. Still, how dismal it would be to live in such a place.

We passed at least twelve doors before the vishku halted before a door that looked like all the others.

"Here we are." She opened it and a fresh scent of soap wafted out as we stepped into a vast space littered with wood tables. On the far wall, windows opened into what must be an interior courtyard and multiple hearths burned on each side wall.

Sindri scanned the area, eyebrows pinching together. After no one appeared, she raised her hands and clapped. "Lärling Duran! Where are you?"

At the far side of the room, a strawberry-blond head popped up between two long tables. "Vishku Sindri! I didn't hear you enter!" His cheeks turned red, making his short beard look blonder.

"What are you doing?" the vishku barked, inferring guilt as I had.

"Scrubbing the floors, as you requested," Duran replied as Sindri barreled forth, Vale and me behind her.

Duran popped back down, out of sight. I swore I heard faint cursing and the ruffling of pages before he rose again, patting his long white tunic down as if trying to be presentable.

"Lärling Duran!" Sindri admonished. "Were you reading?"

The dwarf's face fell, and I smothered a laugh. Vale shot me an amused glance.

"No, Vishku. I—"

Sindri was upon him, hands reaching into the folds of his tunic. From them, she extracted a small leather-bound book and waved it around. "Then what's this? It's not helping you with your duties." She tossed the book on the table and shook her head. "I should send Prince Vale and Princess Neve from the House of

Wisdom. But I've given my word and would hate to disappoint the new princess."

The dwarf threw his hands up to reveal misshapen fingers on each hand. "Only here could someone get in trouble for studying!"

"You're meant to be serving the House of Wisdom for a prior offense." Sindri scowled. "Shall I add another punishment for not doing your job? This one with a chaperone."

"Skies, no," Duran murmured. "I won't do it again. Promise." He picked up the book and handed it over. "I apologize, Vishku Sindri."

For a moment, the vishku said nothing, and when it seemed like she would deny him, she took the book. "I want this room done before dinner."

"Th-that's too soon!" Duran sputtered.

"Prince Vale and Princess Neve wish to speak with you. After they leave, you'd better work quickly." Though Sindri's tone was strict, I caught a glimmer of amusement in her eyes. "And see them out when you're done, Duran."

Vale and I nodded our appreciation, and the vishku left. The moment the door to the corridor shut behind her, Duran let out a frustrated whine.

"I should have been a blacksmith!"

"You never would have lasted." Vale laughed. "Your father would have been tough on you—tougher even than Vishku Sindri—and you wouldn't be able to spend hours and hours just reading."

Duran shuddered. "You're right. Plus, the forge is

hot. Stars, I hate that." His annoyance seemingly out of his system, Duran turned his big blue eyes on me. "So, you're the new princess? You really chose *him*?"

A laugh burst out of me. "I guess I did."

"A delight, fair Princess Neve. Seeing you with this lug tells me that there's hope for me yet." Duran winked at Vale, who shook his head as though he expected nothing less than the dwarf's sass.

"We need your help, Duran," Vale said.

"I assumed so," the dwarf replied, palms up and his eyes to the sky. "I'm always getting this one out of binds."

"What a tall tale."

"It's been true—at least twice."

Vale cocked his head as if reaching farther back into the recesses of his memory. "Yes, well, this request has to do with my new wife and must be kept secret."

Duran's countenance shifted. The playfulness dimmed. "Secret, eh? Why?"

"Because," I piped up, "it's illegal."

The dwarf opened his mouth, but I cut him off.

"And before you ask, I cannot tell you why I require it."

He shut his mouth, then opened it again. "Do you possess mental magic?"

"No." It wasn't even a lie, not as far as I knew. "It seemed a natural thing to ask, after being confronted with illegality."

"Hmm, she's far too clever for you, Vale." The dwarf used Vale's given name. Only those in the

Aaberg family and Vale's other close friends did the same. Well, and Sayyida, but she didn't adhere to many social norms.

"She's cleverer than you know," Vale replied, and as heat rose in my cheeks, I looked away to gather myself. "Now, about why we've come. Are you willing to help us, even if there are legal ramifications?"

Duran took a moment, his right hand fiddling with his long white tunic before nodding. "You're lucky I love you like a brother."

"That I am." Vale inhaled. "Duran, can you acquire a dose of the Liar's Salvation potion?"

The dwarf's eyes widened. "Why would you need that?"

"We can't tell you," I repeated.

"Right . . . of course." The dwarf swallowed. "Well, we have all the ingredients to make the potion here. Whether there is some already brewed and bottled, I cannot say."

"Can you check?" I was hopeful we'd get to leave with a dose today. That would mean one more moon of being able to defend myself from anyone prying into my past.

"Not with you in tow." Duran gave a humorless chuckle. "Most potions are brewed and stored at the base of the White Tower. I'll have to go there to check. Which I can't do until tonight—not without rousing suspicion." He gestured to the mop and the bucket not far away, forgotten by him, not even noticed by me.

"And if there isn't any in stock? How long does it take to brew?" Vale asked.

I stiffened. I hadn't even considered that might be an issue. The vampires had always had the potion on hand, but what if it took an entire moon cycle to create the potion?

"I believe it takes around a week to mature."

Too long. I had six days. I shot Vale an alarmed look.

"Check to be sure, will you?" The prince placed a steadying hand on my shoulder.

"Yes. And if I need to, I'll brew it in secret." Duran's gaze flicked to the door before returning to Vale. "I can look for it in the storerooms tonight and send you a message tomorrow? To the castle?"

"No, I'll have Filip come here and take the message from you," Vale said. "This can't get in the wrong hands."

Duran shrugged. "Whatever you want."

"Thank you, friend." Vale inclined his head. "I think we should go. Wouldn't want to keep you from your work for too long. Vishku Sindri wouldn't approve."

Duran rolled his eyes. "If only I could make you help as payment without rousing questions, I would."

The pair hugged, and Duran took my hand and kissed it. The hairs of his short beard tickled my skin before he lifted his face to grin at me. "You wouldn't happen to have a single sister, would you, my princess?"

Though pain sliced through me at his question, one

that I'd been wondering more often of late, I smiled. "Not that I know of."

"A shame." Duran released my hand and bowed. "I'll send word, and perhaps a dose of your brew, tomorrow. Should I show you out? Or do you know the way?"

Vale pressed his hand into my lower back. "We can handle it."

We left Duran to his work and found the long, gray hallway empty. I exhaled. "Hopefully, they have it on hand."

"Agreed. If not, though, Duran will find a way to brew it."

I prayed to the stars that he was right.

CHAPTER 19

NEVE

My wings burned as I whipped around, blocking an attack from Sayyida. She howled in frustration as she soared by me, and Sian, my team member for the day, appeared to take her on.

I barked out a laugh at her frustration, but my relief was short-lived as Filip came at me next.

"Head in the game, Princess!" Filip's wooden sword struck mine. "No one is here to protect you!"

I parried a second attack before retaliating with one of my own. "Nor you!"

He scoffed, performed a twirl in the air, and attacked again. "As if I need it. I feel great today."

Admittedly, he'd been doing well. The difference between Filip in the middle of his magical growth spurts and Filip at his full strength was striking.

Sweat dripped down my face as we fought and flew.

Below, Vale watched, assessing the teams. Today it was me, Sian, and Marit, against Sayyida, Filip, and Saga.

It had surprised me when the princess arrived with Sayyida. Saga claimed to want to learn more about self-defense with her friends, and her brother wasn't about to deny her.

Truth be told, the practice wouldn't hurt Saga. I was already better than her and Marit.

"Argh!" Filip grunted as I soared above him, wings straining with the effort to move fast, flipped, and hit his honey-brown wings from my inverted position.

From below, Vale clapped. "Ingenious, Neve! Filip, you're out! Saga, you too!"

My heart leapt. Of those on the other team, only Sayyida remained. I spun in midair to find her, taking a moment to marvel at how much more dexterous my wings had gotten. Daily physical training and swordplay had enhanced my reflexes, which Vale had already deemed very good. And though we'd only been partaking in aerial training for two days, my wings were benefiting from the exercises.

Soon, I wouldn't fear flying high in the air. I'd ride the winds like I'd been born to do.

For now, though, I soared toward Sian as he took on Sayyida, a wide grin on his face. The young Nava captain was bright red, revealing how hard she was battling the experienced warrior.

She was so focused on Sian that Sayyida didn't even see me coming. Heart pounding, I lifted my wooden sword and brought it down as she jerked out of the way, twisted, and stabbed me in the arm.

"*Ow!*"

"Out, Neve!" Vale called.

"Thought you had me, huh?" Sayyida laughed. "Not likely, Neve—hey!"

Sian finished her off by zooming over and giving a swat to her thigh. "Never turn your back on your strongest opponent."

"Yeah, Sayyida," I teased.

"Shove it," she shot back as she dropped to the ground and marched off.

Sian and I followed, clapping our hands together in victory as our feet hit the floor. "You flew well, Princess Neve."

"Thanks. I feel a lot stronger." I shifted my wings so that they pressed down my back, into a resting position, and winced. "More sore too."

"Have you taken to the mineral baths?"

I swallowed. As a slave, I'd washed in a bathhouse with natural mineral pools, and I'd heard Frostveil boasted something similar, but I hadn't gone to them. Not after what had happened back in the Vampire Kingdom. The day I'd killed a vampire.

The day I'd risked my life for a new beginning.

"I'm not partial to them," I lied. For now, I'd stick with Vale's vast tub.

"Perhaps a sauna, then? I find those always help when I've overtrained."

"The one in the city?" The only one I'd seen was the fancy one in Lordling Lane.

"We have one inside the palace," Saga chimed in from behind. I twisted to find her skipping toward us. "I want to go too, Neve, so let's do it! Sayyida will come too."

"I will not," Sayyida shouted. She stood with Filip, and the pair looked to be plotting how best to beat me and Sian next time. Sore losers, both of them.

"You will," Saga muttered as she closed in. "We should go now."

"You're already done training?" Sian smirked. "You didn't last very long."

He wasn't wrong. It was still early in the morning, and we usually trained until lunch.

"We have the theater tonight." Saga's hands landed on her slender hips. "And I bet Neve has to pick up her dress still."

I did. Or at least, I had to send someone to do so for me.

"So, you see, Sian, we have time to sauna, eat, and then go to the shop before we have to get ready for the show," Saga continued.

Sian chuckled. "Very well. I suppose it takes females a long time to get ready."

"Nearly as long as you." Vale strode our way. "Don't pretend you don't try to look pretty at the theater, Sian."

The males began to verbally spar, and Saga turned

toward me, rolling her eyes. "What do you say to a girls' morning? We've seen each other most days but always with Vale. I don't blame you since you're a newlywed, but, well, I'd like some time alone with you and the girls!"

A smile grew on my face at being included, considered part of the group. "I'd love that."

I lay back on the wooden bench as Saga poured water over hot black rocks.

"Good?" Saga turned back to the bench and lay down, allowing her towel to fall.

Though the sauna was open to anyone in the palace, when the royal family wished to use it, the Clawsguard cleared it out. We were alone, Saga, Sayyida, and I.

I'd been naked around slaves at the Blood Court. Both in the baths and in our bedroom. There wasn't much privacy there. But since arriving in Winter's Realm, I'd either had my own room, or Vale had granted me privacy whenever I wished.

Too much privacy, I sometimes thought, though he was following the letter of our agreement. No way I could be upset about that, even if my body disagreed with me.

In the sauna, however, we were free to drop the towels and relax in the way nature intended.

"So, Neve, which gown are you going to wear

tonight?" Saga asked, her blue eyes closed as she breathed deeply in and out.

"I'm not sure." I wiggled my bare toes and stretched out on the hot wood.

During the days when there'd been no Courting Festival events, Saga's personal dressmaker had come to the castle to take my measurements. I'd given her an idea of what I liked, the colors, cuts, and fabrics. She'd claimed she had a few gowns in the works that matched what I liked. With a few embellishments fit for a princess, she could have them done by today.

Vale had been ecstatic. Every time I wore crimson, Roar's colors, he frowned, though he hadn't actually said anything.

Truth be told, I was pleased to have a new wardrobe too.

"One of the royal blue gowns," I said, weighing my options.

At least half of the dresses I'd ordered were royal blue, but I'd chosen gold and shades of white, the other Aaberg hues, as well as variations of purple and a lighter blue—my preference. Vale had given me far more flexibility than Roar, who had curated my closet.

I shrugged. "House colors."

"*Gross*," Sayyida sang. "Don't be such a suck-up, Neve."

Saga cracked her eyes open and pointed a finger at Sayyida. "As if you don't wear Virtoris blue and black every chance you get! Don't be hard on Neve for trying to get in my parents' good graces. I think royal blue will look very nice on you, Neve."

"I can't help it if Virtoris blue goes with my eyes," Sayyida mumbled.

"You sound like Sian." I laughed when Sayyida scowled at the mention of the male who'd beaten her. "Oh, get over it, Sayyida. Sian is a great warrior. And you can't win every time."

Sayyida sat up. "I beat my brother every time."

"When there's no magic involved," Saga corrected.

"But at swords. Or any other weapon."

"Well, perhaps one day you'll beat Sian too." I offered a rowan branch. "If he keeps working with you, you'll be more likely to do so."

Sayyida cocked her head. "You're right." She paused. "You're not the middle child, are you?"

My eyebrows knitted together. "What?"

"Well, you're good at negotiating and that makes me think of a lot of middle children I know."

Saga laughed. "You're a middle child, Sayyida. And you're not very good at negotiating, just fighting to get your own way."

"*Anyway*," Sayyida said loudly, ignoring the princess. "Then I realized that I know so little about your family. Aside from your father, Fates rest his soul. Do you have siblings?"

I swallowed down the hot air. The matter of my family, or lack thereof, was coming up more often. I supposed it was only natural. People were curious about me, the female who had been engaged to a warden and then wed a prince. Although I should have taken it as a sign that people were trying to get to know me, it always made my heart ache.

Once, I'd had a family. Once, someone had known my true name—not the one my slave master, Lord Aldéric, had given me. Once, I'd been loved and belonged to others.

A sob ripped out of me.

An alarmed expression crossed Saga's face. "Neve? What's wrong?"

I forced down the lump in my throat and gave myself a shake, determined to rid my body of the sorrow. Of the cold somehow seeping into me despite being in a hot, dry sauna. "Nothing. It's nothing."

"Afterworld burn me. It's not nothing." Sayyida shifted to sit up and her black curls cascaded down her back. "What did I say?"

She looked so earnest, so like she cared, that I wanted to tell her everything. The actual truth.

It wasn't the first time I'd considered this. Since Saga had learned who I was, the idea had drifted in and out of my mind, fleeting but present.

"She won't say anything," Saga whispered, which only made Sayyida's stormy gray-blue eyes widen.

She picked up her towel, wrapped it around her, and came closer. "I won't say a thing. Saga knows I will take secrets to the afterworld."

Sayyida might be a sore loser and rowdy, but she'd always shown she was a true friend.

Perhaps telling Sayyida was smart. She had access

to many ships, knew the crews, and when and where they were sailing. One day, when there wasn't so much attention on me and Vale, perhaps Sayyida would help me stow away on one. Then I could put distance between me and the Vampire Kingdom, and Vale would be free to find and wed his soulmate.

Something in my chest pinched. I curled inward at the pain but forced myself to straighten out. As much as I didn't like the idea of leaving Vale, we had a deal. And I couldn't force him to continue to be with me when he wanted to find his soulmate.

"I'm here," Saga whispered and placed her hand on mine. "If you want to tell, I'm here."

I took her hand and met Sayyida's eye. "There's lots about me that you don't know."

Sayyida shrugged. "Isn't that the same with everyone?"

"Not to this degree." I took a deep breath and told her everything.

Ignoring one of the Clawsguard's assurances that 'he'd get it,' Sayyida opened the door to the dressmaker's shop for Saga and me, her eyes still wide with wonder. They'd looked that way since I'd told her my story. Who I really was and what I needed to do.

Things were still sinking in for her, which I found understandable. I often couldn't believe my own circumstances, and I'd lived through every minute of them.

"Guards, remain out here," Saga instructed. "One to the back door. We'll be fine inside the shop."

I swallowed. The only reason Vale had let me leave the palace grounds without him and venture into Avaldenn with Saga and Sayyida was because his sister promised to take six Clawsguards. Vale would want the soldiers inside the dress shop with us, but if Saga thought they were fine out here, they probably were. It was unlikely that a vampire assassin could have already made it all the way to Avaldenn from the Vampire Kingdom. The Blood would have only gotten the news that I'd killed Gervais a day ago. Perhaps two days, if the winds had been favorable.

We're fine. Completely fine.

For a couple more days, at least.

The inside of the dressmaker's shop smelled like spiced tea and snow lily. My throat tightened because when I smelled snow lily, I thought of Clemencia.

Was she well? Was Anna? Caelo? We hadn't received word of their well-being from Lord Riis. I made a note to pull the Lord of Tongues aside at the theater and ask him.

"Look at this!" Saga ran her hand over a dress displayed on a mannequin near the front. "So stunning!"

Sayyida shrugged, but I agreed with the princess. With exquisite beadwork on the bodice and a flowing chiffon skirt that shimmered in the midday light, the dusty pink gown was fit for a queen.

"You should try it on, Saga," I encouraged. "It nearly matches your hair."

"Perhaps she would make me one that's an exact match." Saga cocked her head. "I—"

"Thought we heard you!" Two familiar figures appeared from deeper in the shop. A slim nymph followed, her race obvious by her rounded ears, lack of wings, and vivid blue hair, from which small white flowers grew.

Baenna and Eireann Balik smiled twin smiles, and for the first time, they reminded me of Filip and Sian, rather than the other way around. I had seen little of the Balik ladies since I wed Vale but had seen much of the Balik brothers.

Saga faked a gasp. "I can't believe you two are here! Have you already bought up the shop?"

"Like you don't have bespoke items on hold." Baenna rolled her eyes playfully at the princess. "But yes, Father said we could get whatever we wanted, so we're stocking up. The southlands don't have the same quality of dressmakers. Or assistants." Baenna shot the nymph a grin, and the female blushed prettily before turning her attention to us and curtsying.

"Welcome, Princess Saga, Lady Sayyida." The nymph turned to me. "I'm afraid we have not met?"

"Neve," I said.

"*Princess* Neve." Saga patted my arm. "You'll get

used to it." She looked at the dressmaker. "Princess Neve recently wed my brother, Prince Vale."

The nymph's eyes went wide. "Congratulations on your recent marriage, Princess Neve." She curtsied again, dipping and rising with a smoothness that few managed. "My mistress is in the back, putting the finishing touches on the gowns you ordered. I'll tell her you're here. Feel free to look around while we get your orders ready for you to try on."

She disappeared to the back of the shop, and we spread out. I lingered near the front of the lovely shop, taking my time to examine the stitching and running my fingers over the varied material the dressmaker used. To my delight, I found no flaws. Saga had chosen an excellent dressmaker.

I'd found at least two more dresses I wished to add to my order—plainer ones to wear day to day, when the door to the shop opened, letting in a chill.

I shivered, hoping the new customer would close the door quickly.

"They'll let anyone in here these days, won't they?" Drawled a voice I recognized.

I heaved a sigh and turned, already knowing who I'd find.

Since the wedding, I'd done well in avoiding Calpurnia Vagle and her uppity friends—Hadia and Adila—both of House Ithamai, the noble house of the east. I'd only seen the trio in the crowds the day King Magnus paired Sayyida and Marit with the jarls. Seen but not spoken to them. My luck had run out.

"Hello, ladies," I said as if Calpurnia hadn't been talking about me. "Dress shopping today too?"

Adila scoffed and her snow-white wings went rigid. "Shopping? We only order bespoke."

"That's nice," I said, well beyond caring. No matter what I did, these three were set on disliking me. I wouldn't try to change their minds when, in the grand scheme of things, they mattered very little.

Hadia eyed the plain dress I'd been examining. "You're not going to buy that, are you? A princess, even one who used to be a whore, should dress better."

The insult ran off me like water as my eyes dipped down to her dress. The dark purple material was rich in color and the embroidery of a set of scales—representing the justice their mother was so fond of—had been done well enough. But there were flaws. Flaws in the stitching, in the cut, in the way the dress hung off Hadia's body.

"A daughter of the Warden of the East could dress better too," I remarked. "Those stitches are coming out." I pointed to the hem of her dress. "And the cut, well, if this dress is bespoke, I'd consider getting it altered again to fit properly."

Hadia's cheeks reddened. "You wouldn't recognize quality if it hit you in the face."

"Dressmaking is one thing I'm sure of." I lifted my chin. "Another is that it's, perhaps, not the best idea to insult someone of a more elevated title than you. Princess is higher than lady, correct?"

The ladies, Vagle and Ithamai, exchanged furious glances but said nothing.

"That's what I thought." I smirked.

Calpurnia opened her mouth, probably to retaliate, when the dressmaker's assistant appeared. "Princess, I have a room set up for you so you can try on the dresses you ordered."

"Thank you," I said before sparing the ladies one more glance. "Have the day you deserve."

The trio gasped, but I'd already turned my back on them to follow the nymph with a wicked smile on my face.

CHAPTER 20

VALE

The strong scent of sage and vinegar nearly bowled me over as I entered the healer's sanctuary. *Stars, something must have really needed cleaning for it to smell this bad.*

"Prince Vale, may I help you?" a healer greeted, her hair a mess, but her tone bright.

"I've come to visit my friend, Sir Qildor, if he's awake?" I lifted the bag I'd brought with me, filled with the knight's favorite treat. "And I brought meat sticks. He's permitted to eat them, correct?"

"He can eat whatever he likes. No wine or ale, of course. They hinder healing, but meat sticks are acceptable. And yes, he's awake. Others are visiting him."

"Oh." I craned my neck to peer around her but didn't see Sir Qildor or anyone else I recognized in the beds. "Who is visiting him?"

Should it be his family, I did not wish to intrude.

"Lord Virtoris and Lord Balik."

"Vidar and Sian?" I found it unlikely that the high lords of the great houses would be present, but best to check.

"Yes, my prince."

Great minds thought alike, it seemed.

"Show me where he's resting."

The healer led me deeper into the sanctuary, to the private rooms for longer term patients. Back here it was relatively quiet. Such a drastic change from the day I'd carried Neve in here and pulled glass from her cuts. The day I knew I wanted to learn more about her.

The healer stopped and knocked on a closed door before opening it slightly. "Sir Qildor, the prince is here to see you."

"Vale?" Qildor asked hesitantly.

"Yes, Prince Vale."

"About time," Sian said loudly.

"It is," I agreed, moving into the room as the healer stepped aside and shut the door behind me. "I should have come earlier."

I should have come every day.

"Are you well, Qildor?" I tried to ignore the guilt I felt at his situation.

My friend, my brother in the cabal, smiled from where he sat in his bed, leaning back against the head-board, a cup of tea in hand. "I am. Thanks to you."

"No, it's thanks to me that you're in this situation."

Qildor's face fell and his violet eyes darkened.

"Don't say that, Vale. The king made his choice. Not you."

It was all he dared to say; the closest he came to speaking ill about my father on the matter. A smart faerie.

"How are your wings?" I eyed the bandages.

"Better by the day." Qildor motioned to one of two empty chairs. "Sit, Vale. We have much to catch up on. I hear that you're training the new princess?"

"With the help of Sian and Filip." I nodded to Vidar as I sat next to the heir to House Virtoris. "Sometimes Vidar, Luccan, and Thantrel too."

"I wish I could come more often," Vidar admitted. "But Mother is set on me helping her get Sayyida out of her engagement. Each morning I sit in a meeting with yet another house, speaking to another male who wants to wed my sister."

"And why not Sian?" My eyebrows pulled together. "House Balik should hold more sway than most."

"Agreed," Vidar agreed. "Once Sayyida told Mother about wishing to wed Sian, Mother brought the idea to the king. He dismissed it so quickly he might have expected the request."

Impossible. But I suspected Father had denied their request because he still believed that Lord Balik might have the Ice Scepter. Guilt churned in my stomach.

I hadn't yet told Sian about the king's thoughts regarding Lord Balik. Partially because I wanted to find the Ice Scepter, and partially because, in my heart, I didn't believe Lord Tadgh Balik had the Scepter. He was too noble to keep something that wasn't his. My father's suspicions against Lord Roar made far more sense.

"I see," I said, resigned.

"Can we turn to happier matters?" Qildor asked. "Like that gift you brought me? I can smell it from here."

I handed over the bag of meat sticks and Qildor pulled one out and took a bite.

"Stars, so good." He closed his eyes momentarily. "They serve the blandest food here. I miss eating in the grand hall with you and my fellow knights."

"We miss you too," Sian assured him. "Though, of late, we've been taking our meals in private. The king has been in a foul mood."

"Let's not dwell on that." The less we spoke of my father, the better.

"Agreed." Qildor took another bite of his meat stick. "So, tell me, Vale, how is married life?"

Only then did I realize I was the first of my best friends to wed. I supposed they were all a touch curious.

If only I could confide in them that my marriage was not normal. That it wouldn't last.

My skin prickled, as it did when I thought of Neve leaving, and that I'd never see her again. I didn't like the idea but doubted she'd be persuaded, even though I suspected that she had feelings for me too.

"It's unlike what I imagined," I admitted. "Better in some ways, worse in others."

"His wife is a feisty one." Sian winked. "She's bossing you around already, Vale?"

I laughed, along with my friends, but shook my head. "Not really. It's more . . ."

That I don't know how much time we have.

"That I worry about what's to come," I finished.

"The vampires," Vidar breathed. "They could be here within two days, you know."

My eyebrows wrinkled. "That seems early."

"Not all the Red Assassins live in the mountains," Vidar replied. "I believe they have an island too, due north of Sangrael."

I straightened. "I didn't know."

"I only saw it on my last voyage. It was clear in a place where there's usually always fog. A keep, a red one decorated with bleeding roses choked by thorns. Like in the tales."

My fingers tightened around the arms of my chair. Had I been a fool to allow Neve to go shopping with Saga and Sayyida? Even with six Clawsguards at their sides?

"It might not be them," Vidar admitted, "not like we docked to check. But it's likely."

"I'll keep that in mind," I muttered, annoyed that he hadn't brought it up earlier. Then again, he probably didn't know Neve was out shopping with his sister. It wasn't like Sayyida would gush over such an outing.

"Is that why you're training her?" Qildor asked. "In case an assassin slips through the castle walls?"

"Yes."

"She's doing well too," Sian added. "Princess Neve was not a natural at holding a sword, but to watch her fight—now that's natural. Like she's been doing so all her life."

Because she had been fighting all her life. Just not in the way Sian assumed.

"She's catching on," I agreed. "And she's fast. That helps."

"Also helps that her instructor is in love with her," Sian teased. "You must be giving the princess additional *lessons*. Am I right, my friend?" His tone was suggestive, not unlike the thousands of other times we'd spoken as a friend group, but I barely heard what he said. No, I was stuck on the fact that he thought I was so in love with her.

We'd hoped to play it off like that, but I was never sure how realistic we were being. If one of my best friends was buying the act, we had done a good job.

Or was there nothing to buy?

Father had asked if I was in love with Neve.

Burning Fates, was I?

I'd never been in love before, and I felt things for Neve that I'd never experienced. That I wished to protect her, almost to an outrageous degree.

Allowing her to go shopping without me, guarded by six elite soldiers nonetheless, had taken a tremendous amount of convincing.

I swallowed.

I . . . I think I do love her. Stars, when did that happen?

"Vale, you all right, brother?" Vidar asked. "You look pale."

"I-I'm fine."

Physically, anyway.

Vidar didn't look so sure, nor did Sian. Qildor was too engrossed in his third meat stick to notice my internal crisis.

He used the very stick to point at me. "You should get her a sword of her own. Custom-made like that one you gave Caelo on his nameday. I bet Master Smith Urgi would love to make a sword for a princess."

"Good idea," I agreed because it was. Neve had been using practice swords and occasional live steel to get used to the weight, but the swords we kept on hand were too big for her. I was willing to bet that she'd love a custom-made blade. "I'll stop by the forge as soon as—"

Someone knocked.

"Come in!" Qildor called out, his face brightening at the prospect of more visitors.

Filip Balik strode in and met my eye. "I have your message from Lärling Duran, my prince."

I stood. After we'd finished morning training, I'd sent Filip to the House of Wisdom to receive an update from my friend. It had taken the squire longer than I'd anticipated to return, which I hoped meant that Duran had been retrieving the Liar's Salvation for him.

"Duran?" Vidar leaned forward and placed his elbows on his knees. "What's he up to? I haven't seen him in so long."

"Studying. Like usual," I replied. "Excuse me. I have to read this. Qildor, I hope you continue to recover. I'll stop by again soon. I shouldn't have waited so long."

"Don't worry about it, old friend. Good to see you." He held up his meat stick. "Bring more next time, will you?"

"I'll have more sent tonight, *and* bring some with me when I visit," I promised.

Always observant, Sian's eyes narrowed and fixed on the letter, but no one said anything as I left the room, then the healers' sanctuary. I made my way down the corridor for a couple of minutes before stopping in an alcove and tearing open the letter.

Our stock was empty. I am already making more of what you require, but I was wrong in my guess that I'd need a week to brew. It will, however, take six days. As that's my day off, I can bring it when I visit my father.

I appreciated that he'd kept the letter vague and hadn't named either me or him. I'd burn the missive too, to be safe. If anyone discovered their new princess was drinking Liar's Salvation, many, especially in the palace, would be angry.

I folded the letter and stuck it back in the envelope. The Liar's Salvation would be done in six days, but the full moon was five days away. Which meant Neve only had five until the potion in her veins stopped working. We couldn't rush the potion brewing process, so there would be a single day in which she couldn't lie.

A single day in which her magic should appear.

Would it be powerful? Weak? Would it unravel or

burst from her? And would the appearance cause problems?

I swallowed down the anxiety rising inside me. There was no use in chasing worries that may never come to pass. No matter how we spun this, Neve would be like any other fae.

CHAPTER 21
VALE

The reindeers grunted as the sleigh eased to a stop in front of the grand gold doors of the Royal Theater.

From the moment she'd met the Winterborn creatures, their bone-white antlers large and branching like trees, Neve had seemed as enchanted as I'd been the first time I'd ridden a reindeer drawn sleigh. Horses were used for everyday riding and warfare but the noble and royal houses used white reindeer on special occasions. Ones in which we wished to make a statement. A night of theater mixed with Courting Festival Events was certainly one such occasion.

Neve leaned over me to peer out the window. Her silken hair touched the skin of my hands and sent chills down my spine. Her eyes glowed beneath the oversized faelights ringing the great domed building. "It's so beautiful."

The awe in her voice pulled at my heart. After

hearing the news that Duran wouldn't have the Liar's Salvation ready in time, she'd paced until it was time to prepare for the evening. But even as she applied cosmetics, seemingly calm and still, I saw the anxiety in her every stroke of rouge and lip paint.

However, when faced with the Royal Theater and all the pomp that went with our attending the production, her worries seemed to melt away. I hoped that the show would continue to keep her anxiety at bay.

"King Einar Falk built it over a thousand turns ago," I said, exiting the sleigh. Two Clawsguards rode reindeer on either side of our conveyance. One made to dismount and assist the princess, but I waved him off and extended my hand to help her.

"The ruler before Harald?" she asked as her hand landed in mine and she stepped down.

"His grandfather," I corrected. "King Birger ruled before King Harald."

"Well, it's stunning. It looks almost new." A gale of wind whipped by, and Neve pulled her black cloak tight around her and blinked up at the theater, made of glittering white stone. In that way, the playhouse resembled Frostveil Castle, but that was where the similarities ended. The theater was far smaller than the castle and only three stories high, with two wings reaching out from the large central dome where the plays took place. On the outside, carved in the white stone, were snowflakes, all different from their neighbor. Near the door, pixies dressed in fine attire threw their sparkling dust upon the snow and the pathway, adding to the magical ambiance.

"Mother is a patron of the arts. As was Queen Revna Falk and Queen Dagnia Falk before her. I supposed they all did their best to make sure the theater didn't fall into disrepair."

"They did well." Neve shuddered as another frigid wind blew in off the sea. "But I might lose my nose to the wind if we stay outside a moment longer."

"Imagine the fright you'd give the people if your nose simply fell into the snow."

She chuckled, and I pressed my hand to the small of her back, guiding her up the steps and to the doors. The Clawsguards fell in line behind, quiet as ghosts. As we neared the building, two fae dressed in black uniforms opened the doors for us and bowed. The pixies throwing their sparkling dust paused too, inclining their heads.

In the foyer, hundreds of commonfae dressed in their finest attire watched our entrance, but a male usher waved to get my attention as he neared. "My prince! This way, if you please." He gestured for us to follow. "I've been told that before the play, the nobles will be gathering on the third floor."

Neve and I had hoped to time our arrival so that we wouldn't have to socialize beforehand. There would already be enough of that at intermission. Unfortunately, it seemed we would not be spared.

I nodded. "Show us up."

The usher cleared our way through the crowds and

up the staircase. With each step, the din of the crowd below grew fainter, and soon enough we were at the top, faced with a much smaller gathering.

The families of the Sacred Eight were present, my family too, as well as a few jarls and ladies of lower houses. Not everyone who was attending the Courting Festival had been invited. Only about half, but I still thought that was quite enough. Despite being less crowded than below, the foyer was suffocating.

Each head turned and took us in. I didn't miss when Calpurnia, my cousin on my mother's side, scowled and pointed at Neve. She stood nearby with the young ladies from House Ithamai and House Qiren. All six appeared unimpressed by my wife. Aenesa Qiren going as far as to wrinkle her nose and turn away. I bristled. With night-dark skin, a tall, curvy figure, gleaming green eyes, and wings that were complemented by the beaded emerald dress she wore, no one could deny that Aenesa was beautiful. She'd indicated her interest in me before, but I'd always thought she had a nasty streak, and that wasn't even taking into account her mare powers, which only added to my reluctance to get to know the female. Now a married male, I particularly did not like that she seemed inclined to insult my wife.

Neve, however, had noticed their expressions and beamed as she unfastened her black cloak embroidered with white bear paws near the golden clasp and allowed it to drop off her shoulders.

"Do you like my dress, ladies?" She swished the skirt of her royal blue gown. Though I knew almost nothing about dresses, I liked the way this one hugged her torso and the full curves of her hips and then flared out. Completing the look was a glittering sapphire and diamond tiara borrowed from Saga. I thought that Neve had never looked more like a princess.

Those in my cousin's group said nothing until Calpurnia gave a tight nod.

"Lovely," she replied, her lilac wings pressing tight down her back in frustration.

"Aenesa?" Neve prodded.

The Lady of House Qiren sighed and, with seemingly great effort, forced herself to look at my wife's dress before her emerald gaze landed on me. "Does the prince like it?"

One would think that would be over now, but apparently, I'd have to make my loyalties much clearer. "I do like it. Very much. Not only does she look beautiful, but I appreciate that we match." I gestured to my own royal blue jacket embroidered with gold thread around the wrists, as much embellishment as I'd allow.

Aenesa's lips pursed. "I agree. It's lovely."

She sounded as though she were trying to speak through a mouthful of snow. I bit back a laugh.

"Thank you. It's one of a kind." Neve handed her cloak to a servant who appeared at her side. "Well, I believe my husband and I must do the rounds. Do enjoy the show."

Amused by my wife's antics, I turned to the Clawsguards, waiting to follow. "Hold watch at the perimeter."

We swept into the room, and I leaned in close. "Calie looked like she had gryphon dung under her nose when she had to say something nice to you."

"As did the others. And Aenesa Qiren, stars, is she mad that you're no longer available." The way Neve smiled up at me made my heart skip a beat. "Guess they'll have to get used to it. I'll fish for compliments and flaunt my handsome husband around them every chance I get."

"Diabolical."

"Thank you."

"Let's take in the room." We walked around the bulk of the crowd, stopping only when a servant offered Summer Isle wine.

I'd handed the first glass to my wife and had selected my own when Mother appeared, resplendent in a gown of gold.

"You two look lovely." She eyed Neve's tiara. "I suppose we shall have to get you a few of your own, my dear."

"Saga seems to enjoy sharing. There's no rush," Neve replied with none of the brazenness in her voice that she'd exhibited the morning Mother learned of our marriage.

Then again, Mother was being civil too, so perhaps Neve was sensing her energy and reciprocating in kind. I appreciated that. Mother might be upset with me, but I still loved her and wanted to please her.

"I will say that the jewels in that tiara suit you." Mother turned her attention to me. "Vale, darling, your father and Rhistel are in the family box. He wishes to speak with you before the play."

"Ah." I shot Neve a sidelong glance.

"I can take her." Mother placed a gentle hand on Neve's elbow. "I don't believe that you've met some of the most influential jarls and ladies—those who head lesser houses. Have you, Neve?"

"I haven't," my wife replied. There was no fear in her eyes at being left alone with Mother. As she did every morning, Neve had taken the Mind Rönd Saga had supplied. And if there was one thing I was certain of, it was that Neve could verbally keep up with anyone here.

"I'll see what Father wants." I kissed Neve on the cheek. "I'll be back as soon as I can."

Neve smiled at me, an adoring wife, and we separated. I turned and made my way down the hallway that led to the royal box, the largest, most lavish box, with the perfect view of the stage, set in the center of those of the Sacred Eight. Completing the circle around the playhouse were other boxes, less ostentatious, owned by jarls, noble ladies, and wealthy merchants.

I'd nearly reached my designation when the door to my family's box swung open. Two Clawsguards stood outside but didn't move a muscle, telling me that it wasn't my father or Rhistel who were leaving. Had it been, they'd have stepped back and prepared to follow the king or heir wherever he went. I only had to wonder for a moment as to the person's identity when Lord Riis shut the door to the box.

He brushed down his midnight black jacket and inclined his head. "Prince Vale. I see the king wishes to get quite a lot of business done before pleasure."

"As ever." I paused, a million questions burning inside me, but one rose to the surface above all others. "A moment of your time, Leyv?"

He joined me, far enough away to be out of the Clawsguard's earshot. Since seeing my mother leave Lord Riis's suite, I'd been torn. Had they once been together? And if so, did it matter?

It wasn't like Mother and Father had married for love—nor pretended to be a love match now. Most royal marriages weren't like that. No, theirs was an alliance between two powerful houses that had been instrumental in the White Bear's Rebellion. And at present, they didn't share a bedchamber, nor had they for much of their lives. They were seen together at public functions and that was about it.

Yet, if Lord Riis and my mother had an affair while she was married to my father, that made him much less trustworthy. And I'd given him so much power over me. Over Neve. That made me uneasy.

Despite being certain that the Lord of Tongues did not possess the Ice Scepter, I had to play this with intelligence. Had to use Lord Riis to keep Neve safe. Others too . . .

"Has there been any word from Caelo?" I asked, thinking of the brother of my heart and hoping he was safe.

"They made it," Lord Riis replied. "Everyone is safe

and sound. He's also received my message to remain there."

"Thank you," I replied. "Neve and I appreciate it."

"Of course." Lord Riis paused. "Is there anything else?"

A gleam in his eyes made me think he suspected something of me. Did he feel that the king was suspicious of him? If so, what did he think it was about?

"Nothing," I replied. "My father is waiting for me."

Lord Riis stepped aside. "Enjoy the show, my prince."

We parted, and Riis's heavy footsteps rang down the hallway, back toward the pre-show party. I rolled my shoulders back and entered my family's box.

Large enough to seat twenty, the royal box was painted in swaths of blue and gold, House Aaberg's colors. A selection of cheeses, fruits imported from the Summer Isles and the Elven Kingdom, breads, and cured meats were spread out on a table before the king. Three bottles of fae wine awaited, each one rare and expensive.

Below, the semi-circle playhouse spread before us, empty, the seats a royal blue. Above, the great dome was painted deep gold save for the middle, which was enchanted glass. The glass dome allowed theatergoers to take in the starlight on a clear night but didn't allow in daylight during earlier shows. The curtain spread across the stage, a red waterfall that contrasted with all the blue.

Rhistel and Father were the only ones present, both

holding goblets of wine. If I dressed to minimize embellishment, Rhistel did the opposite. He, too, wore Aaberg royal blue with gold embroidery, though his gold artistry covered his entire jacket as well as the tunic beneath. His pants were simpler but clearly made of fine fabric. Father also wore our house colors though his sense of style lay somewhere in between mine and my twin's, a regal, slightly understated balance.

"About time," Father said when he saw me. "Take a seat."

Rhistel said nothing, just looked out over the seats below and at the stage. That suited me as well as it did him.

"Now," Father said after I settled into my seat next to my brother. "Have you seen anything of note since we last spoke about the Scepter? Rhistel?"

I leaned forward and rested my elbows on my knees to better see Father.

"Not a thing. I even had a drink with Lord Balik as you requested, Father. He seemed normal, as did his magic."

I arched an eyebrow. "You had Rhistel questioning Tadgh Balik?"

Father gave a single nod. "I'm considering wedding him to one of the older daughters of the southlands. His pick."

I thought of Baenna and Eireann, the eldest daughters and most likely to be considered for such a match. They were Saga's close friends, but as they were also Sian's sisters, I'd spoken with both many times over the turns too. Though both ladies were not too young, around twenty-five turns, and well educated, which Rhistel valued, I couldn't picture either of the Balik ladies with my brother.

Then again, I couldn't imagine my brother married to *anyone*. He didn't invite that sort of union. The Courting Season we had held not long ago had proven that.

Differing from a Courting Festival in the sense that during a Season, *Rhistel* held all the power, but he had stupidly used that power to choose no bride. During the current Festival, however, *Father* held the power over who would marry who. Not just for his own children, either, but for the entire kingdom.

Save me, of course, though I wasn't about to rub that in when the king was not being negative about Neve. At the moment, anyhow.

"I was going to bind you to one of the Balik ladies, Vale," Father added, likely noticing that I was deep in thought. "After all, their house heir is your squire, so you're already bound to the rulers of the southlands. Tightening that knot seemed wise . . . lucrative . . . but then you took matters into your own hands and upended my plans." He snorted. "Alas, I'd rather have the Baliks in my grasp than not."

"Because you think they hold the Ice Scepter? Or other reasons?" I asked.

Rhistel rolled his eyes. "Do you really care, brother?"

"Of course I do. Why would you assume otherwise?"

He turned his gaze on me, a twin to my own. "You've been so preoccupied with your bride; I figured that matters of our house mean little to you."

I swallowed. My brother and I had many differences. At times, I flat-out despised him. But looking into his eyes, I could tell that this was a rare instance where he was being real—vulnerable. He wished for me to care about our house, and in a way he was right. I'd done a poor job of showing that in the last week.

"I care," I assured him. "And I'm sorry that now the responsibility of securing alliances falls on you and Saga. I do not regret marrying Neve, but I regret that you have even less choice than before."

For a moment, my twin stared at me until his face relaxed and a slight smile bloomed. "I suppose I could do worse than a Balik wife. They are both quite attractive."

"As if that matters." Father frowned. "Alliances do not require attraction. That's what harems and whores are for. Now, back to the matter at hand. If Tadgh Balik is showing no signs of deceit, nor a marked increase in power, then we shall move on to Lord Riis. I still have reasons to suspect him."

"I have been dying to know what those are, Father," I said. "Truth be told, I see none, and he doesn't even have the bloodline to use the Hallow." I nodded to the door. "Not to mention, he was just in our box. So you trust him in some regards?"

"Should I not speak to my spider, that would only raise red flags," Father replied. "Plus, he is handy. Lord Riis is trying to find Warden Roar for me."

"And?" I pressed.

"No sightings. He has not retreated to Guldtown. Nor has anyone spotted him on the Queen's Road."

"The storms have been bad," I mused. "Perhaps he's holed up in a small inn?"

"Or he has found Riis's spies and paid them off," Rhistel added. "Do not dismiss the depths of House Lisika's pocketbooks."

Never. The great house of the western territory had always been the wealthiest in Winter's Realm. Their mines supplied much of the kingdom's gold and, though they'd been mining them for centuries, never seemed to run dry.

"So what of Lord Riis?" I circled back to my previous question. "What makes you suspect him? After all, he lives in Avaldenn." To my knowledge, Leyv hadn't visited his own castle in the east in over a turn. "And regularly attends court at Frostveil. Why are you suspicious?"

"His sons," Father replied. "Over the turns that I'd known him, I've noticed no power difference in Leyv. However, his eldest bastard-born grows ever stronger. Lord Riis might groom his son to use the Scepter."

Luccan *was* more powerful than two turns back, but now that I knew he was a gatekeeper, I thought it more likely he was extending his magic in that way.

"Are you saying that *they* have winter magic?" Rhistel asked.

Father shrugged a single shoulder. "We don't know who Luccan's mother is, it's not unrealistic to think that she's a Falk bastard and has a thread of winter magic in her blood. The Cold King sired bastards before his trueborn children. His father before him sired even more."

From what I'd heard of the Falk king, that was true. He hadn't married right away when he took the crown, and he had his own father's harem at his disposal. It was only when he married Queen Revna that the Cold King stopped sleeping around and visiting his harem. But by then, there were white-haired younglings all around Avaldenn, each of their mothers claiming they were of royal blood.

Calder Falk, my father's own sire, had only added to that proliferation of Falk bastards. Though I wasn't about to mention that. Talking of Calder Falk was always touchy with Father.

"Lord Riis has always been secretive about who birthed his *bloody bastards*," the king added.

"Luccan is now a true Riis," I said, annoyed that he kept emphasizing that word. Like many at court, Father still thought of the Riis brothers as bastards, but it was no longer true. "You legitimized him. Arie and Thantrel too."

"Only to hold sway over Lord Riis for the Festival. Still, that decision could prove more fruitful than I ever imagined. It has allowed me to observe Leyv's sons.

Mark my words, there is something *off* about Luccan Riis. I want eyes on him, and Vale will do it. You're already close to him, are you not?"

My stomach tightened. I should have seen this coming. Of course, Father would use my connection to Luccan to his benefit.

"Very well," I said, not about to argue when we were all being civil.

I wasn't entirely sure about Lord Riis or where his loyalties lay, but I was absolutely certain that Luccan had nothing to do with the Ice Scepter. I'd have to find some way to prove my friend's innocence.

"Good." Father took a long sip of wine. "Now that we've covered everything, I'm prepared to make more matches before this bleeding play starts." He looked at me. "Tell the Clawsguards at the door to have the ushers open the playhouse."

I did as he requested and minutes later, Mother and Saga appeared. Vidar walked arm in arm with my sister. He inclined his head in greeting, which I returned. Neve walked through the door after them. My pulse quickened.

I held out my hand. "How was it without me?"

She came closer, pressed her lips to my cheek, and kissed it, then whispered, "Fine. Your mother really did introduce me to people. Perhaps she's making amends?"

Perhaps. I trusted Mother more than Father, but I underestimated neither. Mother might simply be watching my new wife, looking for a weakness to exploit that could rip apart our union.

She said she wanted me happy, but I'd always thought she really meant she wanted me happy as long as *she* approved.

"Come," I said. "We're in the front."

We took our seats. Mine next to Rhistel, and Neve on my other side, by Saga, who, since my marriage, had been moved down one seat. Not that my sister minded. If anything, she appeared delighted to have Neve at her side to gossip with.

"Oh look! That's Avalina Truso!" Saga pointed to the stage where a willowy dryad with long green hair pulled aside the heavy red curtain and peeked out to wave at someone in the crowd. "I hope she sings in this play. Wait until you hear her voice. It's divine! And, oh stars alive!" She gasped as a male faerie with wings nearly as dark as my own joined Avalina at the curtain. The pair shared a jest and began laughing, as did those in the crowd who could hear them. "Neve, that's Neris Ibold! All the ladies are half in love with him."

Happy to let them gossip, I tuned them out. The fae on the lower levels entered the playhouse and took their seats. Fae from all walks of life attended the theater, and they all shared an air of excitement. It warmed my heart to see my people living a life they loved.

Some in the villages, the same people I'd often had to protect from attacks, weren't so lucky. They didn't have the safety of the city but found themselves victims of orcs and goblins and other dark creatures that came down from the mountains and out of the deep woods, seeking easier food sources. To take the village's food because the mountains had become too harsh. And as long as the Ice Scepter was lost and the magic of Winter's Realm spiraled, those same village people would continue to grow more vulnerable.

Perhaps even those in this room too. If it got cold enough, so many would die.

But on this night, we were together and warm and safe. We were indulging in our culture and laughing. I eyed my wife sidelong, feeling lucky to be here, especially with her.

Once the theater filled, trumpets blared, and my father stood. He addressed the crowd below, as well as the nobles in their boxes. Lord Riis and his sons had joined us in ours—the favored few. Or those that Father wished to keep a close eye on.

"Tonight," Father's voice boomed, "I have five more matches to make, and all of you lucky fae will bear witness."

Below, many gasped, delighted to be included in the Courting Festival in some small way. In the other boxes, the nobles who would be affected had mixed reactions. Some wore looks of excitement, while others appeared hesitant.

Father's eyes gleamed and a charismatic smile crossed his face as a hand swept down and to the right. "So without further ado, the matches are Jarl Xandri Ra and Lady Yulandia of House Polia."

Two members of lesser noble houses based in the east, bannerfae to House Ithamai. Father continued to rattle off names, ending in five matches, and finally the tension in my shoulders eased. The crowd clapped for the newly betrothed.

Father named no Sacred Eight, none of my friends —no one who had witnessed my wedding to Neve. The matched couples even looked pleased.

Father too. No doubt those matches would benefit our house, though I wasn't sure how, but Father always had a plan.

"Now," the king proclaimed, lifting his glass. "Let the play begin."

CHAPTER 22
NEVE

On the stage, the actors raced and whirled and swung their fake weapons. Occasionally, false blood sprayed, and someone fell. All of this was, somehow, still done in time with the orchestra despite the scene depicting the sheer chaos of the White Bear's Rebellion.

Before coming to this kingdom, I'd never given much thought to the rebellion. Now, though, the signs of it were everywhere. The White Bear's Rebellion had restructured the kingdom in ways the fae of Winter's Realm hadn't seen since Queen Sassa Falk unified all the high lords and ladies. She gathered the many kingdoms and queendoms of Winter's Realm, all under her banner—the Falk banner.

The events playing out before me only solidified the rebellion's importance.

Two greater houses, gone from this world. Villages and smaller cities leveled. A king fell, a king rose, and the fabric of the kingdom tore and knitted back together with royal blue and gold threads.

But this play didn't just tell the story of House Aaberg, of how the White Bear, King Magnus, brought together many noble houses and obliterated the Cold King Harald Falk. No, it focused on the people of Winter.

I'd wondered about my own losses, the family I might have had once upon a time, and this play made it clear I was far from the only one who had lost loved ones.

In the center of the stage, Avalina Truso played a mother kneeling over her lost son. A son who had fought for the White Bear and died for him. The mother was the narrator in the story, the voice of the commonfae, and I could see why Avalina had been cast. Why the queen and Saga favored her.

The dryad possessed a presence that none gracing the stage could match. Even as the play drew to a close and the chaotic final battle of the White Bear's forces whirled and fought around Avalina, I couldn't tear my eyes off her.

"Burning moon, she's too good," Saga whispered, her voice tight as tears ran down her pale cheeks. Was she moved by the truth of the performance or merely the performance itself?

Vale, unlike his sister, had been relatively silent for most of the play, sometimes leaning closer to me, whispering historical additions to scenes.

Still, quiet as he was, emotion rippled across his

handsome features. He'd been too young to fight in the rebellion, but he'd been in battle since. How many mothers had he seen kneeling over their loved ones? Mourning the losses of their children?

My questions dissolved as the music below swelled, stealing the very air from the room as the soldiers on stage cleared out. Only Avalina and the actors portraying the White Bear and King Harald Falk remained. They fought one-on-one, two white-haired warriors, covered in fake blood, fighting for their lives and circling the distraught mother.

Avalina Truso didn't seem to notice the males. She continued to wail, to cry over her son's body. The long white dress she wore, stained with red from the fake blood that had flown off prop weapons, only added to the chills rushing through me.

Then, in perfect timing with the epic music, the White Bear stabbed the Cold King, and as King Harald fell, the music dimmed too.

One would have expected the actor playing King Magnus to stand over the fallen king, to proclaim his right to rule. Perhaps for the lords and ladies who had supported him to appear from the sides and kneel.

There should have been pomp. There should have been a celebration for ending a cruel tyrant. A king who, by all accounts, had turned on his own people during the end of his rule. Instead, the faelights blinked out and the White Bear left the stage. The fallen body of King Harald remained.

As did Avalina Truso and her dead son.

The music played on, soft now, haunting, and as Avalina's wails died out, I held my breath.

The dryad was silent for a moment, her gaze still on her son, her body trembling. I leaned forward, as did a hundred others. We waited for her to speak, to rise and follow the king, to do *anything* but kneel over her son's body.

So when Avalina raised her tear-streaked face, she had everyone's attention. With a haunted expression, she stared out at the crowd and opened her mouth. The orchestra stopped playing just as her song filled the room.

"*We love our land. Our people. The frost and snow and ice and storm of Winter's embrace.*" Avalina's voice was clear and bright, yet also contained depths I'd never heard. She had to have been gifted such a voice by the dead gods. It was simply that lovely.

And it was not only her voice that held us enthralled, but her words, which were spoken not in the common tongue, but in High Fae. A shiver ran down my spine at the ancient language, one that Yvette, the human woman who had acted as my mother, had learned through books. This was the language of my ancestry, taught to me by a gracious and brilliant human. Understanding it required me to perform clunky mental translations and yet, the language still struck my heart. I fell a sentence or two behind in Avalina's song, but the words didn't fail to move me. They were simply so much more poetic than the common tongue.

"*But our land and people are dying a true death. A final death.*"

"*We must rise.*" As she sang, Avalina Truso rose and swept in a circle around the stage, gesturing gracefully to the depiction of Winter's Realm. To where the fallen had lain not long ago and where pools of fake blood still stained the wooden planks of the stage.

Pausing in the silence, the actress stopped moving and slowly turned her lovely, angular face up to the royal box.

"*For twenty turns, we have weakened and died. Slowly. In hushed whispers. In tears, our brothers and sisters in the country-side bury their younglings when Winter claims too much.*

"*Why do we stay quiet? Why not ask for what is promised to us?*" She raised a hand, five fingers splayed.

"*Protection.*" Her hand closed into a fist, which she shook. "*A tempering of the cold, of the death that only grows.*"

"*Why have we not demanded it of our leader?*" A slender finger pointed at our box. "*Is it because we know he cannot save us? Is it because he is not so unlike the one before?*"

I stiffened, but Avalina plowed on, her voice strengthening with the words she sang. Her eyes shined with sorrow that burned from the flame of anger that even an actress as talented as Avalina could no longer hide.

"*We must find the one to bring back the magic. To claim Winter. We, the fae, must stand behind the one who is true to the land. To us.*"

She knelt, dipped her fingers in the false blood, and

began to draw a symbol. "*Long live the trueborn heir and wielder of Winter's Touch.*"

She ended her song, and, delayed, I gasped, my blood freezing in my veins. Beside me, Vale stiffened. The symbol Avalina had drawn was the one I'd seen painted on that dilapidated building in Rall Row. The symbol of the Falk loyalists.

Vale leaned forward. "Be ready for anything."

"What in the stars?" Saga whispered, already hitching the skirt of her gown up, clearly ready to flee.

On the stage, the actress rose and stood resolutely, illuminated by a flood of faelights. In the crowd below, many tilted their heads, wondering what she'd said. Neighbors translated for others and when they were done, faces paled, and eyes drifted up to the royal box. One old fae stood and ran from the playhouse.

Avalina Truso brought a fist to her heart and the curtain fell.

A gasp ripped from me. Across the red curtain was the same treasonous symbol Avalina painted on the floor.

King Magnus shot from his seat and thrust a finger at the stage. "Bring her to me. I—"

Fae soared from the rafters, from behind the curtain, from within the crowd of commoners now rising to exit as fast as they could. All of those in the crowd had been wearing cloaks, not unusual for a cold winter's night. Now those in the air shucked off those same cloaks, revealing daggers at their sides and painted hawks on armbands wrapped around their biceps. Rebels—at least fifty of them.

"Neve, with me!" Vale pulled me up to stand with him. At his side, Rhistel rose too and lost no time in sprinting to the door.

"We should help others!" I looked at the many boxes, at the younglings filling them. "We can defend ourselves."

"I'm not armed." Vale yanked me into the aisle. "But the rebels are. We must get out of here."

We made it up three steps before shattering glass froze Vale in his tracks. Unable to help ourselves, we turned.

From the center of the dome, now shattered, two dozen more fae dropped, starlight blazing at their backs. "The trueborn heir will stop Winter from killing us!" an older male faerie roared, but all my attention was on another faerie, one clad in black fighting leathers and flying on silver wings, her long black hair whipping behind her as she soared our way.

The black-haired female lifted her bow, arrow already nocked, and aimed for the king.

"Father!" Vale yelled, but the Clawsguards in the box were already there, ready. Sir Lars, the king's most faithful, threw himself in front of King Magnus in time to take the arrow into his own heart. The other pulled the king from the box.

Rhistel was gone. Saga and the queen too. We should have already fled as well. Vale might not be the heir, but he was an Aaberg in line for the throne.

And yet, my feet were frozen to the floor.

The rebel aimed her arrow at the king . . . she looked like me.

Black-haired, yes. Glacier blue eyes, yes. But her wings were silver like mine. Her face was of a similar shape. Her eyes and lips too. We were about the same age, and we might be cousins.

And then there was the way her eyes narrowed on the king in hatred . . . I'd looked at him that way too.

"Move!" the king bellowed. He was racing from the royal box too, leaving his Clawsguards to fight.

Vale lifted me off my feet and swept me out of the room.

I wanted to scream for him to stop, for him to wait, but as the black-haired female came closer, another arrow at the ready, I swore at my stupidity. I was in the royal box, and she hated the Aabergs. Hated the name I bore.

I was a target too. I let him take me, let him carry me from the box. In Vale's arms, we raced down the hall, to the third-floor foyer, and into utter madness. We paused at the edge of the room; our bodies pressed up against the wall.

"Let me down," I said, and Vale did so carefully. Seeing as I swayed slightly as my feet touched the floor, I was thankful for his care. There was just so much happening. *Too much.*

Rebels swarmed the area, taking on lords and ladies, many of whom fought with magic, not steel. It was the largest display of power I'd seen yet, and the breadth of magic in the room, how the fae wielded it, made my mouth fall open.

Among the crowd, I spied Lord Riis. Somehow, he'd acquired a sword and was masterfully fending off two rebels and spinning, steel in hand, as another came for him. Sassa's bloody blade! I'd only ever seen that sort of deft fighting from Vale and Sian.

The third rebel attacking Lord Riis fell, and he whirled back, taking out another with his fist. The last backed up, eyes shifting to us, to Vale, who looked ready to jump in despite not being armed.

Lord Riis pointed with his blade. "Below. Help is needed below. Arm yourself, Vale." He gestured to a body not too far away.

A Clawsguard lay dead on the ground. I recognized him as one I'd seen following Rhistel.

"My brother," Vale breathed, taking in the Clawsguard, knowing who he'd been protecting.

"He's not here," I assured him. His body, had there been one, would be close by. And no doubt a rebel would be gloating over killing the heir.

I despised Rhistel, and he and Vale had a complicated relationship, but they were still brothers. Still *twins*. The anguish lining Vale's face said it all. No matter the turmoil between them, he'd be devastated if something happened to Rhistel.

"Vale, help is needed below." I motioned to the sword near the fallen Clawsguard. "Take it."

Vale picked up the sword and pulled a dagger from the soldier's side sheath. "For you. It's all too likely that someone will attack me. If they do, let me take them. Keep running for Frostveil and defend yourself."

Anger rose in me at his insistence that I leave him. I was about to tell him I'd do no such thing when I heard a scream. "Vidar!"

Another female voice joined it. "*Brother!*"

Ice flew through my veins.

"Saga and Sayyida." I ran to the top of the stairs.

Below, commonfae streamed from the theater, around the rebels who were doing their best to slaughter noble fae.

It took a moment, but I found who I was searching for. Sayyida and Vidar—the sight of the latter stopping my heart. A rebel had struck Vidar in the belly and blood seeped through his fine gray tunic. The rebel laughed as the heir to House Virtoris fell to the ground. Their victory was short-lived, however, as Sayyida's water magic surged from her, the torrent picking the rebel up and slamming him against a wall so hard I doubted that he lived. Across the room, Saga was cornered, fighting off a rebel with only magic.

Like Vale, Sayyida had procured a sword to use in tandem with her magic. The steel flashed with tight, controlled strikes as Sayyida circled her brother, who had fallen to the ground. She protected Vidar from a half dozen attacking rebels who saw their chance to kill the House Virtoris heir. All the while, Sayyida's gaze bounded between Vidar, her brother, and Saga, her best friend.

"Vale, we have to help them." Far more rebels were

attacking Sayyida, trying to harm both her and her brother. "I'll take Saga. Fewer rebels targeted her."

He didn't need to reply, for we were already leaping over the balcony and soaring toward the ground. Vale went for Sayyida, and I heard when he added his sword to the mix.

I only hoped that they were fast enough to save Vidar. Pushing my wings, stronger from days of training, I didn't falter as I flew toward Saga.

The princess had been using winter magic to fight off her attacker. I assumed Saga was giving her attacker everything she had, and if that were the case, it only revealed to me how strong King Magnus was with winter magic.

Whereas he could freeze someone to the ground and transform a whip into an even more terrifying weapon, his daughter fought with small bursts of cold wind and an occasional hurled icicle. Creating the latter drained her. She looked pale and sweat dripped down her brow as she tossed one icicle as long as my forearm and then collapsed.

The projectile sailed right at her attacker, who whirled about to avoid being impaled. She saw me, then twisted to face the princess again. Saga was still on the ground, passed out from the effort of wielding magic.

The rebel turned to me, and her eyes sparked with an inner fire. "One princess down. One to go. Hopefully, you're as weak as Pink here." She leapt at me.

The moment she was within reach, I slashed at the rebel with my dagger. The blade struck, running across her collarbone. She fell back with a grunt as I landed, holding the dagger over her.

"I don't want to kill you, but I will if you continue to hurt me or Saga. If I let you up, will you stop fighting and run?"

The words shocked me as they left my lips. This person had tried to hurt, possibly kill, one of my only friends. And I would let them go?

I didn't have time to examine the insanity running through my mind, for the rebel sneered at me and pushed off the ground. Blood flying from her cut, wings beating powerfully, she launched herself at me again.

But before she slammed into me, a dagger came whirling from above, slicing her right wing in half. She screamed, and I spun to find Lord Riis still fending off rebels above, shooting glances my way.

He'd sent the blade. He might have saved my life.

But *I* needed to finish this.

I spun to face the rebel, and though there were tears in her eyes, she stood again. The fury in her face made it clear that she'd never stop fighting.

"How can you ally with them? Don't you see what they're doing? The land is dying. Magic is spinning out. We're weakened. *We're dying.*"

I swallowed, understanding. Empathizing, even. Killing off the land, people dying because of it, I understood why the rebels would fight for that.

"I know. I've seen it."

"And yet you still sleep at a White Bear's side. You still wear the gowns and go to the plays and eat the finery. The villages starve and yet, *here you are*." She spat at my feet.

"I haven't always lived like this," I murmured, shame welling inside me.

"You do now."

"I—"

"Long live the trueborn heir!" she screamed and came at me.

Before I knew what I was doing, I raised my dagger and sank it into her chest. Blood sprayed. But I barely noticed the hot gush as her eyes widened. They dipped down, so mine followed. I gasped.

I glowed, a silvery-violet hue that was stronger than the other times it emanated from me. As if my magic had been dying to get out, to help me. To save my life. The light flickered again, and then the light vanished, just as the life in the rebel's eyes dimmed to nothing.

For a moment, I forgot how to breathe. I'd killed her. Without even really knowing that was what was about to happen, it had.

My throat tightened as I took her in, my gaze darting to the hawk insignia on her armband, to the dagger I'd pushed into her chest.

She would have tried to kill me. Had aimed to injure or kill Saga too, and yet . . . This was my first fae kill. One of my own people, not a vampire monster I despised with all my heart. I dropped the dagger.

"You should never let your guard down," a voice said from behind.

I whirled to find an arrow aimed at me. The faerie

who looked so like me. Closer now, I could see that we shared yet another resemblance. She bore a vertical scar, slashing over her left eye. Not an identical twin to the crescent scar over my temple, but the similarities, when combined, still caught.

She seemed to notice the resemblance too, her ice-blue eyes going round, her lips parting in shock. That second of hesitation was all Vale needed to come at her from the side to slash his blade.

The archer spun to safety, dropping her bow down as she did so. And when she faced Vale again, and saw his sword raised, likely measuring it against the likelihood of her drawing her arrow and aiming in time, she chose correctly and ran.

"Warrior Bear and the princess in here!" she screamed.

"We have to run," Saga hissed. I spun to find that she was awake and rising to stand. "There are so many."

Vale growled, and in his eyes, I could see that he wanted to fight, wanted to hunt down the fae who would have put an arrow through me.

"She's right, Vale. We need to go." Behind her, I saw Vidar, still on the ground, bleeding out. "Vidar needs serious help."

With each minute, fewer fae rushed from the theater, the theater in which I could hear the clashing of swords, the groaning of downed people. No doubt Clawsguards fought under the dome of the playhouse, keeping most of the rebels contained inside. Unable to stop myself, my gaze dipped to the very rebel I'd killed. She stared up at me, lifeless and cold and resolute, with that same sneer on her lips.

Vale still didn't look convinced, but fifty soldiers burst through the front doors. One soldier paused when he saw Vale. He eyed Vidar, covered in blood, and the four bodies of the rebels that Sayyida and Vale had felled.

"Get Lord Virtoris out of here." The soldier's attention strayed to Saga, Sayyida, and me. "We've got this under control."

Someone, likely the king as he'd been one of the first to flee, had sent help.

"*Please*, Vale. Let's go," I urged him. "Help Sayyida carry Vidar."

This time, his friend's name worked like a spell. He blinked, turned to the Virtoris siblings, and marched over.

"They got his belly," Sayyida croaked from where she knelt over her brother. "I don't know how to move him without ripping it more."

"There's no way to know, but we have to move fast. Help me lift him into my arms." Vale motioned to Sayyida, covered in her brother's blood. He set his sword on the ground. "As gently as we can. I'll carry him."

She nodded, clearly relieved that someone with experience was there to help.

Vale had once carried me in his arms. On yet another day, when the rebels had attacked. He had made it look easy, carrying me and running from the terror of the attack, but Vidar was much larger and taller than me. Together, carefully, Sayyida and Vale lifted the Virtoris heir until he was in Vale's arms. After examining the wound the best he could, Vale exhaled. "I don't think we made it worse. Now, Sayyida and Neve, watch my back as we run for the palace. Saga, you take Neve's dagger."

Vale motioned down to the sword. "Neve, this is for you."

I understood how momentous this moment was. Vale was asking me to protect him, to protect his friend.

I would not fail him. I picked up the sword. Sayyida and Saga were already in position, one on each side of Vale. I positioned myself behind him, sword at the ready. "Run like the wind. Let's get Vidar to safety."

CHAPTER 23
NEVE

W e'd eased Vidar into one of the last sanctuary beds before complete and utter chaos descended. One after the other, soldiers were assisting fae victims of the rebel attack into the sanctuary.

Vidar's wounds were more serious than most, so the healers set to enchanting his injury. The moment they were sure he was stable, the ancient Master Healer on duty relayed that to the group and suggested we leave the overcrowded sanctuary. As she did so, I couldn't help but notice the long necklace she wore outside her tunic. The same eight-spoked wheel beneath four stars in the shape of the goddess of healing's constellation. The symbol I'd seen outside the sanctuary. It clicked then that the symbol must be that of the healing profession.

"Let me know if he needs anything. Or if something changes," Vale said to Sayyida, who was not about to leave her brother's side, despite the Master Healer's urgings. Saga, too, was remaining to support the Virtoris siblings.

"I will. Thank you, Vale. I"—Sayyida swallowed—"I couldn't have held off so many if you hadn't come."

He nodded. "You were doing well, but there were too many."

"I need to double down on my training." Sayyida's face hardened. "They almost took Vidar and, well, he'll be an amazing Lord of Virtoris Island one day, and he has powerful magic, but . . ."

"He could do with some additional lessons too," Vale said kindly. "Your brother was always better at captaining a ship and diplomacy than sword work."

"Stars, I've *always* told him that." Sayyida gave a soft smile. It was so far from the sassy one I'd seen spread across her face the day she'd taunted Vidar over being a better swordsfae. At yet another event destroyed by the rebels.

"We'll go. Have you sent word to your mother, Sayyida?" I looped my arm through Vale's, only to find his sleeve drenched in blood. Vidar's blood. That should have repulsed me, but I seemed to have become desensitized. Probably because I, too, was covered in rebel blood.

"A few minutes ago. I'm sure she'll be here as soon as she receives it."

"Good." I angled Vale toward the door. "We'll check on him later."

"Thank you. Truly." Sayyida turned to her brother

and Saga, watching her betrothed on the bed with red-rimmed eyes.

My heart gave a hard squeeze for the princess. I was certain that Saga preferred Sayyida to Vidar, but as she was royal and such a match could not create heirs, the king would not make it. Despite that complication of the heart, Saga did care for Vidar.

As Vale and I exited the healer's sanctuary, I heaved a heavy breath. "I hope he heals quickly."

"He will," Vale said, his voice tight. "The healers won't let him down."

"It must be difficult having two close friends in there."

"More than you know."

Silence fell over us as we walked down the hallway, arm in arm, our pace slower than usual.

"Is that common?" I asked.

"Is what common?"

"Rebels attacking events. It's happened twice since I've been here."

Vale snorted. "The Courting Festival is drawing them out. Before this, we'd have rebel attacks, or more minor issues, once every six moons. The deepening cold is provoking them to attack more often."

The fae I'd killed had mentioned the cold, right before I'd taken her life, a fact that I was trying desperately to forget.

Vale stopped, and because we were attached by the arms, I did too. "I didn't ask how you were."

I blinked. "What?"

"When we got to the sanctuary, I didn't check on you. Are you well?"

My teeth dug into my bottom lip. When Vale said things like that, it was even harder to deny how wonderful he was. How much I didn't want to leave him.

"No," I answered with a long exhale. "I don't think I am."

Suddenly, more soldiers appeared, helping the injured fae. My mouth shut, not about to talk about what happened with others around.

As if sensing the reason for my hesitancy, Vale pulled me into a room off the hallway. From the looks of it, the space was used to store healing supplies. A long table littered with cauldrons, bundled herbs, and books dominated the center of the room.

"Tell me, Neve. What happened?"

I drifted over to the table, picked up a sprig of dried lavender, and exhaled. "Well, I killed someone."

"One of us."

He meant not a vampire.

"Yes."

"I've done more killing than I like to recall—even if it was for a noble cause. Only time will heal what you feel, and even then, not completely."

"Yes, but that's not the only thing that's getting me down." Not only was it true, but I wished to move on from the topic of the rebel quickly. Intellectually, I knew that had I not killed her, she would have ended my life, but my body still felt heavy with remorse for killing a fae. Hence, I welcomed the distraction that had been plaguing my mind.

He arched an eyebrow and waited.

"For the last few days, I've been doing a lot of thinking about my family."

"Anna? Those in the Blood Court?"

"No, though they're family too. I mean my blood family, if I have any left here." My voice wobbled, and Vale was there, wrapping me in his muscular arms.

"I'm so sorry."

A tear tracked down my cheek. "You've helped me more than anyone else. I-I." I paused and drew in a breath, needing to share more with him, to unload. "Did you see that female during the attack? The rebel who looked like me?"

He drew back. "Where?"

"The archer." I peered up at him. "She had black hair and blue eyes, but we looked alike in other ways. That, and things people have said, I guess it has gotten to me."

He lifted a hand and wiped away the wet streak the tears had left before moving up to my temple and caressing the scar there with such tender care. One would think his big hands, calloused from battles, could not be so gentle, but they were.

"Neve, I *am* your family," Vale whispered so devoutly that the words sent chills down my spine. "Even if this ends with you running as far as you can from Winter's Realm, which I would not blame you for, *we're family*. I'll never be able to stop thinking about you." He swallowed. "I'll always care for you."

His brown eyes softened as if he wanted to say more, as if he was holding back something important. I had a hunch of what that might be, and though it scared me to death, it also invigorated me.

Vale, the male I'd married, a prince of the realm, had feelings for me. As I did for him. We'd started off distrusting the other, moved on to vague dislike, then intrigue. Trust and caring had snuck up on me. Now, what did we have?

My breathing deepened as his gaze intensified.

Married, by law, and even in the eyes of the Faetia, but were our hearts inching closer?

The Faetia had blessed our union, and yet we'd brushed it off. Said that we'd follow through with our plan.

Were we fools?

Before I questioned that too, Vale's head dipped, and his lips caught mine.

A soft whimper of pleasure left me and deep inside, something stirred. A feeling that had never been awoken in me, one I wanted more of. By the dead gods and the Fates and the stars and the Faetia and whatever else there was, his kisses were pure magic. Nothing like the other kisses I'd shared with boys and then human men. Nothing like I imagined.

They wiped away the pain, the sadness, and allowed me to exist in the moment. As messed up as that might be after what we'd seen, I allowed myself that small mercy and leaned into him.

Vale's tongue swept into my mouth, and I accepted it, met it with a dance of my own as his hand found my back and somehow pulled me closer.

How did I feel so protected with him? I'd only known Vale for less than two weeks, and yet it was like I knew him, deep inside. And he knew me too. Wanted me. Try as I might to remind myself that I had to leave this court, had to flee at the first chance, I wanted him too.

Stars, I was in so much trouble.

He pulled away with a sharp intake of breath, though he remained close enough that I still felt his exhale graze my lips. "Neve," Vale whispered. "Are we sure?"

A laugh trilled out of me. "*Sure?* I'm not sure of much, but I know one thing." My fist wrapped around the front of his shirt, stained with blood from the fight, just as I was. Not that I cared. Perhaps later I'd feel disgusted, but right now, all that mattered was him and me and our pounding blood rushing through our bodies as we found a moment of peace together. "If you stop kissing me like that again, I'm going to have to teach you a lesson during training."

A devilish smile spread across his face. "Promise?"

"You're impossible." I lured him in slowly.

As our lips met again, Vale's hands moved down and around me. He cupped my rear, his fingers digging into my flesh.

"Bleeding skies, I love this arse," he growled.

"There's a lot of it to love," I said, my voice breathy at the rough passion in his touch.

"Thank the dead gods for that," he murmured and lifted me.

I squealed and my legs wrapped around his middle as he carried me to the table. With one hand, Vale swept aside the bundles of herbs and books, clattering them to the floor before he set me down as gently as one would a porcelain object.

The pulse of pleasure inside me was tightening, the pressure building, and my eyelids fell closed as my hands tangled in his black hair. Beneath the long top layer, my fingers grazed the shaved portion. He didn't wear it up often, but when he did, he looked even more like a warrior than usual and always set my heart racing.

His hands traveled from where they'd been exploring my arse up, to my wings, where his touch became more delicate, reverent, as he explored their contours.

I shivered. Faerie wings were already sensitive and, for that reason, usually kept pressed down our backs, covered up, or vanished. Vale's touch, though, seemed to make mine a thousand times more tender. *Needy.* Craving more, I pressed my wings into his hands, hoping he'd linger.

Instead, he paused and pulled away again.

"What did I tell you about pulling away?" I

murmured, surprised to hear my voice was deeper, almost a growl to match that of the prince's.

"Neve, you're glowing but not your hands. Your whole body."

My eyelids flew open, and I gasped.

He was right. I was glowing, this time more strongly than before. Perhaps differently too?

"It's your magic," Vale said, his hand moving to my chest and pressing into my heaving bosom. "It's unraveling. Desperate to get out. Pulsing within you." His dark brown eyes lifted to meet mine. "You've never felt that before, have you?"

"No. The potion has always worked the same way, never failing. But since coming here, I've sometimes felt different. I've glowed a few other times too. Just my hands though."

"I think it's because you're home. You belong in this kingdom and the magic recognizes you, Neve." His hand drifted to my cheek and cupped it. "You're going to be stronger than you could have imagined."

"It's good that Duran is making that potion, then."

"It would be harder to hide the change. Your magic might adjust silently, but it might also explode out of you when given the chance. Like when younglings go through their magical changes."

"I'm a few turns late." I laughed, shifting in a way that rubbed against him, making me instantly aware of the long, hard length in his trousers.

My eyes widened, as that same length twitched, and suddenly, my magic, vibrant as it may be, was forgotten and we were kissing again, our hands exploring one another's body. We stayed that way for a few blissful moments before Vale changed it up, his lips moving down to trail tiny kisses down my throat.

I tipped my head back, heart thundering, blood pounding in my ears. Fire flushed through me, heating me everywhere and depositing that flame spreading between my legs.

"Vale," I panted, unable to take the teasing for another moment, "I want you inside me."

An animalistic sound left his throat, and he ground me closer, rubbing at the flames between my legs, electrifying me. A thrill ran through me at the thought of him filling me, of our bodies connecting so deeply.

"Now," I added, in case he hadn't gotten the message. "If you don't, I'll have to leave and take care of things myself."

"I swear, if you did that in my suite, I would go mad. You couldn't keep me off you."

"Then why aren't you on me *now*?"

A rumble of a laugh left him and his powerful hands spread my legs farther. I lifted myself a bit as those deft fingers moved beneath my skirts, tugged at my undergarments, and pulled them down. They were off and on the floor in an instant.

Vale went to undo his pants, desire gleaming in his eyes, and I sought to help him, to *feel him* as soon as possible.

We'd not even gotten the top button undone when the door to the healers' closet flew open.

"Blazing moon!" I pulled Vale closer to cover the parts of me that were exposed, cheeks blazing hot.

"By the dead gods!" the same ancient Master Healer we'd spoken to in the sanctuary covered her eyes. "Prince Vale, I pulled you from your mother, wiped your nose, and set your bones as a youngling, but this is *too* far. As if you and your new wife don't have the entire palace to *couple*. Can you *please* find another place to carry on? In case you haven't noticed, the sanctuary is in an uproar, and we need supplies!"

There was far more annoyance in her voice than embarrassment.

That was fine. I had enough embarrassment for both of us. Vale too, judging by the redness blooming on his cheeks.

"Master Healer Nissa, I'm so sorry. We—"

"Are newlywed and went through a harrowing experience that has your emotions running high. Yes, yes, I understand, Prince Vale. What I don't understand is why you're *still in my healers' closet* and not far away where I can go about gathering supplies for the injured and pretend like this didn't happen."

"We'll leave right away." Hand extended, Vale helped me off the table. We were nearly out the door when Nissa cleared her throat.

"Your wife has left something behind."

We twisted and somehow Vale's cheeks became even redder when Nissa pointed to my lacy undergarments.

The old healer's eyes dipped to our bloody attire.

"And might I suggest cleaning up before you engage in any other sexual activities? It's quite unhygienic."

I bit my lip, trying not to die laughing as I ran out of the room and left Vale to retrieve my undergarments.

I'd passed three doors by the time Vale caught up.

"You left me!"

"Of course I did. That was mortifying." I let out a nervous laugh. "And also, somehow . . . hilarious?"

"*For you.*" He patted his pocket. "Whereas I'm trying to hide my erection while picking up your *soaked* undergarments."

That sent me over the cliff. Laughter bubbled out of me, and though Vale still looked like someone had painted his cheeks red, the lines of his face relaxed a touch. "You're finding too much joy in this."

"All we can do is laugh, right? It'll be a story to tell one day!"

His face split into a grin. "One day, huh? Are you making plans to stick around?"

I stopped laughing. I'd been envisioning Vale and me, whispering and chuckling over some shared joke as younglings played around us. Younglings with my hair and his dark, warm eyes.

My heart clenched at the vision, no matter how unrealistic. How unwise and dangerous. If I stayed here, I'd be on edge for the rest of my life. Or at least until his father, mother, and even Rhistel died.

Yet, I couldn't bring myself to wish for that vision to disappear.

"I'm not sure." I watched his eyes light up from within. "I—"

Fast footsteps came down a connected corridor, and a young dwarf soldier covered in blood rounded the corner. "Prince! The king has been looking for you."

Vale's expression changed. "Did he make it out without injury? What of my mother and Rhistel?"

The soldier nodded. "They're all fine, my prince. That's not why I've been sent to find you. The king has called a meeting of lords and ladies."

"Right now?" Vale asked.

"They're all waiting for you, my prince."

Vale looked at me, and I understood. I wanted him to stay too. But he couldn't, so I laid a hand on his arm. "Go. This soldier will escort me back to the suite."

"And guard the door," Vale said. "Most Clawsguards were detained at the theater. *You* will watch over my wife."

The soldier's eyes bulged. Watching over Vale's wife was, no doubt, one of the biggest responsibilities in his career.

"I'll guard her with my life, my prince."

Vale took my hand and kissed it. "When I return, we can revisit our conversation."

CHAPTER 24
VALE

I strode into the council room, consumed by Neve, our kiss, and what had almost happened, only to find my father in a blind rage.

Immediately, I pushed the thoughts of Neve's legs wrapped around my torso and of the wetness of her lacy undergarments when I'd picked them up—those same undergarments that were burning a hole in my pocket—to the back of my mind.

I needed to be present. Resigning myself to my fate, I took my seat next to Rhistel.

"My king, Prince Vale is here now," said Lord Balik, the high lord of the southlands and Filip's father. He sat close to the king, as stoic and confident as ever. Like his children, High Lord Balik had warm brown skin, honey-colored eyes, and golden hair that was only slightly lighter than Sian's. Shockingly, he wore even more gold than I'd ever seen Sian wear, which was quite a lot. The precious metal dripped from Lord Balik's ears, his wrists, and around his neck. "Might we start?"

"Vale." Father turned to me. "It's about bleeding time. Shut the doors."

The soldiers moved to do so and the sound of the large doors shutting echoed through the room large enough for twenty, as everyone within sat in silence.

Tonight, each head of house in the Sacred Eight, save for Lord Roar, was present. As were ten influential jarls from around the kingdom and five Clawsguards, all covered in blood and standing, rather than sitting at the large circular table that dominated the room.

Though her father, Airen Vagle, Lord of Coin, and brother, Eirwen Vagle, sat on the other side of Father, Mother was not present, a notable observation. It hinted that Father didn't suspect anyone in this room of treason. If he did, he would have sent for his mind-reading wife.

"Tell us all what happened after the stars-damned rebels arrived." Father gestured to the Clawsguard. "How many casualties? How many rebels were caught?"

One Clawsguard stepped forward. Not Lars, Father's most trusted guard, but another that took the opposite shifts to Lars. Though I was not close to the old guard, I hoped Lars survived the arrow he'd taken for my father.

"My king, ten jarls, three ladies, and many common fae were injured." The soldier paused.

"Continue," Father growled in a way that told me he already knew what the soldier would say.

"And we caught no rebels. Though our forces killed many at the theater."

I thought of those I'd ended and of the one Neve killed. How many more had met their doom tonight?

"That is all," the guard said and stepped back.

"Actually, it isn't," I corrected. "Vidar Virtoris received a bad injury. He is being cared for." I looked at Lady Virtoris, noted her red eyes. It was probably killing her to be here, at the command of her king, when her son and heir was in the healers' sanctuary.

"Apologies," the Clawsguard said.

"This is happening far too often." Father waved the guard back. "Two attacks in less than two weeks! We must get a hand on these rebels. Put them in their place."

I gaped. Was he not going to even acknowledge Vidar's injuries? Lady Virtoris sat at the table too, and she would not forget such a slight.

"They spoke about an heir returning," Father continued, his cold, glacial features turning red. "So they've sussed out a bastard to use as a figurehead for their rebellion. We will find him and squash this nonsense. Tonight."

"Tonight?" Nalaea Qiren, High Lady of Silks, leaned forward and her long inky hair spread onto the table as her piercing green eyes found my father. "Then who will go, Majesty?"

Not her. The words hung in the air, unsaid but plain in the line of her full lips.

I'd always suspected that, at one point, Nalaea Qiren and my father had had an affair. If that was the case, none of the affection they'd shared then was on display now.

"I lost two of my personal guards." Lady Nalaea held up two fingers. "They are among those you haven't allowed into the palace but accompanied me to the theater upon request. You will not allow them to be with us, but you are fine with them dying tonight? And now I assume you wish for us to send more of our household guards, although you do not permit us to use them?"

Father glared at her. "As you said, we do not permit your servants and guards inside my palace during the Courting Festival, so I see no problem with sending them out tonight. What else are they doing?"

"Dying. Or cleaning the blood off their brothers and sisters in arms and wondering what in the stars is going on in this filthy city!" Lady Qiren slammed her hand against the table. "It isn't enough that we all had to bring soldiers to swell the royal army when we journeyed here? Now you wish to use those guards who wait in taverns at our own expense for us to return home?"

She wasn't the only high lord and lady to take offense. Even calm, Tadgh Balik appeared irritated, though only the slightest furrow of his brow gave that away.

"I can spare much of my guard." Lord Riis leaned

forward. "As I live in the city most of the time and have businesses here, many live here anyhow, and they all know Avaldenn well. They can help lead those whose soldiers are not as familiar. I can also send out spiders. See if they can find a rebel hideout. The city gates are now closed, so if they have a hideout, they will flee there."

Unless the rebels had a secret way out of Avaldenn, they were still here, possibly even residents. Father wouldn't allow the city gates to reopen until he'd had his fill of rebel blood.

"At least Lord Riis is willing to do good for the kingdom." Father scowled at Lady Nalaea.

The conversation turned to exactly how many guards could be spared per noble house and who in the royal army would lead the extra units. Through it all, Rhistel and I remained silent. This was no normal operation. I was betting that Father would want to use me for something specific. Something of shock value.

Rhistel's silence was out of character, though. Even if this was not his realm of expertise, he was the heir. Any chance to show his leadership and strength should have been taken advantage of.

One possible reason for his silence struck me. Had the rebels gotten to him? Had they cornered him like they had Saga? I snuck a glance at my brother and noted his wan complexion.

"Now that that's settled"—Father leaned back, looking marginally appeased after the first moments of dissent—"the soldiers will search through the night.

We'll find where they're hiding." My father turned his cold eyes on me. "At the ninth morning bell, Vale will lead the final forces out into the city to find rebels."

Immediately, I understood his reasoning for not sending me out tonight. Under the cover of night, few would see the rebels pulled from their hiding places. Or who had discovered them.

In the light of day, however, *everyone* would see the rebels being dragged out of their holes like mice, and they'd see the king's own blood had found them. Even if the night search teams found each and every rebel, the king would make sure to set a scene. And that I would star in the charade. Father was obsessed with bringing glory to his name, and by extension, his noble house.

"Very well, Father." I inclined my head.

"Good. Now, let's begin. Soldiers to the castle yard within the half hour." Father stood, pushing his heavy chair back in the process, and stomped away. Slowly, the high lords and ladies and jarls followed until only Rhistel and I remained in the room.

"Did they injure you?" I asked.

His eyes, the same shade of brown as my own, flickered in my direction. "Do you really care?"

"Of course I do." Tired of this question, I loosed a long exhale. "We're brothers."

"Days ago, you had me by the throat over some female."

I cringed, hating that he was right, that for many turns Rhistel and I had not been like brothers. That

Sian, Vidar, Luccan, and Caelo were much more like brothers to me.

Rhistel had taken liberties with his powers, and I could never forgive that, but that didn't mean I didn't care. Deep in my heart, there would always be a place, a weakness, for my twin.

"You're pale. Did the rebels hurt you?" I asked again.

Rhistel didn't answer right away but finally, he shook his head. "They killed a Clawsguard. He was the closest thing I had to a friend."

The resulting pause stretched on, awkward and miserable. I had to be the one to break it. "I'm sorry. I hope he received a quick death."

Rhistel snorted. "A warrior through and through." He rose and, without another word, left the council chambers.

A gold-cloaked Clawsguard stood outside of my suite when I arrived.

"Where's the soldier I left with my wife?" I asked.

"The queen sent for three of us to be pulled from the search for rebels and stationed at her children's doors. I dismissed the other soldier."

"I see." I grasped the door handle. Mother had always been protective, so I wasn't surprised. More like I was shocked that I hadn't seen her personally yet. "Do you know where the queen is?"

"I believe with the princess." The Clawsguard's face softened. Everyone loved Saga and after what had happened, Mother would be particularly fierce over her baby.

"Good." I let myself into my suite. The fresh scent of soap, perfumed with something floral, made my spine straighten. "Neve?"

"In here!"

Her voice came from the bathroom.

"Get in here, Vale," Neve added, her tone dipping, becoming more sultry.

I opened the door to the bathroom, peeked in, and my knees weakened. My wife was in the bathtub, beneath a mound of bubbles and red petals strewn into the steaming water. The top of her voluptuous breasts bobbed in the water, beneath a grouping of silken red petals. When she lifted one leg out of the water, petals stuck to her smooth skin as she pointed her toes.

"How did the meeting go?"

A chuckle escaped me. "You expect me to remember anything that happened when you're like that?"

She shrugged and lowered her leg, a devilish glint in her violet eyes. "The healer said we needed to clean off. The tub is big enough for two."

My heart rate amped up as I entered the room. "How convenient."

"As if you don't know firsthand."

"I don't. You're the only female who has ever bathed in my chambers."

Her eyes went round and for a moment, she appeared not to believe me, but it was the truth.

"Please don't tell me you're untouched," Neve said saucily, apparently having recovered from the shock of being the first female in my tub.

"Do I look like I know nothing of a female's body?" I stood over her now, my hands so close to her, itching to touch, to caress her silken skin.

Neve smirked. "Not at all, thank the stars. Now, are you going to just stand there, husband? Or are you going to put this tub to the test and join me?"

CHAPTER 25

NEVE

I held my breath and trailed my fingers through the red petals I'd sent the servants to fetch from the palace greenhouses.

Would he get in the water?

I'd had far too much time to think this seduction over, to consider if it was smart.

It wasn't. But bleeding skies fall down on me if I gave a damn anymore. Vale and I had been attracted to one another since day one. We'd shared a room, and a bed for many nights. We were becoming increasingly familiar with one another. I liked him, and my body wanted his.

Surely it wouldn't hurt to give in to desire? The fae were known for being very sexual, and I would bet many coins that Vale had had many casual flings. He was a prince of the realm, for stars' sake! Fae must throw themselves at him every day.

So I'd made a choice to seduce him, and I hoped he met me halfway.

Please, you big, handsome lug, get in the tub!

After what felt like an age, he took off his boots and pulled his shirt over his head. I swallowed. Soon, I'd be able to run my hands over those stunning muscles. As I'd wanted to do for so long.

The bloodied shirt fell to the ground, and he stared at me as if still questioning this choice. "You're sure?"

"I am. Are you?"

A lengthy pause in which I about died followed. Then his hands went to his pants and before I could blink, the pants were on the floor too.

"I wanted to make sure you could handle me, wife."

The prince hadn't been wearing undergarments and now he stood before me, nude and glorious.

Every line of him was sheer perfection, even those that were scars, which he had many. His tattoos, which I'd glimpsed many times since we'd been living together, were only decorations on a more beautiful canvas.

And his cock . . . a delicious ache grew inside me.

Vale watched me watching him, a faint curve of his lips the only tell of his amusement. When I could drag my eyes up, up, up, back to his face, he winked.

"Do I meet your requirements, little beast?"

"Aesthetically, I believe you'll do." I winked back. "I hope you know how to use what the stars gave you, my prince."

He snorted and came to stand at the edge of the

bath, his malehood so close, already stiff and standing proud. "I think I'll measure up."

He raised a leg and sank it into the tub so that the water rose and covered the bosom I'd ensured was barely exposed. The other leg followed, and the prince settled into the large tub, the water level rising with his bulk, his legs extending to rest on each side of mine.

Across from me, Vale placed his arms on the sides of the tub and smirked. "Why don't you come here, little beast? I'll wash your back." He lifted a cloth from the pinewood table beside the tub.

I rose in the water, just enough that everything below my navel was still hidden. The air, far cooler than the water, caressed my breasts and my nipples hardened.

A soft intake of air was all I needed to hear to know that Vale appreciated the sight.

"Make room," I purred, parting the bubbles and petals as I came closer. I settled between his legs and his firm shaft pressed against my rear. Playfully, I rubbed up and down.

"By the dead gods, Neve," Vale ground out. "Are you against foreplay?"

"I have no idea what you mean, dear husband."

A dry chuckle and Vale's sudsy hands were on my back, rubbing, pulling me closer. His cock pressed harder against me, and my sex clenched.

"Two can play at this game," Vale whispered into my ear, drawing chills down my spine. His hands moved in slow, circular motions on my back, making good on his promise to wash me, though it didn't take long before they were moving, gravitating to my breasts. My breathing tightened as his fingers landed on my nipples and pulled them lightly.

I let out a whimper as our bodies slid together in the warm water.

"What was that, dear wife?"

I swallowed. He was enjoying teasing me far too much.

"I said, what was that?" He pulled at my nipples again before one of his hands crept up, the fingers splaying over my neck. The other hand dipped lower, down my belly, parting my thighs. With slow, languid circles, he rubbed the swollen apex of my thighs.

My body became boneless as I relaxed into him, rested my head on his shoulders, and twisted to kiss his neck as my hand lifted to tangle into his long, black hair. I pulled lightly at his roots.

A low hum of pleasure escaped Vale. "Do it again."

I took a handful and tugged. As I did so, he applied a bit more pressure to my sex and a gasp ripped out of me.

"Stars, Vale!"

"Soon you'll be begging those stars for more."

I sucked down a breath right as he pressed hard on my swollen nub and began rubbing in faster circles. No comeback came. No innuendo.

His other hand slipped from my neck and landed on my hip. "By the dead gods," he growled, gripping the flesh there, pulling me harder into his chest.

I didn't reply, couldn't. The prince seemed to have obliterated any thought in my head. All there was, was him and me and the pleasure he gave.

"Come for me," Vale whispered as he slipped two fingers inside me and curled them forward all while keeping his thumb on my clitoris.

I whimpered because the truth was, I was close. So close.

"More," I rasped. "Harder."

He chuckled, low and deep. "As you wish."

The pressure increased as he plunged his fingers in and out. The tension in my core wound tighter, the pleasure imminent. The bath water seemed to heat. I ached for more, more touch, more feeling, *more him.*

And he gave. Stars, did he give. With every arch of my back, every whimper and moan, the prince pulled me tighter.

The water in the tub sloshed out, spattering the floor as I writhed.

"Come, Neve. I want to hear you come. For you to clench around my fingers."

"I'm close. I—"

His fingers curled again, his thumb pressed hard into my clit, and stars exploded in my eyes. A moan tore out of me as my sex pulsed.

Vale sighed, and the hand on my hip came back up as he grabbed my chin and directed my face to his. "There she is."

His lips were on mine, his tongue tasting me, his

mouth swallowing my sounds of pleasure as the prince rode out my orgasm.

I was panting by the time it rolled to an end, and Vale's lips parted mine. I opened my eyes to find his own already watching me. Desire burned there.

Though I felt boneless, desire flamed in me too. I wanted more of him. Would there ever be enough?

Planning to take what I wanted, I turned and straddled the prince.

"You're insatiable." One corner of his lips curled up in a handsome smirk. "Because I know I didn't leave you wanting."

"Not even close," I agreed. "But you seem to be." My hand dipped beneath the suds, and my fingers circled his cock.

Stars. My fingers didn't even touch when they wrapped around it. From the smug look on his face, Vale knew how big he was.

Well, he wasn't the only one with impressive attributes.

I released him, sat up straighter, and arched my back so that my breasts emerged from the sudsy water. Red marks marred my pale skin, a memory of where Vale had massaged my breasts. Nipples hard, I leaned forward and allowed them to brush Vale's chest even as his eyes dipped downward, widened.

"You don't play fair, do you?"

"Where's the fun in that? Besides, I happen to know an incredible pair of breasts easily distracts you"—I brushed a hand along his chest, savoring the feel of his skin against mine—"and I intend to use mine to the fullest."

"No complaints there."

"Didn't think so." With one finger, I lifted his chin, seized his lips with mine, and rolled my hips against his.

A groan left the prince, and my lips curled up at the corners. I loved the feeling of power I had over him, nearly as much as I loved feeling us, so close, so . . . right. Never in my life would I have thought I'd find someone who made me feel this way, so alive, so protected, even so cherished. And though I wasn't sure what I'd do in the future, I intended to enjoy every second Vale and I spent together now.

"I need to see more of you," Vale whispered against my lips. "Hold on."

Before I could so much as pull in another breath, Vale's arms wrapped around me, and he pushed up. His powerful legs found purchase on the tub and suddenly, we were standing. Or he was. I was straddling his waist.

"Vale!" I laughed. "Be careful!"

But I didn't need to worry. We might be dripping wet, but the prince was sure-footed and strong as he stepped out of the tub. I got one delicious glimpse of his backside in the mirror before he strode out of the bathroom.

"We're soaking," I protested. "We'll get the blankets wet."

"Who cares?" Vale rasped.

A moment later, he stopped, and I fell atop the blankets. His eyes raked over me as if he were a male finding a feast after many days of starvation. Never, in all my life, had I felt so raw, so exposed. Nor so seen.

Then, without so much as a warning, the prince grinned and pounced on top of me.

"Wait!" I giggled when his teeth tugged at my earlobe and his fingers found my sex again.

"*Wait?* Why do you torture a male so?" Vale drew back, his eyebrows pulled together.

"Because I plan to torture you in a completely different way." I took his shoulders, sat up, and pushed him down onto the mattress. Catching on, Vale allowed his weight to fall.

He grinned the grin of a male who would rather be nowhere else. "I love a female who takes charge."

I didn't answer, just began to kiss a trail down his chest, savoring his taste mixed with the smell of our bath until I reached his cock.

Beneath my lashes, I glanced up to find Vale watching me with anticipation. My lips curled up as I cupped his balls and tugged lightly.

A groan escaped from his lips as I wrapped mine around the tip of his cock. A slow kiss, the taste of him on my tongue, and my heart raced.

Having control over him, one of the most powerful fae in the kingdom, was intoxicating enough, but when he pushed his torso up and his hands dipped down, gripped my hair and tugged as I worked at his cock, I swore I was seconds from another release.

So I pulled back, slowing my rhythm, wanting to make this sort of exquisite torture last.

I'd been with human men before, done all there was to do with them, besides fall in love. As a slave, love was simply too dangerous. But one didn't need to love to spend time learning about others' bodies and allowing them to learn about mine.

Never had I felt like this with another person. Never had I held this equal sense of both immense power and wanting to pleasure another person. It was a high unlike anything I'd ever hoped for.

"Bleeding skies, Neve," Vale growled after only a few minutes of my lips around his cock. "I'm close."

I felt it, the way his cock twitched, the build-up. Wanting to give as well as I'd gotten, I gripped his balls again and tugged.

Vale groaned, and I swallowed his hot release. When he was done, his hands stroked my hair, and slowly, lingering with that heady sense that supplying pleasure gave, I lifted my head and licked him clean.

"You're going to be the end of me, little wife," Vale said when I was done.

"I'm trying to show you that you aren't the only one with talent in this relationship."

He barked out a laugh. "As if I could ever think such a thing." I shifted off him, but before I settled on the bed, he held out a hand.

Desperate for his arms around me again, I went to him and settled on his lap when Vale kissed me. With the feel of his calloused fingers and the taste of him still on my tongue, I might explode with pleasure. And when he pulled away and gave me a lazy smile, I wondered how I hadn't already.

"Lie with me," Vale whispered.

"What?"

"Let's lie down. I want to be next to you."

My eyes widened. "You want to cuddle?"

"Is there something wrong with that?"

"No, but if someone had told me that the famous Warrior Bear was a cuddler, I wouldn't have believed them."

"You say it like it's a bad thing."

"Only unexpected." I kissed him softly, savoring each second. "And I want to."

With one arm, he scooped me up and laid me down. Vale's arm wrapped around me and pulled me into his body.

I relaxed into his touch. It would be very easy to stay here forever.

CHAPTER 26
VALE

I grabbed Neve's hips, pulled her close, and nuzzled her neck. Her hair smelled so good—floral, like the bubbles in last night's bath.

"Don't tell me you're waking me up to get lucky," she groaned, her hand cupping my jawline and stroking in a way that made my cock jealous.

"I doubt I'll ever get my fill of you." I teased aside that curtain of silvery-white hair and kissed her neck, which, despite her rather weak protests, made her wriggle her plump, perfect arse into me.

I went rock-hard.

"Stars, Vale!" She twisted to meet my eyes. "I didn't know male . . . parts got hard that fast."

"*Parts*?" I burst out laughing. "Who knew your mouth could be so chaste?"

Neve gaped. "Excuse me, but I am a lady!"

"A lady who had her lips all over my—"

She slapped a hand over my mouth but grinned

devilishly, as if she was remembering last night as fondly as I. "Stop ruining a pleasant morning with this attitude!"

She looked simultaneously so indignant and cute that I laughed again. "Very well, little wife."

I twisted her so that her whole body faced me and traced a line from her lips to her right nipple, then tugged at it gently before taking her lips in mine.

She moaned. I would bet a thousand golden bears that if I had put my hands between her thighs, she'd be soaked, ready for me, wanting.

A low growl rose in my throat at the thought of burying myself into her, of hearing her cries of pleasure.

"Vale." Neve pulled away with a breathy whisper. "I want you, but I'm tender."

"In a good way, I hope."

"Well, yes, but still tender."

"As long as you can only sing my praises, I'm happy with this." I pulled her closer.

She scoffed. "Sing your praises! It's not like I'll be bragging openly!"

I grinned, loving getting her worked up in more ways than one. "And why not, wife? You can't deny that I used those fingers *oh so well*. More than once, if I recall right."

Her cheeks tinged pink too, probably remembering how, after we'd had our fill of cuddling, I'd made her come a second time with just my fingers.

"So you *do* remember," I teased.

She scoffed. "If I'd known you'd be like this, I would have thought twice about seducing you."

"I very much doubt that." I captured her lips in mine. "You were a female with a mission. I've never seen anything so sexy."

A lazy smirk spread across her face. "Happy to please."

I ran my hand up and down her side, relishing how her hips were the perfect handful. I'd never been more turned on, more attracted. I'd never wanted someone more.

Stars, I wanted her to be my soulmate.

Amongst the fae, once soulmates mated, a mark appeared on their skin. A twin mark signifying they belonged with one another.

That their souls twined together within the web of Fate.

Before sex, the stories claimed that one would feel strongly drawn to their soulmate. I felt that way with Neve, but perhaps that was only because she was so beautiful, so strong, and, because of her past, so unlike the ladies I'd been brought up to see as potential wives.

Plus, soulmates were rare. I didn't know a single faerie who had met theirs, and it was possible that I never would either.

Would I be willing to give up searching for my soulmate for Neve? Would Neve even want that? Posing such a question required more courage than facing down a horde of orcs.

"What are you thinking?" she asked.

"About last night," I admitted. "About us."

Her eyes widened. "What about us?"

"I—"

A knock at the door startled her, and I groaned as the bell tower outside tolled the ninth bell. I swore as my father's orders came rushing back to me. I was supposed to be in the yard, preparing to lead soldiers into the city to yank rebels from their hiding places.

"Prince Vale!" the Clawsguard at the door called out. "There's a soldier here telling me they are waiting for you in the yard."

"I'll be right there!" I yelled before brushing back her hair and drinking in her beautiful face again. "I have to go."

"Right." Neve nodded. "Maybe we should talk later?"

"I'd like that," I agreed and, frustrated in more ways than one, rolled out of bed.

I changed into my royal blue army uniform and went to my personal armory to retrieve *Skelda*, my sword. Once I was ready, I peeked into the bedroom again.

Neve sat on the bed, now covered in a silk robe, her feet tucked beneath the fur I kept over the foot of the bed as she drank from the flask filled with the Mind Rönd potion. Once she gulped down her daily dose, she waved.

"Be careful out there."

"What are you going to do today?" I pulled on a black fur cloak and teased my wings through the slit so they remained free. Just by looking outside, I'd need the extra warmth. The snow was falling thick and fast.

"I might skip training. I feel like I could use the rest."

"Take it then. Until later." I yearned to kiss her but held off. We needed to talk about how we'd taken our relationship—a fake marriage—a step further last night.

And I needed to decide if I was going to be transparent with Neve about the depth of my feelings.

"Good luck," Neve replied, and though I hated to turn my back on her, I left my room to hunt rebels.

Five bells later, my toes ached from the cold. Not only was the snow making it difficult to see, but the winds screamed off the Shivering Sea, souring everyone's mood. I shivered, scanning the street and considering ducking into a shop to question the shopkeeper. Not that I expected any valuable information.

I was beginning to think the rebels were far more intelligent than we'd bargained for.

The night before, the search parties had discovered a paltry three rebels. And that was only because the rebels had been trying to recover the bodies of their dead.

"Prince Vale," a voice called out.

I turned and squinted through the veil of falling snow to find a young female soldier dressed in a royal blue uniform running our way. She wasn't in my search party, though I recognized her as a soldier who often worked in the city.

"Yes?" I asked when she skidded on the ice to a stop before me.

"Soldier Barisia, my prince." She bowed. "We have a rebel building surrounded and think you should come."

My spine straightened, and I waved for my squad's attention. "Everyone, follow her."

We ran through the city and soon enough, the buildings changed. They became more run-down. Dirtier. The fae watching us as we carved through the street wore thin clothing.

Rall Row. I'd been here only a few days ago. With Neve.

The look on my wife's face when she'd seen the poverty still sent chills through me. Though she hadn't said as much, for the first time in the city, Neve had seen fae who had lived somewhat like she had in the Blood Court. And she hadn't liked it.

Neither had I.

And somehow, even though the area had been bad for some time, lately it seemed worse. More destitute.

I caught the eye of a young male dwarf as we passed, sadness heavy in the lines of his face. I might have saved many fae in the villages from orcs, goblins, ogres, trolls and other monsters. But these people? I'd failed them.

"It's right there." Soldier Barisia took a sharp turn and pointed.

In the distance, the House of Wisdom towered above the shanties, but Soldier Barisia was drawing my attention to something much closer.

Bleeding skies, it can't be.

But it was—the same run-down building Neve had asked about the other day. The one with the sign of the rebels loyal to House Falk.

"How are they still there?" Flabbergasted, I stared at the red hawk drawn across the boarded-up door. "It's been sealed off and—"

"They must have built a tunnel that we missed when we searched the place before because you're right," Soldier Barisia interjected, interrupting a prince, a testament to how excited she was to share the news. "There's no door or window that isn't boarded up. It was done so well that they felt safe sleeping in there."

A tunnel. That they'd dug a tunnel was astonishing. Even if they had earth and fire fae at their disposal, the ground here was often frozen solid. It might have taken many moons to form a tunnel that fae could squeeze through.

"If you didn't enter, how do you know it's them in there?"

"The boards have small cracks, so while we can't get them off easily, we can see through. One of us snuck up and did so, and no one inside caught us. Their guard must have fallen asleep or something, but there are about a dozen fae in there. One closest to the wall had a rebel insignia on their armband. We haven't moved in to wake them because we know the king wants you to be here." Her tone soured. "We've stayed quiet and kept our distance."

"Your party will be with me when we root them out," I assured them, wanting them to share in the glory they'd earned.

The line of her jaw softened a touch. "Thank you, my prince."

"Who has what magics?" I asked the band of soldiers who had found the rebels.

They rattled off their powers, or lack thereof, as was common with fae affected by the blight. Quickly, a plan formed. Soldier Barisia had water magic, another soldier had air magic, and I possessed winter magic that manifested in the ability to produce powerful, icy gales. Between the three of us, we would force the rebels from the building. Soldier Barisia would use the frozen water in the ground to flood the area, effectively rendering the tunnels—if they existed—useless. Simultaneously, another soldier and I would work to blow down the shanty. Two other soldiers would make sure the street was clear of civilians. The rest would wait to capture those who ran by any means necessary.

"Ready?" I prompted the two fae helping me with the initial assault.

They nodded, and I gave Barisia the signal to go. Though I couldn't see her magic, I recognized the strain on her face as she melted ground frost, snow, and ice, turning it to water to flood any tunnel inside the shack.

Her assurance that she could manage a feat such as

this one indicated she was powerful. Still, it took Soldier Barisia a good ten minutes before she let out a long breath. "There was a single tunnel. It's flat in places but now those should be flooded. They'll think twice about using it to escape."

"Keep it up for as long as you can," I said.

She couldn't hold the water stagnant. Eventually, it would move downward. Her priority was to continue flooding the tunnel with water to deter rebels from using that means of escape.

"We'll take care of the rest." I called air.

Streams of frost-filled gales coming in off the sea bent to my magic's will and with a wave of my hand, they slammed into the house. Beside me, the other soldier did the same, though with less power behind his strikes. Still, between the two of us, the boards shook, and the glass that remained in the windows rattled.

"There's movement inside," a soldier who claimed to have better-than-average hearing spoke up. "Better hurry."

"Continue bombarding," I said to the other soldier. "Let's blow it down."

His eyes narrowed in concentration as I pulled more power from my depths.

Snow-saturated wind swirled above me, gathering, making the soldiers shiver as it whisked away their body heat. When I felt as though I couldn't control any more air, I released the wind.

The first gale struck, and wood flew off the building, slamming into surrounding homes. Another strike.

More wood ripped off. I sucked in a breath and gathered strength before hitting the building again. At the fourth gale, the door blew off, two shutters too.

"Hold." I held out an arm for the other soldier working air to stop. He did, dropping trembling arms to his side.

The other soldiers braced themselves, waiting for the rebels to rush out. For an attack.

"Two ran out the back!" a soldier cried.

"Go!" I wound up to send a fifth gale. Sweat froze on my brow, but I didn't falter, didn't hesitate to use my power to the maximum as I sent a torrent of wind at the shanty.

Wood creaked, and the entire structure, already so unstable, shuddered.

"Assistance," I ground out, and the other air worker stepped in, giving it his all.

The combined efforts proved enough, and before our eyes, the building began to crumble.

"Be ready!" I gave the order a second before a rebel fled out the front.

A barrage followed, flowing from the building like water as I continued to batter the shanty with wind, ensuring its destruction. We would leave them no place to hide, no alternative route.

Soldier Barisia was red-faced, as was the other air worker, and as other soldiers chased rebels, some felling them quickly, pride welled inside me. We would be victorious. This would be enough to cool Father's fury.

Mere minutes later, the building collapsed. Screams

came from within, and a few more fae ran out the door, some soaking wet. They *had* tried the tunnel and found themselves in water.

As the structure came down, I released the gales under my control and gripped my sword, preparing to chase. And that's when I spotted her.

A female faerie with long black hair and blue eyes. The one who had tried to kill my wife.

When she saw me, she pivoted and raced around the downed shack.

I thrust my sword at the fleeing female, already rushing her. The clanging of metal disappeared as I raced after the black-haired female. Down one street of shacks, then another.

Fates, this female is fast. I put on as much speed as I could muster after expending so much magical energy.

She ran like the wind. And when the rebel tossed yet another glance over her shoulder and saw me slowly but surely gaining, she took a chance and leapt into the air.

I had to admire her guts. Flying was faster than running, but with the high winds, it would be difficult and left her with no cover.

My wings spread, and I was about to follow her when a person ran into the center of the street a half-block ahead of me. The flicker of motion distracted me, but that wasn't the only thing to catch my attention.

His hair was long and white, and his eyes were red, as was his attire. On his breast grew a thorn-choked rose.

Red Assassin.

I stumbled, and in that time, the fae female dropped out of the sky, disappearing some blocks away. My heart sank at the realization that I'd lost her.

And that she wasn't the only person I'd lost.

The vampire was gone too.

CHAPTER 27

NEVE

I sprawled across the bed Vale and I had disheveled. The bed that still smelled of him and me and acts of passion that made my heart race.

The book I'd been pretending to read fell from my hands. Try as I might, the story didn't hold my interest, not when a spicier one that I'd love to reenact with Vale had been playing in my mind. Wishing to feel closer to him, I reclined and scooted over to his pillow. I breathed in the sandalwood and snow scent and my toes curled.

Fates, I was in so much trouble.

I'd known there was a risk when I'd seduced Vale, known I already liked him too much for our tryst to be considered 'just fun.' What I couldn't have predicted was how utterly perfect we'd be together.

How good he'd made me feel. How I'd brought him pleasure too and loved every second of it. How much I'd miss him the moment he left.

I set the book on the bedside table and looked

around Vale's suite. My room too, for as long as I stayed in the Winter Court.

How long would that be? Probably a shorter amount of time than I wished . . .

Before, the question had seemed absurd, but with Prince Gervais dead, only Lord Aldéric, my old master, would recognize me for the blood slave I had been. To my knowledge, Lord Aldéric had never been to Winter's Realm. It was possible, though not probable, that my past might never come to light.

Of course, there were still the vampire assassins. Whether the Blood Court believed me to be a normal fae turned princess, or they learned my true past, they would still send someone to avenge their fallen prince.

The truth was that if I had a *real* choice, if my decisions didn't put myself *and* those I cared for in danger, I'd choose to stay here. To be with Vale. To search the land of my blood, the place that felt so right, even if I'd barely seen any of it. And maybe, if I was lucky, meet my long-lost family.

A sigh left my lips as I sat up and searched the room again, desperate for something else to consume my mind. Something that wouldn't root out so many emotions—some of them conflicting.

If only Vale was here to distract me.

I chewed on my bottom lip, my gaze going to the door as if to will him through it. When he didn't appear, I decided I'd ask the Clawsguard on duty if he'd heard anything.

I walked to the door and opened it to find a guard I

didn't recognize. The dark circles under his eyes spoke of exhaustion. He'd probably been one of the guards at the theater, or maybe searching the city all night for rebels.

"Have you heard from Prince Vale?" I asked, hopeful.

"Nothing yet, Princess Neve," the guard replied, his face softening. "I'm sure he's fine and will be back soon, though. Do you require anything?"

"No, nothing. Thank you." I closed the door and began to make my way back into the bedchamber when I passed the place where the invisible door to the hidden part of the castle was.

I paused, turned to the wall, and feeling ridiculous but willing to try anything to keep my mind occupied, I spoke to the wall. "I have time to kill and no one else is here. Perhaps you'll let me in today?"

The wall remained a boring wall. No glowing. No handle appearing from nowhere. Nothing.

Suddenly, annoyance rose inside me, and I glared at the wall. "You know, it would be great if I didn't have to fear for my life to enter. I might need a distraction, so how about you open up and . . ." I trailed off as a memory from Luccan's house bubbled to the surface.

Luccan made gateways, portals that worked within this realm but didn't connect us to others like the human world. What was *this* hidden door, if not a very short gateway? I held up my palm.

Did it need a blood offering? Would it recognize my

blood as someone it had let through before? A safe person, I supposed.

I had nothing but time and a burning curiosity to learn if I was on to something. I darted into Vale's personal armory and plucked a dagger from the wall. The blade sliced shallowly across my shoulder, making me cringe before I returned to the wall.

Barely daring to breathe, I pressed my palm into my shoulder, wetting it before swiping that blood against the wall.

It glowed, and my heart raced with anticipation. It had worked!

Elated, I waited for the door to materialize before letting myself into the hidden part of the palace for the third time.

Like always, this area was quiet, as if it mourned a past it clung to. I shut the door behind me and drew a line of blood on the paint. Though I suspected that someone, at some point, came back here and cleaned, it was unlikely they'd stumble upon my marking while I explored.

I had no destination in mind, no goal. And yet, I found myself going the same way as last time: to Queen Revna's rooms.

Perhaps I'd read more of her diary. Even gazing upon her jewels again would be fun. I had yet to learn if the brooch was, in fact, a phoenix opal.

I should ask Vale to take me to the library tomorrow. He wouldn't min—what in the stars!

At the intersection in the distance, where I would have gone left, a short, hunched figure crossed in front of me. She didn't notice me, preoccupied as she was with carrying, and likely trying not to drop, a heaping plate of food.

A human.

She had to be. Although I was far away and she wore her long gray hair down, covering what I suspected were rounded ears, she didn't walk like a fae of any race. She lacked the grace the fae exuded. Not to mention her clothing was of poor quality, which fit what a human in the castle would wear. Here, they were slaves, like in the Blood Court.

Was that the person who had been cleaning back here? And what was she doing with the food?

I cocked my head, trying to puzzle out the curiosity. Did I dare follow her? The question persisted for only a moment before my feet decided for me.

I trailed at a distance, careful to keep her in my sight but not alert her to my presence. In truth, it was all too easy. Compared to fae, humans had weak senses.

Plus, this one was old. Her hearing had probably worsened with age, something that didn't happen to my kind unless they were ancient.

The woman walked with purpose, down one corridor, then another, and another. I tiptoed after her, dipping into alcoves now and then just to be safe. My precautions proved unnecessary. She didn't look back once, hinting that she felt sheltered here.

I cringed. This might be the only place she felt that

way. Was I about to shatter that belief? What would she say if I revealed myself?

She couldn't be loyal to the king or House Aaberg, otherwise the castle wouldn't let her back here. For that reason alone, I didn't think she'd turn me in.

The woman stopped. I ducked into hiding again, behind a large vase that held nothing but had once probably been filled with giant flowers. Or something else beautiful and showy.

A creaking met my ears. She'd opened a door. I peered around the vase in time to see the human disappear through a door, not even bothering to shut it behind her.

I exhaled and followed. When I reached the doorway she'd passed through, I frowned. It led to a downward staircase.

Beyond the first ten or so steps, only darkness stared back at me. How did the old woman see in there?

Perhaps she didn't need to. If she'd taken the steps many times, she might do it by feel.

Stars, what is she up to?

There was only one way to find out. I descended the steps slowly and carefully. After only a few, I learned that they twisted, and trying to remain unseen and unheard, I eased to the far wall and ran my hand along it to help me navigate. As it was pitch-black in the stairwell, I had no idea how far it descended. And though I couldn't see the woman, I was certain I was still following her. No air flowed in and out of the stairwell, and the scent of roasted meat and bread lingered in the air.

I followed my nose, halting only when I heard another creak. Air rushed up at me, and my nose wrinkled. Not too far ahead, the human was leaving the stairwell. Wherever she was going smelled musty. Moldy. Gross.

Did the slave quarters smell like that? No slave would live in filth. Not if they could help it.

Taking a few more turns around the staircase, I stepped down lightly, my gaze catching on another door. This one, too, she'd left open, though only a hairsbreadth.

The one at the top of the stairs had been wide open. Here, she'd been more careful. As though someone else might see it but also kept it available to her if she needed to flee?

Hand trembling, I reached out and eased the door open.

The dank stench hit me, and I gagged. Burning moon, it was far worse than I'd anticipated. Like feces and piss and rot. It took a moment to gather myself and scan the area.

Cells lined the wall on my right side, stone on the other. Rocks littered the hallway, and when I peered up, holes in the stone ceiling stared back at me.

The human turned, rounded a corner, and disappeared from sight. However, only seconds later, a faint light flared. She'd lit a candle or a torch.

Whispers, or perhaps they were talking at a normal

level, but they were so far away they sounded like whispers, met my ears. She'd stopped to speak with someone.

From the looks of it, I stood in the castle dungeons. The cells faced me, cold and empty. Overall, this area seemed to be unstable and falling apart. Why would they keep anyone down here?

I tiptoed forward, straining my ears with each step.

When I reached where another hallway intersected the one I stood in, I stopped. The talking had ceased, but I picked up on sounds of chewing loud and clear. The human couldn't be far away and now she was feeding someone. Dying to know who it was, I eased forward to peek around the corner.

The human didn't notice me as she passed a roll through the bars, then a leg of chicken. As the cell she faced was on the same side of the hallway as me, I couldn't see into it. However, the imprisoned sounded male. Could he be another slave?

That didn't sound right. In the Vampire Kingdom, if a slave misbehaved enough, they'd either be sold or killed.

Was a rebel in the cell?

That struck me as odd too. In the White Bear's Pit, I'd witnessed King Magnus sentencing other rebels to death after their crimes. And even if Vale and his soldiers had captured any rebels since last night, why would this slave be feeding them? They'd only have been imprisoned for hours.

Unable to help myself and counting on the human's

inability to see well or far in the dark, I leaned forward, hoping to glimpse the person in the cell, but then my foot caught on a crack, and I fell forward, catching myself with my hands.

A gasp rang out, and I looked up in time to watch the slave stand and sprint in the opposite direction. I pushed up and ran after her. When I reached the cell she'd crouched in front of, I leapt over the abandoned plate of food.

"Wait!" I called out before remembering I might not be in the hidden palace anymore and a jailer could be down here. I promptly shut up and used my breath to sprint after the human.

Thanks to her stifled gait, she didn't make it to the end of the hall before I caught up and grabbed her.

"Stop. Please," I hissed. "I don't want to hurt you. Or tell on you."

She fought, but I yanked her to face me, and for the first time since I'd been following her, I got a good look at her face.

My lips parted. I recognized the human. She'd been in the kitchens the night of the Courting Festival's opening ball.

The slave stilled. Her eyes went wide, and her hand trembled as she reached up and touched my scar.

"You," she whispered. "*You're alive.* You've come back and you've hidden so well. I've been too scared to make contact, but . . ." She didn't finish but flung herself at me, wrapping her arms around me.

I stood there, dumbfounded, as the slave held me in

her trembling arms. This human knew me. Or, at least, she thought she did.

"I'm sorry." I pulled away to take in her watery gaze, her trembling chin. "I didn't mean to scare you, harm you, or anything of the sort, but I have to know . . . who do you think I am?"

CHAPTER 28
VALE

I slammed shut yet another shanty door.

"Nothing?" a soldier asked.

"No," I replied, my emotions barely restrained. Considering I'd been trained in the army to keep my emotions in check under pressure, that said quite a lot. Today we'd found a cache of rebels, but in many other ways, the search hadn't gone to plan.

While searching for the vampire, I had come across three fae in a home—all drained of blood. From the looks of them, they'd been a family: a mother, father, and youngling of around Filip's age. It turned my stomach to remember them, bloodless and frozen on the floor of their hut.

And they weren't the only bloodless fae we'd come across. Far from it.

"Any sighting of the vampire?" I asked, hoping for some good news.

"We've been all over Rall Row, my prince. Asked as

many of the residents as we could too. No one has seen one." He eyed me, and I could feel him questioning if I'd *really* seen a vampire.

A part of me almost wished I'd hallucinated the creature, but I hadn't.

"The Warrior Bear is as useless as his father!" one rebel, a mouthy, reedy, young male, cried out from where ten others were being kept under guard. "I don't know why anyone gave you control of Winter's Realm when you can't even find a *so-called* vampire in a city of fae. You'd think they'd stand out, wouldn't you?"

As much as I hated to admit it, the rebel spoke true. In a city of fae, a vampire would be obvious. Especially one with red eyes and wearing the uniform of the Red Assassins.

Then again, if anyone knew how to hide, it was those very assassins, which told me one thing: the vampire recognized me.

He'd wanted to be seen.

Wanted to get to me.

There had to be more, for the King and Queen of the Blood Court would not enlist the Red Assassins and send only one killer to seek their revenge and murder Neve. How many more roamed the streets of Avaldenn?

My throat tightened and, needing to move, to do *something*, I stomped over to where the rebels huddled together against the wind and snow.

"None of you saw a vampire?" I demanded. The entire group had slept through the night in Rall Row.

Judging by the trail of corpses we'd found; the vampires had hunted in the same area.

"Course not," the same mouthy faerie spat as he pushed his chest out. He was going for intimidating but missed the mark so widely that it was almost laughable.

And yet, a vague sense of pity arose in me when I looked at the rebel. He was much too thin to strike fear in any heart.

"We were holed up in that shack," the youngling sneered and spat at my feet. "Didn't see much in there besides each other, did we?"

"Unfortunately for you, that trend will continue." I turned to my soldiers, having had enough of this rebel. "Let's take them to the castle."

"Sounds good to us," the same young male rebel jeered. "Maybe then I can ask the king when he plans to do something about winter killing so many in the country."

"You'll be heading straight to the dungeons," I replied. "An improvement on your latest accommodations."

The male glared. "So you don't care! Winter will soon seize the city too. No one can push back the true cold when it comes for you!"

"Gag him," I instructed Soldier Barisia. The last thing I wanted to do was hear that rebel, or any of them for that matter, spout off about how my family had failed them.

It wasn't like we were blind to the changes in the

kingdom. Or that the cold truly came in harder and faster than ever before.

These past days, I'd allowed myself to become distracted. Mostly with Neve but also with my friends and the few good days we've had. And while I didn't regret the time spent with them, particularly not the night before with Neve, in the tub, in my bed, with her lips wrapped around my cock, I needed to do better.

I needed to remember why the nobles of the court were here in the first place, for I had played a large part in bringing them here.

If one of the noble houses had, indeed, taken the Ice Scepter during the aftermath of the White Bear's rebellion, the chances that they were here and brought the Scepter with them were high.

But so far, none of the soldiers we'd put in place at the beginning of the Festivals had seen anything of note. Nor the spies Lord Riis assured us were looking for fae of unusual power or those lurking in the libraries or around the Crown Drassil tree.

Of course, not even Lord Riis knew exactly *why* he was monitoring these people. It would help if he did, but with Father now suspecting his own spymaster, I didn't think that would happen. Not unless I convinced him otherwise.

I didn't believe for a moment that Lord Riis possessed the Scepter, but while Father wanted me to spy on Luccan, I could not. He and the rest of the Riis brothers were my dear friends. Lord Riis kept a dangerous secret for me.

I wouldn't throw them under my sword. Not when they'd done so much. Even if I held other questions in regard to Lord Riis and my mother, where the Scepter was concerned, none of them applied.

I'd try again to convince my father of their innocence too, right after I told him we needed to send more guards out into the city to hunt for vampires.

CHAPTER 29
NEVE

A smile broke on the old human's face. "When you fell, your hair covered your features. I thought you were a visiting noble or even the Aaberg princess. If I'd known it was you, I wouldn't have run." She shook her head and tears streamed down her cheeks. "But *it's you*."

"Who is *you*?"

She blinked once. Twice. Then let out a soft, incredulous laugh. "You're not a rebel then?"

"No, I'm a . . ."

What in the world would I say? An ex-blood slave? Not a chance I'd admit that to someone I didn't trust.

"Who do *you* think I am? You seem to have recognized me twice. The first time, I believed you had made a mistake, but now I'm not so sure. You know who I am. Or you think you do." My hand drifted to my scar. "Why do you keep fixating on my scar?"

"Because you got that scar on the last night I saw you." The human took a step back.

For a moment, I prepared for her to run again. My confusion only doubled when, instead, she curtsied. Yes, I was married to Vale and a princess, but was this the time?

"That night, in lieu of the bedtime routine, the queen tasked me with preparing you and your sister to flee from the castle," the human continued as she rose, clearly oblivious to how my heart stopped at the mention of a sister. "That same night, you disappeared into the palace walls, held by female fae soldiers dressed as commoners. As much as I wished to guard you myself, they'd been chosen because they could run very fast and protect you better than me."

A pained look crossed the human's face. "Before you disappeared, your sister reached for you. She didn't want to be parted and when she reached out for you, she scratched your temple deeply. You were too young for your fae healing to be in full effect. I remember thinking that would leave a scar if you lived."

I'd fled the palace? With soldiers? And this old human had wanted to protect me? But why?

"*Please*, be out with it." My arms trembled. "What's my name?"

She clasped her hands together and held them under her chin. "You are Princess Isolde, twin to Princess Thyra, the lastborn daughters of King Harald Falk and Queen Revna Falk."

My knees buckled, and I caught myself on the wall before collapsing.

The human stared at me, concern evident in her clear green eyes. "Are you well, Princess Isolde?"

Isolde.

"You've made a mistake," I said. "A scar like mine can't be so uncommon."

"On fae, scars are always uncommon," the human replied, her tone knowledgable. "Scars only remain if the injury was particularly barbaric—usually from a battle. Or if the fae was scarred very young, before their healing abilities matured. That's what happened to you. I'm certain of it." She paused and gave me a soft smile that I interpreted as her trying to calm me.

"You resemble your aunt, though I can see some of both your parents in you too. Your sister seemed to favor your mother's coloring, though you were both only two turns when you fled, so that may have changed." Her hand fluttered to her heart; the gesture so affected that it raised another question.

"Did you know them well? The king and queen?"

I didn't believe her, and yet, I was entertaining her. My heart raced at the implications.

Her face softened at the mention of the queen. "I knew your mother very well. Your father, less so. I came from the Skau household with your mother when she married the king."

"Why did you come with her?" This was a human slave. Why would the old Queen of Winter have her close when servants and slaves were plentiful in the palace? And, to hear the slave tell it, the queen had let her watch the queen's children.

"I was your mother's friend."

"But you . . . How old are you?"

"Seventy-two."

I supposed that worked out. After thirty turns, fae didn't age at the rate humans did.

"Revna, a high lady before she was a queen, didn't get along with the other fae ladies. But she found me interesting—the daughter of a slave of House Skau raised to be a servant through loyalty. A human, only a couple of turns younger than her. Though most would call it impossible, we became the best of friends and that bond only died when she did." The human's face fell. "I miss her every day."

Her lips trembled. Though much of what the human said was unbelievable, I did believe she'd loved Queen Revna.

"What's your name?"

"Emilia."

"It's good to meet you, Emilia."

She lifted her gaze to meet mine. "You don't believe me."

A pause filled the cold, dank air of the dungeons before I shook my head.

"You should meet someone." She took my hand, so familiar with me, although we'd just met.

For some reason, I didn't pull away. I sensed that she wasn't a threat. Only confused.

She led me to the dark corridor we'd rushed down.

This time, as I wasn't running, I took it in with greater detail. Like in the other corridor, all the cells proved empty. Some had caved-in ceilings too.

Why keep anyone down here? If they wished for the prisoners to die, there were many legal ways to do so. To have the ceiling collapse on top of you would be horrible.

We reached the cell Emilia had been visiting, the candle she'd lit still flickering against the iron bars. I peered inside to find a male on the ground, his long, thin legs out in front of him. His clothing was filthy and full of holes. I could only imagine how cold it would be down here with such horrible attire.

He should have been miserable, but when he saw me, his blue eyes lit up. I blinked. He looked so familiar though I couldn't put my finger on who he reminded me of.

"Karial," the male rasped. "You're alive!"

"No, my prince. Karial perished at the hands of an assassin, remember?" Emilia said, her tone softer than before. "This is Princess Isolde, your brother's daughter." She eyed me sidelong. "Though she doesn't yet believe me on that score."

Prince. His brother's daughter.

"*Prince Calder?*" I gasped.

No wonder his eyes struck me as familiar. I'd seen them in the face of King Magnus. And now that I knew who he was, other resemblances stuck out to me. The square jawline. The white hair, though you could only tell by looking at this male's scalp. Otherwise, the long curtains of his hair were so dirty they appeared almost brown.

"It is me," the prince replied, still looking at me as though I was a star blazing red in the night sky.

"But everyone says you died in the White Bear's Rebellion. Like everyone else in your family."

"Not killed," Emilia whispered. "They glamoured another to look like my prince and killed that person. Once the gossip spread and no one corrected it, that word became history."

Prince Calder let out a huff. "Down here, I'm as good as dead."

"No one has come down here?" I gestured around.

"These are the eastern dungeons. They aren't stable, and hence, no longer in use, so few come down here to feed my prince or occasionally change his blankets, clothing, and bucket. All of them appear to be under a spell."

I studied the prince with pity.

"So yes, the king has kept his father down here all these long turns." She eyed me. "But as we know, there are others in his family who survived."

Says you.

"Who is Karial?" I asked.

"My younger sister," Prince Calder replied. "She married into the Royal House of Sahar in the Summer Court when she was quite young, but I was told that Magnus still killed her and her children to exterminate the Falk line." He swallowed. "Not that the Summer

Court could ever prove it, but I am sure that's what happened."

My heart clenched for the male in the cage. Living as he did would be difficult enough, but to lose your entire family in the way he had . . . stars. Perhaps it was better that I didn't know what happened to my family.

"In you, I see much of sweet Karial," Calder said softly, "though your eyes are your mother's. Your hair is much like your father's."

"I think you two are mistaken," I said, unable to take the awe and adoration in their eyes. "As much as I'd love to have been born royalty, I was not. I—"

"What is your magic?" the prince interrupted.

"I don't know."

His eyebrows pulled together.

"I—" Stars, I had to tell them about my past. Otherwise, my explanation made no sense. I supposed I had enough leverage to do so, knowing that Emilia fed the prince, and that the prince was even down here. And I didn't get the feeling they'd tell anyone.

"I grew up as a blood slave in the Vampire Kingdom," I admitted. "They gave me a potion to nullify the magic in my blood. It lasts a moon cycle and will wear off in three days. But I've never known my magic. So, as you can see, I can't be who you say I am."

"*The* Blood Court!" Emilia let out a cry. "Princess, I'm so sorry! We meant to get you to safety, but we failed you!"

"I understand the potion," the prince said, not bothering to apologize like Emilia. Nor comfort her as he thought something over. "I have ingested it for many turns." He paused, his face growing serious. "If you have winter magic, and it's powerful, then you are, most likely, who Emilia says you are."

"But that can't be true. Others have to have that kind of magic. Bastards, for one. And the noble families have intermarried over the turns," I protested and then snorted at myself with how ridiculous I sounded, like I might actually belong to a noble family.

"Winter magic runs strongest in my family," the prince said, not caring about my protests. "That's why Sassa Falk could unify the houses into one kingdom."

Thanks to Clemencia, I learned the basics. The Shadow Fae had come to conquer the Kingdom of Winter and all in it had needed to unify and fight or else die. They'd bowed to Sassa Falk, and she'd led them to victory, banishing the Shadow Fae before they decimated the kingdom and moved south, as the histories told us was their goal.

"There are too many coincidences," Emilia said. "So try as you might to fight it, I'm right, Princess Isolde."

"*Neve*," I corrected her.

"In public, yes. However, to me you will always be Isolde, daughter of my dear friend and a female I would give my life for," the slave countered, rolling her shoulder back.

I stared at her. The first impression I'd gotten of her that day in the kitchens, had been that she was a fearful creature. Now I was sure that I'd mistaken shock for fear.

"I'm sorry, but you're mistaken," I said. "I can't remember my family, but the idea that I'm a long-lost princess? That's ludicrous."

"But you being a blood slave," Emilia mused. "That makes sense."

"How?"

"You were meant to go west. Thyra was to hide in the east."

"Did she make it?"

"I don't know. I assumed you both died." Emilia closed her eyes. "But you went farther west than your mother and father intended. Beyond the western territory of House Lisika even." Her eyebrows drew together. "I wonder why."

I sighed. My curiosity would be the end of me. "Where was the Princess Isolde supposed to go?"

"A lesser house in the west. One that remained allied with King Falk during the White Bear's Rebellion. Your parents hoped they'd take you in."

"Hmm," I mused.

"You need to show her proof," Calder interjected. "She needs something tangible." He looked at Emilia. "Is there anything in the castle that can convince her?"

Emilia cocked her head before nodding. "Perhaps."

"Go then. Show her."

"What about your food?" Emilia pointed to the plate. "I can't leave it here or, if it's one of the days a guard appears, they'll realize that someone comes down here."

"Imagine the shock if they learned that someone saved me from starving in these decrepit dungeons, despite their best efforts," he growled. "Unless the ceiling falls in on me, I'll survive until you can come again. Go. This is more important."

Emilia picked up the plate, and Calder passed her the bones he'd already stripped of meat. "I'll return soon," she assured the prince before turning to me. "Come. I assume you followed me down the stairwell?"

"I did."

She arched an eyebrow. "The castle doesn't let just anyone in."

"No Aaberg loyalists," I confirmed.

"But you're married to the Warrior Bear."

"He's different. I have no loyalty to King Magnus. Nor the heir. Not even the queen."

Emilia nodded. "Very good."

We left Prince Calder, brother to King Harald, in his cell, though before we turned the corner, I couldn't help but take one more look at him.

He watched me too, his eyes shining with what looked like hope.

Emilia led me up the dark stairwell, through the hidden part of the palace, to Queen Revna's suite.

"I used to spend so much time here." Emilia sighed

as we entered the living quarters. "If she were still alive, your mother would look the same as when I'd last seen her, and I'd be old. There is no way I could drink fae wine with her like I used to. How unfair."

Anna and I would be the same one day.

"My best friend is human," I said, a pang of sympathy for Emilia slicing through me. "Well, one of them."

It used to be that Anna was my only best friend, but I was accumulating others whom I didn't think I could live without.

Clemencia, Saga, and Sayyida were among those who had stolen my heart. The males in Vale's cabal were more distant, but I could envision myself growing close to them too. That was, if I was foolish enough to stay, which despite my daydreaming about being with Vale, I was not.

Was I?

"So you came here as a servant?" I didn't want to venture down the path of Vale and me at the moment.

"A personal servant to the queen."

"I don't understand why they kept you as a slave after."

My meaning was clear. If you'd been so close to the queen, why didn't they kill you?

"King Magnus and Queen Inga don't see humans like your mother did." Emilia shrugged. "Of course, Queen Inga, as my friend's lady-in-waiting, knew that Queen Revna liked me. But she didn't understand how deep our friendship went. It's likely that after Queen

Inga was crowned, she forgot all about me. And in time, I no longer looked as I once did." She gave a dry laugh. "We humans don't have magic, but invisibility is a sort of power. Here, we use it to the fullest."

That I understood. I would have given a lot to be invisible to vampires in the Blood Court.

"In here." Emilia shuffled into Queen Revna's bedchambers.

Though I'd been in those same chambers, this time, I hesitated. She seemed so sure that I was a princess by blood. What was she going to show me?

"Come in here, Princess Isolde."

I sighed and followed her. Again, the paintings on the wall stole my attention, particularly the one of the twin girls, their backs to the painter as they ran away hand in hand.

Their faces remained hidden, and their hair was too short for me to really discern the color. If I had to guess, I'd say white—a typical Falk hair color—and dark brown, but with such sparse hair, it was hard to judge.

"You were both born with hair, but it fell out. Your mother had that painting done at one turn old," Emilia explained, smiling at the painting and correctly inferring my thoughts. "She loved the image."

"Why not show our faces?"

"She had other paintings. One I'm about to show you."

I joined her at a nightstand, one drawer already open. She pulled out a watercolor painting and handed it to me. "Your mother painted this one herself. She didn't like them to be on display because she didn't think she was very good. I disagree."

I took the painting and gasped. The queen was an excellent artist. She captured two girls, the twins, her daughters, as they played with stuffed unicorns. In this one, their hair was slightly longer.

One's hair gleamed white, the other black. One's eyes were violet, the other's a stunning glacial blue. One's smile was my own though with far fewer teeth. That same girl had my nose. It was the first head-on image I'd seen of the royal twins, and there was a resemblance. A strong one.

My hand trembled.

"You look so much alike." Emilia pressed.

Yes. Even with twenty turns between me and the girl in the painting, the resemblances were plain. I dropped the painting as my breath became thin.

"Isolde! Are you well? Can I do anything for you?"

I spun, taking in the room, the place where the castle had led me days ago. Here, voices spoke to me. They answered me when I asked for help.

I'd ask again.

"Please," I begged the inner castle. "Is she right? Am I Princess Isolde? Is that why you let me back here?"

Across the room, the doors to the glass cabinet in which the queen held her crowns flew open. One crown glowed a silvery purple.

Welcome home, Princess Isolde. Many voices spoke as one, stealing my breath.

Tears filled my eyes. "Why didn't you tell me before? Why not when I read the diary?"

We were not sure. Not until you bloodied the walls.

Bloodied the walls. The way I'd entered the hidden castle today.

"So you just let me in before because you felt bad for me?"

You were in need of sanctuary.

We. Not the single female voice, and yet so familiar. Like when I touched the Drassil tree of Traliska, many spoke. An image of a Drassil filled my mind. The last time I'd touched one had been during my wedding to Vale. When the Drassil, or more specifically the Faetia, had blessed our union.

I bristled. Why would the voices of the Faetia do such a thing? If I was a Falk, and he an Aaberg, then we were enemies.

My hands slapped over my mouth.

Oh stars. But Vale was only an Aaberg in name. His father had been born a bastard by blood. A *Falk* bastard. My cousin.

And Vale is his son.

CHAPTER 30
VALE

My band of soldiers returned to Frostveil Castle with the rebels in tow, and I led them down to the western dungeons. Though I should have been proud that we'd captured so many rebels, my mind wasn't in the moment but consumed by the memory of the vampire.

Right after seeing him, before searching the city high and low for more of his magical order, I'd sent a missive to the Clawsguard watching the door to my suite. The reply had come quickly, and the guard had assured me that all was quiet in the palace.

Neve was safe.

For now.

I needed to speak with Father about increasing her guard, and of the drained bodies we'd found in the city.

First, though, the rebels.

I descended the stone steps into the dank dungeon. Behind me, footsteps echoed in the low-ceiling tunnel.

Some rebels fought—probably the mouthy young male among them—but mostly they appeared resigned to their fate.

When I reached the bottom of the steps, I discovered we weren't the first troop of soldiers to return. A dozen other rebels glared at me from behind bars, but they weren't alone in the dungeon cells.

From behind bars, actors from the Royal Theater stared back at me. Avalina Truso, the best-known actress in the kingdom, being one of them.

Someone had thrown her in one of the first cells closest to the stairs. From the moment we locked eyes, she looked daggers at me, her fine-boned hands clenched at her sides, trembling from the cold of the dungeons, which was even worse than outside.

Saga and Mother would be disappointed to learn she was down here, but perhaps Avalina deserved this fate. Her song indicated rebel proclivities, but the others?

I walked down the aisle, my heart sinking deeper with each step. The rebels were being held on the right, the actors on the left. A quick count told me that thirty other actors were imprisoned. I didn't believe for a second that they'd all known the theater was going to be used for a rebel attack.

"Why are they here?" I asked the guard on duty, gesturing to the cell of actors and actresses.

"King Magnus said to bring 'em here, I guess?" the guard replied. "That's what the soldiers who brought 'em in said."

Why didn't he mention this to me?

"Have we questioned them?"

"A few."

"And?"

The guard shrugged. "They're still locked up. I didn't do the questioning, my prince."

"Lock up the rebels," I instructed those following me. Determined to take matters into my own hands, I approached a cell containing three adult male actors, one faerie, one brownie, and one dwarf. I didn't remember them on stage. Maybe they'd been in one of the chaotic group scenes.

"You were in the play *The White Bear's Rebellion?*"

"We were, my prince." The brownie bowed his head and his mop of long dark hair flopped forward, covering his face. He wore a thin house coat and shivered as violently as Avalina. The rest looked much the same, in night clothes or house coats. It seemed that none of them had been allowed to dress for the dungeons when soldiers pulled them from their homes.

"Have you been with the Royal Company long?"

The brownie nodded. "Five turns for me." He pointed to the faerie wearing loose pants and a robe only fit for lounging in one's house. "Sven joined at about the same time."

"I've been there for a season," the dwarf replied, his voice deep and raspy.

"You're ingrained in that culture."

The brownie's hairy cheeks blossomed red, likely anticipating where I was going.

"Were you aware of the rebels plan to attack the night of the production?" I asked outright. "Had there been rumors among the company? Were they helping the rebels?"

"I didn't know," the faerie, Sven, piped up for the first time. "And I've got a family and four mouths to feed. Had I heard, I would have quit."

"Not told the authorities?"

"That too," Sven said, though I didn't quite believe that part. *Now*, he would have told someone, but back then? Questionable.

The brownie and the dwarf also claimed that they hadn't known about the rebellion. As Liar's Salvation wasn't cheap and was extremely hard to come by, I felt certain that they told the truth.

I moved down the line of cells, asking others. The vast majority hadn't been informed about the attack. Only a few admitted they had helped the rebels. They didn't appear to regret their choice.

I didn't ask them all, but enough to know that most of the imprisoned didn't deserve to be in our dungeons. An issue that had to be remedied.

As I passed by Avalina Truso's cell, she leaned closer. "Aren't you going to ask if I knew?"

"It seems clear to me that you did." I paused. "But for the sake of fairness, did you help the rebels?"

A slow, controlled smile spread across her face.

"I did, my prince. I was the mastermind behind the attack, the production, the final scene that told the truth of the White Bear's Rebellion. And I shouldn't have stopped there."

"What more could you have portrayed?" I retorted; my throat tight at her smug expression.

She let out a laugh. "So much, my prince. You're too young to know all that happened, but scandal abounds in the Court of Winter. It always has." She arched an eyebrow. "And your family has been at the rotten heart of the most salacious scandals for so very long."

"What do you mean?"

"I believe you should ask Queen Inga that question." She looked down at her nails, some of them broken and ragged. "I have to say, to play your mother is a dream role. Such a complicated female."

I stared at her, unsure of what to say until I decided to say nothing. I turned away from the actress and left the dungeons in search of the king.

I found my father in his personal library, a goblet of wine in his hand. Mother was there too, the pair seemingly deep in conversation, a rarity. In public, the royal pair presented a united front. In private, they were rarely together—not unless they were scheming.

"Mother. Father." I approached the pair but stayed standing.

Mother smiled at me, and Avalina's words rang in

my mind. I pushed them back. This was no time for rebel nonsense.

"How many did you find?" Father asked, his eyes leveling me as Mother shifted to give me her full attention.

"Eleven." Of the group of rebels we'd found, only two got away.

I repressed a shudder as I recalled the black-haired female running, how she'd leapt into the air and how I'd been about to follow. That was until a vampire walked in front of me.

"There are more," Father growled. "At least fifty were in the theater."

"That's not counting the ones who burst through the dome," Mother added.

"The other search parties found quite a lot of them too. And some bands of soldiers have not returned yet."

My father snorted. "It's not enough. Search teams will continue night and day. No one will come in and out of the city. Nor sail from Avaldenn. It will remain this way until I'm sure we've caught *them all*."

My mouth dropped open. To halt movement in and out of the city for a day was a big deal. To do so indefinitely? Madness.

"Father, I—"

"You will not sway me, Vale," my father said.

The hard lines on his face said as much, and as much as I wanted to argue, I saw the wisdom in moving on. I had other battles to fight, two I might fix now.

Besides, if this embargo went on for too long, he'd see how foolish it was and call it off.

"There are other matters I'd like to address."

Father inclined his head, and Mother set her drink down. I had their full attention.

"There are actors and actresses in the dungeon. Some are guilty and should be there, but many are not. We should release the ones who are innocent."

"*Absolutely not*," Father scoffed.

My jaw tightened. "Why not?"

"I'll be frank, Vale. I care not if they're guilty or innocent. They were *there*, and I will keep them until I see fit to release them. In doing so, others will think twice about working with the rebels in the future." He took a drink of wine, his face reddening with the annoyance I'd stoked.

"This is a bad idea, Father."

"When you rule a kingdom, then you can make the calls," Father replied. "Until then, you do as I say. Your role is to control the army. And to always bring honor to our family, which sometimes means reminding others of how powerful we are." He looked at Mother for support, but she said nothing.

Avalina's words came back to me. I was sure Mother and Father had secrets. What married couples didn't?

But why would an actress know of them? Or think she did?

"It's wrong," I said. "You might cause more ire than inspire loyalty."

"I will *demand* loyalty."

Stars, he was the most stubborn arse I'd ever known. I'd get nowhere with this issue when he was like this. Perhaps instead I'd recruit the cabal to free the innocent actors, or, more accurately, the members who weren't stuck in the healers' sanctuary. I'd speak with Sian about it later.

Loosing a sigh, I moved on to the topic that had consumed so many of my thoughts since I'd seen the vampire. How to protect my wife.

"I have one other matter to discuss," I said.

Father chuckled humorlessly. "Out with it then, son."

"I spotted a vampire in the city. Assassins who have come for Neve. They have already attacked and drained many fae in Rall Row. I request more guards around her at all times. At my door. At the base of my tower. Wherever she is, I want them there."

Father arched an eyebrow. "They're busy at the moment, rounding up rebel scum."

My fists balled up. "We can spare a half dozen."

"You can't be sure the vampires are assassins."

My mouth opened, then closed before opening again. "He wore the thorn-choked rose of the Red Assassins on his breast."

"Until I hear from Lord Armenil, I'm not inclined to assume that the vampires will attack someone of my house." Father paused and sipped his wine. "Not to mention the castle is *crawling* with soldiers already, Vale. Your request is unreasonable."

Did he hear what he was saying? Was he even going to acknowledge the deaths in Rall Row?

"You think wanting soldiers around *my wife* until we've learned who the vampire was, and if there are more, is unreasonable? What of everything you've said today? What of your inability, no, your disregard, for protecting your people? For doing what is right!"

Father shot to his feet, his ice-blue wings fanning out in irritation. "Do not speak to me about what is right. Do not dare to question what I do for our House. *For this family.*"

"Neve is your family," I growled, then, realizing I could go at this from another angle, I tried again. "She may carry the next Aaberg prince or princess."

The spark of hope that flared in my chest at my own words surprised me. Neve and I had been intimate, but had not had sex. And we certainly had not dared to speak of younglings. Our marriage had been a farce, temporary from the start.

And yet, the idea of younglings with her eyes and my dark hair set my pulse thrumming.

"She might," Father agreed. "But there is no proof of that, and if there ever is, then we will take better care of your princess." He waved his hand. "Now, leave. I must speak with your mother."

The words he didn't say rang more loudly in my ears than the ones he uttered. Father would protect Neve in public. However, if a vampire assassin slipped through the castle gates and took her life, he would not be fussed.

Only Mother's slight moment, a small shake of her head, stopped me from fighting on.

She was right. I'd known it from the start and yet somehow, I'd deluded myself in the last few days into thinking I could reason with Father.

I'd been wrong.

He loved me. Loved all his children, and though I didn't believe he loved Mother, he did respect his wife for her vast power and status.

But Neve, even while she bore his name, was still his enemy. He didn't care if they killed her.

I couldn't forget that again.

"I'll take my leave then." I spun on my heel, and before Father or Mother could say a thing, burst out of the room.

He'd always been willing to hurt others to achieve his ends, always been brutal in his retribution, and I hated that about him. Hated how I had to reconcile the father I knew with the king who would burn entire cities —and had—to get what he wanted. His rebellion had proven as much.

But this time he'd gone too far by neglecting the female I loved.

Yes, loved.

I could no longer deny the fact. Or tell myself I only wanted her body or adored her spark. One didn't experience the fury pulsing through my blood for anything other than love.

I sighed, my emotions a ball of blackness rolling

through me, and rounded a corner, only to find Lord Riis striding toward me.

He waved. "Prince Vale, a moment?"

"I'm in a bit of a hurry." I should have already stopped by my suite, should have told Neve what I'd seen in the city.

"I'll be brief." Lord Riis stopped in front of me. "How is Princess Neve? After the attack?"

"She's fine. Shaken, but alive." My throat tightened up as I recalled how close she'd been to dying. "Thanks to you. I'm sorry I didn't say that sooner."

Leyv placed a hand over his heart. "I'd do it again."

That was more than I could say for my father. My brother too. Possibly even my mother. It hurt that the only person in my family who cared for Neve, besides me, was Saga.

Lord Riis might have secrets. He might have even had an affair with my mother, and perhaps they were still carrying on. At first, that idea had shocked me, but now that I'd had time to calm down, I wasn't sure I cared.

They'd been friends since they were younglings, and my father didn't love my mother. Respected her power, yes. Feared her. If he was smart, he would. Admired her bloodline—of course.

Love? If they'd ever had that, it had died long ago.

However, Mother had affection for Lord Riis. Because of this, I didn't think she knew that Father suspected her childhood friend of holding the Ice Scepter.

But I did. And Lord Riis had not only asked after Neve's health but also protected me and my wife. I was in a great debt to him and, seeing as my father's suspicion regarding the Lord of Tongues was ludicrous, it was time I returned the favor.

"I have to tell you something, Leyv."

The seriousness in my tone got his attention right away. "Yes?"

"I must swear you to secrecy before telling you. The only people you can inform are Luccan, Arie, and Thantrel, and only if it seems they're in trouble."

I wouldn't be able to live with myself if my friends were hurt because of my father's delusions.

"Very well."

"The Courting Festival was not called only so that the king could create alliances to benefit his house."

"I assumed it was to force you and Prince Rhistel into marriage," the Lord of Tongues quipped. "That's not correct?"

"I can't say that it wasn't on Father's mind," I groused. "But there's a stronger reason behind the Festival." A quick glance around assured me that no one was approaching. "Many have speculated about this in the past, but I can confirm that the Ice Scepter has been lost since the time of the Falk reign, hence the increase in storms and the fall in temperature." I paused, thinking about the blight that affected the health of so many fae, but chose not to add that. It was only a theory, not proven that the blight was connected to the disappearance of the Ice Scepter.

"Father has recently learned that a noble house stole it."

Lord Riis blinked. "Well, people have wondered why we haven't seen the Scepter. Why, like so many other Falk items, the king hasn't retrieved it from the royal vaults and carried it on formal occasions. Or when he blesses the Crown Drassil."

Which Father did four times a turn, two more times a turn than his predecessor King Harald Falk. It had always been a source of pride for my father. I could not deny the other points. Father didn't venture into the royal vaults for the Scepter because it was not there. Just as many other Falk items had gone missing.

"Did King Harald use it when he blessed the Crown Drassil?" I'd been too young to pay attention to the actions of the previous king and queen.

"Not always, but if Winter was getting out of hand" —he arched his eyebrows—"like it has been, he brought the Ice Scepter out. The Crown Drassil, any Drassil tree really, needs to be fed magic—a tribute if you will—and the Ice Scepter is a powerful magical object."

"So it keeps the magic of the land under control not only in the hands of the ruler but by using the Drassil's connection to the land? They're all three connected?"

"Or perhaps the Cruel King liked how it looked." Lord Riis shrugged and gave a half smile, perhaps to lighten the tension rolling off of me. "I spoke more with Queen Revna than her husband. Besides, what has this got to do with me?"

"The king suspects you might have it."

The spymaster paled. "I'm not from a noble blood-line. I have not a drop of winter magic."

"That's why I don't agree with him, which I have said to him. He, however, thinks that the increase in Luccan's magic is suspicious."

"He has grown stronger since he started making gateways." Lord Riis swallowed. "This is my fault. I asked him to create ones connecting our properties, for safety."

"Yes, well, I thought you should know. To protect yourself. And the knowledge might help you and your spies in finding a real suspect now that you fully under-stand what you're looking for."

"Thank you, Vale," Lord Riis whispered. "I can see that this has cost you."

I'd promised Father, Mother, and Rhistel that I wouldn't tell anyone else about this. And now I'd broken that promise. Twice.

I'd broken my honor.

"It's the right thing to do. I owe you for saving Neve. For masterminding how to protect her as best as anyone could. I should be thanking you, Leyv."

Lord Riis opened his arms and embraced me.

I stiffened, unused to such closeness if it didn't come from Neve, Saga, or my best friends. Lord Riis hadn't hugged me in many, many turns.

But he once had. Once, I called him uncle. Once, he'd brought me gifts, and I'd loved practicing swords with him.

"Thank you," Lord Riis said, still embracing me. "Thank you, Vale."

"Of course," I murmured as we broke apart. "You've always had a place in my heart and Luccan, Thantrel—even Arie—are some of my closest friends."

The sadness in the Lord of Tongues's eyes lifted a touch. "You have no idea how happy I am to hear that." His hand, large and rough, clapped on my shoulder, squeezed. "I believe you have a wife you need to be getting back to?"

"I do," I said, relieved for an out to distance myself from the cloud of emotions rolling between us. "Good day, Leyv."

We parted, though I still felt the spymaster's eyes on me until I turned the corner.

I was at the door to my suite before I knew it, so great was the depth of my thoughts. The Clawsguard on duty opened the door for me.

"Welcome back, my prince. I'm sure the princess will be happy to see you."

I nodded, slipped inside, and inhaled. The room smelled like smoked vanilla. Like Neve.

"I'm back," I called out, half hoping she'd respond from the bathroom, and I'd find her waiting for me in the tub again, violet eyes calling me closer.

But there was no response. Only silence.

In his letter, the Clawsguard at the door had assured me that Neve had not left our suite. Was she asleep?

"Neve?" I asked, more softly, in case she slumbered.

Still no reply, but when I ambled down the short

447

corridor that opened into my bedroom, she was there, sitting on the bed, staring out the window at the falling snow.

"Neve? Are you well?" I approached the bed and sat near her feet.

My weight pried her from a trance. She turned, looked at me, and swallowed.

"No."

"You've fallen ill?"

She'd been fine that morning. More than fine. Neve had been happy, but the female before me appeared anything but.

"I think so." She looked at her hands.

Something in her voice hinted that she wasn't telling the entire truth.

"Did something happen?"

"Nothing."

"All right . . . Well, we found many rebels," I said, hoping to engage her.

She said nothing. No matter how sick she felt, I had news. So I told her about the house in Rall Row, the infiltration, and chasing the black-haired faerie. That captured her attention, albeit briefly. Then she continued to stare at her hands.

"I lost the rebel when I saw a vampire."

Neve didn't look up. She didn't blink. It was as if she'd gone as cold as ice.

"They managed the journey quickly." Her voice trembled as she spoke.

"The question is how," I said.

She didn't reply.

Flummoxed and hoping to pull her from her idleness, I plowed onward, telling her how the white-haired vampire had appeared before me and then disappeared as if he were playing a game. Then I told her about how we'd taken the rebels to the dungeons. How I'd seen the actors there.

At the mention of the performers, her eyes filled with tears that she wiped away.

When I finished, including my time with my father and Lord Riis, Neve let out a long sigh.

"Is that all?"

"Yes." I swallowed. "Can I get you anything, Neve? A tea? A tonic? I've never seen you like this."

"No, I feel fine, but off."

What did that mean?

"Do you want to get out of the suite?" I asked. "Take a walk around the castle? Perhaps we should visit the smithy, Master Urgi, and have a sword made for you. In case the worst happens."

Neve's eyes closed. "No. Please, Vale. I want to be left alone."

Then, before I uttered another word, she lay down and turned her back to me.

I swallowed, watching her for a moment before I stood and went to the bathroom. Once alone, I placed my hands on the sides of the sink and looked in the mirror.

Something was wrong with Neve, and I couldn't

help but wonder if I'd upset her. Or did she regret what we'd done? How close we were getting? That if we grew closer, it would jeopardize her desire to leave.

My heart ached because I regretted nothing of the sort.

CHAPTER 31
NEVE

Vale and I strode down the hallway, answering a summons from the king.

Tension stretched tight between us, a reminder, as if either of us needed one, that we hadn't spoken for hours. Even now, when we should be putting on amiable faces for the public, silence rang between us, making our footsteps, and that of the guard following us, echo in the white stone corridor.

I was thankful for the silence, for in my head, I was screaming.

Vale and I were related. We couldn't be together.

True, royals had wed other royals for centuries and most of them shared blood, but I hadn't grown up with that expectation. How ironic then, that I'd already wed a royal. Been intimate with him too. My stomach rolled at the thought.

But what do I say to Vale?

Since he'd returned and told me about the rebels,

453

the vampire, and the imprisoned performers, Vale had been watching me closely. He wanted to help. Possibly blamed himself for the distance between us too.

Was it better that way? Maybe I should continue to distance myself? Would that hurt him less than knowing the truth?

As we stepped outside, into a snowy courtyard filled with nobles, the queen, the heir, and the princess amongst them, my questions fell away. The people formed a loose line, and as we passed, each one studied Vale and me. Though I wanted to lie in bed and cry, I put on a show.

A false smile graced my face as a wicked wind blew tendrils of my hair into my vision. I nodded at a few people and pulled the muted sable cloak around me tighter as I followed Vale through the dense snow, which hadn't stopped falling since yesterday morning. Even a city as used to the snow as Avaldenn couldn't keep up with the snow removal.

"It's colder than a mage's touch out here," Saga said as we joined her.

I stood between the royal siblings, wishing I could switch places with Saga, but that would look too odd. Newlyweds wanted to be near one another all the time, right?

The princess's hand appeared from beneath the hand-dyed, pink fur cloak she loved. She gestured at the area. "What's the event?"

"You don't know either?" Vale asked.

"No. About an hour ago, a message arrived at my room, telling me to come here."

"Father is being mysterious," Vale murmured.

"Not sure I like that."

Neither did I, but I said nothing. Saga noticed too because she side-bumped me.

"Is your mouth frozen shut?" Her tone was light and teasing.

"Kind of," I replied, trying to give her a true smile.

Saga cocked her head, hinting that I'd failed at my attempt. "Neve? Is something wrong?"

"No," I lied and rubbed my hands together for something to do. "Like you said, just cold."

Vale looked away.

Saga exhaled and a puff of white filled the air. "I guess there's trouble in paradise."

"I'll fill you in later," Vale said.

I suspected he would tell her about the vampire. A good idea. Perhaps Saga would see it coming and be able to warn him when assassins descended on the castle.

We didn't have to suffer the uncomfortable silence hanging over our trio for too long as seconds later, a lur horn sounded. I straightened, seeking the horn blower, and found him by the door, the bronze horn to his lips as he blew again, and the king appeared.

"A lur horn?" Saga whispered. "Why?"

I understood. They were only blown during a time of war. Chills ripped down my spine as the king stomped into the courtyard, his face like ice and a white fur cloak flowing behind him.

Thankfully, my own cloak hid the tightness that took over my body as the king passed us by. For two decades, King Magnus left his father to rot in the dungeons. He had imprisoned not just rebels but innocent performers. And, of course, he didn't care at all if I perished in a vampire attack.

If he knew my ancestry, he'd welcome it.

And what would Vale do if he found out?

I swallowed down the pain that came with that question. Vale had affection for me, but if he knew that I was of the Falk line, would he hate me as much as his father hated the Falks? Besides my disgust with myself, that was yet another reason I'd been keeping my distance from the male who had been so kind to me.

The male who, despite reason, I still felt a pull toward.

Stars, I hated myself.

As it was, the king didn't even spare me a glance as he passed us. Instead, he stopped between two Clawsguards who had cleared a space for the king.

"Bring out the prisoners," he bellowed with no preamble.

My lips parted. The rebels were already being executed?

"What happened to the idea of a trial?" I whispered to Saga.

Not that the one I'd seen with the White Bear had

been much of a trial at all. Still, I was shocked that the king wasn't putting on a show for his people.

"I don't know. This is unusua—" A gasp flew from her lips.

Footfalls in the snow sounded and a quartet of soldiers led out the performers from the Royal Theater.

My heart stopped as the guards herded the actors and actresses toward the wall. At my side, Vale grew stiff.

"I spoke to some of them. They're innocent," he growled.

I swallowed, studying the performers. Most appeared terrified; trembling and shuffling and some tripping before they made it even halfway across the courtyard. They had to be freezing too, not dressed in anything remotely suitable for the outdoors.

"Father, you can't." Vale broke from the line of people.

Few appeared surprised. And Rhistel, nestled between two Clawsguards farther down the line of people, smirked. I was sure he wanted their father to blow up at Vale.

Would he?

"Stand back, Prince Vale," the King of Winter retorted as he pushed Vale back with a gale of icy air. Then, as the king had done in the throne room when he whipped Sir Qildor, ice formed on Vale's boots and crawled up his legs. Frost formed on his lips, silencing him.

"No," I whispered. No matter how disgusted I was

with myself, no matter how much distance I wanted to put between us, that pull, that reaction to be with him and help him, was still there. As instinctual as breathing.

I took a step, only to be stopped by Saga grabbing my arm and pulling me back in line. "My father will do it to you too. Vale's not hurt. Believe me, he's endured much more, and besides, you can't help him. Or them." Tears fell down her cheeks, dripping off before freezing on the ground.

Her blue eyes were stuck on Avalina, standing at the forefront of the performers, now all lined up and waiting. The actress Saga admired looked so proud, so brave and resolute.

"These fae were present and complicit in the attack on the Royal Theater." The king's voice boomed, silencing anyone who dared to so much as whisper. "They are, by extension, rebels, and I sentence them to death."

"I had no idea that the attack was to happen!" one, a brownie in a thin, filthy shirt, cried out. "Many of us weren't involved!"

"They weren't!" Avalina screamed in agreement and gestured wildly to those she stood with. "But I was. I let them in. I concocted the whole plan." She lifted her chin in defiance and glared at the king. "So if you want to kill someone, kill me. Punish me. Make an *example of me*. But spare them."

A low rumble left King Magnus's throat, sinking my stomach. Avalina had signed the death warrants of those around her.

I braced myself seconds before the king called his magic, freezing each performer to the ground. Like with Vale, ice climbed up their feet, their legs, stopping at their hips. The cold power spiked in the air, and unlike the first time he'd used it, *inside me*.

I startled and looked around. No one else seemed to have had such a reaction. I swallowed. Yet more proof that I was who the castle said, who Emilia said, who Prince Calder said.

The winter magic soared above us, a whirlwind of frost forming into icicles. The performers cried out, and everyone heard because unlike when he'd silenced his son, the king hadn't done so to the rebels. He wanted them to scream. Wanted us to hear it.

Inside, my blood pounded as what the king was about to do became clear, as the very power he wielded affected me in a way I didn't foresee. It flowed through me, awakening something inside me that begged to be let out. To save them.

But before I could so much as breathe, the king's icicles spun in the air, their tips pointing at the performers.

"I will spare no one who questions my reign," King Magnus growled before he sent the icicles soaring at the performers. "I will punish those who act against me. As I punish those who do not come forward and inform on betrayal in the kingdom."

The weapons hit their marks. Blood sprayed upon the snow. Fae screamed, both those being murdered and those in the crowd.

At my side, Saga wept, and I dimly recalled that she possessed winter magic. Did she feel what I'd felt? Or did she weep for those killed?

The king turned to the crowd, his eyes blazing with fury as he pointed to the line of dead or dying fae.

"No one will build a boat for them to sail into the afterworld, for they will not be allowed our Sigling ritual. They have showered dishonor on themselves. On their families."

Some gasped, but the king barreled on, uncaring, hard as ice.

"Their bodies will be tossed into the sea, weighed down by rocks." He spared the performers one last smug look before marching out of the courtyard, hurling one last line over his shoulder as he went. "They will not drink from bottomless horns nor dine in the starry halls of the afterworld. They will *never* find peace, not even in death. Remember that before you consider acting against the House of Aaberg."

CHAPTER 32
NEVE

I awoke to a cold bed and a heart full of dread.

I had two days until the potion that suppressed my magic ran out. Two days until anyone could ask me anything, and I'd have to answer them truthfully. Something so simple might spell my end.

What if Vale asked what was wrong? What would I say?

Since the execution in the castle courtyard, he'd been as quiet as me. Protective still. Hurt, definitely, but quiet.

Angry. Sad. A million other things.

I didn't know exactly, but who wouldn't experience a storm of emotions after seeing so many people die for doing their job? For being around others who bore the guilt.

King Magnus had declared that if anyone knew about the rebels, or even suspected, they'd better come forward to save their own skin. To do otherwise was treason. The King of Winter had sowed fear, and I didn't doubt he would see his harvest.

No one in the city would take in rebels. No one would want to help them. Would the ones they were still searching for be able to get out?

According to Vale, there were a few who had escaped. The black-haired girl, for one.

The door to the bathroom opened, and I breathed a sigh of relief when Vale exited, fully clothed. "All yours."

"Actually." The word came out garbled, and I cleared my throat. That happened when one talked little. "I want to train today. I can go alone."

Hurt crossed his face, and I cringed. I hated causing him pain, but it was all I'd been doing since I learned the truth of my ancestry. I'd ignored him, distanced myself from him, been short and far too quiet.

My stomach roiled at the wrongness of it all.

"I should go to assess you. Few are better," he said, and when I didn't argue the point, he added, "But unless I have advice for you, I'll keep to myself."

His question as to *why* I was keeping him at arm's length hung in the air, plain in his beautiful brown eyes.

Desperate to break the connection between us, I looked at the floor and leapt from the bed. There was no use in arguing that he should be there. As the most accomplished warrior in the kingdom, Vale was also an ideal instructor and though I sometimes felt like it might be better to let the vampires take me, I wasn't ready to give up yet.

Getting away, running south, and trying to forget what had happened, I could do that. I could even try to forget Vale.

But die?

I might hate myself for what I'd done and how much I was hurting Vale, but when it came down to it, I wanted to live.

"I have to put on pants and a shirt, and I'll be ready."

"Wear fighting leathers today," Vale replied, his tone level.

I didn't ask why, only set to put on the appropriate clothing for what I hoped would be hours of physical exertion.

Within minutes, a Clawsguard was following us through the castle. No one spoke on the way, and though the silence between us was becoming more common, it still made my heart ache.

Thankfully, when we arrived in the training room, others were present. Sayyida fought with Filip while Sian assessed their style and abilities. Luccan, Thantrel, and Arie were present too, warming up, and in Arie's case, stretching on the ground.

"Father said we needed to train more," Luccan said as we neared the crew. "What with the rebel attacks and all. And he told Arie that he had to come too. No excuses, not that Arie complied with that command."

The middle Riis brother frowned at the jab, but I

nodded, understanding the deeper meaning. Vale had told Lord Riis that the king suspected the Lord of Tongues might be in possession of the Ice Scepter. Lord Riis probably wished for his sons to train to defend themselves against the king and his soldiers—as much as against the rebels.

"It can't hurt." Vale eyed me sidelong before catching himself and looking away.

My cheeks burned. Before, I'd have basked in his attention, wanted it. Craved it, even. But now, it reminded me of our shame, a shame only I knew about.

"Want to spar with me, Princess Neve?" Thantrel swaggered closer, his emerald eyes gleaming with playful confidence and those fiery wings rustling.

"No," Vale answered for me. "She's not there yet. She'll fight with Filip or Sayyida." He paused for a heartbeat. "And today she's using live steel."

My spine straightened. Save for that one time I'd sparred with him using live steel, Vale had insisted I continue to practice with wooden swords. Everyone I'd trained with had done the same. It was a precaution. One that would be removed when he thought I had enough control over a weapon.

"Thank you," I murmured.

"You've already done so. At the theater." Vale didn't look at me as he spoke. "And I know you're strong enough to hold and wield steel now. So it's time to push your abilities further. Today you'll fight with a sword and two stakes."

Neither of us knew when a vampire would attack,

but one day, they would come. When that day arrived decapitation, a stake to the heart, and infernos were the only ways to kill the bloodsuckers.

If only I were a fire fae. Anything other than what I am.

Any excitement about my magic appearing was gone. If Prince Calder was correct and winter magic came out of me and I was powerful, King Magnus would feel it.

Bleeding skies. I had to get the Liar's Salvation in my hands, not to lie, but to keep my magic at bay.

"Filip!" Vale called out.

"Wait your turn!" Sayyida yelled from where the pair had taken their sparring into the air. "I almost have him!"

She proved her point mere seconds later, slashing her sword against Filip's chain-mail-protected belly and cheering. "Point for me!"

For the first time in over a day, my lips broke into a smile. It felt so foreign on my face, almost painful, but the way the pair landed and Sayyida performed a victory dance pried me out of my misery.

"Filip, over here." Vale gestured for the youngling to join us.

The squire ran up, and I wasted no time assessing him. Today, he appeared coordinated, which told me he wasn't going through a magical growth spurt at the moment.

"My prince." Filip bowed when he reached us.

"*My prince,*" Thantrel mimicked and bowed, arms

wide in exaggeration. "Simpering stars, Filip, are you for real?"

Vale's lips twitched, but Filip insisted on always treating Vale in this manner, even if Vale wouldn't have minded a more casual relationship.

"Just because you have no manners, doesn't mean others should stoop to your level," Filip sniped at Thantrel.

"So the lad does have teeth!" Thantrel barked out merrily. "There's hope for you yet, young Balik!"

"Enough taunting him," Vale interjected and set his gaze on Filip. "I want you to spar with my wife today. With dulled steel so she can better get used to the weight of real swords. Do not hold back."

My wife. I swallowed and forced myself not to show the way my stomach roiled. Once a protection, now it made me think of our taboo night together.

"Very well." Filip turned to me, patting at the woven metal chain mail he wore. He and Sayyida had been fighting with steel rather than wood, so they'd needed the protection. "There are extras by the weapons."

I nodded. "I'll be right back with those."

"And holster two stakes," Vale added. "If anything so you can get used to their presence and weight at your sides."

"I know."

"I'll be off to the side. Out of the way."

I didn't miss the Riis brothers exchanging looks of

surprise. Usually, Vale stood close by, and I'd have wanted him to be there.

I pushed all that aside as I retrieved weapons and additional protection from storage. Moments later, Filip and I were sparring, and I relished the movement. It allowed me to forget about everything else.

Forget who I was, the danger I was in, and about the person I cared for. The person I was distancing myself from. The person I was hurting.

While I sparred, none of that occupied my mind. Not if I wanted to grow stronger and have a chance at living.

Filip leapt and his honey-gold wings caught air as he soared over me.

I fell into a crouch, out of the reach of his blade.

"Thought I'd be able to get you out fast. Sayyida taught me that one today."

"You'll have to try harder," I shot back.

And he did.

The next five minutes were a whirlwind of attacks, me on Filip, the squire on me, rinse and repeat. We both used our wings, and each time I did so, I breathed easier. Thanks to training, my wings grew strong. So strong that I no longer doubted their capabilities.

Maybe I can fly away from vampires for the rest of my life. I leapt back as Filip came at me again, blade arching and missing.

"Come on, Neve!" Sayyida yelled.

I chanced a glance to the side. The others had

stopped practicing to watch. Why were we the center of attention?

"Head in the fight!" Vale boomed.

I whirled as Filip attacked again. That had been close.

Attack. Parry. Attack. Parry. We continued, falling into a rhythm and both breathing hard as sweat dripped down our faces.

"Imagine a vamp!" Sian shouted.

Would that work? I had no idea, but I was willing to try anything, do anything, to win this sparring match. To gain some real confidence against a person trained to fight.

In my mind's eye, sweet Filip became the now deceased Prince Gervais. My heart rate ratcheted higher.

Well, that was something I could work with. I needed to hone my fear.

So I forced myself to remember the prince's cruel laugh. The sharp pain when his fangs punctured my neck. How scared I'd been when he drank from me, and my blood slid down his throat.

"No!" I rushed Filip.

He sidestepped me, but now fear fueled me in addition to my desire to win, and I spun, slashing with my sword.

His blade caught mine, and I saw the brief widening of his eyes before he pushed me back. I stumbled and Filip was on me again. *No.* Prince Gervais was on me, and I envisioned Anna there too. Right behind me. I was protecting her again.

I found my footing and leapt over my adversary. He followed me, pivoting, reaching long with his sword, his weight all on his toes in anticipation of an easy strike. A win.

That was when I pulled a fast one, fluttering my wings to reverse my direction. Falling back the way I'd come; I attacked and swiped Filip clean across the back.

"You got him, Neve!" Sayyida cackled. "You're down, little Balik!"

But he didn't stop. Instead, Filip caught his balance and turned back to me.

Not fast enough, though. Not this time.

My sword swiped Filip in the side, clanging his chain mail. The young Balik stared down at where I'd struck him, as if in disbelief.

"Guts are spilling, brother," Sian chortled. "You're done."

I lowered my sword. I'd done it. Vale had told him not to take it easy on me. I'd beaten him with no help, no hindrance from a magical growth spurt on his part.

Maybe I'd be able to protect myself.

I had to keep practicing. To do better. Grow. Be better.

I had to be able to defend myself against someone like Vale. At that, my elation dimmed. I hated that if Vale learned who I was, everything could very well change. He might see me as an enemy rather than a person worthy of his help. Of him.

Filip was still gaping down at where I'd swiped his side. My eyebrows knitted together and worry for the squire seeped in.

"Did it hurt?" I asked. The chain mail should have kept him protected.

"No." Filip lifted his gaze to meet mine. "Good job. I have to say, I didn't expect that, Princess Neve."

"By that, you mean for me to win?"

His cheeks took on a pink hue. "Yes."

"Well, I have to say, I didn't either."

Filip's face loosened and his honey-colored eyes warmed. "Another round?"

"Another round."

"I'm done," I proclaimed, wiping my drenched brow. I'd practiced for five hours and reached my limit.

"You did well today," Vale said, and I caught his nod and smile before I looked away. When he spoke next, his voice was more restrained. "But you've been at it for a while. Rest would be good."

Rest. That meant returning to his suite. Or perhaps I could seek Saga?

Sayyida was gone already, as were Sian and Arie Riis.

"Yes," I said. "I think I'll go speak with Saga. We can have a ladies' day."

Vale didn't reply right away. "If you wish. I can escort you to my sister's chambers—"

"I think I'll take a Clawsguard." I motioned to the door where two stood. "You'll have one go with me anyway, right?" I risked looking at him, risked feeling that heartbreak and ill feeling all over again.

Stars, would it ever end? Or would I punish myself for something neither of us had known for the rest of my life?

"I will," Vale agreed, reluctant lines forming on his handsome face. "Take Sir Arvid. He's the stronger of the two."

"Thank you." I managed a small smile. "I'll see you later." I took three steps before Vale stopped me.

"Neve?"

I swallowed, turned.

"Remember what I saw. Be careful. The castle is the most protected building in the city, but there are always weaknesses to exploit."

"I will," I assured him, knowing that it was killing him to let me out of his sight, but equally knowing that I needed this time apart. "And I'll be back tonight."

He nodded. The look of rejection on his face threatened to cut me in half, so I turned away. What could I tell him that would explain why I'd become an ice queen?

And I could not tell him the truth.

Bleeding skies, I needed that potion.

Vale had informed me that Duran said it would be a day late. It was the best he could do, and that terrified me. I had to hope that, when my magic appeared, it was weak. I was weak. So weak that King Magnus wouldn't sense it.

And that over the course of a day, Vale wouldn't ask too many questions.

I returned my chain mail, sword, and stakes to the storage area and pulled my hair back so that it no longer stuck to my neck. As ready as I would get, I exited the storage area to find Vale talking to Filip. They seemed engrossed, which relieved me, and I made for the door.

"I'm going to see Saga," I said to Sir Arvid, one of the Clawsguards waiting for us. He looked behind me at the prince. "Alone."

His eyebrows shot up. "Shall I take you by your suite first to wash?"

Point taken. I was sweaty and stinky, but Saga would have to deal with that. I needed some space from Vale.

"No, show me to the princess's chambers."

Sir Arvid led the way. Though I'd been to Saga's rooms before, I'd never come from the training facilities and Frostveil Castle was vast. I was sure there were parts of it I'd never seen before.

Like the Crown Drassil on site. And the library.

I paused at that last thought. Perhaps I could make a stop at the library on my way to Saga's rooms. I had yet to learn if the brooch from Queen Revna's room—*my mother's* room—was a phoenix opal.

"Sir Arvid, before we go to Saga's suite, can you take me to the Royal Library? I want to research something."

"I suppose so," the Clawsguard said. "It's a quick detour."

"Perfect. The princess isn't expecting me, anyway."

He changed course, and I allowed myself to be led through the palace. On the way, we passed many fae, some servants, some courtiers. The latter stared at me, though less than they had that day in the solarium. The novelty of my marriage to Vale was somewhat wearing off.

Sir Arvid took a turn, and we found ourselves in an empty hallway. I looked around.

"Quiet in here, isn't it?"

"The library isn't a popular destination," the Clawsguard replied.

"That's a shame."

"If you say so."

I assumed the soldier didn't read much.

The hallway ended in a set of double doors made of pine. Upon their face, a true artist had carved a white raven and dusted it with some sort of stone that glittered in the light coming in through the window. In this kingdom, the white raven was a symbol of one of the dead gods' messengers and wisdom. Sir Arvid opened one door for me, and I gasped as I entered the Royal Library.

I would not have known from the outside, but the library had been built in one of the castle's towers. The circular room spun up at least seven stories, and from the bottom, a viewer could gaze up at all of them.

I inhaled, savoring the scents: parchment, ink, and

something unnamable. The weight that had been pressing down on my heart lightened a touch. There were so many books. Tomorrow I'd convince Vale to let me spend the day here. I'd bring a dozen Clawsguards with me if it made him happy.

"May I help you, Princess Neve?" a voice asked.

I twisted to find a female fae. She was short, like a dwarf, but without the bulbous and large facial features of their kind. My eyebrows pinched together until I placed her fae race.

A leprechaun. I'd never seen one before. From what I'd learned, they almost exclusively worked in coinaries and lived around their places of employment. I'd had no reason to go to a coinary.

"Good afternoon," I said. "I'm looking for a visual reference on rare gems. A phoenix opal, if you have it."

She nodded. "Come with me."

The bottom level of the library was chock-full of shelves and books. The librarian wound through them until we reached a shelf across the room. She stopped and peered up at the books.

"This section is on rare gems. I believe this book"— she stood on tiptoe to pull a green one down from the fourth shelf from the bottom, almost out of her reach— "will have the information you're looking for. If it doesn't, or it's not to your liking, I'll help you find another."

"Thank you," I replied, taking the book.

"Can I do anything else for you, Princess Neve?"

"That'll be all."

She nodded and gestured through the stacks. "There's a table by the windows over there. Three stacks over. Sit, if you wish." Having said what she needed to say, she left.

I did wish to sit, so I went to the table, and Sir Arvid followed, a bored expression on his face. Settling in, I sighed as the wooden chair creaked beneath me.

The first library such as this one that I'd ever had access to was Roar's. And while House Lisika's library was nice, the Royal Library put it to shame.

I opened the book and found that the gems and stones featured were alphabetical. Smiling, I went to the proper section and found an image of a phoenix opal.

It looked like the one in the brooch. I leaned back, conflicted. Lord Riis had said that phoenix opals were beyond valuable. Originally, I'd wanted the brooch because it was pretty, though a part of me wondered if it would be a good piece to use as currency.

Now, though, I knew it was my mother's.

Another moral issue for another day. I shut the book and stood.

"Sir Arvid, we can—" I turned and found that someone else stood in Sir Arvid's place.

CHAPTER 33
NEVE

"Prince Rhistel." I frowned at the heir.

What was he doing here? And why hadn't my guard announced him to me? Where *was* my Clawsguard? I peered around the heir, trying to find Sir Arvid.

"Have I lost your interest already?" Rhistel smirked. His face was so like Vale's and yet, so not at the same time. Whereas Vale's face radiated warmth and strength, Rhistel's was shrouded in mystery and cunning.

Annoyed, I met his gaze, wondering what to say to someone I didn't want to be around but couldn't ignore.

"I didn't hear you approach," I settled on.

The heir smirked. "What are you doing in the library?"

Ah, yes, Rhistel was touted far and wide as the scholar prince. Knowing him, he thought this library was his and his alone. Pompous arse.

"Looking up precious gems. I'm almost done."

"Eyeing the crown jewels, are you?"

I scoffed. I already possessed one of the rarest and most expensive jewels and it didn't belong to his family. "Merely curious."

"As am I." Rhistel came closer, a dangerous gleam sparking in his eyes.

I took a corresponding step back. "I was leaving." I spun, prepared to walk away, when Rhistel grabbed my arm and yanked me back around.

"I'm afraid you're not." His eyes burned into mine. "I have to understand what Roar and Vale see in you— besides the obvious, of course. Beauty is tempting, but to ensnare two of the most powerful males in the kingdom, there has to be more to you than a pretty face and a pleasing figure."

As he spoke, his hand trailed downward and grabbed mine. I hissed and realized that where he touched me, we were skin to skin.

Rhistel wasn't wearing gloves.

I'd only seen him remove them once. That day in the solarium. The day Vale had gone berserk. My heart rate spiking, I tried to pull away, but suddenly, the room dimmed and my mind clouded.

Perhaps before I delve into your simple mind, I'll see for myself if you truly are merely a tempting morsel. Rhistel's voice wound through my head. *Kiss me. And make it good.*

A small part of me recoiled, but I lifted onto my toes all the same, mouth parting for the prince in front of me.

Stop, Rhistel said, though his mouth did not move.

Hovering on tiptoes, I froze.

I blinked and tried to force my feet to the ground, tried to put distance between Rhistel and me, but to no avail. Though a part of me wanted to scream at the thought of kissing him, I was powerless to stop it. What in the stars was happening?

A slow grin bloomed on Rhistel's face. *I have to say, I like you better like this, Neve. Docile. Silent. I—*

Pain ripped through my body, and the lights in the library brightened, blinding me. I gasped as all my faculties engaged, and I found myself still on my tiptoes and Prince Rhistel laid out on the floor.

"Princess Neve." A voice drew my gaze up from Rhistel. Filip stood before me, his eyes wide with horror. "Are you harmed?"

"What? No, but I-I'm not sure what happened." I looked around. "Or where Sir Arvid went."

"He left. Prince Rhistel spoke to him and the Clawsguard left the library and then the prince approached you and you—you almost kissed him, Princess Neve."

I shook my head. "I would never do that. Not willingly."

"I know why you did." Filip looked down at Rhistel, his toe pushing at the prince's ungloved hand warily. "But we have to leave before he wakes. I snuck up on the prince from behind so he didn't see me, but if he knows I was the one who hit him over the head, they might execute me."

"Fast then," I said, wanting answers but also not wishing to put this youngling in danger.

We rushed through the stacks. Luckily, the leprechaun librarian was nowhere in sight. We didn't see her when we passed through the large pine doors, nor Sir Arvid, nor the Clawsguard who should have been following Rhistel. I kept my mouth shut until Filip led me into a hallway with a few people.

Making sure those wandering the halls weren't close enough to hear but *were* close enough to be witnesses should Rhistel come looking for us, I turned to Vale's squire and kept my voice low. "Did Vale tell you to watch me?"

"He did." Filip swallowed. "I was watching from the third floor."

I nodded, trying to piece things together. The memory of Rhistel's voice in my head was strong. He'd wanted to search my mind—a power Queen Inga had. Though Vale had never told me Rhistel shared it.

He would have been able to because, for the first time in my hurry to leave the suite that morning, I'd forgotten to take the Mind Rönd potion.

But Rhistel hadn't only said he wanted to read my mind: he'd told me to kiss him.

And I would have. I would have kissed him. He forced me somehow.

I gasped, putting the pieces together.

"Filip, I think Rhist—"

"*Don't* say it here," the youngling cut me off, terror

in his voice. "Wait until we ask Prince Vale. Where no one can overhear."

I nodded, anxiety mounting, and by the time we made it to Vale's suite, I was dying for answers. The Clawsguard at the door let me in. Filip hung back, but I waved for him to follow.

"Vale? Are you in here?" I called out.

He appeared at the end of the short corridor that funneled into his bedchambers, a smile on his face.

He was happy that I was calling out for him. I winced at the realization but didn't have time to feel too bad. Not with my questions burning their way up my throat.

"We need to talk," I said. "About your brother and the magic he's been hiding."

All the blood left Vale's face. "What do you mean? What happened? Didn't you visit Saga?"

"I asked Sir Arvid to take me to the library first. Rhistel was there. He touched me without his gloves on." I arched an eyebrow.

His mouth opened, then closed before opening once more. He had no defense. He knew that I knew.

"Filip," Vale started, "perhaps you should—"

"No. He deserves the truth too. If it wasn't for him, your brother would have delved through my head." I swallowed. "And he tried to make me kiss him."

Maybe, had I done so, he would have demanded more. Rhistel had threatened as much in the past.

Vale's expression hardened to steel. "You swear it?"

Filip's eyebrows pulled together. Fae couldn't lie,

and he didn't know that I possessed that ability. At least for two more days.

"I do," I said.

Vale inhaled deeply and closed his eyes. His fists were tight balls of fury, and when he opened his eyes again, a warrior stared at us.

"I must swear you both to secrecy."

I arched an eyebrow. "We deserve an explanation."

Everyone did. If what I believed about Rhistel was true, he was incredibly dangerous.

"You do, but I must insist," Vale said. "I've been sworn to secrecy too, if that makes a difference."

Then I understood. Vale valued honor above almost everything else. He might not get along with his brother, might hate him at times—as he appeared to now—but he'd made a promise. He would have kept it to his dying day, but we'd cornered him. Or, more accurately, his brother had been reckless and exposed himself.

No matter how you spun the coin, the truth was about to come out.

"I swear," I said.

"Me too," Filip added.

Vale gestured to the settee. "Sit."

He looked like he needed to take a seat more than we did, but Filip and I obliged while Vale created a thick barrier of air in front of his door. If the Clawsguard was listening, he would no longer be able to hear.

When Vale approached, I couldn't hold it in any longer. "He's a whisperer, isn't he?"

Vale winced, and his hand scrubbed over the back of his neck. "Yes."

"Aren't they supposed to be killed when they're young?"

Filip had gone pale and didn't seem to have a voice. That was fine. I would ask the questions for both of us.

"They are," Vale agreed. "But my brother is the heir to the kingdom, and this power didn't develop until Rhistel was nineteen turns—almost twenty. That's very late."

"No one noticed?" I pressed.

Vale looked away. "I was the first he used his whispering powers on."

Oh. I sensed a story there and not a good one. But before I could decide whether I wanted to hear it, Vale continued.

"After that, Father told Rhistel to wear the gloves. But before that, we allowed the rumor to spread that it was from Rhistel's winter magic. It only took one time of him pushing himself and nearly freezing someone to death for others to believe it."

"You staged that?"

"We had no other choice."

"But"—Filip sat up—"can't whisperers lie?"

"What?!" I sat up straighter. Saga hadn't mentioned that part.

"They can," Vale answered, shooting me a look. "It's the only fae power known to allow us to lie."

"Another reason they are not allowed to live," Filip added.

Yes, I understood The Liar's Salvation potion was illegal, though even if it wasn't, most wouldn't use it anyway as it nullified magic. That made fae weaker, and in this world, power was everything.

"That's how they can make up stories," I whispered.

"Which is what happened when Father helped Rhistel stage the event that led others to think the heir possessed winter magic that was so strong he needed to wear ice spider silk gloves. The rumor sprouted from my brother's own lips."

My teeth dug into my bottom lip. "What do the gloves do?"

"They're ice spider silk," Vale repeated, as if that explained anything.

"And?"

"The silk negates any use of magic," Filip said, and I remembered he'd mentioned that before and finally understood. The silk kept the heir's power restrained.

"The ice spiders are in the Ice Tooth Mountains," Filip continued as if he couldn't help himself. "My people hunt them because otherwise they will hunt us, but the silk, if one can find a nest, is priceless."

"Rhistel still hasn't completely mastered his magic, so he's supposed to wear them everywhere," Vale said. "I'll kill him for removing them. For doing that to you."

I did my best to ignore how the protective comment made my heart stutter. Vale and I couldn't happen, no matter how much my body and heart wanted it.

"Ice spiders are the Riis family animal," I murmured.

Vale nodded. "There's a reason Lord Riis took that animal as his own. He has the power to negate others' magics. Just like the ice spider."

"Oh," I breathed. That would be powerful indeed.

"How often has the heir used his magic?" Filip asked hesitantly.

I could tell that he hated having this conversation. The squire probably considered it disrespectful to Vale. Filip was so loyal that sometimes it made my heart ache.

"Not for many turns." Vale cleared his throat. "At first, he used it when he could get away with it. That's one of the reasons we grew apart. I couldn't abide by his choices. But once"—he let out a pained breath— "Father caught him and had Sir Lars beat him. It was the only time Father has ever done so to any of us."

Rhistel was a whisperer and whisperers were like vampires in the sense that they read minds and controlled minds. I shuddered with revulsion. No one should ever be able to do that.

"Unless you two have more questions, I need to go speak with my brother," Vale said when Filip and I fell silent. "Alone."

"No," I retorted firmly. "Filip knocked him over the head to get me out of there. Rhistel didn't see him coming, and no one saw us leave the library. But if you go looking for revenge, he'll ask questions. That puts Filip at great risk."

Filip squirmed. To save me, he'd acted on impulse. But he'd only been there in the first place because of Vale's orders. He would not be harmed for that.

"It might kill you to do so, Vale, but you have to pretend like this never happened. Let Rhistel wonder what happened too. How I got away."

Vale's eyes darkened.

"*You must*," I insisted. "No one in this room needs more danger aimed at them."

A muscle fluttered in Vale's jaw as he nodded. "Fine. I'll do nothing, but if he tries to control you again, I can't promise I'll stay quiet a second time."

CHAPTER 34
NEVE

For the fifth time, I reread the opening line of the chapter before sighing, closing the book, and setting it in my lap.

When I was a slave, reading was always my escape; the only thing I did for myself that I loved. But since I'd come to the Winter Court, reading hadn't been able to occupy my mind.

Next to me, Vale shifted, deep in slumber. Though I still found it uncomfortable being next to him, asking to sleep in another room would be unwise. Gossip about the newlyweds' bedroom arrangements would spread around the court like wildfire. Additionally, not sleeping in the suite would leave me less protected.

Thankfully, Vale was a prince of honor, and since I'd distanced myself, he hadn't tried to initiate anything. When it was time to sleep, he merely slipped into the bed, his back to me, and fell asleep.

A murmur interrupted my inner turmoil, and a

scowl formed on Vale's handsome face. I reached for him, stopping right before my hand landed on his head.

My instinct was to soothe him, to stroke his long black hair and whisper that it would all be fine.

A lie, but sometimes we did that for those we cared for.

My heart clenched. How could the Fates be so cruel? They'd twisted me together with Vale, ensured our paths intertwined, and bound us with an attraction unlike any I'd felt with another. Only after we'd allowed ourselves to act on that attraction and be vulnerable with one another, had they revealed the truth.

Worse, I couldn't tell Vale why I'd backed off. Why I'd gone from seducing him to a fae made of ice.

I hated myself. I almost wished I'd never learned the truth because at least while I was still with him, I could be happy.

Twisting, I gazed upon him. Would he be able to stay silent when he next saw Rhistel? Too much was on the line for Vale not to. Especially if Rhistel used his powers on his brother and saw that Filip and I knew of his magic.

Would Rhistel do such a thing? I wasn't sure exactly what happened when Rhistel first tested his magic on Vale all those turns ago. What had he made Vale do? Say? See?

My stomach twisted. I needed to distract myself once more. I lifted the book again, my fingers caressing the worn edges, only to catch on where the binding gaped.

I sucked in a breath, my gaze catching on the gap. This was Brogan Lisika's book and with everything that had been happening, I'd forgotten that I found one of Brogan's notes to Roar.

Perhaps some fae would have hesitated at reading the private note from brother to brother. I was not among them. Roar gave me the book. Roar betrayed me. I no longer held any responsibility or affection toward him.

At the very least, getting it out of where Brogan hid it so well would keep me occupied.

I worked the edge of the paper glued to the binding. As it was an older book and already partially gaped open when I tossed the book across the room in anger, that part was easy. Bit by bit, the paper lifted.

When enough of the paper separated from the binding for me to peek inside and find a small, folded note, I turned the book upside down and shook the note out. It dropped onto my lap. Folded up, the creases were white, the missive clean. Two decades old, Brogan's hiding spot kept it free of dirt.

Mindful of the note's age, I opened it with careful fingers, and, despite everything that was weighing me down, I smiled.

Brogan had been around ten turns when he died, so this note was from a child, and it showed. The handwriting was trying so hard to be fluid and neat but missed the mark. I knew almost nothing of Roar's brother, but by glancing at the page, I recognized a lord in training.

Setting the book on the side table, I gave the note my full attention.

Little brother,
I hope that when you finally find this, you're feeling better because I want to visit the mines when I get back. Mother won't let you go if you're still ill, though, so do hurry and get well.
I'm already dreading the journey. Mother and Father and me in a sleigh for weeks! My ears will bleed with Father's jokes. Actually, now I wonder, did you get sick on purpose?
Perhaps I should sneak into your room and join you.

I shook my head and held in a laugh. Yes, a youngling wrote this. One on the cusp of entering his preteens when fae, much like humans, became far more moody, dramatic, and unreasonable. At least that was what Yvette told me when I'd been around the same age.

As much as I am tempted, you know I won't. Mother would be furious. Besides, healers have been sleeping at your bedside day and night. They're as obsessed with you as they are with that baby. Did you know that Father says that I'm to marry a Balik female and you get the baby! Apparently, she is from an important family, but it does make me laugh. Imagine, you wedding a baby! Then again, you are quite short. I think that makes you a perfect match!
Too bad she has that hideous scar by her eye. Mother doesn't think it will go away. She's too young, she says.

House Balik has a mage in their castle. I'll ask about baby scars when I'm there. You'll owe me if I can save your baby wife from being scarred for life!

I sat up straighter, my hand drifting to the crescent scar over my right temple as what Emilia had said came rushing back. When I'd escaped from the castle as a babe, my parents wanted me to go west and sent my sister to the east.

Guldtown was about as far west as one could go in Winter's Realm.

I bore a scar by my eye, and yes, I'd been born into an important family. Despite me being but two turns when the rebellion ended, the late Lord Lisika would have met the royal children. Had he recognized me? Or perhaps the maid tasked with protecting me had told them?

Emilia had said that my family tried to send me to a noble house that remained loyal to the crown. There, I'd have been safe. That couldn't have been House Lisika. In the White Bear's Rebellion, the house of the snow leopard fought beside Magnus Aaberg.

I swallowed. Those answers may never come, but another epiphany hit, washing them from my mind.

The day Frode threw me at Roar's feet, he'd fixated on my eyes and my scar. He'd said that all fae acquired scars as they aged, and if we were worthy, they told a story.

My skin crawled. Did Roar recognize the scar? Had he put two and two together that I was the baby who had, somehow, ended up in his family's castle? His father told Brogan that I was from an important house.

On the day we'd met, Roar had been quick to take me in, to want to help a bedraggled female. At the time, he'd given a good enough reason for me to see the value in partnering with me. Now I wondered how likely it was that he suspected who I was.

Roar had been very insistent in his pursuit of me. Had he known, or at least strongly suspected, that I was a missing princess?

At that, I paused. *Missing* . . .

I'd been told that the Falk line went extinct. Not that the princesses were *missing*.

And yet, Prince Calder rotted in the dungeons . . .

A slow, horrible idea dawned on me. Had my family used decoys to trick the White Bear's Rebellion into thinking they'd killed off me and my sister? My guts twisted.

Stars, the idea was too awful to imagine. A part of me wished to disappear into the hidden palace right then, to find the human and ask, but at the late hour, she probably wasn't there. Plus, there was more to the note.

One part of the trip I am looking forward to, though, is playing with the Scepter. Father says we can't talk about it, but that when it's the three of us in the sleigh, I can touch it. Imagine, Roar! What if I cause a snowstorm?

I sucked in a breath. A scepter that could cause a

snowstorm. If Brogan Lisika wasn't bragging about playing with the Ice Scepter, then I was a troll.

I continued on, but the rest of the letter proved fruitless, just brotherly teasing and musings about whether Brogan's potential wife would be more attractive than the scarred baby.

Once I reached the end of the page, I exhaled. This note, the one correspondence that Roar never found, told two of House Lisika's secrets. One: that I, a Falk princess, had likely been taken there at some point, and two: that many turns ago, the Lisikas possessed the Ice Scepter.

They'd lost me. Despite my value as an eventual bride to one of their sons and a bargaining chip, somehow I'd ended up a slave in the Vampire Kingdom.

That begged the question. Had they also lost the Ice Scepter?

Only one way to know.

Confronting Roar after I left Avaldenn had been high on my list of things I needed to do. Now? A trip to the west was inevitable because Warden Roar Lisika owed me, and the realm, answers.

CHAPTER 35
VALE

I awoke to find Neve staring down at me.

"Good morning." I breathed in her smoked vanilla scent, surprised that she was looking at me at all. I wasn't sure what was going on with her, or between us, but as much as I wanted answers, I didn't feel it was my place to pry.

Maybe we'd rushed into a physical relationship. Perhaps she still had things to work through from her past. Or she worried about us growing closer and her leaving.

"I have something to show you," she said, her voice raspy. Dark smudges ringed her eyes.

"Are you ill?" I sat up.

"No"—she cleared her throat—"but I didn't sleep. You'll see why." She held out a piece of paper. "Read it."

I took the paper. It felt worn beneath my fingers and

as I read, my eyebrows pinched together. "Who is this from? And to?"

"To Roar. You'll see that near the end, from his older brother, Brogan." Neve patted the book on the nightstand. "It was in the binding."

"What?"

"Roar told me they often hid notes for the other to find. This was Brogan's favorite book, and he hid what appears to be his last note to Roar inside it." She pulled her knees up to her chest. "Read the note, Vale."

I wiped the sleep from my eyes and did as she asked, skimming over the childish taunting of male younglings. When we were younger, Rhistel and I had also teased one another about the females Mother had often tried to push on us. I was about to ask Neve why I was bothering with the letter, when my gaze trailed downward and caught on the word scepter.

I sucked in a breath, moved up the page, and read. When I was done, I looked at Neve. "You think the Lisikas have the Ice Scepter."

"Or they *had* it."

For a moment, I sensed she wanted to say more, but when she turned back to me, her violet eyes were serious.

"Vale, what's Roar's magic?"

"He's a shapeshifter."

Neve's lips parted. "I'd not expected that. Into what animal?"

"Potentially any, though I've heard him say that he favors the animal of his house, the snow leopard. Most shapeshifters shift into only a few animal forms, so he might have mastered a few more by now."

"Perhaps a snake," Neve muttered.

I laughed. "I'm shocked that wasn't his first shift."

For a moment, amusement gleamed in her eyes, but then she caught herself and looked away. "But his family married into the Falk line at least once. Tore Lisika was Sassa Falk's king consort. Roar helped the Drassil tree in Traliska. So he has winter magic too, right?"

"He does. Having at least a small bit of winter magic is possible for anyone in the great houses of Winter's Realm," I conceded. "They've all married into each other at one point. Usually more than once, so there's a little of Falk blood in all of us. I have seen Roar wield winter magic before, though his magic isn't strong."

Neve studied me for a long moment. "Right, so he does have the power to use the Scepter, if he has it, but I really don't think he does. I mean, his own wings were affected by the blight, and don't people say that's related to the Scepter's disappearance? Like its disappearance caused a flux in the magic of the kingdom?"

"That's what some whisper," I agreed, "though no one can prove it. My question is, how in the world could his family lose such an item?" I shook my head. "I can't see *that* happening."

"Well, I don't know!" Neve threw her hands up. "People lose precious things all the time."

I sensed a subtext there. "Why didn't you sleep?"

She huffed out a breath. "Just worried."

"About Rhistel?"

"Yes."

She was lying. I wasn't sure how I could tell, but I got the distinct sense that my brother was not her primary concern. Though, now that I was reminded of what he'd done, my blood began to boil. Last night, I'd dreamed about confronting him, about teaching him a lesson.

"I'm going to get ready to train." Neve shifted and stood. Her nightgown had been bunched up and fell around her shapely legs. Legs with thick thighs and muscular calves wrapped in a softness that I longed to touch again.

My cock began to harden, ready as it ever was where she was concerned. Thankfully, Neve had already turned and left. The bathroom door shut behind her, and our moment of revelation and connection was over.

She doesn't want me here.

The message rang home every time Neve turned her back on me during training. Each time, it hurt a bit more.

Sometimes I caught glimpses of the Neve I'd been getting to know, the night before we'd explored one another's bodies. But it was always gone in a flash, like a shooting star disappearing into the night sky.

"What's wrong with you two?" Luccan came up beside me. "You seem off."

"I'm not sure," I admitted.

"You didn't say something stupid?"

"Likely I did," I replied with a chuckle. "But I don't know what."

"Hmm, well, she's having trouble today." Luccan met my gaze. "I think you're distracting her. That and she looks like she didn't sleep. Do us all a favor and, if you want your wife to be able to fight off vampires, go take a walk? A run? Whatever, just get out of here. I wish to teach her how to throw axes today, so she needs to concentrate."

"That would be irresponsible," I retorted.

My friend gestured to the sparring room floor. "We're in the castle, the most protected building in all of Winter's Realm. But even if no other soldiers roamed the yard or halls, you really think that Than, Sian, Filip, and I are going to let anyone touch her? Come on, Vale."

I exhaled. I trusted Luccan and Sian wholeheartedly. Filip and Thantrel, while I wasn't as close to them, were devoted to me too. My friends wouldn't allow harm to come to my wife, and with all the tension between us, I should have welcomed the time to myself.

But I didn't. No matter how chilly things had been, I still hoped that whatever Neve was going through would thaw. That soon we'd be able to be normal together again.

That our relationship might even deepen.

I didn't dare bring that up to her, though. Not in her current state. I only wished she would tell me what troubled her. I suspected it was far more than the threat of vampires arriving in the city.

"Fine," I agreed grudgingly. "I'll take a walk."

"Good call." Luccan punched me in the shoulder. "That way we can show Neve all the slick fighting moves Sian and I have."

I arched an eyebrow. "What moves?"

"Tricks that we keep a secret from you," Luccan replied. "Otherwise, you might claim them for your own."

I chuckled dryly. "As if I need them. I'll wipe the floor with you two."

Luccan pushed me to the door. "Now go. I'll tell your princess that you'll be back later."

I nodded, and, throwing a glance over my shoulder only to find that Neve's back was to me, left the training facilities. At the door, I pointed to my Clawsguard.

"Stay with my wife. If someone wishes to speak with her and you don't recognize them, get Sian Balik to stand with her."

"Very well, my prince," the guard replied.

I went on my way, still conflicted over leaving Neve. In truth, she was in good hands, but that didn't change the fact that I had a duty to her. Not that I could realistically be with her all the time, anyway.

Father was still searching for rebels, and it was only a matter of time before he sent me into the city again. More than anything, I didn't want to go. The king's massacre of those actors haunted me, and, rebels or not, I didn't wish for anyone else to suffer that fate. If only I'd called my cabal together faster, then those fae might still be alive.

A sigh left me as I climbed the steps, into a busier part of the palace. Fae watched me. Some even waved. Apparently, the stigma I'd brought upon myself by marrying Neve without Father's blessing was wearing off.

When do I tell Father?

The moment Neve had given me Brogan's note, and I'd read about House Lisika's treachery, I should have gone to the king. I should have told him everything. But something had stopped me. At first, I'd only been disappointed that Neve and I still seemed at odds. Now, though . . . I couldn't help but think there was something in the letter itself that had stopped me, even if just subconsciously.

Perhaps I needed to return to my suite and read it again.

Deciding to do exactly that, I pivoted from wandering to striding for my chambers. As I'd chosen to locate my suite far from the rest of my family, and in a less elaborate part of the palace, the crowds of fae thinned. Most visitors to the palace liked to stay in the nicer parts of Frostveil, public places where they might bump elbows with the king, queen, heir, or their delightful princess.

That suited me.

I was about five minutes from my room when a

figure I knew as well as my own turned into the otherwise empty hallway ahead of me.

Rhistel's back was to me. Hence, he didn't notice his twin lumbering behind, fists clenched and proverbial steam spraying from his ears.

No Clawsguard followed my brother. He'd slipped away or perhaps whispered his guard into remaining somewhere.

At the thought, my anger boiled over, and I picked up my pace. "Rhistel!"

My twin stopped, and even from a distance, I could see the tense lines in his shoulders as he turned to face me. "Brother."

"That's all you have to say? *Brother?*"

I wouldn't throw suspicion on anyone, but my promise to Filip and Neve that I would keep quiet about what Rhistel had done was being tossed to the wind. I couldn't allow him to violate those I cared for. As no one was around, this was the best moment to confront my twin.

"Were you hoping I'd break into song and dance?"

"You used your magic on her," I growled, closing in on him. "I told you to stay away from her. Not to speak with her, and you tried to control her."

"I tried to get her to kiss me." Rhistel shrugged. "Wanted to see what all the fuss was about."

"Have you no shame?"

"When it comes to your commoner wife and understanding why my brother would give up so much to be with her? No, I do not." Rhistel snorted. "Now I'm fated to wed a Balik because of your choice. Have you met those females? Utter nightmares."

My mouth fell open. At the Royal Theater, he'd called the Balik ladies lovely, said he could do worse. What had changed?

"I'll never forgive your selfishness, Vale."

I blinked at the last dig, the small kernel of sympathy and curiosity for my twin's plight gone in an instant.

"You'll never forgive *my selfishness*?" I took a step closer to Rhistel, and he had the good sense to back out of my reach. "You whispered my wife. Like *you* did to me."

"Fates, not this again," Rhistel moaned. "I couldn't control it then."

"Not that you would have wanted to." His first whispering had resulted in the single most mortifying moment of my life, and my brother had loved every minute.

"Perhaps not," Rhistel admitted. "I don't regret trying to get to know your wife better." His eyes narrowed. "How did she escape, anyway?"

I swallowed. This part of the discussion was off-limits.

"You know, don't you?" Rhistel glowered. "I'm going to assume it wasn't you. I'd have woken up with a black eye." He lifted his hand and tugged off his glove. "How about I see for myself?"

"You can't."

"I'm the heir. One day, no one will be able to stop

me from what I wish to do. I believe I'll start that now."
He tugged at the glove again, and I reacted, hurling my
fist at his nose.

Bone cracked. Blood spurted. Rhistel fell with a cry.

"How dare you strike me!" Rhistel rose, blood
seeping from his nostrils. "You think it'll keep me away
from your commoner? You've only made her all the
more enticing, brother. If you don't keep her locked
away, I'll find her. That is, if the vampire assassins don't
first."

My vision went red, and I lunged at my brother. But
he acted quickly, water materializing from the air and
streaming into my face.

When it vanished again, he went for his glove. "I'll
have you offer her up to me even. It will be all your
idea."

Like the great white bear in the Pit, I charged, slamming into my brother, hurling his body over my
shoulder and tossing him against the wall. He saved
himself, though, conjuring water to soften the blow and
then slamming it back at me.

I retaliated with a screaming gale that blew the shutters from the windows lining the empty corridor.

"You can't do whatever you wish, Rhistel!"

"I can. And I will." He lifted his arm and water
poured from the ceiling, and not a trickle, *a deluge* of
freezing water.

It kept coming and coming and with each second,
my breath grew thinner.

Had I been less heated, I would have understood

that I wasn't underwater. That all I had to do was take a dozen steps in either direction, and I'd be fine. But nearly drowning as a youngling wrung all rationality from my brain, and I defaulted to fight mode.

I leapt at Rhistel and perhaps only because he'd expected me to lose my head, he didn't move in time. I crashed into him, knocking him to the ground, and began pummeling him with my fists.

Blood sprayed. On me. On him. On the floor and walls.

Rhistel roared. "Get him off me!"

Somewhere deep in my mind, I must have known that I was going too far, but I didn't really hear him, didn't stop.

"Prince Vale, please! Stop!" a voice called out seconds before hands grabbed me to pull me off my brother. Like an animal desperate to avoid being caged, I fought back, fought to be free. "You're killing him!"

Killing him. My heart stopped its frantic pounding, and I stilled.

"Thank the stars," a second voice said. "Get help. A healer. The heir can barely breathe."

Those words brought me back to reality, and I took in my brother, as if for the first time.

His face better resembled ground sausage rather than the face I'd grown up with—the one that looked so much like my own. Blood covered him from chest to crown and pools of red crept across the white floor.

I drew in a shuddering breath. Bleeding skies, what had I done?

CHAPTER 36
VALE

I waited outside Father's bedchambers, my hands fisting and unfisting to let off nervous energy. As a youngling, I'd stood in this very place many times, waiting for punishment, though never for an act so serious.

Never for nearly killing my twin brother.

Rhistel had been rushed to the healers. Since then, I received only one update—that he lived, but had I gone on for even seconds longer, his fate might have been different.

I would have killed him.

His blood still caked beneath my fingernails, a memory of an act that felt like a blur. My twin had hurled insults at me, at Neve, but when he'd said he'd make *me* give her to him, I'd lost it.

I'd do no such thing, but if it came from my lips? If I said it in front of her?

Would Neve believe me? Would she remember she was mine?

But then, she wasn't, was she? As much as my body and heart yearned for her, she was her own fae, and so much distance separated us.

Footsteps fell down the corridors, fast and heavy. I twisted to find my father striding toward me, his face red and set in hard lines. Had he been the kind to beat his children, I would have expected that. As it was, Father either had others dole out physical punishments or he had disciplined us in other ways.

Was this the day he froze me in a room again and left me for hours?

Father reached me, stopped, and motioned for his Clawsguard to stand outside. "Vale, with me."

We entered his bedchambers, and it was obvious he'd recently had someone, a female, inside. Lacy undergarments were strewn across the floor.

"How could you be so stupid?" my father growled the moment the door shut behind him and the silencing charm was in place.

"I-I don't know," I replied. It was common knowledge that I was, in fact, the stupidest Aaberg. Though my actions today had taken the cake. "He made me so mad that I lost it."

Father's ice-blue eyes were hard, unforgiving. "Is she your mate?"

Of all the things I'd expected him to say, that was not it.

"Do you have a marking?"

"No," I replied. "She's not."

It pained me to admit it, but aside from my territorial need to protect her, the usual signs of being a mate weren't present. No markings. No sense of wholeness from the other. No mind link—though that one seemed rather rare, from what I'd read.

Neve and I had none of that.

"And you'd still beat your brother nearly to death for her? You are a fool."

"I'll take any punishment."

"Of course you will." Father sighed. "And not just from me. You realize Rhistel will never forget this. Never forgive you. I have half a mind to send you south to the Summer Court because when he becomes king, I don't know that he'll let you live."

I said nothing, but the truth of his words resonated in my bones. And yet, leaving Winter's Realm, leaving my home felt unbearable.

"But for now, I still have use for you," Father said, and my head snapped up.

"What?"

"I would send you away, but I need you." Father went to his drink cart and poured a glass of whiskey. "You will leave Avaldenn to hunt rebels. Find their hideouts. You will obliterate them. Only bring back their leadership or the Falk bastard among them."

"Fine," I said, somewhat relieved. "Neve and I will leave—"

"You will not take your wife."

I stiffened. "Why?"

"She is too much of a distraction."

"She is *my wife*. I won't leave her."

"You will. Now, get out before I change my mind and truly punish you. Be out of the city in two days' time."

I wanted to argue, wanted to deny him, but what was the use? He would insist, no matter what I said. But that did mean I would yield to his demands. Not this time.

I would go hunt rebels, as was my duty, but my wife would go with me. I'd do anything to get Neve out of the city—our ultimate goal, anyway.

But one thing gave me pause. I still had knowledge about the Ice Scepter, and my father was right in front of me. Yet, I hesitated to share that news.

The grounded part of me couldn't help but think that there was something in Brogan's letter I wanted to review before I told Father. And, petty as it was, I also simply didn't feel like helping him right now.

"Why are you still here?" My father pointed to the door. "You're dismissed."

I nodded and left his chambers, my findings still buried inside me.

Later that night, I sat at a corner table in the Warmsnap Tavern.

Duran and the Riis brothers had heard about what had happened. How, I wasn't sure. I'd avoided the training facility, avoided my friends completely, and yet, Luccan and Thantrel had found me and pulled me from the castle.

I hadn't even had a moment to see Neve before we left, but Luccan assured me that Sian, Filip, and my Clawsguard were still watching her. That she was safe.

Likely furious at me too, considering I'd done what she asked me not to do.

"Here, drink up." Thantrel shoved a horn of ale into my face.

"I haven't finished my first." I pulled the horn from its stand and took a glug.

"This is an incentive for you to hurry. Drink and let those worries drift away." Thantrel snapped his fingers and a nymph barmaid appeared with a second horn stand. She set it on our table, all the while looking longingly at Thantrel. Normally, I'd find the female's black eyes disconcerting, but somehow nymphs were always beautiful.

Not as beautiful as Neve, though. I took another drink to dim the guilt I felt at not being with her, even if my friends assured me that she was fine.

The youngest Riis brother grinned. "Thank you, Tricieal. You're always around when I need you."

"Always," she replied, batting her eyelashes. "Anything else, my lords?"

At my right, Duran rolled his eyes and shook his head. Thantrel's flirtations with both males and females often irritated him.

"No." Luccan arrived behind his brother and the barmaid. "We're fine. Thank you, Tricieal."

The nymph sauntered off, tossing Thantrel no less than three flirtatious glances over her shoulder before disappearing into the kitchen.

"How many whores are in love with you here?" Duran grumbled.

"Tricieal isn't a whore. She's a barmaid. But can you blame them?" Thantrel gave a devilish smile.

"Your father is the proprietor of the establishment where they work," Duran shot back. "Isn't that a conflict of interest?"

"I never force a lady," Thantrel replied with a smirk. "Or anyone, for that matter. If they want to share a night with me, and I with them, who am I to deny them the pleasure?"

"You're so full of yourself." Luccan eased into the seat on my left. "Sit, Than."

His brother obliged, and as Luccan was as broad across the chest as me, the circular table felt much smaller. That would make it harder to escape the inter-rogation I felt coming.

"So, you kicked the shit out of Rhistel, huh?" Thantrel asked. "Stars, I wish I'd been there."

"I regret it," I said. "He'll never forgive me."

"You're brothers. Of course he will."

At nineteen turns, Thantrel was younger and knew Rhistel and I had a strained relationship, but nothing more. To most, we could pretend to be cordial—sometimes even felt it. Luccan and Duran, however, knew me better.

"But Father doesn't think so. Hence why he's sending me away."

"What did you fight about, anyway?" Thantrel asked.

"Rhistel is displeased that he'll have to marry a Balik. Apparently, I was supposed to."

"Your brother would marry no one if he could help it. He'd continue to put coin into our father's pockets and frequent upstairs." Thantrel gestured to the staircase in the tavern that led up to the high-end pleasure house owned by Lord Riis.

"He comes here that often?"

"At least three times a week." Luccan raised an eyebrow.

Was Rhistel in love with a whore? I doubted I'd ever know. My brother would never speak to me again.

"Who does he visit?" I asked.

"Mistress Rambi is a favorite," Luccan said. "But there are others. I can look at the ledger, if you wish?"

"Do."

Luccan took a drink of ale. "Your wife did well today, Vale. After you left, it was like she could concentrate again."

"Would you like to tell us what's happening on that score?" Thantrel leaned forward and placed his elbows on the table.

"Not particularly."

"Maybe we can help," Luccan pressed. "You shouldn't be having marital issues this soon."

Duran watched me closely. Of all those at the table, he knew Neve was hiding something and that she needed to lie for some reason. I trusted him not to say anything, though, especially seeing as Thantrel was present. Thantrel was a turn too young to be a member of the cabal.

"We're adjusting," I said because if that wasn't the truth, I didn't know what was. "Did she learn anything new today?"

"She threw axes well enough. And Sian showed her a few tricks," Luccan replied. "Told her not to show them to you, though." He winked, and I rolled my eyes. "And I have to say that her flying is getting better and better."

"We were thinking she should switch to magic soon." Thantrel paused. "Actually, what is her magic? I've never seen her use her powers."

To buy time, I drank a few more slugs of ale, finishing the first horn. The ale warmed my belly.

"I don't know," I said. "Neither does she."

Thantrel gaped. "But she's . . . What? Twenty-two turns? That's old enough to have had her power—even for late bloomers."

"Twenty-three," I corrected him. "And she has never trained with her magic, but we've seen it a few times. It's something we're planning on working on trying to tease out."

Tomorrow, her powers would be freed. I didn't

know how they'd materialize. As an explosion? Or would the grip of the Liar's Salvation potion over her magic loosen gently?

"I've read that those from small villages put less of an emphasis on training their magic than those at court," Duran said. "And Neve is from a small village in the west, so that makes sense."

I wondered what Duran believed a commonfae from the west would need to lie about?

"Perhaps we start small then," Thantrel mused. "This will be fascinating to watch someone learn magic as an adult."

"How about we focus on weapons for a while longer?" I said. "When she's ready to use her magic, she'll bring it up."

Thantrel leaned back in his chair and swung his leg up to cross at his knee. "So protective."

"What?"

"You growled at me."

No, I hadn't.

Had I?

Stars, why had I agreed to come out with these jesters?

"Give me that ale." I reached for the second horn Thantrel had brought and took three more long swigs.

"You should slow down, Vale," Duran whispered.

"Not everyone is as small as you, Duran." Thantrel shook his head. "Vale can hold his ale."

I didn't argue as I took another swig, knowing the

ale would be the best way to drown the worries swimming in my heart.

CHAPTER 37
NEVE

Vale snored next to me, still completely dressed after stumbling into the suite drunk with Sian right behind him, explaining that Thantrel Riis was to blame.

I'd heard what Vale did to his brother and had a guess as to why he'd nearly beat the heir to death. Though I was furious with Vale for confronting Rhistel and putting Filip in danger, I didn't wish to speak with him in his current state.

I shook my head. He hadn't lasted a single day before blowing up at his brother.

And yet . . . despite my anger, I couldn't help but feel a sliver of happiness too at knowing that what he'd done, he'd done for me. Because he had feelings for me.

At that forbidden thought, my stomach rolled. I swallowed and turned the page in the book I was pretending to read. Why was I so attracted to a male I couldn't have?

So many times since I'd learned the truth, I had tried to think of the fact that Vale and I could not be together as a positive. In theory, it made it easier to leave when the time came. Now that I knew who I was in blood and bone, I hoped that day came sooner rather than later. As a Falk by blood, Frostveil Castle was the most dangerous place in the world for me and tomorrow, my magic might appear for the first time in my life. I cast a glance around the room, feeling closed in. Trapped.

Perhaps, instead of locking myself away in this suite tomorrow, I should hide in the hidden part of the palace?

It might be the only place the king couldn't find me. And maybe I could see Prince Calder too? Emilia had assured me he was the only prisoner held in the eastern dungeons. His own winter magic was bound, but Prince Calder might still have advice for me on how to control mine.

It was an idea . . . one I would entertain more in the morning. I sighed and dedicated myself to trying to get some sleep when a loud *thunk* froze me in place before my head could even hit the pillow. I straightened again, ears straining in time to catch footsteps. A moan.

My skin tightened just as the door to the suite burst open and the scent of blood rolled inside.

My heart surged into my throat as I leapt to my feet and found crimson eyes staring at me. He wore all red and his tunic bore a rose strangled by thorns on his breast.

Vampire.

Beyond the monster, a longsword had stabbed the Clawsguard into the door, and in the vampire's hand was a stone bearing a rune. It glowed, telling me that whatever magic the stone possessed was active. It likely allowed the vampire to get through the protections on Vale's door.

"Prince killer." The vampire pocketed the stone and pulled a thin-bladed sword from his back. The metal whined, sending terror through me. "Prepare to die."

"Vale!" I screamed. "Get up!"

He moved behind me, grunted in surprise, and sucked in a breath. Having lifted the blankets, the reek of ale rolling off him was even more potent.

Stars, would we be able to fight this vampire off?

"*Skelda.*" Vale darted for where he kept his prized blade, always within reach since the threat of vampires hovered over us.

If only I'd been so prepared, I wouldn't be staring down a vampire assassin with nothing but a book within arm's reach. And though it was tempting to search for another weapon, I didn't dare take my eyes off the assassin.

Vampires were the fastest of all magical orders. He might blur over in a second.

But he did not. The vampire merely watched us, a hint of amusement in his red eyes, when Vale stumbled over and placed his body in front of mine.

"A drunk faerie and an unarmed prince-killer? What a waste to send so many of us."

Stars. How many?

"How did you get into the castle?" Vale growled.

We'd always known it was a possibility—a distant one, but always possible. Still, it seemed that to be confronted with a weakness in his home's defenses was too much for Vale. He had to learn how this vampire had done it.

"With a trail of blood behind us." The assassin took a step forward. "If you step aside and let me have the prince-killer, I'll allow you to live, Prince. They sent me to bring back only one head."

"Never," Vale growled as he lowered into a stance I'd seen many times while sparring. "Neve, remember escaping last time!"

I swallowed. Vale wanted to buy me time to escape out the window. To fly away.

"Escape?" The vampire laughed. "That won't be happening."

He rushed forward. Vale raised his sword. *"Neve! Go!"*

But as the vampire prowled closer, as Vale slashed his sword and the vampire dodged it, I remained frozen in place. Vale and I might never belong together in the way I longed for but leaving him was off the table.

I bounded over the bed, desperate to find a weapon, but as the vampire was between Vale and the armory, I had to get creative. Casting a glance around, I spied long, thick icicles out the window. They weren't stakes, which had to be wood, but they were something to work with.

I darted to the window, opened it, and frigid air burst in.

"Fast!" Vale yelled beneath the clanging swords, clearly under the impression that I was leaving him.

Instead of launching out the window, however, I extended my wings, preparing them in case I slipped, placed a hand on the thick pane, and leaned forward.

The icicles hanging from the top of the tower had tripled in size since I'd last noticed them. I gripped one and pulled with all my might.

It didn't budge.

"Fates, come on!" I hissed as Vale's cry of pain sounded behind me. I tried again, this time engaging my wings to keep me from falling out the floor-to-ceiling window and grabbing on with both hands. Again, the ice held firm.

I swallowed down a lump in my throat. I needed to think of something else. I whirled, prepared to use any item inside Vale's room as a weapon, and caught the moment the vampire's blade sliced across Vale's chest. As the prince was wearing regular clothing and not armor or chain mail, Vale cried out and shifted to protect his innards. The vampire took that moment to throw a punch that landed on Vale's temple.

"No!" I screamed as the prince toppled, blood seeping into the fabric of his shirt.

"Time to earn my fee." The vampire kicked Vale's blade aside and prowled closer, an evil glint in his eyes.

Suddenly, my hands grew cold. I looked down to

find them glowing—a silvery violet light. Was this a sign? Did I need to use this? My magic?

Desperate, I raised my arms, extended them in front of me, and hoped that something, *anything*, would happen.

Nothing did.

The vampire sneered. "Weak in magic too. How did you kill our prince?"

Any sensible fae would have lunged out the window and flown to safety, but I couldn't move. Not with Vale on the ground like that.

If I left, would the assassin decide to leave no witnesses and kill Vale? Would we both die here today?

Heart pounding in sharp, staccato beats, I tried to force something from my hands. Again, nothing poured out.

Tears pricked in my eyes. Was this my debt to be paid? If so, I hated the Fates, hated the Faetia, hated the very stars in the sky and the dead gods.

A motion behind the vampire caught my attention. Emilia was rushing forward, a stake in hand. I gasped, but the vampire was too set on me, too ready to win his prize.

He didn't sense the stake until Emilia had already leapt up and planted it deep in his back. Momentarily, red eyes went wide, then fell flat, as the vampire collapsed.

I stared down at the human, head shaking. "How did you know we needed help?"

"Do you think I'd speak to you, tell you who you

are, and then leave you alone?" Emilia gestured to the wall, where the hidden door was ajar. "I've been coming here each night, waiting. I was late tonight, but also, it seems, just in time."

"T-thank you," I breathed. "We have to help Vale."

"You have to run," Emilia retorted. "I heard the vampire. There are more."

"Help me carry him. We're taking him into the hidden palace."

The human stared at me as if I'd grown a second head. "He's an Aaberg."

I stepped over the vampire and knelt by Vale. His eyes were closed, and blood seeped from his wound. The cut was the length of my forearm, but I took hope because it also appeared cleanly done. The vampire's blade had gone straight across, and it did not seem too deep. "And Vale isn't like the king or the heir. I will not leave him."

I was certain of that, however, if I moved him, would I make the injury worse? As if sensing that I was there, Vale's eyes fluttered open and locked on me.

"You didn't run." He grabbed at his head and blinked. "Why?"

"There are more coming." I swallowed. "Vale, I'm going to ask you to stand. We'll help you walk, but I don't think I can lift you on my own."

Strong I was, but Vale was a *huge* faerie.

"I can move," Vale grunted as he used his left arm to push up and wavered.

Barely. His muscles trembled and his breath caught.

Those injuries might be nothing compared to what was happening in his head, but there was no time for negativity. We needed to run, get to Luccan Riis's home, and, if possible, alert the palace guards that vampires had breached the building. The assassins might be here for me, but in no way did I think they would spare the throats of other fae. Our blood was too delicious for them to have much self-control.

"Emilia, come here," I instructed.

Vale's eyebrows pinched together. "Emilia?"

The human appeared at his side. "Prince Vale, nice to make your acquaintance."

Any other day, the shock that rippled over the prince's face would have made me laugh. I would bet that a human slave had never addressed him so informally, with no curtsy, no deference, but Emilia wasn't your average human. She'd been keeping another prince alive for two decades, and she had no loyalty to the family she served.

"I'll watch his right," I said, knowing that Vale would need more support there, and I was stronger than the old woman.

As Vale fought to stand, Emilia and I positioned ourselves at his sides in case he needed assistance. In the end, he stood on his own and barely wobbled, which I took as a good sign.

"This isn't the first time I've been sliced open," Vale muttered when he saw me eyeing his wound. "Hurts every time."

"You got hit in the head too," I said. "But we'll take

care of that and find a way to close the sword wound," I assured him as we walked to the door, still open, waiting for Emilia.

On the way, Vale paused over *Skelda*.

Not wanting him to bend over and topple, I scooped up the blade. "I'll carry her for now. Worry about yourself."

He frowned. "Give it to me if we see another assassin."

Though I wanted to argue that his sword arm had to be compromised with such a large injury, I understood that, even injured and unsteady, he could wield *Skelda* with far greater skill than me.

"Fine." I nodded, while already plotting ahead. If it came down to it, I'd pass Vale the sword. But I also wanted a weapon.

First, though, Vale to safety.

I paused, the first niggling doubt that the castle would accept him leaking in. What if Emilia and I went through and he was stuck here? More assassins might come at any moment, and once they saw their dead colleague, I doubted they'd spare Vale, even if he wasn't their bounty.

Emilia shot me a dubious look as we stopped in front of the door in the wall, which hadn't disappeared since Emilia sprinted through it to save me. I suspected she'd been thinking the same as me.

"Vale first." I placed my hand on the wall. "He saved my life. Has done so many times. You can trust him as I do. That being said, your princess demands he be let inside."

Vale's eyebrows knitted together. He didn't know that this part of the palace was sentient. It had spoken with me, so why wouldn't I try to do the same and bargain with it?

The hidden palace didn't answer, but the door remained in place. Open and ready. I supposed we'd just have to try.

"Go on in." I nodded to Vale.

He shuffled closer, and I held my breath as he touched the doorjamb, then slowly crossed the threshold. I exhaled, as did Emilia.

"You're right about him," the human whispered as poor Vale stood there, watching us, confusion and pain clouding his eyes.

"I know. Now you go, Emilia. I need to get a weapon."

"Get the stake holsters. Mine too." Vale placed his hand on the wall for support.

"I will. I'll be right back." I dashed over to his personal armory. As I'd been inside many times, I knew exactly where to go. I grabbed *Skelda's* sheath and a smaller, sheathed sword for me. I plucked the belts up and threaded the blades through before grabbing four stakeholders and doing the same. The belts were growing cumbersome, but I was to the point where I only needed the actual stakes. In two quick steps, I opened the stake drawer and plucked one, two, three, and finally four out, putting them in the holsters one by one.

I'd closed the drawer when voices came from down the hallway.

"Karpov should have finished her by now," a female said.

"She sleeps with the prince," another voice, also female, replied, excitement lacing her tone. "Perhaps they're fighting."

My heart leapt into my throat. I would bet my life that Karpov was the vampire Emilia had killed. More had arrived.

Gripping the belts heavy with weapons, I ran out of the armory and to the door to the hidden palace, aware that the footsteps in the corridor grew ever closer.

"Here." I shoved the belts at Emilia, who looked alarmed to be touching weapons and fumbled them.

"There she is!" a voice hissed.

I twisted in time to see two vampires standing over the dead Clawsguard, one with her finger pointed at me. "Get her."

I gripped the door and slammed it shut, catching their blurring forms as I did so. The moment the door shut, I pushed Emilia away, but I needn't do so.

Two thuds hit the other side of the wall.

"Where's the handle?" one growled.

"It was here!" the other answered, confusion and anger lacing their tone.

I patted the wall. "Thank you."

"Not to beg for attention," Vale said, his voice weaker than before, "but I need to get this wound taken care of before we go to Luccan's so I don't tear it open further."

I turned and took in the gash through the shirt. It seemed like the bleeding had lessened, but it still looked bad. The only positive sign was that the vampire hadn't hit anything vital.

"I can help," Emilia said. "I keep supplies back here."

I nodded and lent Vale my arm. "Lead the way, Emilia."

CHAPTER 38

NEVE

As we walked the hallways of the hidden palace, I kept my gaze on Vale while he took in everything around him with wide eyes.

"There is so much history back here," he murmured when he caught me staring.

"I guess your father did away with everything else relating to the Falks?"

"He burned everything he could. Some of it in a castle fire. Some in a bonfire. Or that was what I was told."

We followed Emilia into the same wing in which Queen Revna and King Harald—my parents—had lived and Emilia stopped next to a room that was only one away from Queen Revna's room.

"The old queen's healing workshop." Emilia waved us inside. "She set it up for storing potions, so I keep the ones I've stolen in here."

"Stolen!" Vale huffed as I escorted him inside and

over to a large, padded table in the center of the room, a spot meant for the sick or injured to lie down. "How do you manage stealing from the healers' sanctuary?"

"Most fae don't notice humans, do they?" Emilia arched an eyebrow and when Vale didn't comment, she continued. "We're deemed beneath them and therefore your king doesn't care to watch us. I slip a potion from the healers' sanctuary in my pocket here and there. A few herbs another time. After many turns of doing so, I have a storehouse."

She really did. Though the room was far smaller than the healers' sanctuary, or even Vale's suite, the tall shelves along each wall appeared well-stocked with herbs, flasks of liquids, and labeled tins.

I didn't worry about closing the wound. I'd never have sewn up skin before, but the wound wasn't too deep, and I knew how to use a needle and thread. I might not be as skilled as a healer would manage, but I'd make sure the wound was sealed. Vale's healing abilities would do the rest.

He would live, of that I was sure, but I needed him to be strong in a very short amount of time. Strong enough to run through Avaldenn and find safety.

"We need a potion to amplify a fae's accelerated healing, if such a thing exists, one for head injuries and staving off infection," I said to Emilia, who swung into action.

"Here." She plucked down three bottles from a shelf. "I'll set out the doses too."

"How did you learn the correct doses?" I didn't see

instructions on the bottles and while a human could easily steal potions, learning to use them was another matter.

Emilia's cheeks pinked. "Queen Revna taught me."

"So you're still a Falk loyalist?" Vale accused from where he perched on the table.

"Until I die."

"Why? If they kept you as a slave, why continue to be so loyal?" The words tripped off his tongue. His family kept slaves, and Vale knew they likely wouldn't be loyal of their own accord.

"I wasn't a slave to the Falks. I worked for Queen Revna as a servant." Emilia's chin rose, but even as her defiance bloomed, she continued to measure doses for Vale. "She taught me things regarding healing. It has come in handy when helping the other slaves."

Vale looked stunned speechless, and I patted him on the back. "Take the potions, and I'll clean your wound."

Emilia finished measuring, and Vale did as I said.

"Arms out," I instructed.

Vale moved his arms as much as he could and, slowly, I took off the shirt he'd been wearing when he passed out from his night of drinking. Blood had already crusted to his skin, but as I'd suspected, the slice across his chest wasn't too deep or wide, thank the stars.

"Is there a numbing solution? Or potion? Or whatever?" I asked Emilia.

She nodded and pulled a balm from another shelf. "Rub it around the injury."

"I should clean it first."

Emilia beamed. "A natural, like—"

"A cloth damp with vinegar?"

In no way did I wish for Vale to discover who I was now. Thankfully, he hadn't been paying close attention to the exchange. The prince was too preoccupied with the room, which aside from holding potions, herbs, and the like, also showed off images of the queen and her family.

One was a relaxed family portrait. In it, the twin girls—my sister and me—were sitting on our mother's lap. We were young, likely not even one turn, but now that I knew who was whom, I recognized my eyes in the portrait.

Did Vale?

I side-eyed him, but he gave away no recognition.

Finally, he turned to me as Emilia handed over a wet, sour-smelling cloth. Anticipating what I'd need next, she also set down a small kit containing a needle and thick thread.

"I can't believe this is all back here," Vale murmured. "I've wanted to see it for so long and here I am."

"Thank the stars for it." He winced as I started dabbing the injury. "Sorry. I'll be as gentle as possible."

"Do what you must. I can handle the pain."

From then on, I worked in silence, cleaning the wound and trying not to notice that this was the closest we'd been since I learned about my ancestry.

Once the blood was gone and the wound was clearly visible, I sighed.

"You lucked out." I palmed the numbing balm and began rubbing it on his skin. "That blade could have hit so many things if he'd run you through with it."

"Assassins know how to strike to disable rather than kill. For all the vampire's bluster, he inflicted this wound on purpose."

Killing a born prince, while poetic justice, perhaps, would invite war. At least if I died, the Blood Court could say that it was the dead gods' vengeance or something of the sort, but Vale was innocent and royal by blood. We were not the same.

Except we actually were. I was just the only one of us who knew just how similar we were.

"How long does it take for the balm to work, Emilia?" I asked. She'd been sitting by, waiting to be of help.

"Only a few minutes."

Vale blinked and rubbed his head.

"How's your head?" I asked, concerned for what I could not see. The chest wound, while messy, was far less mysterious.

"I think I'll be fine," Vale said. "My temple throbs, but part of that could be from the ale. I had too much last night."

I held back my *'you don't say?'* comment. Vale might not even remember Sian, who'd been acting as an additional guard down the hallway until Vale returned. His friend had needed to help the prince into the room. No use in making him feel bad that if he'd been clear-headed, he could have dealt with the vampire more effectively.

"Emilia, can you get him water and food?" Then, noting his clothing and my own nightdress, I added, "we'll need new clothes and cloaks too. Can you find some?"

We only had to go to Luccan Riis's place, but that was far enough for a vampire to recognize us. Cloaks weren't just ways to stay warm but excellent disguises.

"I'll take care of everything," Emilia assured me. "The balm should be working well by now. The needle and thread have a spell on them to keep them clean, so you needn't worry about those." My heart gave a stutter. I hadn't even considered how the tools might be different.

"You can do it. I'm sure of it." Emilia gave me an encouraging smile and left the room.

"Are you ready?" I picked up the needle and thread Emilia had set out for me. The thread was smoother to the touch. The needle curved at the end too. Though it seemed preposterous, I hoped that some of my mother's healing gift passed down to me and I'd excel at suturing. "Because this might hurt," I said as I finished threading the needle. "I'm sorry if it does."

"I can handle it."

"I've never sewn up skin."

"I have, but I can't do it on my own. Not with the angle of this wound, anyway." Vale nodded down, and I tried to envision him awkwardly sewing up his own upper chest. Yes, that would certainly be a sight. "One stitch at a time, Neve. Go as slow as you need. We're safe."

I nodded at his assurance and went to work, pulling together the skin at the end of the wound and applying one stitch at a time, like Vale had said, and I'd seen Yvette do once to a slave who tripped and cut open their leg. The materials we had differed. Tonight, I had proper healing supplies, while Yvette had needed to boil normal thread and the needle, but the idea was similar. One step at a time, one stitch.

At times, I needed Vale to pull his skin closer together, which he did without complaint. I worked tirelessly, trying not to notice how the lines of the tattoos on his chest were not quite straight anymore. How I wasn't stitching perfectly. Instead, I focused on Vale, making sure I wasn't hurting him. Had I not been paying attention to the times that his breathing deepened, I would have thought that he was unaffected.

"*Tell me* if it hurts," I insisted. "I can pause and give you a moment."

"It's not that," Vale said. "I can feel your magic."

I stopped stitching. "Excuse me?"

"With each touch, I can feel your magic. It's faint, but there. Do you sense it loosening?"

The truth was that since my hand froze, I had felt off, though I put that down to everything that had happened. When Vale mentioned my magic loosening, though, it made more sense.

Beneath my skin, something bubbled softly. If I didn't pay attention, I could ignore it, and as I'd been paying attention to not harming Vale, he'd sensed it more than me. It showed how in tune with me he was, and that made my stomach sink.

"I didn't feel it until tonight," I replied, focusing on his chest and not his eyes, searching for something in me that I couldn't give him.

"It's there," he assured me. "Soon it will be free. I like how it feels—familiar."

Thankfully, at that moment, Emilia returned with food, bread, and two cold legs of chicken, before leaving again to retrieve clothing. When she got back the second time with an armful of garments, I was halfway done with the wound. The human came over and examined my work.

"You're doing well. Only a couple of those stitches are sloppy."

My face fell.

"Don't speak to her like that." Vale glowered at the human before meeting my eyes. "They'll hold."

Unlike with garments, I'd been going for functionality, not beauty. Though it felt vain, to be told my work was ugly still struck me, but Vale's assurances helped.

"I didn't mean it to be a criticism. Most people take many moons to stitch up a wound so well." Emilia held up a wrinkled hand, and for the first time, I noticed she trembled, ever so slightly. "I would have offered, but I'm old and my hands aren't as steady as they once were."

"It's fine," I said. "As long as it closes his wound and doesn't become infected, I'll consider this a triumph."

"And how's your head, my prince?" Emilia asked.

"Save for the ache, which I'm still blaming on the

ale, I feel normal." Vale pressed his hand against his temple, which was red but not swollen. A good sign.

"The potions are working." Emilia turned to where she'd set down the plate of food. "Eat while she finishes. If I need to get more, I will."

He took the plate and did as the slave requested, while Emilia helped me hold the sides of the wound closed and gave occasional pointers.

I wasn't sure how long it took for me to sew Vale up, but when I finished, I breathed a sigh of relief. "Try for no sudden movements."

"Until we run," Vale said.

"I guess so. That's still the plan?"

The truth was that we had the option to wait out the night back here. No one would find us, and, for as long as we needed, Emilia would bring food. Vale would be able to heal fully. We could wait until Duran had the Liar's Salvation ready. Perhaps even send Emilia to get it.

"I think it would be best for you to leave Avaldenn," Vale said. "Once you're safe, I can send a message to the castle for them to hunt down the vampires, but I have little hope of them being found."

"They're that good?"

"The Red Assassins are among the best of their trade in Isila." Vale let loose an exhale. "With their stealth, great speed, and strength, vampires are the perfect assassins."

I swallowed. "I heard there are more."

"I think you should go too, Princess Neve," Emilia said softly, which earned her a glare from Vale.

"And how exactly is it that you two know one another?" he asked.

Despite Emilia saving us and supplying everything I needed to help Vale, he didn't trust her. I supposed the fact that she could access this part of the castle was enough for him to remain suspicious.

"I met her back here after Rhistel came looking for me in the suite," I lied, not wanting him to put the pieces together that Emilia might be related to the change in my attitude toward him.

"Why didn't you tell me?" he asked.

Internally, I cringed. I should have seen that one coming. I'd told him about the diary, about how the queen suspected his mother and Lord Riis of being in a relationship—why would I leave Emilia out?

"I asked her not to," Emilia piped up. "You'll understand that it doesn't look good for a slave to have access to this part of the palace, does it, my prince?" She eyed him. "Even if I've done nothing but serve House Aaberg for turns, it casts suspicion on me even if I've done nothing wrong."

"Except be faithful to the Cruel King," Vale spat back.

I swallowed dryly. Thank the stars I hadn't told him about my ancestry.

As if she intuited my thoughts, Emilia cast a sidelong glance at me. "The Falk family was good to me, and despite what others say, King Harald was not all bad."

Grateful for her, I changed the topic. "Emilia, you wouldn't have non-healing potions back here, would you?"

"Some. What are you looking for?"

"Liar's Salvation."

Emilia blinked. "I'm human, as are most of those whom I treat. We don't need a potion to lie. And even if it would still be good, Queen Revna would never keep such a potion on hand. It's illegal."

"I know." I also knew that once my magic appeared, it might give away my secret. Even if I was out of Avaldenn, I could be in danger. It all depended on how Vale took the news.

"I wish we could wait to leave until we meet your friend and get the Liar's Salvation," I spoke cryptically to Vale. Emilia might do anything to help me, but that didn't mean she would protect Duran. I hated having to be so careful around both of them.

"It's not worth it." Vale slipped off the table. "I can have Luccan pass a note to Filip, and he'll get the potion tomorrow. They'll send it on to us. I promise they're trustworthy."

Emilia snorted, which earned her a glare from Vale. I held up my hands, not wanting to deal with their animosity when their goals were the same—to keep me safe.

"Vale, if you can run, I think we'd better get moving."

"I'm ready," he said. "The clothing?"

Emilia nodded to the pile, which she'd set on a smaller table that had likely once been littered with healing tools. "Choose what fits."

We went to the table, and the moment Vale picked up the first shirt, he stiffened.

"What is *this*?"

He needn't ask. While the shirt was midnight black, the amethyst cuffs embroidered with silver hawks made it all too obvious that the clothing was from House Falk.

"What else did you expect her to find back here?" I whispered.

"King Harald wasn't quite as big and muscular as you," Emilia added. "But that's one of his larger tunics. I hope it works for you, my prince."

Vale's cheeks reddened.

"Put it on," I hissed. "You'll be wearing a cloak over the tunic, anyway."

He grunted but complied, tossing on the tunic and then the plain black cloak Emilia had found for him. Once Vale was taken care of, I turned to the pile of clothing Emilia had gotten me. She'd chosen pants rather than dresses. To the touch, the material was very fine—something only nobility used.

"Queen Revna and King Harald hunted together often when they visited House Skau's castle, so she had excellent outdoor wear. You're the same size as her." Emilia came up beside me and pulled a sweater out. "This will be warm too."

"Thank you," I whispered, fingering the thick

sweater and pants my mother used to wear. I pulled the trousers on beneath my nightdress and turned to face the wall when I shimmied the dress over my head and slipped the sweater on. It was indeed warm. Quite soft too. I ran a hand over the material of such good quality that it looked as good as new, though no one had worn it in decades.

We gathered our weapons and put on our thick cloaks. I eyed Vale. "Are you sure you're fine to go?"

"Once we're out of the palace grounds, we're flying," Vale replied, his wings lifting from their compressed position.

"Agreed." Vampires were the fastest creatures in Isila, but they didn't have wings. "Emilia? Can you show us the best way out of here?" I only remembered how to get back to Vale's suite, which would be the opposite of useful.

"Where would be best to exit?" Emilia asked.

"The eastern side of the palace," Vale answered.

She let out a hum and then nodded. "There is a way that will lead you to the outside."

"After you, then." I gestured to the door, and we followed her into the hallway.

Emilia turned left, and despite myself, I glanced right—at my parents' bedrooms. Both doors were ajar, probably from Emilia rummaging through their things.

"Neve?" Vale asked. While I'd stopped, he and Emilia had kept walking and were now waiting for me. Vale with confusion in his features, Emilia with a sad understanding. "Is something wrong?"

"I . . ." I trailed off, unsure how to answer his question, all the while the doors pulled at me.

The castle—maybe my parents even—had wanted me to find this place, to come back here, and now I was leaving. Running. Hiding. I'd yearned for my family, but I was abandoning what little I had left of them.

"One minute." I dashed for my mother's suite.

Vale swore, and his heavy footsteps told me he followed me into the queen's suite before pausing on the threshold of her bedroom.

I, however, approached the desk and pulled open the drawer. The diary was there. I shoved it in my cloak pocket. Should I never return, it would be my keepsake.

I turned to Vale. "We might need coin too. Do you have any on your person?"

He shook his head. "There might be a coinary, though. Depending on where the gateway goes."

"I have a better idea." Though I'd once thought to use it as currency, I hadn't thought to grab the phoenix opal when the vampires attacked. Thankfully, that would not be an issue. There were many jewels back here.

I left the bedroom and entered Queen Revna's vast closet, where I pawed through my mother's jewelry. Knowing that it was hers, that it might have been mine one day, and that each piece was a connection to my past and that I might have to sell it hurt, but I shoved down my emotions. All the while, Vale followed, his movements still a touch clumsy from the ale in his blood, a stunned expression on his face. Once I'd filled my pockets with rings, necklaces, bracelets, and brooches that would fetch hundreds, if not thousands, of gold bears, I was ready.

"Let's go."

Vale nodded, and we left the queen's suite to find Emilia in the hallway, ready and waiting. But I stopped again.

King Harald, my father, had slept across the hall from my mother. Despite his horrible reputation, he was blood. I wanted something from him too.

I entered the old king's rooms and Vale gave a huff. "Neve! We have to hurry! The longer we take, the better prepared the vampires will be in the city to hunt anyone who looks suspicious."

"I'll be fast!" I said, sure of what I wanted as I rushed to the sword case and smashed the glass.

"What in all the nine kingdoms?" Vale hollered, but by the time he raced into the room to learn what I'd done, I'd already wrenched the sword from its case, placed it in the sheath, and slung the sword strap over my shoulder.

"*Now*, I'm ready."

CHAPTER 39
VALE

S o many questions bubbled through my mind. Neve already had a sword and stakes. Why had she felt the need to take that particular blade?

None of what I'd seen made sense, and I didn't think it was because of the ale still pounding through my system in spite of the food and water the human had brought me.

That same human, Emilia, was directing us through the palace, and I had to be ready to protect and fight the moment we exited the castle. So, as much as I wished to question Neve, I needed to focus.

"Up ahead, we'll have to cross a hallway in the main part of the palace," Emilia announced as we reached the bottom of a staircase.

Though it was difficult to tell because I'd never been back here, I sensed that we'd made our way to the ground floor and were, perhaps, near the servants' living quarters.

"Is it a well-traveled part?" Neve asked.

"Not this time of night. And it's the only instance in which you'll be vulnerable before going outside." Emilia gave Neve an encouraging smile.

The slave seemed very attached to Neve, which I found odd. As Neve was a princess and my wife, I'd expect servants and slaves to show her respect, if nothing else, but every time the human looked at Neve, she seemed a bit . . . sad?

Something wasn't adding up. As soon as we were safe, and I was clear-headed once more, I intended to do some digging.

"Thanks for letting us know," Neve said with a stoic nod. "We're ready."

"Good"—Emilia stopped and turned to face the wall—"because the exit is right here." She pressed her hand into the wall, right where a handle molded into her fingers.

"How many are there like that?" I despised the jealousy in my voice even as I spoke, but it rankled that the human walked around back here and shared some sort of secret with Neve.

"Doors?"

I nodded, and Emilia appeared thoughtful. "I've used around two dozen."

"Others can use them too?" I asked. "Besides Neve, I mean."

"Yes." Emilia eyed me, suspicion clouding her eyes for the first time. "But you'd have to kill me before you pulled their names from my lips."

"Which won't be necessary," Neve cut in. "He's curious. Vale has wanted to come back here for a while."

The human glared at me, but Neve must have assured her for she twisted the handle, shifted something on the other side—a tapestry by the sounds of it —and peeked outside. "The coast is clear."

We followed her through the door, ducking under a tapestry, and into the hallway. I recognized the area right away and shock set in. The labyrinth inside the palace was far vaster than I'd imagined, and I'd studied the blueprints of the parts that had disappeared.

Were there parts that hadn't made it onto the blueprints? Rumors of such things abounded. Of rulers who had constructed areas of their castles, hidden them, and killed off the builders to keep their secrets.

Had the Cruel King done so? Or another ruler before him?

Or perhaps all the ale and my injury really did have me more turned around than I thought. As Emilia shuffled across the hall and shoved aside another tapestry to place her hand on the wall, I figured that was as likely as not.

The wall shimmered beneath the human's touch and, again, a door appeared, the handle a moment later. Emilia opened it and crossed the threshold. Then Neve. I was about to follow when a gasp caught my attention. I twisted and froze.

Calpurnia, clad in soft, slippered feet, had rounded the corner—a cup of something steaming in her hand.

I cursed myself for getting too drunk and not being on guard, for not having heard her coming.

"Vale," she whispered. "Where are you . . . how are you . . .?"

"Vale," Neve hissed from inside the hidden passage. "Come on."

Calpurnia straightened. "That's her!" A blink of shock crossed her tanned face. "Bleeding skies! That's how she got away that day! She——"

I stepped into the hidden passage, shutting the door behind me. Eyes wide, I met Neve's curious stare. "Calpurnia saw me."

"What!"

"She recognized your voice too. We must hurry."

Neve swallowed. "What will she do?"

I couldn't be sure. Calpurnia wouldn't wish to hurt me. But Neve? If given half the chance, she'd tell my father that Neve had access to this part of the palace. Another reason for him to dislike her. Perhaps to suspect her too.

"Hurry!" Emilia hissed. "You must leave as quickly as possible! The door isn't far."

Relief did not flood me at her claim, for once we reached outside, we weren't safe. We simply had a new problem. Neve had heard the assassin say there were more of them. How many? Frostveil would be difficult for many to breach, but many could be waiting in the city. The one that broke into my rooms was not the same vampire I'd seen in Rall Row.

Those thoughts consumed me until, again, Emilia stopped in front of a plain wall.

"This will lead outside. Near a servants' entrance. The one covered in ivy."

"We're familiar with it," Neve said. "Thank you, Emilia. I wish you could come with us."

"I do too. But I'll wait here for you, if you ever wish to return home. Ever loyally yours, my princess."

Neve swallowed, and to my great astonishment, she hugged the human.

I stood off to the side, uneasy. Not that I disliked humans, more like I rarely thought about them and knew little about them. They were often out of my sight, and overall, rare. Once, bringing human slaves into this kingdom had been far more common, but not for many centuries. Now, most of the humans in Winter's Realm were all born here. They did not belong in their world, wouldn't fit in, but fae didn't see them as equals. We gave them only one option—living and serving in the three pillars of society: the noble houses, the House of Wisdom, or the Tower of the Living and the Dead. In turn, each noble home or foundational institution fed, housed, and protected the slaves.

I wasn't alone in thinking that the exchange of freedom and everything one might dream of in that life was not a fair exchange for food, shelter, and protection. I was, however, in the minority. It was an uncomfortable circumstance that I did not like to think about.

However, Neve was at ease around them, likely because she'd grown up with many humans. Seen them brought over from their world even, for the laws of Winter's Realm did not exist in the Vampire Kingdom.

The pair broke apart. Emilia stuck her head outside again and proclaimed the coast clear.

I slipped my hand down to find Neve's, but she pulled away.

"We need to keep our hands ready to fight," she said, not meeting my eyes.

"Of course," I said, though I'd rather connect with her, feel her skin on mine as we ran for our lives.

"Good luck." Emilia cast another smile at Neve and nodded to me before we stepped outside, closing the door behind us and bracing against a great gale of wind that about blew me over.

I reached out and steadied Neve as she stumbled back into the castle wall, which had reverted to sheer stone.

"Stars!" Neve breathed, teeth chattering already and eyes blinking as snow whipped into her face. "It's absolutely freezing out here."

"And windy. That will hinder flight," I murmured, already reassessing how we'd have to flee. "If there aren't breaks in the wind, we'll have to run through the city."

Neve's eyes widened. "Maybe we should go back inside and wait? See if the winds die down? It will be difficult to see through such thickly falling snow."

"Remember what Vishku Sindri said? That the coming winter storms would be the worst we've seen in many turns?" Snowflakes melted on my skin as I waved my hand through the air. "This must be what she meant. Who knows how long it will last?"

Neve rubbed her hands together. "I suppose the wind might blow our scent away, but it might also blow it to them. Those vampires in your suite will remember it."

"Yes, but they might still be inside and, anyway, they don't know the city like I do," I said.

For a moment, she looked like she wanted to argue but ended up giving a single nod. "You're right. I think it's time for me to leave, anyway."

My mouth fell open, and my stomach dropped to my knees. It had always been the plan for her to leave. Now that it might actually happen, I wished to tell her the truth: that I *never* wanted her to leave.

But since we'd taken our relationship to a physical level, Neve had pulled back—maybe exactly because she was leaving. I didn't know. All I knew was that she wasn't interested in staying here. Staying with me.

"So what do you say we make a run for it?" Neve pointed to the closest part of the castle wall, visible through the snow-filled wind. "Fly over that wall? Even with the winds, that short of a flight should be doable, and I don't remember guards being near there. Actually, the thick snow in the air might help in that regard. No guards will see us."

Not that it mattered. Calpurnia already had. Still, I nodded. "Let's go."

We raced for the wall, my most recent injury tugging slightly and my ankle weaker than normal. I might have underestimated the injuries, but I pushed through, relieved for one thing: that Neve was correct in thinking that the snow was doing us a service. Though soldiers manned the walls, it was unlikely that they'd be able to spot us this far away, anyway.

But vampires could see very long distances. Did they wait out here somewhere? Biding their time until we fled?

Or did the assassins believe we'd remain hidden in the palace? It was anyone's guess. I only hoped that wherever the other assassins were, it was far away from the palace and Lordling Lane.

We reached the wall and wasted no time leaping into the air. No longer pressed down against my back, my wings caught the wicked winter winds, and I shuddered.

Up we went, and as we descended, fighting the wind as we did so, I searched the street. My heart pounded, expecting a vampire to leap out at us at any moment. Not any vampire either, a Red Assassin. Prince Gervais had been difficult enough to kill, but if the stories about the Red Assassins were true, they'd be ten times more difficult.

My fear was for naught, though.

As far as I could see, which, thanks to the snow, was not as far as I would like, no one roamed the street. Considering how dark and cold it was, few would be out tonight. That would both help us spy vampires and make us a potential target.

"Stay close," I said to Neve as we landed. "Keep

your hand on your stake. Wings ready to fly if we need a quick escape."

She shifted the sword she'd taken from that lavish room in the hidden palace. I didn't know whose room it was, though it had to have been someone important—being so near the one that had clearly been Queen Revna's suite.

I didn't need to ask if the book was the diary she'd mentioned. The diary interested me too. My mother had been Queen Revna's lady-in-waiting, and Queen Revna had written about my mother and Lord Riis. Though I'd decided to trust the Lord of Tongues, that didn't mean I did not want to learn more about his past. About if he'd been more than a friend to my mother—if once, they'd loved one another.

We plunged into the city, walking quickly down the streets, as one would if they were desperate to get out of the cold. Perhaps in such weather, running would not look too odd, but I would not risk it. Not unless we saw a threat.

As we wound through the streets, we were met with only snow and wind. On a night such as this, no one had even kept their horses outside.

We'd reached the square where Ragnor's Pies and many other food stalls waited with the doors closed and windows shuttered and rattling against the gales. As the square was wide open, I could see that no one was around.

"Across," I said, and we strode into the square.

We were halfway to the other side when I sensed

that I'd been wrong. We were not alone. Someone was watching us.

"Eyes open," I murmured. "I feel—"

"Oh my stars!" Neve pointed to a table pushed up against a stall and tied down with rope.

I swallowed. Someone appeared to have fallen asleep at the table. In a cold such as this, I doubted anyone could survive sleeping outside.

"We have to check on them," Neve whispered.

"We have to get to Luccan's," I corrected, hating myself. Whoever that person was, he was one of my people. A fae of Winter's Realm.

But so was Neve. I'd made a promise to keep her safe, and more than that, I loved her.

My heart gave a hard thud, as it did each time I thought of how desperately and quickly I'd fallen for my wife and how she seemed to have changed her mind about me.

"It will only take a moment," Neve said. "I don't have a good feeling about him or her."

"I don't either."

"Dead or not, we still *have to* check, Vale."

I sighed, and the air streamed white from my lips. "Hurry."

"Sir? Miss?" Neve strode up to the fae and shook them. "Can you hear me?"

No response came, and though before she'd put on a practical front, anticipating that we might be met with death, my wife's face fell.

"Let me check their breathing," she said. "Then we can go."

She placed both hands on the person's shoulders and lifted. The moment we caught sight of his face, I knew it was a lost cause. Not only was the fae dead, but blood dripped down the front of his torn-out neck.

"The vampires did this," I growled. "They attacked a fae of Winter's Realm."

"They did," Neve said, setting the male down with trembling fingers. "He's dead. Let's go—"

"*What?!* No burning boat? No prayer to the stars to honor him?" a female voice sounded from somewhere unseen, silky and powerful.

I spun and located her by the gleaming of her daggers in the moonlight. She crouched on top of Ragnor's stall, a slice of a smile cutting across her face.

"If you're going to leave him there, he wasn't worth much at all, then, was he?" she purred. She leapt off the stall and landed as light as a snow leopard into fresh powder. The thorn-choked rose on her breast jumped out at me. She belonged to the Red Assassins' guild. "Good thing we used his blood for something useful then."

"Behind me," I murmured.

"Oh, if I want a drink from that pretty neck, it won't matter where she stands," the vampire sang. "That is, unless you are more than what you seem."

She paused and studied my attire. "Lovely clothing, though outdated. And you're quite muscular and seem to be ready to fight off an enemy." Her eyes traveled to Neve.

"Stakes." The vampire's sharp fangs lengthened. "Now, why in the world would anyone in this kingdom be carrying stakes unless they *expected* to come across a vampire?"

"You can never be too safe," Neve growled. "You're about to find that out for yourself."

The female vampire let out a throaty laugh. "Am I, little dove? Are you the one we're searching for? If you are, speak up. The faster we take your head, the sooner we can leave this frozen wasteland. The fae blood is delicious, but not good enough to stay here."

"Wife." I angled to take control of the situation before Neve admitted her identity to this cold-blooded killer. "We should—"

"I'm the one you're looking for," Neve proclaimed. "I killed Prince Gervais. Given half a chance, I'd do it again too."

A stream of curses left my lips. By the dead gods, could Neve not hold her tongue for a second! As exasperated as I was, however, I didn't dare take my eyes off the assassin as she lifted two fingers to her mouth and a shrill whistle cut through the night.

"Little silver dove, you have felled a prince. Now, let's find out if you're up for taking on the Red Assassins."

CHAPTER 40
NEVE

Two long, slender blades flashed in the moonlight as one vampire soared our way. Vale shoved me back, pulled his sword, and deflected the projectiles.

The vampire's lips formed a cunning, deadly smile. "This will be far more fun than I'd thought."

She leapt and Vale met her in the air, their swords clashing together.

"Neve, run!" Vale grunted.

I wanted to call him an idiot for thinking I'd leave him, but the three new figures with glowing red eyes rushing into the square were far too distracting.

"Vale, there are more!" I pulled the sword on my belt from its sheath.

"Fly!" He grunted.

But like in his suite, my body wouldn't let me, and neither would my heart. I might be filled with shame over what we'd done, who we were to one another by blood, but that didn't change the pull I felt to Vale, nor how much I wanted him.

I would not see him killed for me.

So, as the new trio rushed for us, I pulled my blade back and prepared to attack. My best shot would be to decapitate one of the bloodsuckers in one fell swoop and then turn my attention to the others. If I lasted that long.

As they neared, a sense of cold washed over me, dread, I supposed, but I kept my stance, watched, and waited for them. Vale was busy with the female and, as the others were here for my head, I was sure they'd run right past them and come for my jugular.

When I could see the whites of their eyes, the cold spiked, deepened, as if it pierced me through the heart. I began to glow. I gaped, but before I figured out why, the vampires skidded to a stop in front of me.

"You're the one who killed our prince?" one asked, his eyebrows knitted together in confusion. "And you face us *like this*?"

Another sneered. "What did you do, glow him to death?"

I tried to answer but couldn't. Like in Vale's suite, I was immobile, but this time, it was my entire body. My mouth froze. Arms and legs too.

My heart fluttered wildly. What was happening to me?

"She's struck dumb!" The third laughed and hooked a finger toward Vale and the female vampire.

"Looks like Samiya gets all the fun tonight. Take the moonstruck one's head and earn our bounty."

No, no, no! I tried to move again but couldn't, and when one of the trio took a step toward me, I was sure I was doomed.

But I wasn't. They took another step, and for a second, it was like icy fingers squeezed my insides. Then a blast of blue light shot from me, cold as ice, and froze the trio in place.

I gasped when the light stopped, catching my breath and blinking as the cold that had immobilized me loosened and my sword arm fell.

Had that happened? Had my magic saved me?

The answer was plain. The vampires stood before me, frozen in a strange light blue ice. Behind, Vale and Samiya fought, both as skilled as the other, but the vampire was faster.

My fingers glowed brighter.

Maybe not for long.

I raised a hand, and again, frigid fingers squeezed me from the inside.

"Please," I whispered. "Save him."

And when Samiya's blade arched for Vale, cutting the end of his cloak off as he spun out of the way, my magic did as I asked. Blue light surged from me, uncontrollable and wild, and hit the vampire.

She screamed, slowed.

I sucked in a breath as Samiya blinked and her arm twitched. The second blast hadn't been as strong as the first, so she wasn't frozen like the others. However, my power immobilized Samiya's arms long enough for Vale to swipe his sword. Her head soared away, and he spun, his eyes going wide at the sight of me.

"What in the nine kingdoms was that?"

"My magic," I said, teeth chattering because the cold lingered deep inside me. "I-I-I don't know how."

"Is that *ice*?" He gestured to the trio, covered with glinting blue ice. At the motion, I glimpsed beneath his cloak to his tunic. It looked wet, probably with blood. My handiwork had not held well, though Vale was not likely to admit as much.

Seeing as he was still standing, not on the ground in pain, and awaiting my answer, I swallowed down the truth. "I don't know, but we can't leave them like this. They'll drink from more fae. Let's kill them and run."

He looked like he wanted to say more, but I raised my sword and, with as much might as I could put behind the swing, decapitated one vampire. Seeing me act brought Vale back to the moment, and he took care of the other two.

Once done, we stared at each other, four bodies surrounding us and red blood—showing that the assassins had all recently fed—spilling on the snow.

"Are you hurt?" I asked.

"I'm fine. The stitches opened but I can push through. You?"

Guilt clawed through me that he'd been injured, and I had not. "Not a scratch. Let's get to Luccan's. We'll be safe there."

"You will *die here*," a voice growled.

I craned my neck around Vale to find three more vampires slinking off the street. By the stars, how many were there?

One with long white-blond hair lifted a bow and arrow and aimed.

Vale gripped my hand, and his wings opened. "Fly."

My wings snapped out, and together we launched into the air. We rose above the roof of the tallest building and even though the snow swirled and wind battered us, I was thankful for Vale's quick thinking. That we'd been fast enough to avoid another fight. That—

An arrow flew between us, then another to my right, but either the archer had poor aim, or the snow and wind were throwing him off. I was guessing the latter, for it was slowing us too.

"Let go," Vale said. "And make your flight path erratic."

Though releasing his hand was the last thing I wanted to do, I understood his line of thought and complied. As two targets, we were harder to hit and as the arrows came at regular intervals, only one of the vampires had a bow and arrow. All the others could do was track us as we flew through the gales and the snow. And if we got to Luccan's and dropped into his yard, inside the warded gates, they'd never reach us.

It took forever, and at least two dozen arrows flew by before I caught the lights of Lordling Lane below.

"That's it, right?" I yelled into the wind.

"Yes. Luccan's is the one that—*bleeding stars!*"

An arrow sliced through Vale's wing, and he grunted as he dropped toward the ground before catching himself.

"No!" I zoomed toward him and extended my hand. It was miraculous enough that he'd caught himself, speaking of too much training and a strong will, but any minute now the wind could fail. "Let me help."

"I'm too heavy for you." Vale winced, though he still took my hand. With both hands, I squeezed his fingers as tight as possible. It was taking all that he had to stay in flight.

"We need to land," Vale panted.

"They're down there. Can you make it to Luccan's?"

His answer came as he dropped again, this time pulling me down with him. Retaliating, I strained my wings to stay aloft, but Vale was right. He was far too heavy. We were so close, and yet close only spelled death. To get us to safety, I had to think of a different way.

"Vale, I'm going to try to use magic again." My pulse fluttered at the mere idea. "But I have to let go."

"Do it. Buy us time."

I had no idea if I could do so, if I still had enough power left inside me. My magic shouldn't even be making an appearance until tomorrow at the earliest, but something was affecting it. I hoped that something was the desperate need for survival.

One of my hands released Vale and together we

descended like a rock tossed into a lake. With each passing second, the vampire's red eyes glowed brighter. The one with the bow nocked another arrow, and I seized the moment.

Unsure if it was necessary, but not knowing any better, I aimed my free palm toward the white-blond archer. "Please work!"

Again, a deep cold settled over me. Vale hissed, hinting that he felt it too, but I didn't take my eyes off the archer as he pulled back the arrow.

A second before the arrow would have flown, cold burst from me again. This time, I was more prepared for the sensation. Frost grew, as if from the cobbles, up the vampires, leaving only their necks and heads bare.

I sucked in a breath. So the cold didn't fully come from me. It felt like it did, probably because I was unused to using magic and it overwhelmed me.

"Brace," Vale yelled because the ground was coming at us fast.

I shifted my attention in time for my feet to slam into the ice-covered stones. The impact shot up my legs, ripping a scream from my lips as my knees buckled. I fell forward and shot my hands out so that they caught me scraping against the stones. Blood welled, but Vale took those bloody hands and pulled me up.

"Next time, bend your knees a lot."

"*Next time*. Bleeding moon, there had better not be a next time!" I muttered.

"There might be, if we don't hurry." He gestured to the vampires and then pointed to Luccan's home, now within sight. "I don't think your power was as strong this time. Can you run?"

Though my legs cried out in agony, I had no choice but to make them work. "Yes."

We ran, and against my better judgment, I twisted to locate the vampires.

Though they were still stuck in place, their arms were moving, ripping at the thick frost so that they might free themselves. Seconds before, frost had covered their entire bodies, and now there was much less.

Pushing through the pain in my legs, Vale and I sprinted down Lordling Lane, which, thanks to the weather and late hour, was empty. We were nearly there when another arrow cut across the top of Vale's injured wing. He stumbled and fell.

"Vale," I stopped.

"Get up," he hissed, clearly in pain. "Run."

I held out a hand. "With you. Only with you."

He took it and though it was his wing that had taken the arrow, the fall impacted him too. He limped ever so slightly.

Fates alive, would we make it?

"I love the chase!" one vampire roared, and I just knew if I turned, I'd see them blurring toward us.

"Come on, Vale!" I pulled ahead of him, tugged at his arm, hoping I wasn't ripping his injury open even more as I tried to get him to move faster.

He grunted but picked up his speed, and through the swirling snow, Luccan's gates appeared.

We closed in, my heart thundering with each step.

Somehow, the vampires weren't on us yet, but with their great speed, they might be within seconds.

"Blood, Neve," Vale ground out. It was taking everything he had to run. I had to do the rest. "Blood releases the wards for us."

I pressed my bloodied hand into the gate and the metal turned hot. The lock opened. Panting, I pushed it open, and we stumbled through.

I slammed the gate shut behind us and the lock latched in time for the male vampire with long white-blond hair to run into the metal. I cringed as Vale stumbled and went for his sword once again.

"No. Get inside." I wheezed because though the vampires could break metal, they weren't. The wards had set back in place already. "Get to the front door."

Pain cutting through my legs and palms, we ran the rest of the way down the path, up the steps. The moment our blood touched the door, it opened.

I exhaled and rushed across the threshold, only to be stopped at sword point.

"Get that out of her face, Thantrel," Vale growled.

"Sorry." The blade disappeared. "I'm the only one up and heard the alarm when the gate opened."

"But we're allowed through it," I said, confused.

"That doesn't mean we don't want to know when someone, even a trustworthy someone, arrives." Another voice joined, and I peered past Thantrel to see Luccan pulling a robe over his naked chest as he came down the steps. "Vampires?"

"At the gate. Three of them," Vale confirmed.

Luccan looked at Thantrel. "Up for a bit of archery practice?"

"Always. I'll join you when I'm done."

"Be quick. And wake Arie." Luccan rolled his eyes. "Arie would sleep through a dragon landing on top of the house."

"Arrows won't kill them," I said before Thantrel left. "Only stakes to the heart, decapitation, and lots of fire."

Thantrel winked. "We have all sorts of arrows, beautiful. Trust that we've got it covered."

I chose to believe them. After all, I'd killed a vampire with a small stake fashioned after a killing device from the human world. The Riis males could be equally inventive.

Thantrel left, and Luccan waved for us to follow him down the stairs. "To the sparring room. You have to go."

He was right. Even if those vampires were dead, we had no idea how many more roamed the city. And they'd already proven they could enter the castle. Avaldenn wouldn't be safe anytime soon.

Slower than I would have liked, Luccan led us downstairs. At the bottom, we found the sparring room, dark and cold.

Luccan waved his hands and the faelights in the corners blinked on, converging on the hidden gateway. "We will join you once we finish off the vampires and make sure no more have followed. You remember what to do?"

"Yes," I assured him and held up a bloodied hand.

"The others will find you healing supplies when you arrive."

"*Others?*"

"You'll see. Go." Luccan pointed to the portal. "My brothers and I will be right behind." He ran back up the steps, leaving Vale and me alone.

"Ready?" my voice wavered. The portal wasn't only an escape route, but a chance at the freedom I'd been grasping for so long. And yet, even though things between Vale and me could not be as I'd come to hope for, I was scared.

Once we walked through, once I made this first step to leave Avaldenn, I would truly leave behind the life I might have had. One with Vale. Maybe even in a messed-up way, the one I had been born to.

"Let's go," Vale said and, pushing aside my inner turmoil, we staggered to the portal and swiped our bloodied hands across the wall.

It shimmered, and a circle of light appeared and expanded until it was large enough for us to walk through. I peered inside, seeing nothing but smelling something familiar.

Snow lilies?

"Together?" Vale held out his hand.

"Together," I replied, and we stepped into the light.

Not ten seconds later, the gateway spat us out and a scream met my ears. My heart leapt as my eyes adjusted to the darkened room, lit by only the blazing fire in the corner, and found Anna and Clemencia, slack-jawed and wide-eyed.

"What in all the nine kingdoms?" Anna whispered. "You scared the crap out of me, Neve!"

"I wasn't planning to do so."

"Yes, well . . . why are you here?"

Clemencia shook her head. "I'm still mad at Lord Riis for making us ride *for days* through all that snow when there's a gateway to here."

I laughed. "A valid annoyance."

In fact, I was annoyed that the Riises hadn't told us the gateway came here so we could visit our loved ones. Lord Riis claimed that it was to everyone's benefit that we didn't know where they were. While I understood his reasoning, I didn't like it.

Sir Caelo entered the room, a tray with three wine goblets in his hand. He blinked when he saw Vale and me. "I didn't know you two would be joining our party. Good to have you here, Princess Neve. Brother."

Only then did I remember how late it was. Vale had been out for hours, then sleeping, and then we'd been chased by vampires. And this lot had just been drinking all night!

Life was so unfair.

"Why are you two bloody?" Clemencia asked, coming closer, her face paling as she took in our hands. "Oh, Prince Vale—your wings!" She bolted to the door and stuck her head out to speak to someone in the hallway. Once done, Clemencia turned back to us. "A servant will get a healer. Now, tell us what happened."

"It's a long story, but we're fine. Nothing vital was

injured." Vale shucked off his cloak, wincing as he did so, lending less sway to his words.

"He has an injury to his chest too," I admitted. "I tried to suture it, but I didn't do a good job and it was reopened."

Anna stood too. "In this tower, we seem to have nothing but time. Not that I'm complaining." She took the goblet Sir Caelo offered. "The service here is immaculate."

"She has gotten far too used to thinking of me as a servant." The knight's tone was dour, but his smile said he actually didn't mind. That same smile dropped when he took Vale in more closely. "Are those silver hawks on your sleeves, Vale?"

"They are," Vale muttered. "Again, long story."

"I can't wait to hear it." Anna sat once more and gestured to the empty chairs around the fire, eagerness in her dark, upturned eyes.

We took the offered seats as Sir Caelo slipped out of the room, only to reappear with two more goblets and three bottles of wine. He handed me a goblet. "I figured we needed a lot more than one bottle for the tale you're to tell."

"Thank you, Sir Caelo."

"Just Caelo," he said as he poured for me. "You're married to this one here, and despite all his flaws, he's a brother to me." He threw Vale a mischievous glance before meeting my eyes again. "That means you're family."

I smiled. Though we'd spent little time together and

didn't know each other well, I'd already begun to think of Caelo less formally. After all, I'd allowed him to guide Anna and Clemencia here and had heard many tales about him and Vale. I felt like I knew the knight and hoped that we could deepen that feeling into something true.

Vale took the goblet and let his friend pour his glass. "We do have quite a tale. But let's wait for the Riis brothers to arrive. They—"

The gateway shimmered prettily again, and the Riis males entered the room. Arie swore as he stumbled and Luccan caught him.

Thantrel grinned at the sight of the wine. "You'd better fetch more goblets, Caelo."

"I'm not your servant." Caelo's chin lifted. Apparently, acting as one for us and Anna was fine, but not for Thantrel. "Get your own."

"Blazing stars, I'll get them." Arie shook his head. "And when I return, someone had better explain why I was ripped out of my bed in the middle of the night and brought to Riis Tower."

So that was where we were! Riis Tower was the home of Lord Riis's family before the king raised him to be a lord. If my memory served, it was in the midlands, near House Vagle's castle.

We settled in with our drinks, and the others caught us up on what they'd been doing since arriving at Riis Tower—which seemed to be a lot of relaxing. When Arie returned, he did so pushing a small cart weighed down with bottles and tins and the like. At his side, walked a healer, her occupation obvious by the wheel and star pendant on her necklace, identical to the one Master Healer Nissa wore.

It was Vale's and my turn to tell our story, but with the healer present, I was unsure. I studied the female faerie. She had long black hair, and the first signs of lines around her eyes, hinting that she was at least a century old. Her dark brown eyes looked kind and serene. Trustworthy?

"Should we . . ." I asked the Riis brothers, eyes slicing to the healer.

"The servants in this tower are the most loyal you'll ever meet," Luccan replied. "They've served my family for many turns—long before Father's line was noble. They will say nothing."

"The young lord speaks true," the healer piped up. "I'm loyal to House Riis and if you are a friend, I am loyal to you."

"She's a friend," Luccan confirmed. "Now, please Healer Yellana, help Prince Vale."

"Of course." The healer continued her inspection of his chest, which was still bleeding, though not as badly as I'd feared.

Before Vale began telling our tale, I did so, and as I spooled the thread, I made sure to leave out the use of my magic and Emilia, as the knowledge of both would create more questions. Most of which I wasn't prepared to answer. Not even from Vale, who eyed me as I omitted both. The story worked anyway and the idea of the hidden palace and fighting off Red Assassins entranced our friends. When I was done, I leaned back and sighed. "And here we are."

"Far more exciting than Riis Tower," Anna breathed. "I can't believe you went through all that. Fought off so many vampires!"

"I'm envious *of you*," I said to Anna, Clemencia, and Caelo. "Frostveil has been trying."

Vale frowned. "But not all bad."

"Not all bad," I amended, sensing he had taken my claim personally. Although, if he learned the truth, perhaps he wouldn't agree.

Though I tried to reassure him, questions brimmed in Vale's eyes. He hadn't brought up my use of magic, or Emilia, and as I'd left them out, I'd trust that he wouldn't say a thing around others. But that did not mean I wished to remain under that curious, pain-filled gaze any longer. Vale had questions, and I had secrets to keep.

"Is this balm for minor cuts?" I asked, plucking a familiar-looking balm from the healer's cart.

"It is, my lady."

"Can I take it? For my hands?"

The healer blinked. "Of course. I have more."

"Good." I cupped the balm. "Anna and Clem, can you show me to a room? I think I'm ready to retire for the night."

We left the den, and though my heart screamed not to, I cast a glance back at Vale. The look of hurt, confusion, and betrayal on his face nearly shattered me.

CHAPTER 41
NEVE

I awoke alone, in an enormous bed, a cold fire bubbling under my skin.

"What in the nine kingdoms?" I whispered, sitting up and rubbing my arms for a moment before my vision cleared from sleep and the scene before me set in. "Oh, no!"

In the weak morning light, frost crawled across the room like a spider. Icicles dripped from the canopy, and there were fat snowflakes on my blanket.

Worst of all, the diligent lady-in-waiting and friend, Clemencia, stood at the edge of the room, watching me with wide eyes.

"Clem," I breathed.

"I came in here because I heard you shout in your sleep."

I had? I didn't recall a nightmare. Then again, perhaps I'd been yelling about whatever was happening in my room.

"I found this." She waved her hand wildly to encompass the room, her voice smaller than seconds before, her teeth chattering from the chill. "So please, what's going on, Princess Neve?"

"I—" My insides seized.

My throat tightened because this time, I recognized the signs of what was about to happen. All my life I'd wished for this day, the day my magic appeared, and I learned what it was. Now that the day was here, I only wanted it to never show.

But, like last night, I had no control over my magic. It pushed to come out of me and this morning, it bubbled out of me like a brew in a cauldron set over a roaring flame.

"Princess Neve." Clemencia came closer, her steps small and hesitant. "Are you hurting? I can go get the healer."

I shook my head because a healer was the last thing I needed. No, I required someone who might know how to restrain my magic. Somehow, though my throat felt coated in frost, I croaked. "Get Vale."

She whirled and ran to the door, slipping on the ice on the floor before catching herself and flinging the door open. "Help! The princess needs help! Get Prince Vale!"

A nearby door opened.

"What's wrong with her?" Anna's voice, still groggy from sleep, hit my ear and a moment later, she appeared in the doorway. She'd put me in the room between hers and Clemencia's, and my oldest friend hadn't left my side until . . . Well, I supposed until I fell asleep because I did not remember when she left.

"Her magic is appearing!" Clemencia shouted. "Help! It's being violent with my lady!"

"What!" Anna shrieked, and though I still felt like a glacier was crushing me, I could still make out Anna's distinct footfalls, the way her clubbed foot dragged ever so slightly as she ran to the bed.

"Neve." Anna's voice trembled at my name. "Are you hurting?"

I raised my hand, showing her how blue my skin had turned before a flurry of snow burst all around me. I yelped, and Anna reared back.

"I'm going to take that as a yes," Anna murmured. Dimly, I heard Clemencia, still yelling for help, but as a fresh wave of cold rushed through me, the room fell away.

I stood in a forest, before a tree with purple leaves. A Drassil tree.

Vaguely, I knew I wasn't really in the forest. If I concentrated hard enough, which I could only do in fleeting seconds, I still felt the bed beneath me, heard an echo of someone talking. Anna? Clemencia?

But the tree looked so real. As though if I reached out to touch it, I'd feel the bark rough against my fingertips.

Was I dying? Was my magic killing me and this was some hallucination to make it less painful? Because though I still felt like I was freezing, it was working.

Perhaps this led to the afterlife. If so, it wasn't so bad. Sort of peaceful.

For a moment, it stayed that way. But when the tree's leaves danced and a faint light emanated from it, I sensed that was about to change.

"Hello?" I asked, feeling foolish but also justified. The Drassils had spoken to me before. Why not guide me into the afterlife too?

Isolde, that familiar female voice, the same one that spoke when I'd saved Anna. *You must go back.*

I pushed aside the fact that now the tree, or maybe the Faetia, was acknowledging my bloodline. "Back where?"

To Winter's Realm. To those you love.

I sucked in a breath. So I really was dying?

"How?" I asked, not sure if I wanted to follow through. Here it was pleasant and peaceful and in that room in Riis Tower it was . . . Well, anything but peaceful.

You decide to take your place in the world. You claim your life.

"I never wanted the life I have."

It is yours all the same. You go back. You claim your name, then decide if you want the rest.

"And what if I don't? What if I want to leave and go south with Anna? What if I want to forget about my mistakes?"

You cannot.

I swallowed. "Why? Is this the price I must pay?"

The voice didn't answer, and for a moment, I feared our conversation had finished until they spoke again.

The price is unpaid. Until you claim yourself, it will remain so.

"I'll hurt people."

Like Vale. My magic perplexed him, and I'd already hurt him with my actions. But all of that would be nothing to what he'd think when he learned of my bloodline. "I don't want to do that."

Think of those who will suffer if you do not. The fae of winter.

A deep breath sank into my lungs. For the first time, I saw what, perhaps, others would have seen so long ago. Claiming my name, my ancestry, would come with more problems. *Huge* problems. It would mean many fae would wish to kill me.

But I could also help others—those who had been like me.

Perhaps even the slaves in the Blood Court. Heat built inside me as purpose thundered in my heart.

If you think of them, you are worthy of the crown, my daughter.

Daughter. My heart rate ramped up. The voice I'd been hearing, the voice that spoke when I saved Anna. It was my mother's voice?

My hands began to tremble with the revelation that, yes, my mother had been a healer. She'd been there that night and helped me save Anna. Stars, how could I have been so stupid?

"Mother? I wish I could see you."

No sooner had I said the words than the air in front of me shimmered. A female shape materialized out of the shimmering and where once nothing stood, a faerie watched me. A crowned faerie.

A queen with eyes of blue I'd seen in paintings.

A sob wrenched its way up my throat, and the image of my mother gave a sad smile.

"Why haven't you done this before?" I lifted a hand and gestured to her form. She wasn't solid, and yet seeing her, almost lifelike, was more than I'd ever dared to hope for.

"Communication comes at a great cost. Just as it does when I speak to you without a body. Speaking to you this way, I will deplete faster. Turn back to stardust faster." She spoke normally, though her voice was the same as when she'd had no body. "But you need me more than ever before so I will stay as long as I can."

I wouldn't lie and say it was enough. It would never be enough, but it would have to be for now. "I'm so scared. Of so much."

That smile returned, sad and longing and understanding. "I would be worried if you were not. Much is to be done to bring the kingdom back from the brink. But remember this, my love—fear is normal. Fear is a reaction. Courage, however, is a choice."

A pretty line, but much more difficult to act on than to say.

"I want to help others," I admitted. "Those who have no power most of all. But how?"

"No one knows how to lead, not really. Not until they do it."

I wasn't sure how true that was, but any question

flew from my mind as my mother's form began to disappear. First her feet, then legs and arms and body. It happened so fast that within seconds I was trembling and committing her face to memory.

"Are you gone?" I whispered, wishing I'd asked a million more questions. That I'd been faster.

For a little longer.

"Why didn't you tell me before? Why didn't you tell me my given name? Who you were?"

You were not ready. Not in heart, soul, or mind. I would have only put you in more danger.

"But I am now?"

Yes, my love. You are ready now. I am sure of it. First, you must go west. Back to where it began.

West, to Guldtown? To confront Roar? I'd already wanted to do so. Nothing would stop me now.

"Mother?"

Go, Isolde, before it is too late. Make your family proud.

"I don't know how," I said.

You will figure it out. You . . .

Her words died, and the cold inside me intensified. My heart raced.

I stood on a precipice. If I didn't return now, if I didn't fight back the cold clouding my veins, I'd never return at all.

So I made a choice.

CHAPTER 42

VALE

Neve's eyelids fluttered, and for the first time in what felt like a thousand turns, I took a full breath.

"She's waking up, right?" Anna choked from blue lips. She shivered violently but refused to leave the room. As we did not want the human to pass out, Caelo had started a fire, and the temperature in the room was rising, albeit slowly. "Please tell me you see that she's waking up."

"I think so." I placed a hand on my wife's shoulder and winced at how the cold shot up my arm and stole my breath.

Though I'd been upset that she hadn't wished to share a bed with me last night, that she'd left me with so many questions, perhaps it had been for the best. The room was so cold, as was she. Had I slept in the bed with her, I might have frozen to death.

How did she survive?

"Neve?" I rubbed her shoulder, trying to force some heat into her skin. "Can you hear us?"

"She's still so blue," Clemencia whispered from where she stood behind Anna. "Should we have a bath drawn?"

Yes, Neve had turned a stomach-churning shade of blue, and her skin was freezing to the touch. She truly looked as though she'd been frozen inside a block of ice, but she breathed normally.

"It can't hurt." Luccan shot a glance at Caelo, Arie, and Thantrel, grouped together at his right. "Than and Arie, the servants are sleeping. Can you draw the water? Caelo, maybe toss another log on the fire? Get it roaring hot."

Caelo stoked the hearth as the two younger Riis brothers ran from the room into the adjoining bath chamber and began preparing the tub. My gaze followed them, taking in the bedchamber covered in ice. The room was barely tolerable to stand in, and everyone inside shivered.

Everyone except Neve.

What was going on?

Was this winter magic? I suspected I'd witnessed her wielding it last night too, but this was far beyond anything I'd seen.

"Not the price." The words slipped from Neve's lips and her eyelids fluttered harder, ratcheting up my heart rate. "Not the price to be paid."

My eyebrows slammed together. She'd asked about

a price before. Of hurting people. Whispered of her mother too.

Magical releases could be powerful, but Neve seemed to be experiencing hallucinations. I'd never heard of such a thing. Then again, I'd never heard of a faerie coming into their magic so late in life, either. Perhaps, for someone in Neve's circumstances, this reaction would be normal. I hoped she came out of it unharmed.

"I still have to pay the price," Neve spoke again, her voice becoming more frantic.

That should have been a cause for distress, but as she spoke, her breathing deepened. Beneath my hand, she grew a touch warmer, and color returned to her cheeks. She really was coming back to us.

"Neve, we're here." Anna took her friend's hand in her own. That small display of connection, of love, had to have hurt. Anna was human and thus, more sensitive to pain than the fae, but while Anna shivered even more violently than the rest of us, the human did not flinch back or release Neve. "*Please*, come back."

Anna's words worked like a spell, and Neve's violet eyes flew open. They landed first on me, then darted to Anna and Clemencia. My wife exhaled and some of the panic left her eyes.

"You're all alive. Of course you are, but when she left, I wasn't sure."

"Who is *she*?" I asked, and Neve tensed as if she hadn't been aware she'd spoken out loud.

"I—don't—" Her mouth closed, and her eyes

flared. "I mean, she was—" Again, her mouth closed, and her fingers lifted to cover her lips. "Bleeding skies, I can't lie."

I removed my hand, and it formed a fist before I caught myself and loosened. Why had she needed to lie? We were hovering around her, worried for her life. Why would Neve want to tell us an untruth?

"Then don't," I said, trying to sound calm, nonjudgmental of what she'd said, how she'd wanted to lie to us. "Who is she? And what was this price you spoke of so many times?"

Despite my efforts, the words came out harsher than I'd intended, and when Neve looked at me again, fear clouded her eyes.

"Wait," Anna interrupted. "Neve, let's get you near the fire. You're still blue."

My wife lifted her hands and stared at them, aghast. "Holy stars."

"You were worse just moments ago, my lady. Before we lit the fire." Clemencia came forward to help Neve stand.

Though I knew I should have assisted my wife, I did not. I merely watched as Clemencia and Anna helped Neve to the hearth. The snow and ice that had filled the room hindered their movements, though at least it hadn't seemed to get worse.

Neve had conjured it all. Had created this room of pure winter. Now that she was back and thawing, would everything melt? I had so many questions, so I followed the females, watched as they settled Neve into a chair in front of the hearth.

"Once you've warmed a bit, there's also a bath being drawn," Clemencia informed Neve. "It might be too much of a shock for you right now, though." She paused, tears filling her dark eyes. "We thought we'd lost you, my lady. That the release of your magic killed you."

Neve extended her hand out for Clemencia. "I'm sorry I didn't tell you everything before. That I had no magic. That I could lie. You must have been so confused after I killed that vampire and . . . Stars, Clem, I was trying to keep you safe, but I'm so sorry. I should have been more forward with my past—given you a real choice."

The lady-in-waiting nodded. "Anna told me much about your past. Once here, I did ask. Things weren't fitting."

"I'm glad she told you."

Clemencia swallowed. "Thank you for saying that. You are a real friend."

Neve's face loosened a touch.

"And I also wish to say that I'm sorry for your past. You should have never been held there. You're a fae of winter —a holder of winter magic, even." Clemencia gestured to the surrounding room. "This room is not the only place covered in frost and ice. The outside of the tower is too, spanning two rooms in either direction. All from you."

"Seriously?" Neve asked.

"You do not realize this, perhaps, but that means you are likely of noble birth."

No inkling of surprise flitted across my wife's face.

So she had known. Or, at least, suspected. But how? And why hadn't she mentioned it to me? She'd spoken of getting to know her family. Of wanting to know who they were. If she'd discovered a bloodline, then why not tell me? No matter the distance between us, I would have helped.

"She knows she is of noble birth," a deep voice said from the doorway.

Every head spun to find none other than Lord Leyv Riis at the door.

"Father!" Luccan stood. "When did you arrive?"

"Just now. I came calling at your house and saw the vampire ash before the gate. When no one was home, I had a hunch that something had happened. That you'd come here. Arie and Thantrel?"

The pair poked their heads out of the adjoining bathroom. Arie waved. "Here, Father. Running the princess a bath."

"Good." Lord Riis entered the room. "Which brings me back to the matter at hand. You know who you are, don't you, Princess Neve?" Lord Riis's eyebrows arched. "You are protecting yourself by keeping it a secret. However, those in this room have proven themselves trustworthy."

"Some secrets should remain in the shadows," Neve replied.

"Agreed," Lord Riis replied. "However, some deserve to see the light. Yours among them."

"How can you be so sure?"

"I might have worked out who you are," the spymaster replied.

Neve stiffened, and Lord Riis rushed onward. "And I can speak for my house. If I am correct, no one bearing my surname will say a word. Anna and Clemencia have proven themselves to be true friends too. I do not think either would share information to harm you?"

"Of course not!" Anna shouted. "Neve is my sister!"

"I would never harm my lady for she is also a dear friend." Clemencia's voice, though quieter, rang through the room as loudly as Anna's had.

Lord Riis gave a stout nod. "Then the only people we must question are Prince Vale and Sir Caelo."

I sucked in a breath. "Excuse me? She's my wife. I . . ."

I trailed off, not about to admit that I loved Neve when she barely looked at me.

Still, her head swung around, eyes wide as they landed on me. I was sure that everyone in the bedchambers sensed what I'd nearly admitted.

"She *is* your wife," Lord Riis said. "And you promised to protect her. Didn't he, Princess Neve?"

Of course I had. Save for the Riis brothers, everyone present had been there that night—the night I'd proposed and given Neve my name to keep danger at bay.

"Yes," Neve whispered. "But this . . . my secret will shake many. Perhaps asking him to keep his promise now is too much."

Lord Riis stood up straighter. "It might be. But I've also known Prince Vale since he was a babe. I've seen him grow, watched him turn into the male before us today." His voice softened. "To the prince, honor means much. So, Vale, if your wife shares news that may distress you, will you honor your word?"

What in all the nine kingdoms could be so dire that they thought I'd turn against Neve? After I'd thrown myself into danger for her. After I'd seen a friend injured and still said nothing.

After I'd fallen for her.

If they were questioning my honor, then Neve must be hiding something awful.

She had tried to lie. Tried to lie about a price and a female she'd seen. Why?

By the dead gods, the haunted, terrified look in her eyes made me want to rip something apart. Even if it tore *me* apart, I had to know what had done that to her.

"I will honor my vow of protection," I said finally. "Caelo?"

"I stand with you, Vale. Always. Whoever she is, if you are with Princess Neve, so am I."

Lord Riis bowed his head. "Princess?"

"Perhaps I'll start with what I just saw? Answer Vale's first questions?"

She stalled, but I didn't mind. I sensed she needed the courage to work up to whatever she must share.

"As you wish," Lord Riis said.

Neve turned her face up at me. Tears swam in her eyes. "I saw a Drassil tree. And heard a voice."

Like the day we'd wed.

"The voice was familiar and told me I was on the cusp of the afterlife, a sort of in-between land. I think my magic was killing me as it"—her hand swept around, encompassing the room—"did this."

For a moment, she broke eye contact with me and sought Lord Riis. "Apologies for this, by the way. I'll clean it up. Somehow."

Lord Riis let out a throaty laugh. "Let's not worry about such trivial matters. Continue."

"Right." A wobbly sigh left her lips, but she returned to face me again. "The voice was that of my mother, though I didn't realize it right away, only at the end. I asked if I was paying a price because when I saved Anna, the same voice said they could do so. For a price. I thought that meant my life."

Anna's hands flew to cover her mouth. "You didn't."

Neve turned to face her friend. "I did, and I'd do it again."

"But what if it costs your life later?" Anna whispered.

"I have a feeling something else will claim my life. But if I gave mine for yours, it is a price I'm willing to pay."

Anna began to cry, and while Neve looked like she wanted to console her, Clemencia was there, wrapping an arm around Anna's thin shoulders and nodding to my wife.

Neve folded her hands in her lap, stared at them. "The voice said I had to come back, that I had much to do here, people to help, and it was all because of who I was, which I discovered in the hidden part of the palace."

"Why didn't you tell me when you found out?" I asked, prying her attention from her hands. "I could have helped you find your family."

"No, Vale, you couldn't have." Neve stopped and for a moment, I sensed she would try to lie once more, but she took a deep breath and lifted her chin. "We'd never find them because my family is dead. Killed off in your father's rebellion—on his orders."

My heart stuttered. She possessed winter magic, marking her as from a powerful bloodline, a noble one, as Clemencia said. But her family was gone—on Father's orders. Killed during his rebellion.

By the dead gods.

I took a step back, studying her more closely than perhaps I ever had. How her hair was so similar to my father's. The shape of her eyes too. I twisted, taking in the room. I'd never seen winter magic this strong. Not even from him. My heart raced as I turned back to her and caught those violet eyes with my own.

"Neve, are you saying what I believe you're saying?"

Please say no.

Instead, she nodded. "The person I spoke to was my

mother, Queen Revna Falk." A shuddering sob broke from her before she mastered herself once more and rolled her shoulders back. "And I was born Isolde Falk."

CHAPTER 43

NEVE

Vale stood over me, a muscle feathering in his jaw, the concern I'd seen in his eyes before guttering as he considered my secret.

I waited, hoping he'd say something. *Anything.* The seconds ticked by into minutes, and finally, when the pressure in the room grew so thick I thought I might explode, I tried to get through to him.

"Vale, I—"

"I have to go," he said and stomped out of the room.

Everyone else stood still, most not daring to even look at me. Not until Anna took my hand. "Neve might like some time to rest."

"And a warming bath," Clemencia added. "The water is ready?"

Wide-eyed, Thantrel nodded. "It is. We will, umm, leave."

It was the first time I'd seen the youngest, most

605

outgoing Riis brother anywhere close to at a loss for words. Silently, Thantrel left, and his brothers followed, clearing out of the room until only one male lingered on the doorstep. Lord Riis.

"Something else?" I sighed, already exhausted by the day, though it was still early morning.

"You are exactly who I thought," Lord Riis said, "and Vale may take some time to come to terms with the truth, but I believe he will."

"We're related, Lord Riis. Closely so."

And married. Put two and two together on your own.

"I understand your fears in that regard." A small smile curled his lips. "I'll get another room prepared for you, Princess Neve." He turned to go.

"Wait."

Lord Riis stopped. "Yes?"

"How *did* you figure out my identity?" I didn't doubt that he'd known. Out of everyone in the room, he hadn't seemed surprised when I'd spoken the name my parents had given me.

"I'm a spymaster," Lord Riis replied. "I listen. I observe."

"And?"

"The night of the ball, in the kitchens." He pointed to my scar. "The slave looked shocked, like she recognized you."

Emilia. My stomach pitted.

"Did you interrogate her?"

"I questioned her. Without force."

My lips pursed. "And she told you?"

"She did not, but her colleagues had looser lips. I spoke with them too, and bit by bit, I pieced together that Emilia had worked for the Falks. Had been very loyal to Queen Revna." He swallowed. "You'll remember that I, too, knew your mother. I recognized the hairpin Princess Saga gave you that had once been Queen Revna's."

"I remember," I breathed, replaying the night of the Courting Festival's opening ball in my head.

"The night you wore that hairpin, you struck me as familiar. Only later did I realize I'd been recalling your mother. Not so much in your looks, but in the way you hold yourself. And after I spoke to the other slaves, I eventually remembered the human, Emilia, too. She'd worked in the nursery, and Queen Revna always proclaimed her to be the best nanny."

"You deduced who I was from that?" I frowned.

"No, but then you wed Prince Vale and the Drassil tree blessed your union. That it even spoke to you was remarkable. Few know this because there are many stories of the Drassils speaking to epic heroes, but they've only ever spoken to those of noble blood. That narrowed your identity further. That was enough for me to believe I might be right in my hunch." He paused. "Even as my suspicions grew, I had no idea which twin you might be. How did you learn?"

I pointed to the scar. "Emilia and the palace."

"The palace?"

"I can enter the hidden part of the palace. It speaks to me."

But only when it wants to, I didn't add.

Lord Riis's eyes crinkled at the corners. "A spymaster's dream."

"I suppose so." Another question tipped my tongue, one I'd tried hard not to consider, but if anyone would have the answer, it would be Lord Riis.

Perhaps it won't be so bad, and he can pull me out of my torment.

"I have another question."

"Anything, Princess Neve." He cocked his head. "Or shall I call you Isolde now?"

"No," I said.

Though that was the name I was born with, and my slave master had given me the name Neve, I wasn't ready to claim Isolde yet. It didn't feel right.

"Very well." He inclined his head. "You were asking?"

"It is said that King Magnus had everyone in House Falk and House Skau killed." I chose my words deliberately, knowing Prince Calder still lived in the dungeons —that the king had allowed the rumor to spread and instead tortured his birth father by keeping him locked up for decades. "I'm assuming bodies were found and verified? So why do people believe I am dead?"

The Lord of Tongues paled and cleared his throat. "Because after the fighting in Avaldenn ended, soldiers found the bodies of two young girls, toddlers, in the same tower where you and your sister slept. They were burned."

"Burned?"

"Not on purpose. You can't tell now, but King Magnus hurled fire at Frostveil, burning large portions of it. No one could know for sure if they were you and Thyra, but no other toddlers lived in that section of the palace."

"They could have been brought in, though," I said. "They had to be because Thyra escaped too."

The moment the words were out of my mouth, I regretted them. Lord Riis had promised to keep my secret, but he'd said nothing of a sister. If she lived, I might have just put a target on her back.

Lord Riis blinked. "You're sure?"

"That's what Emilia told me, though I'm not sure if my twin lives." I swallowed thickly. "A part of me wonders if someone put the toddlers there as decoys."

"You were—*are*—princesses," Lord Riis said as if that was a valid reason.

Maybe it was valid to my parents, but to me, it was only heartbreaking.

I sighed, and though the ice had left my veins, I found I wanted nothing more than to sit in the hot water and think over all that had happened. "Lord Riis, might we talk more later?"

"Of course. I'll have a servant waiting outside to show you to a new room when you're ready."

"Thank you."

He showed himself out, leaving me with Clemencia and Anna. The moment we were alone, my throat tightened.

"Do you two think Vale will forgive me for not telling him? That he . . ."

That he'd what? Would love me? Impossible. Fae families intermarried, particularly noble houses, but not as closely as we had. A relationship such as ours was taboo, and we would have to dissolve it.

That felt like someone was punching me in the stomach. My body could not fall in line with my head.

"He will, Princess Neve," Clemencia answered.

"Clem"—I stopped her—"please call me Neve."

I'd never shied away from the title of princess, not even when it was all pretend and had nothing to do with my past, but I considered Clem, like Anna, too good of a friend to use a title.

"It's clear in his gaze that he loves you." She paused. "And even if you can no longer be married and have done normal things that married couples do, you will both come to terms with the truth—you didn't know. No one meant harm by it. Quite the opposite."

"He seems like he does what he says," Anna added. "He tried to sneak you out of the city. And helped you kill another royal."

"He's the most honorable person I've ever met," I admitted.

My friends said nothing, and I found I couldn't sit there a moment longer. I made to stand, wobbled, and they were there, holding my arms and helping me to stabilize.

"Thank you," I whispered. "I want to use the bath."

Though every one of my muscles ached, I pushed

through the pain and exhaustion and, with their help, walked to the bathroom.

"You're no longer blue," Clemencia said, her tone soothing. She was always there to help me, and it seemed she was slipping into that role now. "But you need to stay in the bath for a good long while to make sure you're warmed from the inside out. It was terrifying how blue you were."

"Truly," Anna agreed.

I didn't argue, just slid into the tub. Arie and Thantrel had chosen the perfect water temperature. It was not too hot but not lukewarm, either. My muscles loosened and as I allowed the water to warm me, I wondered what Vale would say when I next saw him.

CHAPTER 44
VALE

O utside, the waning moon shone, though it somehow felt like only minutes had passed since I'd last seen Neve. Since I'd learned we were related.

We'd been intimate, and I'd dreamed about taking her and burying my cock in her every way possible.

I'd fallen in love with her.

I swallowed down the revulsion and chased it with a strong ale. The horn was empty, so once again, I held it out.

Sitting in a dilapidated armchair across from me, looking at home in his small family library, Thantrel cleared his throat. "You might have had enough, Vale."

"That so?" I grumbled, fingers walking along the top of a side table. "I seem to remember what happened today. So I would argue not." I stood, intent on filling my horn. The motion threw me off, but I righted myself quickly. Or so I'd thought. The way Arie and Thantrel looked at one another hinted otherwise.

Gryphon's balls. If they're agreeing on something, it must be true.

I sighed. "Fine. Someone get me water. Or perhaps I should go flop in the snow and lie there until morning."

The snow had fallen all day. Perhaps it would continue to do so and bury me. At least then, I wouldn't have to deal with the many thoughts running amok in my head.

"Water." Arie stood up and rushed from the room.

Caelo set his own horn in a holder. "Do you want to talk about it?"

Did I want to talk about how I was in love with my aunt? How she was born of a family line my father despised? How he'd kill her in an instant if he learned? The skin on the back of my neck tightened at the thought. By the dead gods, I needed to get Neve out of Winter's Realm.

But would she want to go? She was a Falk, with as much right—or more—to claim this land.

No, I didn't wish to talk about those matters.

"I'd rather not."

"Fine." Caelo rose from the settee he'd spread out across. "I need to piss, anyway."

He left, leaving me with Luccan and Thantrel. I eyed them suspiciously, a question arising.

"Did you two know?"

Luccan gaped. "That she's a Falk? Of course not! You think we'd hide that from you?"

I'd hidden things from them. Like that my father believed their family might have the Ice Scepter.

"We didn't know," Thantrel echoed. "Father never tells us things like that. To protect us."

"Also because you don't need to know everything." Lord Riis entered the room as if he owned it, which I supposed he did as this was his ancestral home. "Sons, I'd like to speak with Prince Vale. Alone."

"Arie went to get him water," Luccan said even as he rose from the armchair he'd occupied for hours.

"It can wait for what I wish to say."

Luccan nodded, but Thantrel eyed his father with skepticism. "Where did you go? No one has seen you since this morning."

"Another thing you do not need to know. Now, leave us."

My friends left, and I remained looking up at Lord Riis. "Well?"

"I see you haven't taken these revelations well."

I snorted. "One could say that."

"Well, I'm not sure if what I'm about to tell you will make your night better or worse."

"How could it get worse?"

Lord Riis gave a half smile. "In my experience, it can *always* get worse. Though the other side of the coin is true too—it can *always* get better. That this news, while it might be a shock, will have an upside."

I gestured to the chair Thantrel had occupied. "Out with it then."

"Kind of you to offer me a chair that has been in my family for centuries." The Lord of Tongues took the seat. Once settled, he leaned back, the picture of relaxation, though the slight tightness in his jaw said otherwise.

"I spoke with Neve after you left—"

"Isolde," I grumbled. "Shouldn't we call her Isolde?"

"For now, she wishes to go by Neve. Though I take it as a good sign that you care enough to even bring up her birth name."

"Feelings don't just turn off, Leyv."

He gave a single humorless chuckle. "I understand that well."

Something in his tone, a lightness, made me forget the depths of my turmoil. I looked up at him and caught him gazing out the window.

Though I'd paid it little attention, in the distance, if one looked closely enough, you could see the towers of Staghorn Castle—where my mother grew up. Where she'd lived until the day she'd wed my father.

"I left Riis Tower today," he said, turning back to me. "Returned to Avaldenn. Your father is furious that you and Neve have disappeared. Furious, too, that the vampires left a path of destruction in the city, and he has no one to blame."

"I tried to tell him."

"He should have listened. The only good thing in all this mess is he has not noticed my sons are gone."

My stomach pitted. I hadn't considered that either. While the Riis brothers had more leeway than most nobles because they lived in Avaldenn, they would be expected to be at Frostveil Castle for the Courting Festival events. By coming here, Luccan, Arie, and Thantrel had put themselves in danger.

"They should go back," I said. "Father might call an event at any moment."

"I agree," Lord Riis said. "I told them as much this morning, but they would not leave you after what happened."

I swallowed. "I don't deserve such good friends."

"You do, Vale." Lord Riis leaned forward and rested his elbows on his knees. "But to my point—I do not wish to speak of the king or the Courting Festival." He exhaled. "I only mention that I returned to Frostveil because, while there, I told someone where you were."

My spine straightened. Telling someone that we were here would reveal Luccan's gatemaking power. "Who?"

"Your mother. She needed to hear that you were safe, and we had something important to discuss, something we both think that you should finally learn."

He looked uncomfortable, an unusual expression for the male.

"You didn't tell her what you believed about Neve, did you?" The idea made my chest tighten and my blood race.

Lord Riis looked away, and I leaned forward. "Leyv? *You promised.*"

"I did," he agreed. "And I broke that promise, but only to—"

I shot out of my seat, and in two strides, had the spymaster by the throat.

"Mother will tell my father, and he will be even more pleased to kill Neve than he already was," I growled. "I *demand* to know why you broke your promise."

"Because . . ." Lord Riis's voice was strained, but he did not fight back. If he had, he might have been able to break free, for the Lord of Tongues was one of the few faeries larger than me. "Inga had to be convinced."

"*Of what?*"

"Telling you our secret." He could barely get the last word out.

I relaxed my hold on his neck slightly, enough for him to take a full breath. "What secret?"

His eyes locked with mine. "You and Rhistel are not Aaberg by blood. You are *my* sons."

CHAPTER 45
NEVE

The sun was rising outside the windows of Riis Tower as Clem and I searched for Luccan.

Yesterday had been long, and the night doubly so. Despite the passing of time, my mind was still so full of questions, doubts, and fears. Deep down, I knew what I wanted, would never forget that purpose burning inside me when my mother said I had the power to help many. I could not fathom how to reach my goals, but I had one clue, one way to begin.

My mother had told me to go west. Why exactly? I wasn't sure but suspected it might have something to do with the Hallow. Or perhaps my closure involving the situation between Roar and me. I'd wanted to confront Roar since he'd ridden from Avaldenn in the dead of night, and that desire had only intensified when I learned that Roar might have known who I was the whole time, so my mother's suggestion fit perfectly with my plans. West I would go. Hopefully, with Luccan's help.

Clemencia stopped before a closed door. "He takes his breakfasts in here when he stays the night."

My ears perked up. "How often does he visit?"

Her eyes crinkled slightly at the corners. "We really had not been here long when you arrived. You know, with the travel time and all. So he's only visited twice, two days in a row."

"That's a lot for someone who should be at court." I elbowed her gently. "You know, by orders of the king."

Pink roses bloomed on the apples of her high cheekbones. "He has things to do here. And it's not like he takes a lot of time to get back to Avaldenn."

"Things to do. *Riiiight.*" I laughed. "I bet he just wants to flirt with you."

"I won't deny that there's some of that too." Clemencia patted down her skirts. "Now, don't you have something important to ask him?"

"I'm noting this deflection, and you can be sure that I plan on asking you more about the two of you later," I teased and tapped my temple. "But yes, you're right, I should get on with it."

I knocked on the door.

"Come on in!" Luccan called out.

We let ourselves into a bedroom and found Luccan wearing a thick robe, his dark red hair pouring over his shoulders as he read a book.

"Good morning," I said.

He stiffened and lifted his eyes from the book. "Ah, Princess Neve and Lady Clemencia." He pulled his robe tighter over his broad chest. "Apologies for my state. I thought you were the servant bringing me my tea and biscuits."

"Afraid not," I said. "Just us."

"Which is quite good enough." Luccan rose and began picking up his books. "To what do I owe this visit?"

"No need to tidy up." I took a few more steps into the room, which was spotless and sparse. Like in the rest of the home, there was no sign of ice spider imagery to represent the now noble House of Riis. I wondered if the castle Lord Riis lived in—one that I suspected might have been my mother's ancestral home—crawled with those mysterious eight-legged creatures. "I have a favor to ask of you and then I'll leave you to your breakfast."

Luccan straightened. "If I can help, I will. Also, my father spoke for our family yesterday, giving you an assurance that we would keep your secret, but I want you to know that I plan to remain your friend, Neve."

My heart stuttered. Any relationship with me puts him at significant risk. If the king learned who I was— or more likely, *when* he learned who I was, if my budding ambitions went to plan— and that Luccan was aiding me, that would spell his death sentence. But I didn't need to tell Luccan that for I was certain he already knew.

"Even though Vale despises me?" I asked because despite all the other reasons for him to shy away, that one seemed like it would be very important to Luccan. "You two are so close."

"We are. And for the record, I doubt he despises you. Rather, he's in shock."

I'd have been worried if he wasn't but going through the emotions of our falling-out felt very different from expecting them. "Well, I am thankful for your friendship. It's more than I could ask for."

Luccan looked like he wished to say something more, but I wanted to get on with my request, so I plowed onward.

"I came here to ask you to create a gateway to the west. To Guldtown."

Red eyebrows drew together. "You wish to see Lord Roar?"

"To confront him," I corrected. "I've wanted to since he left me high and dry at Frostveil, but when I saw my mother in my . . ." What did one call what I'd experienced?

"My vision," I settled on, "she said to go west. I think she wants me to get closure."

So I can move on to other things, bigger things. Like finding the Ice Scepter and helping the fae of Winter's Realm.

I kept those thoughts to myself. Before I shared what my heart wanted most, I needed a plan.

"I can understand that," Luccan said. "However, at my skill level, making a gateway takes me weeks. It's why I haven't made that many, just those connecting my family's properties."

My mouth fell open. "Weeks? But it would take less time to ride!"

"True. The upside to a properly formed gateway is that you can use it many times."

"Yes, of course. I just didn't expect that timeframe." I sighed. "Well, I had hoped to get there sooner, but——"

"*Although*," Luccan interrupted, a spark in his eyes, "I could try to make a temporary gateway. Mind you, it would still take me a day or so, and it would only last a second, long enough for you to pass through."

I inhaled; my hope renewed. "But it's possible?"

He nodded slowly. "I've never done it before, but I have read about them." He glanced at Clemencia and straightened. "I wouldn't mind trying and stretching my magic."

I smothered the smile I felt growing inside me. Though I believed that Luccan wished to help me, I also suspected that he wanted to impress Clemencia. "I'd so appreciate it."

He stepped up to a bookshelf, pulled a tome from the collection, and skimmed the first page, then flipped through the book. He was about halfway through the pages when he stopped and came closer.

"This is a map of Guldtown. I've only been there once, as a lad, but you likely remember it better than me. Pick a place where you'd like me to open the gateway."

I examined the map, which, with my limited knowledge, appeared up to date. The castle stood out and while going there would be easiest, I also wouldn't put it past Roar to have put magical defenses in place. Those that might injure us if we tried to use magic. After all, in the eyes of the king, Roar had committed treason. It was likely the Warden of the West would have only recently returned home, and not having protections put up the moment he rode through his city's gates would be idiotic. Roar might be a snake, but he wasn't stupid. However, he couldn't keep everyone from Guldtown, right?

My gaze drifted to the city gates I'd first ridden through on Frode's cart. Then I'd been half frozen and dressed in little more than rags. The next time I walked through them would be so very different. I pointed to a spot in the woods near the city gates. "We can come out here. I can walk to the castle from that point."

"Got it." Luccan plucked a quill from his table and noted the spot. "I'll begin preparations. Remember, you must be ready at any second to leave. Once I am close to the final moments of creation, I will send for you, no matter the time."

"I'll be ready," I assured him. "Thank you for your help. For your friendship."

"You're welcome, Neve." Luccan held up the book. "Looks like I'd better get to work."

We left his room, and I turned to Clemencia. "That went much better than expected."

"He's an honorable male. And your lineage might even excite him."

"What do you mean?" I waved for her to follow.

The morning had just begun, but I was ready for the next stage of my plans—training with my unruly magic.

"Luccan doesn't always agree with the king." Clemencia's teeth dug into her bottom lip. "I don't think I do either."

I gaped. Clemencia, my rule-following tutor, was expressing disdain for the male whose word was law?

"How do you mean?"

Clemencia's quickening pace hinted that she might be nervous to answer. "Things I saw at court . . . they did not sit right with me. And I don't think I'm the only one. You must know, Neve, that some will see your name as a way to rid the kingdom of its troubles."

My pulse skittered. My mother had mentioned something similar, but how many others were thinking it?

Stars, what did Vale think about all this? And if he forgave me for keeping my identity a secret, could he also forgive me if I claimed my real name and acted for those I thought needed it most? Which wasn't his father or the other nobles.

Or was any relationship we might have had broken forever? I came to a halt, the thought sending a jolt of physical pain through me.

"Neve?" Clemencia placed a hand on my shoulder. "Are you well?"

I exhaled. "Yes. I came to a rather unpleasant thought and my body reacted."

"Don't discount that."

"I won't."

Though I didn't know what to make of it either.

Dressed in a thick cloak and boots, I tramped outside through the snow.

Clemencia trailed behind me, and I glanced back and up to find Anna watching—as she said she would. I waved at her; glad I'd been able to dissuade my best friend from coming outside.

It was too cold for a human, particularly one who had spent most of her life in the Blood Kingdom's relatively mild climate.

It was cold outside, even for me. The temperature had dropped precipitously last night and hadn't risen again after the sun rose. The frost and ice that my burst of magic sent crawling across the outside of Riis Tower hadn't melted yet either. Though the cold was a way of life in the Winter Kingdom, to me the recent changes toward deepening cold, more snow, and ice and frost, felt ominous, like twilight descending much too quickly.

I glanced back at Riis Tower again, for the first time taking in the building as a whole. It was, as the name implied, one circular tower, large enough for a family of about ten and a few servants. The middle of the tower boasted a courtyard. While I'd been told I could practice there, I'd opted to distance myself, just in case my magic got out of hand again.

The Tower was so plain that I couldn't imagine Lord Riis growing up there. It wasn't a home made for a lord, but a wealthy merchant, which was what the Riis family had been, once upon a time. And aside from the Tower's size, the only other thing that spoke to their wealth was the freestanding log sauna nearby. Public saunas existed in cities, maybe even in larger towns, but few could afford such a private luxury.

"I think this is far enough, Prince—Neve." Clemencia cleared her throat. She had difficulty doing away with formalities.

"Sure." I stopped. "First step, make a clearing."

"Perhaps a path too? For the way back?" Clemencia's cheeks were pink from the effort it had taken to trudge through the snow.

"I'll try my best." I inhaled deeply. "Remember, I'm new to all this."

Even though Clemencia understood that and didn't expect a grand spectacle from me, the admission still had the power to shame me. As a slave, my master had proclaimed my nameday to be on the first day of each new turn. Now, I knew that while he had gotten the correct turn and the day had been a good guess, it was also incorrect. Queen Revna's diary had stated that her twins had been born on Winter Solstice, which was in nearly two moons' time.

I was twenty-three turns old—nearly twenty-four— and I didn't know a thing about my magic. No matter how you looked at it, I was very far behind, and though I had no power over that, a mixture of negative emotions, mostly shame and fear and resentment, still rubbed me raw.

"I'm here for you," Clem assured me.

I wasn't sure how I'd gotten so lucky to have her as first my tutor, then my friend.

"Stand back a bit?" I waved.

Even though she'd already endured my frozen bedroom, she indulged me, taking a dozen steps back.

Ideally, I would have had Vale with me. He was the only one in Riis Tower who had winter magic. But we weren't speaking, and despite Luccan's reassurance, I wasn't sure we ever would again.

A lump rose in my throat. Reflexively, I swallowed. Stars, I needed a distraction.

Time to work magic. I rubbed my hands together, unsure how to start and hoping it would flow.

"How about you focus on directing wind, like Prince Vale does, to make your clearing?" Clemencia offered, ever the helpful teacher, even when she didn't know a thing about the subject.

"Sure," I said because it made sense. Winds were part of winter storms. Plus, I didn't have any better ideas.

I closed my eyes and sank deep into myself, seeking the power I'd felt rushing through me the night before. The magic that, had I not chosen to meet it, rather than succumb to it, would have taken my life.

It didn't take long for it to awaken. All morning, my magic had lain inside me, dormant. Or perhaps I hadn't known how to feel for it until now. After all, I'd seen a light come from me a few times but didn't have a true release until the night the assassins came for me. I still wasn't sure how that had happened, when my magic should have been bound by the potion.

But today, the power inside me hummed to life, filling me in such a way that my eyes flew open.

Clemencia was beaming. "I can sense it! And you haven't created a storm yet, so that's good!"

"Small miracles." I focused on that hum, on that vibration inside me, and marveled at it. All my life I'd wanted to feel the thrum of my power in my veins and for the first time, I was about to control it too.

To my right, unbidden, snow swirled, creating a funnel that reached my hips.

Or maybe not. But a random swirl was much better than a room filled with frost, ice, and snow. Right?

I could work with this, something smaller and less life-threatening.

Hand twisting, I directed the swirling snow up, and to my great delight, it did as I requested. For the next few minutes, I moved the small vortex around, practicing, flexing my muscles. When I'd gotten a handle on it, I released and focused on the ground at my feet.

Using one's hands wasn't necessary to work magic. Other fae didn't, though it did feel intuitive for me to practice using them, and as I was just beginning, I'd allow myself a crutch. I faced my palms to the ground and called air.

The northern winds, much milder in the midlands compared to Avaldenn, redirected, but with far more force than I'd intended and slammed into the ground. An explosion of snow filled the air.

Clemencia squealed, and though my heart was thundering, I let out a laugh. Mistake or not, it felt amazing to work my magic.

Like I was a full fae.

When the air cleared of snow, I twisted toward Clem and noticed someone walking toward us.

Clem noted my distraction, turned, and waved. "Caelo! Good morning!"

"Good morning to you too, Lady Clemencia. Princess." He moved through the snow with strong legs, his pace faster than ours had been. When he reached us, he gestured to the snow. "Impressive work."

"It wasn't intentional," I admitted. "I'm flexing my powers, seeing what I can and cannot do."

"We have a good idea of what you can do."

"*On purpose*," I amended. "I'd rather not nearly die whenever I need to work a feat so impressive."

"That would be preferable, wouldn't it?" He paused. "I heard from the others that you've been sparring regularly. Considering your circumstances, you need to maintain your current physical strength and prowess. Ideally, continue to build on it too. So I came out here to see if you wished to train with the sword today?"

"Yes," I said, lighting up inside. I'd enjoyed my daily physical training sessions.

Caelo's blue eyes took me in with interest. "You enjoy sparring practice?"

"I do. It makes me feel . . ." I trailed off, considering exactly what sparring did for me, "As if I'm no longer a weak slave. Like I might actually be able to defend myself against any threat that comes my way—one day, at least. And I liked just doing something active too, moving my body, learning what I could do, pushing myself."

Caelo nodded. "Your ancestors were great warriors. So great that Queen Sassa unified the many kingdoms of Winter into one before taking on the Shadow Fae. I can see you being a part of her Valkyrja."

"Valkyrja? What's that?"

I'd heard a little about Queen Sassa, but never that term.

"An elite group of fighters, all of them female."

"But females serve as soldiers here, right?" My eyebrows pulled together, unsure why one would need an exclusive group when anyone could be in the army or the Royal Nava.

"It wasn't always that way," Caelo said. "When the kingdoms were separate, things were different. Back then, females weren't always fighters, but in Queen Sassa's court, they were. Her Valkyrja weren't her queensguard, but they were a unit the queen often deployed in battles. Always to astonishing effect." Caelo grinned in a way that made him look much younger than his twenty-something turns. "Reading the accounts of Valkyrja flying into battle on their pegasi was what pushed me to take up the sword."

"Interesting." I made a note to find books on the topic. Perhaps Riis Tower had some. For now, though, I needed to return to practicing. "Can we delay sparring,

Caelo? If I can handle it, I'd like at least an hour of magic work. I have to build those muscles too."

"I'll plan for a session after lunch. Thantrel wishes to join too. That's fine with you?"

"Of course. I'll see you then."

He turned to go back to the tower.

"Uh, Caelo," I blurted.

He faced me again. "Yes?"

"How is Vale?"

"Hungover as a dwarf after the Winter Solstice."

I didn't understand the reference, and yet, I still cringed. "I see."

"Not all because of what you told him."

"What do you mean?"

"He had a talk with Lord Riis last night—one that left him in a foul mood. Before they spoke, he'd already downed many horns of ale, but after . . . Well, I've never seen Vale drink quite so much."

"Any idea what they spoke about?" I asked, unable to help myself.

"No, and the High Lord left before any of us woke. His sons do not know either."

Luccan hadn't even mentioned it. But why would he share that information with me? Technically, I was still Vale's wife, but we were separated in every way that mattered.

"I see." I rubbed my hands together to ward off the cold. "Thank you for telling me. I'm worried about him."

Sir Caelo's full lips spread into a smile. "It relieves me to hear that, Princess Neve."

"Relieved? Shouldn't I be the one worried an Aaberg will come for me?"

The knight scoffed. "Perhaps, but I doubt it will be Vale."

He was the second person to say such a thing. Though I wasn't sure if either was right, my heart leapt at his words.

CHAPTER 46
VALE

F rom my tower window, I watched Caelo trudge toward the castle as Neve resumed practicing magic.

My stomach twisted as, for a second time, she raised a funnel of swirling snow, this time to double her height before losing control. The funnel exploded over her and Clemencia, prompting laughter.

My wife was a Falk, working winter magic. Not with much luck, but it was obvious that despite her lack of refined motion, the magic flowed from her. For a beginner, that meant quite a lot. Particularly after how much of her power poured from her last night. And as she laughed, she seemed in good spirits. Learning was always easier with that sort of attitude.

I could help her, though.

The thought came unbidden and unwanted, and I shoved it into the recesses of my mind.

Technically, yes. I possessed the skills and knowledge

to help. But after how I'd acted, would she even want my help?

Would she wish to speak with me ever again?

I turned away from the window, intent on downing a glass of ale. A servant had made sure to supply me with drink through the night and into the morning. That had never been more apparent than when I took one step and stumbled over my own feet.

Bleeding skies, I hated this world.

Hated how things were turning out.

Why didn't Lord Riis keep his secret? I could have lived my whole life not knowing the truth, even if knowing it made so many things click into place.

Like how my twin and I never wielded winter magic as well as Saga. Certainly not like Father either. How we alone of the Aabergs had dark eyes—a feature everyone attributed to House Vagle, though the hue was uncommon there too. No, those eyes came from Lord Riis.

Most of all, it explained why Lord Riis, out of every noble in the kingdom, made it a point to come to Frostveil often. How he'd sought me and Rhistel out as younglings, given us toys, and played with us. How when he'd had Luccan, and then his other children, he'd brought them to the palace too.

He'd always been there in our lives, a quiet spectator. As involved as it was safe to be. His dark brown eyes always followed us, had always crinkled at the corners when either Rhistel or I made mischief.

It wasn't that he was dear friends with our mother, but that he still loved her—that he always had.

He'd said as much to me last night. Said that he'd often joined his mother, an ambitious faerie born of the merchant class, when she attended my grandmother, Lady Eliana Vagle in Staghorn Castle. In those visits as a young male, Lord Riis fell in love with my mother. They were each other's firsts for everything, and said that, while he'd had many other lovers, none stole his heart.

He claimed to love Rhistel and me too, so much so that it hurt him to have to stay away. He'd managed only because it was what was safest for our mother and for us.

As much as I hated him for shattering my life, erasing every sense of self I'd cultivated over the turns, I understood a female stealing one's heart and claiming it for her own. A male would do many things for that one special female—even have a long-lasting affair under the king's nose.

I poured another glass of ale, downed it, and groaned. The stars knew I'd regret every drink I'd had thus far, but I couldn't stop myself. Drink was the only thing that numbed the pain and the reality of my life, or what I'd thought had been my life.

A knock came at the door.

"Come in," I called, hoping it was the servant who had been checking in hourly. Perhaps with my normal order of ale, I'd get food this time. That might save me some pain later.

Instead of the servant, however, Caelo appeared. When he saw me, he frowned and poked his head into the hallway.

"Water and bread *only*," he said to someone—the old servant, most likely. "And don't bring him more ale. No matter what he threatens. I'll fight him if necessary. Judging by the state of him, I'd easily win."

A soft *'eep'* sounded from the hallway and then footsteps as the servant left.

Caelo entered my room, bright blue eyes taking me in with concern.

"You scared my servant away." I frowned. "I want more ale."

"No more than your face probably scared them." Caelo snorted. "You look awful. The last thing you need is more ale."

Fists tightening, I stalked over to a chair by the fire, which I had not had the will to light, and slumped down. The chair creaked under my weight, old but well-made and sturdy.

"You yelled at Lord Riis last night," Caelo said and joined me.

"What did you hear?" My eyes narrowed. I hadn't considered that anyone would overhear me railing against Lord Riis after he told me his secret. My mother's secret.

Now my secret.

"General sounds of anger. The door has a muffling enchantment on it, but we knew there was yelling. And he left before anyone could question him today. Care to tell me why?"

"Why did you speak with Neve?" I asked, deflecting.

He snorted. "You've been watching her the whole time, haven't you?"

I didn't answer.

Caelo snorted. "She asked about you."

My gaze lifted from where it had dropped to the floor. "She did?"

"Yes." Caelo sat forward and stared me in the eyes. "You should go talk to her."

"She's a Falk, Caelo."

"Most everyone in the Tower heard. And yet, *you're* the only one avoiding her. Avoiding all of us."

"I'm not avoiding everyone. I let you in here, didn't I?"

"I didn't give you a chance to deny me."

"Good thing too. You're quite obnoxious."

"That's why you love me."

A single laugh tripped out of my lips, surprising even me.

"There we go!" Caelo said with a grin. "You need to come out of this funk."

"You say that like it's easy to learn that the female you're married to is a Falk—a member of the house that my own house exterminated like rats. An enemy."

"To whom, though?" Caelo arched an eyebrow.

"What?"

"Whose enemy is she?"

I swallowed, understanding, though it resonated as a

betrayal to my father, or the fae who had raised me as his son and who I still thought of as my father. Truths aside, those feelings hadn't evaporated overnight.

"The king despised the Falks, and I guess he had a good reason, but why would you hate Neve? She was only a baby when the rebellion ended." Caelo shook his head. "I understand you want your father to be proud of you, but there's nothing noble about despising someone who couldn't even dress herself when you took the crown. She should not pay for the faults of her father."

"I agree, but he would hate her for her bloodline. He already hates her for what she's done."

My friend scowled. "If he knew what she'd gone through, he'd be awed."

Though Father would never love Neve, had he heard her story before he'd met her and the events of the Courting Festival transpired, he would have been impressed. She'd escaped slavery and shown great ingenuity and bravery to get what she wanted.

But once he learned of her bloodline, he still would have fed her to the White Bear. Or worse.

"I'm awed," I admitted.

"Brother, you're not awed. You're in love."

I cringed. Was I so transparent?

"Everyone sees it," Caelo added, as if he were a mind reader. "You're disgusted with yourself because . . . Well, yes, we've all worked out the relationship, but"— he shrugged—"you didn't know. No one blames you for it."

I stood, and, never missing a beat, Caelo did too.

"I'm not good enough for her."

"Ah, I disagree. Though I understand not pursuing a relationship now, even if that was what you once wanted."

I exhaled, long and low.

"Still want, then?" Caelo let out a thoughtful hum.

"It's quite annoying that you keep speculating about my feelings."

"I've known you for over twenty turns and even if I had not, you're wearing them on your face, Vale." He paused. "Is something else wrong? Am I misreading this situation?"

"No," I admitted because the truth was, even when I'd thought that Neve and I were cousins, I still loved her. Contemplating how I'd turn that love off had been painful, but now I faced another problem—a bigger one.

"What else is wrong?" Caelo came up beside me and only then did I realize that I'd gravitated to the window once more, to where she'd been. She was still practicing magic.

"You can tell me anything, Vale."

Stars, I wanted to. I'd dealt with my burden all night, and I'd considered telling three people: my brother, Neve, and my best friend. Somehow, it was easiest to envision telling Caelo. And yet, I would need his word. A solemn vow.

"I have a secret that would change the fates of kingdoms." I looked at my friend. "I do want to tell you, but only if you do not tell anyone else. Should this information get out, it will be from my lips only."

Of every other soul in the world, Rhistel deserved the truth too, but all night long I'd wrestled with telling him. Far more than I'd wrestled with telling Caelo. I still was not certain that I would tell my twin.

"You wish for me to make an eiðra?" Caelo asked.

"I do."

"Of course I will," Caelo replied, looking slightly wounded. "Though I hope you believe that, even without one, I would never tell a secret of yours to another soul."

I did believe such a thing. Him, I trusted to the ends of this world, I always had been able to, even when the darkness loomed, so all-encompassing. And yet, I was so insecure with my new identity that I still required this shield.

"On the spark of your parents' souls in the after-life." I extended my palm. "Swear you will say nothing, or their spark be put out."

Caelo sucked in a breath at the harsh demand but did not hesitate to clasp my forearm at the elbow with his hand, and I squeezed his forearm in return. "Vale, I swear on my parents' souls, on their eternal spark dining and drinking in the great long halls of the stars, that whatever you tell me will remain a secret."

An exhale parted my lips. I already felt lighter.

"I am not who you think I am." I paused, the next words battling their way up my throat. "I'm not Vale

Trahal of House Aaberg, but Vale Trahal of House Riis."

Caelo's mouth fell open. "Lord Riis is . . ."

"My birth father."

"Bleeding skies," Caelo swore. "Now that is one thing I would have never expected to come out of your mouth."

"Never something I expected to hear, either."

"He told you last night, didn't he? Hence the yelling?"

"He thought it might help with Neve, because apparently everyone can see I love her. Even if I haven't told her myself."

Caelo chuckled dryly. "I've dragged my feet on such a matter before." Eyes wide, he clapped a hand on my shoulder. "But I have to say, there is one beacon of light here."

"What's that?"

"If you wish, you can be with her now and not feel disgusted." He cocked his head. "And, to be honest, I'm a bit relieved that the king is not your father."

My eyebrows flew up. "What do you mean?"

Caelo dropped his arm. "The king is a bastard, literally and in every other way possible, Vale. You have always loved him, and sometimes he can be halfway decent, but of late? He's become harder, crueler. I heard what he did to Sir Qildor, and I doubt you have forgotten it."

I'd never be able to forget that day, and I knew what Caelo meant. I recognized how my father was changing as winter grew stronger, as his grip on the kingdom weakened.

"I'm not saying you should not love him. I'd never say such a thing," Caelo added. "But knowing you do not have a blood tie could help you stand up to him in ways you have not before. Ways that can be seen in the light, and not only in the shadows."

Not by using the cabal. That's what he meant. Our group endeavored to assist those that my father did not seem to care to help. Though we remained inactive since the Courting Festival began, a fact that haunted me, especially when I remembered the dead actors from the Royal Theater.

"It's not like I don't stand up to him, Caelo."

"Not enough, though."

My hand went to my heart. "Ouch."

"Sometimes the truth hurts. But we need to hear it all the same."

CHAPTER 47
NEVE

I dropped my trembling arms to my sides, annoyed that my magic had appeared, seemingly to do whatever it wanted.

"You're tired," said Thantrel, my tutor and only companion for the morning. He shielded his green eyes from the sun, so brilliant against a backdrop of pristine snow. "You worked too hard yesterday."

Between practicing magic in the morning, sword-play with Caelo in the afternoon, and then volunteering to mend some of the Riis family pieces their servants didn't have the skill to do, Thantrel was right. I'd fallen into bed the night before, exhausted.

And yet, I still had the energy to wonder about Vale for a couple of hours before sleep claimed me.

Only Caelo had seen the prince since the day my magic burst out of me, and the knight had said nothing about their meeting. Not to me, anyway.

"I suppose I should be happy I won't experience any

magical growth spurts." I sighed, blowing a stream of white air from my lips. Though it wasn't snowing at the moment, it was still freezing outside. "It would be embarrassing to be unable to control my magic *and* be clumsy."

The corner of Thantrel's eyes crinkled. "You say that like you *know* they aren't going to happen."

I scoffed. "You're hoping for the opposite, aren't you?"

"Until Filip arrived at court, I was the last in my circle to experience a growth spurt," Thantrel replied. "It's far more fun when you're not the one experiencing it."

"Well, I hope I don't. I have quite enough on my plate, learning magic at all." My hands landed on my hips. "Maybe you're right, and I need to rest."

"You know what helps me the most when I'm exhausted?" Thantrel asked.

"What's that?"

"A stiff drink."

"It's not even midday!"

He shrugged an elegant, lithe shoulder. Unlike the other Riis brothers, Thantrel was slim, his muscles lean. His build must have come from his mother. "Rules are made to be broken."

I laughed. "Says you."

"Trust me. Life is more fun that way."

Considering Thantrel seemed to have a lot of fun, I believed that.

"One more go," I said. "Then I'll allow you to corrupt me."

"Princess, you couldn't handle me corrupting you."

My cheeks turned red at his silky tone, which only made the youngest Riis brother laugh as I turned away from him and called my magic once more.

Thantrel wasn't who my heart wanted, but he was so charismatic and handsome that when he flirted—which was quite often—I became a little flustered.

Doing my best to ignore the faerie behind me, I looked at the evergreen trees, their limbs hanging heavy with snow from the near-constant storms plaguing the midlands since our arrival.

"I'm going to take the snow from the nearest tree and swirl it around the tree," I declared.

"Looking forward to the show," Thantrel replied.

I focused on the tree, willing my magic to rise against my skin again. It did my bidding, the pulse of it weak, tired, as Thantrel claimed. But I could not have that. When I faced Roar, I needed to be strong in every way that mattered. I needed to show him that he had not shattered me.

Not that he'd care, but *I* did. I'd trusted Roar, and he'd broken that trust. More than that, he'd kept secrets from me. And I was certain that he'd suspected my true identity since the moment he'd first seen me, when he commented on my scar.

Magic thrumming, I directed it at the tree, and to my delight, the branches shook.

"More," Thantrel called.

"I'm trying," I gritted out as my arms began to tremble, far too soon for how long I'd been going at it.

I pushed again, and the snow on the branches fell to the ground.

"Wrong way."

"Aren't you supposed to be helping me?" I barked but didn't bother to look at him. He was likely smiling, and that would only infuriate me.

"This is how Father taught us! Are you saying he did it wrong?"

Aside from Luccan, I did not know. The other Riis brothers had yet to show their powers. But seeing as Luccan was trying to create a gateway in a matter of days, I suspected that Lord Riis knew a thing or two about training his sons.

My teeth ground together with the effort of sending more power at the tree, trying to lift the snow, and sweat trickled down my face before, finally, something happened. The snow rose in a thin stream, straight up rather than swirling about.

Almost there.

Another wash of power left me, this time leaving behind the lingering sensation of spikes pounding into my forearms. I winced but didn't let the pain stop me. I'd been through so much worse—and if I wanted to live a life in which I wasn't looking over my shoulder every two seconds, I had to become powerful. So strong that others would not dare to mess with me.

To do that, I had to walk through the fire and reshape myself. I had to believe I'd transformed from the blood slave I'd once been to a fae who could change the lives of those who lived as I once did.

"Like this." I twirled my fingers in the direction I wished the snow to go. Another spike of pain slammed into my chest, stealing my breath for a moment, but I was determined to make this work. I sucked in air. "*Come on.* I want you to—"

From the corner of my vision, a figure emerged from the Tower, then stopped. Normally, I wouldn't care who was watching, but I felt their attention like a fire burning from my feet to my head and I couldn't help but look.

Vale was there, stepping foot outside of Riis Tower for the first time in days. He didn't look drunk or hungover, like I'd imagined he would. His eyes were so intense that they nearly leveled me.

I sucked in a breath, and the control over my power vanished. The snow fell to the ground, and my bones ached.

"Bleeding stars," I breathed, knees buckling.

Thantrel was there in an instant, catching me, but I remained fixated on Vale. On his heaving chest.

Was he angry?

Before I placed my finger on his emotion, Vale twisted and stomped around the tower, out of sight.

I exhaled and tears sprang to my eyes. I wiped them away.

Did he think I wanted to be who I was? That I'd planned that we'd become close, intimate even, all the while knowing our relations?

Was I the only one who still felt this forbidden bond between us?

"He'll get over it," Thantrel whispered, still holding me up.

Swallowing, I stood on my own and gazed at the snow.

"He needs time," Thantrel assured me.

Tears stung my eyes before I wiped them away yet again. "He despises me."

"He's been drinking us out of house and home. I doubt he's clear-headed at all right now."

"I need him to know I didn't mean to hurt him."

"He knows."

I stared at the spot where Vale disappeared. "I'm not so sure."

The fire blazed, warming the den and my aching bones, which despite a full, delicious meal and a hot bath, still had not recovered from my hours of practicing magic.

I sipped the wine from the Summer Isles and relaxed back into the armchair, watching as Clemencia, Arie, and Anna played nuchi.

Anna had learned tonight, and my best friend caught on quickly, a fact that did not surprise me but seemed to charm Arie. Despite losing badly, the middle Riis brother smiled at Anna more often than I'd ever seen him smile.

CHAPTER 47

Almost as often as Luccan stole glances at Clemencia.

As though my thoughts summoned him, Luccan walked into the den. I gaped.

I'd seen him hours ago, checking on him when Thantrel and I came inside from practicing magic. Then, he'd looked exhausted, but since midday, Luccan had declined.

His skin, already naturally pale, was wan and dark circles ringed his eyes. His gait was sluggish, and though he tried to hide it, I spied a faint limp.

I patted the seat next to me, wanting to speak with him before he began flirting with Clemencia. "Join me."

Luccan grinned and, after pouring himself a spirit from a cabinet brimming with bottles of liquor from all over Isila, sank into the neighboring armchair with a groan.

"How are things going with the gateway?" I asked.

"Well enough. I might have it ready by tomorrow. Be prepared."

"I will." I sipped my wine, wondering how to delicately mention that perhaps he was pushing himself too hard.

As it turned out, I needn't worry about tact. Anna put down a winning hand of nuchi and Arie looked up from the game, noticing his brother's arrival.

"Luccan, you look like a steaming pile of gryphon shit!" Arie stood and came over. "Have you eaten?"

Luccan scowled. "I can always count on my brothers to lift my confidence."

"You didn't answer," I whispered. "Have you eaten?"

"Before I came," he assured us. "I need to rest awhile, though. Gatemaking is taxing."

He'd mentioned so before, and while I would have to be blind not to notice that Luccan looked as tired, perhaps more so, than me, he hadn't looked quite this disheveled yet.

"Not that I am not grateful for the work you've put in," I began, "but maybe I should try to find a different way west."

"Staghorn Castle has gryphons," Arie supplied. "Caelo can charm them?"

Gryphons didn't accept new riders easily. Elves charmed them the easiest. Before, when Caelo had commanded ravens, I'd wondered if he was part elf but never asked. Arie's words indicated I was correct.

"The Vagles would never give Neve their racing gryphons." Luccan waved a dismissive hand. "They might even deny Vale, and they're his relations. Besides, there's no need. I'm fine. You two worry too much."

"They worry the right amount." Clemencia rose from where they'd been playing cards. "You need a very deep rest tonight, Luccan."

The eldest Riis brightened when she said his name. I took a drink, hiding my amusement in my cup.

Clemencia's father was very strict, and back before she'd left for Riis Tower, she'd claimed he'd never let her be with Luccan, though the pair seemed infatuated with each other. Her father's reasoning? Luccan was a bastard.

I'd learned that wasn't true. Clemencia, a female living in the far reaches of the western territory, had not known that the king had legitimized Luccan, Arie, and Thantrel, either. Since then, she smiled more—probably believing that her father would approve of their match.

Even if he did not, I did. I hoped they'd be together.

"I'll make sure to get plenty of rest, lovely," Luccan said, his nostrils flaring as Clemencia neared and her scent of snow lilies filled the air. "Using the gateway is your best chance, Neve."

"Very well. But if you fall over, I'm going to Staghorn Castle and stealing those gryphons."

That got a laugh out of the brothers, probably because we were all envisioning me trying to subdue a racing gryphon. The mood lightened, and as everyone gathered around the fire, I wished nights like this would not have to end.

But they would. Eventually, the king would call another Courting Festival event. The Riis brothers would have to go to Avaldenn.

I was to go west and hadn't asked if anyone would want to join. Anna would. Clemencia, too, may wish to return home, although I was still unsure how wise that would be. The queen knew Clemencia, had seen that she attended Vale's and my wedding and had told her husband. Was the king still out for the blood of those who had witnessed our vows?

Thinking of Vale dampened my mood. I glanced at the door and was unsurprised when he was not, miraculously, there. He was with Caelo, the only person he wanted around him since learning who I was.

I was staring at the door when it opened and Thantrel glided in. He caught my eye and winked.

"Missing my handsome face already, Neve?"

I snorted. "Hardly. I . . ."

I trailed off, not wanting to admit I'd been pining after Vale, a male who wanted nothing to do with me. "Where did you go?"

He hadn't dined with Anna, Clem, Arie, and me. I hadn't seen him since our training session.

"Someone had to go to Avaldenn and check that there's not a Courting Festival event tomorrow," Thantrel replied as he poured himself a drink and downed it. "We're still in the clear."

"Thank the dead gods," Arie breathed, his glance going again to Anna. "I despise that event."

"The only person who likes it is Calpurnia Vagle." Luccan rubbed his temples as if just thinking about Calpurnia was giving him a headache. I could relate. "She is so sure her uncle will give the best match to her."

"Eireann and Baenna Balik liked it too," I said, remembering the night we'd gambled. "Did you see them, Thantrel? Marit, Saga, and Sayyida? The Balik ladies too?" Saying their names made me miss them more. How lucky I was to have found friends in such a short time.

Thantrel leaned against the back of my chair, necessitating that I tilt my head up to see him.

"Ran into Saga. I told her where you were but only because she promised not to breathe a word. I didn't see Sayyida or the Balik ladies." He cleared his throat. "As for Marit, I can't say that she is in the best of spirits."

I sat up straighter and twisted in my seat. "What do you mean?"

"Her intended is pushing for them to wed soon."

"But the king said they'd wait until her father returned with news from the Blood Court!" My heart raced at what this could mean for my friend. Jarl Triam had a reputation for killing his wives, and while Marit had been training with us, I wasn't sure she could protect herself.

"Yes, well, the jarl is using the vampire assassins— two more of which have been caught in the city, by the way—as an excuse to push his wedding. He claims Marit needs the protection of a family."

Arie scoffed. "As if the Armenils aren't one of the largest families in the kingdom."

"It's an excuse," Luccan agreed. "Everyone knows the wolves of the north protect their own."

Despite their reassurances, my stomach sank. The only reason there were vampire assassins at all was because of me. My actions.

Stars, I had made a mess of this kingdom.

My mother's words rang in my ears. I'd taken parts of what she said and clung to them, but I wasn't ready to face some of her more ambitious wishes yet.

A former blood slave, even one masquerading as a princess, did not rise to claim a throne. A seat she'd never dreamed she'd set eyes on, let alone command.

Again, I drank, allowing the sweet wine from the south of Isila to run over my tongue and wash away a bit of my anxiety.

"The pack will keep her safe," Arie said stoutly. "I'm sure of it. If Connan were at the festival, I'd return to Avaldenn and make sure he knows to keep an eye on her."

"Connan Armenil?" I asked. "The second oldest in their family, right?"

Clemencia beamed at me, proud that her lessons had sunk in.

"Yes," Arie replied. "He is not attending the Courting Festival."

"Already married?"

"Too ill." Arie swallowed. "He's a great friend of mine, but often ill, so I see him less than I'd like."

"Rune will make sure no harm comes to his sister," Thantrel assured his own brother.

Usually, one teased the other. This was a rare moment of solidarity. It was a night for such things.

I stood, went to refill my goblet, and in need of a change of topic and a lighter heart, I cast a playful glance over my shoulder. "Who wants to lose to me at nuchi?"

CHAPTER 48
NEVE

The last game of nuchi was a terrible mistake.

After the first round of normal nuchi, Thantrel had decided to mix it up. That we should play *drinking nuchi*. By the time I drank my fifth glass of wine, I was certain Thantrel was simply making the rules up as we went along.

But I also didn't care. For the first time since arriving at Riis Tower, we'd laughed and played like friends should. Like those stolen days at the castle when the king had been too furious to call any Courting Festival events. Days of sheer bliss.

The only people missing were Caelo and Vale—one of whom I wanted desperately to see.

And I had enough wine in me to where that felt like a pretty good idea. At my request, Clem had given him a room on the opposite side of Riis Tower from mine, and despite that extra distance around the circular tower, I didn't question my choice. Not until I stood in front of his door, hand raised to knock.

"Stars, what am I doing?" I whispered.

It was late, after the hour of the aura owl. Vale was probably sleeping.

Even so, I'd come this far. Farther than I'd managed in days. Steeling myself, I let my hand fall, once, twice, three times. My nerves jolted with each knock echoing in the hallway, but I forced myself to stay in place. To not run like a coward.

I waited. And waited. A full minute passed, then two, and nothing happened. Was he really sleeping so hard?

No, I'd shared a bed with him. Unless he was drunk, Vale did not sleep *that* soundly.

Was he ignoring me?

My fingers itched to open the door, but I knocked twice more first and waited again. When he did not open the door, I turned the knob and peeked inside.

The room stared back at me, empty, the bed cold.

Where in all the nine kingdoms was he?

"Vale?" I called out in case he'd stepped into the adjoining bathroom.

No answer.

I shut the door and pressed my back against it, exhausted from the emotional journey I'd taken.

"But where is he?" I whispered.

I'd worked myself up to come here, to speak with him. Though terror wracked my bones over what he might say, I also didn't want to give up.

Perhaps Caelo was awake? Maybe they were in the knight's room drinking? That felt right, so I began making my way there but quickly ran into a servant.

She cocked her head ever so slightly, the only indication of her curiosity. "Are you lost, Princess Neve?"

"No, I was looking for Prince Vale. Is he with Sir Caelo?"

The servant swallowed. "No, Your Highness. He's not."

"Do you know where he is?" I noted how she wrung her hands.

"I do."

"Where?"

"I showed him to another room. One he requested to see."

"Take me."

She pressed her lips together. "Are you sure? You two have been——"

"*Now*," I demanded, surprising myself with the force of my tone. I bit the inside of my cheek. "I'm sorry. It's been a long day. Please show me to the prince."

She didn't argue further, just waved for me to follow, so I did, down the corridor and up a set of steps. We climbed and climbed until there were no more stairs. We'd reached the top level of Riis Tower.

"Who's up here?" I asked.

I'd been under the impression that no one slept on the highest level. Largely because it was far from the kitchens and the den where people liked to congregate.

"No one. The prince is . . . visiting."

Visiting who?

I stayed quiet until the servant led me to a door. It was ever so slightly ajar and even from the hallway, I could smell Vale's scent—fallen snow and sandalwood that made my heart skip a beat. He was inside.

I dismissed the servant. Taking a deep inhale, I leaned into the door.

"Vale," I called, sure that since the door had been open, he wouldn't be asleep or in a compromising position, but not wishing to startle him. "It's Neve."

He didn't respond, and unable to help myself, I pushed the door open enough to peek inside. I found his back to me as he looked out the window.

In the distance, a castle gleamed in the waning moon's light. Staghorn Castle—the seat of his mother's family.

"Vale? Are you well?"

His shoulders lowered, his dark semi-diaphanous wings pressed down his back, and still, he said nothing. His unusual actions set my heart racing, and I entered the room and went to him. Only when I stood right beside him did I realize he was crying.

My lips parted at the almost unfathomable sight. Vale Aaberg, the famed warrior. Strong and stoic and honorable. And there he stood, crying.

My stomach pitted. "*Vale?* What's wrong?"

He didn't turn to me, nor did tears stop streaming down his face. Instead, he pointed out the window.

"Do you see those torches in the distance?"

"Of course I do." Beyond the small clearing around Riis Tower, beyond the woods filled with evergreen trees, there was a black castle that flew a flag of green bearing a silver hart. I'd been told it was a short walk away, though I had not ventured that far. "Thantrel told me that it's Staghorn Castle."

"It is." He inhaled deeply. "That's where my mother grew up. Where she lived until she married."

I waited. This was common knowledge. What was Vale getting at?

"You can't see it in the dark, but I know which tower her room was in. In the daylight, she would have been able to see Riis Tower." His shoulders slumped. "I wonder, if all that time, she was thinking of him, just as he thought of her. If she still is."

My lips parted. "I don't understand—"

He spun and gestured to the room. "Lord Riis grew up in this room."

"Oh," I replied, still not understanding, but taking in the room all the same. The bed was on the small side, the furs atop older, and the room dustier than the others I'd seen, which made sense as no one came up here. Otherwise, the space was tidy but unlived in. "You wanted to see the castle?"

"I wanted to see this room." He swallowed and his gaze fell to the floor. "M-my father's room."

I stiffened. "Your father is King Magnus."

"In duty, yes," Vale replied. "It's how Lord Riis could call him my father for so many turns. The king, the male I've always called father, believed he sired us. But he did not. Lord Riis did."

I blinked once, twice, three times, working through the information.

Burning skies. Vale is not an Aaberg. My heart rate sped up.

He lifted his gaze to meet mine. "I'm a bastard, Neve."

The initial spark of excitement that blazed through me fizzled. Poor Vale. He wasn't thinking the same as me. Not at all. To him, his entire identity was being questioned, and as I walked a similar path, though in reverse, I could understand.

"You're a Riis," I whispered. "And you can also be an Aaberg too. If you want." I paused. "I feel selfish for asking, but does this mean that you don't completely despise me? That when you avoided me you were working out your own troubles? Not just what happened between us?"

"I never hated you," he replied. "I felt betrayed and blindsided, but I never hated you."

My primary worry cast aside, I blew out a breath and focused solely on him. "How did you find out?"

I doubted very much that Lord Riis would leave evidence. Should this news get out, get to King Magnus, there was no telling what he'd do. If he'd still love Vale and Rhistel as his own. If he'd disown them.

Perhaps he'd even have them killed.

My throat tightened. I tried to convince myself that the king would never harm a son who had loved him and tried to please his father, despite the many reasons not to. A son who followed through on his father's wishes and then worked in secret with the cabal to right any wrongs the king might have ordered.

But even as I tried to convince myself the King of Winter would do no such thing, I'd never be able to say as much, because I could no longer lie. King Magnus would do *anything* to keep control of this kingdom, harm anyone, cast anyone aside.

My jaw tightened. But King Magnus would never hurt Vale. Not while I breathed.

"Lord Riis told me the truth," Vale admitted. "He even spoke to my mother about it. He claims to have loved her all his life."

"Still?"

"Still." He met my gaze. His eyes were no longer watery but resigned. "I can't say if Mother loves him, but they were together before Mother married my—the king. Rhistel and I were born prematurely, even for twins, though the king did not seem to realize—even then he was busy, planning for the rebellion to come."

"Why would she do that? Did she not love your father at all?" I understood why Inga would feel repulsed by her husband now. He slept with concubines and any female who took his fancy. The start of a marriage, though, that was when people were on their best behavior.

"Their families arranged the marriage. Not a love match." Vale shrugged. "Common enough amongst the noble houses—even those with little power."

Yes, that made sense, but something else did not.

"Vale?"

"Yes?"

"You insinuate your mother knew right away that Lord Riis sired you?"

He paled. "I did."

"So did your father call himself that and Queen Inga agreed to allow him to father you and Rhistel? And then when he acted as a father, she could call him one?"

Otherwise, it would be a lie, and fae could not lie.

Vale cleared his throat. "I have something else to tell you. Another secret. One that cannot leave this room. One that I should have told you much sooner."

"I will keep any secret you give me," I promised, touching my heart.

"Rhistel is not the only whisperer in the family. Mother is one too—hence, she can lie."

I gaped. To have one whisperer in the family was dangerous. To have two? "Do the others in House Vagle know?"

Technically, like Rhistel, the queen should have been killed as a youngling.

"My grandfather does, and of course his wife did, though she is long gone to the afterworld. Uncle Eirwen is the only other to know, besides Father, Rhistel, and me."

"Not Saga?" Then I recalled that Saga had told me, adamantly, that her mother was not a whisperer. "Oh, my stars, she doesn't."

"I only learned of Rhistel because he used his power on me," Vale replied. "Mother assured me it would never happen again. That she'd teach him to act with honor."

A lot of good that had done.

The information made so many things click into place. How only the queen disciplined Rhistel. She was the only one with the power to do so.

"Is she stronger than him?"

"Yes, and Mother has far more control too," Vale assured me. "Please, say nothing. Rhistel is not a male of honor, but Mother has done no wrong, save for continuing to live. And revealing one of my loved ones might reveal the other."

"I said I wouldn't say a thing," I assured him. "I meant it."

I looked at the window where the lights of House Vagle, the great stags of the midlands, glowed. The noble houses had so many secrets. Inga's powers and a relationship with a merchant were salacious, but those secrets were far from the only ones that the old stone castle guarded.

How romantic—the son of an up-and-coming merchant falling for the noble lady. Her falling for him too. If the tale hadn't been crushing Vale, I would have enjoyed it far more.

"What about Saga?"

Vale shook his head. "What about her?"

"Lord Riis and your mother . . . not to be insensitive, but . . ."

Vale let out a humorless laugh. "Lord Riis traveled for two turns and Saga was born right in the middle of his journey. Also, when her hair is not pink, Saga strongly favors Father. She has stronger, more varied, winter magic than Rhistel and me too. I dare say that she is the king's only legitimate heir."

Imagine that. A kingdom in which Saga ruled and Rhistel did not would be a wondrous place indeed.

"I'd always wondered where my dark eyes came from," Vale said. "The Falks generally had light eyes. The Vagles too, save for Calpurnia, but she clearly favors her mother's coloring."

I refrained from commenting that I had no idea who Calpurnia's mother was as he let out a long breath. "Rhistel and I have brown eyes too. Mother always said an uncle looked like us, but now it's much clearer where the coloring comes from."

"Your build as well," I breathed. "Aside from one other male in the western lands, Lord Riis is the only faerie who I've seen who is larger than you. Though Luccan is close."

"That too." For the first time, he gave a small smile. "I suppose that is something to be grateful for. I am one of the Riis brothers now. Already brothers in my heart, now they are in blood too."

"I'm assuming that since Lord Riis has kept this secret for so long, he is leaving you the choice to share the news. Have you told Luccan, Thantrel, or Arie?"

The brothers had been acting normally, but I had to be certain.

"Leyv is letting me tell who I wish—if I wish to do so. And no, the Riis brothers have no idea. Only you and Caelo."

Silence stretched between us, so poignant my heartbeats thundered in my ears. "Why did you tell me all this, Vale? We haven't really spoken in days, and before, I was cold with you. Cruel even."

"I understand why now." He reached out and took my hand. "And isn't it obvious why I want to share? I want you, Neve. I want you to know all about me, even that which I have not accepted yet. I want you to be my wife, in truth."

My breath hitched.

"Not to mention, you shared a rather large secret as well." Vale's face loosened into familiar, happier lines. "You can't be the only one with drama in our circle."

I laughed. "I'd give it all to you if you want."

"Oh, no. We'll share."

I lifted onto my tiptoes and pressed my lips to his. Unlike our last kisses, this one was so very soft, hesitant in a way—as if we were getting to know one another.

The real Neve and Vale.

Or Isolde.

But no. I was not ready to bear that strange, regal name—wasn't sure if I ever would be. Neve might have been the name given to me by slavers, but it was the only one I'd ever known. It would take time to think of myself in another way.

We broke apart, and I beamed up at him. "I wish to be with you Vale."

He grinned, and like a faelight being ignited, all the sorrow he carried vanished.

My fingers slid into his, so comfortable against his skin. "I'm so glad you told me. You have no idea what was going through my head these last two days."

His expression clouded. "I—had a lot to work through. Caelo helped, but I needed time alone."

"And you've worked through it all?"

"No, but that might take quite a while. Perhaps I'll never fully come to terms with it. But I still believe Lord Riis and know that I want you, *Neve Falk*. Or whomever you wish to be, I want you, no matter what trouble that might cause."

I swallowed down the emotion climbing up my throat. "Be sure that it will cause trouble."

"Whatever happens, we'll work through it. You and me—together," he said and kissed me again.

CHAPTER 49
NEVE

I awoke, clothed, in Lord Riis's childhood bed with my arm wrapped around Vale.

When had I fallen asleep?

I recalled making it to the bed and kissing and talking some more and then . . . things got hazy. I had to have fallen asleep first, but as sleep slowly left my mind, I recalled waking up a couple of times to find Vale tossing and turning. Though he'd assured me he was firm in his choice to be with me, he was still troubled. No matter how strong he was, he might remain that way for a long time.

However, as I looked down on him now, the morning light streaming in through the window and dappling his cheeks, he slept peacefully. I eased out of the bed, not wishing to wake him. He needed the rest, and not just because we'd stayed up late talking. No, during our pillow talk the night before, he'd also agreed to come with me to the western territory. To help me confront Roar.

My heart swelled. We'd been through so much, and while I was sure we'd go through more, last night had been healing.

I slipped from the room, down the corridor. I paused only at a window, taking in the conditions. Sunny, though dark clouds loomed in the distance, threatening more snow. When I reached my bedroom, I found Clemencia inside.

She eyed me with barely concealed amusement. "Where have you been?"

"Upstairs. Why are you sitting in my room like a nursemaid?"

"With the prince?" she asked, ignoring my question.

"Stars, you are nosy."

"And you're avoiding my question." Clemencia leaned forward and clasped her slender-fingered hands together. "Did you make up?"

A smile spread across my lips. "We did. And we slept in the same bed."

She squealed, which made me laugh. I pulled out warm clothes to change into, so I could go outside and practice magic. I needed to take advantage of every opportunity to do so because after I confronted Roar, I wasn't sure my identity would stay a secret for long. The moment news that a Falk princess survived the White Bear's Rebellion got back to King Magnus, he would hunt me down.

"What about you and Luccan?" I asked Clemencia, slipping out of my clothing and pulling on scratchy woolen pants and a top. "He eyed you often last night."

She blushed. "Nothing more than flirting has happened. I long for more, but he's been so tired."

I cringed. Luccan worked himself to the bone for me. I owed my friends so much.

"Is he up already?" It wasn't too early but also not so late that I'd assume everyone was awake—particularly after all the drinking. Somehow, I felt fine, a small miracle that I wasn't taking for granted.

"I don't know."

"Let's go find out." I pulled on my boots and my warmest cloak and gestured to the door.

"I'm not dressed properly," Clemencia argued, all the while going to the door, a gleam in her eyes.

"You could wear a sack and he'd still be in love."

"Please, the Riis males are far more stylish than that."

"Except Arie," we said in unison and giggled.

We left and made our way to the courtyard, where Luccan had been working on the gateway. If he was awake, I was certain he'd be there, and sure enough, the moment we exited into the courtyard, red hair glinted in the sunlight.

"Is he *trembling*?" Clemencia gasped.

I nodded. "Let's not startle him."

Luccan was working difficult magic, and I did not want to ruin his efforts, so we rounded him slowly and gave a wide berth so he would see us coming. When he looked up from the spot in the air that shimmered when the light hit it right, he spotted us and gave a single nod.

"I think that means we're good to approach," I said.

My stomach sank more with each step we took toward the gatemaker. Circles ringed Luccan's eyes, so dark they appeared bruised. His lips were chapped, whereas last night they'd appeared normal, and there was a hollowness to his cheeks that hadn't been there hours ago.

He was working far too hard.

"How long have you been working?" she asked when we reached Luccan, and he paused to cast his magic.

"An hour or so." His shoulders slumped as he spoke.

"Aren't you tired?" Her voice dripped with concern, and I could tell Luccan heard it too because his eyes warmed a touch.

"I am, but Arie had to go to the House of Wisdom today, and he woke me to tell me he wouldn't be back until much later. After that, I couldn't sleep."

"Maybe you should take a nap?"

"I'd rather not leave it for that long," he replied. "I'm doing well, and making gateways is easiest when my magic flows nicely."

"Need anything?" I asked, understanding that he was as stubborn as he was a good friend. He'd work until it was done. "We can get you food. A drink?"

"Just to concentrate," Luccan said.

I took that as our cue. "We'll leave you, but please, call if you need anything. I'll come running."

"The next time I call for you, it will be because I'm about to make the final push, and you need to be ready to walk through the gateway. Expect that to be around the hour of the gryphon."

So he thought it would happen at midday when the sun was nearing its peak. I rolled my shoulders back, even more ready to get to work, and thankful that Vale and I had made up last night.

"Perfect," I replied. "Until later."

Clemencia and I left the courtyard, but she only made it but a step inside before she cast a glance over her shoulder. "I was going to offer to be with you while you trained, but . . ."

"Stay with him." I understood her concern. I'd feel better if someone was nearby too.

"Are you sure?"

"Very. Besides, isn't it boring to watch me train?" Clemencia had no winter magic, so she did not offer input. She watched and encouraged.

She smiled. "I like imagining what you'll do when your powers are fully formed."

That was one question I'd been asking myself too.

A storm neared, and I took precautions, settling in to practice near the outdoor sauna. The log building cut most of the wind but still gave me enough space to work magic safely. I wasn't about to go back inside because snow might soon fall. Not when I was just getting warmed up, both in body and magic.

The day before had been a disaster, but today I was reinvigorated. Much of that was down to reconnecting with Vale, though I also attributed some of my extra energy to me getting stronger.

With a flick of the wrist, I sliced off the icicles hanging from the tower roof. Once free, they wobbled a bit, but I used my power to claim control and sent them hurtling at the dead tree I'd been using for target practice.

One struck and the other nine missed.

"Better than yesterday," I murmured, rubbing my hands together.

"What did that tree ever do to you?"

I spun and took a few steps around the sauna to get an unobstructed view of Riis Tower. My heart warmed when I caught sight of Vale trudging through the snow to join me.

"It looked at me the wrong way." I shrugged.

"Fates, remind me only to smile at you."

I waited until we stood face to face and lifted onto my tiptoes, wrapped my arms around his neck, and kissed him. "Did you get enough sleep?"

"I feel better than I have in days."

"Good."

"You should have woken me, though. I could have been tutoring you all this time."

I released him and cocked my head. "Do you actually have winter magic, though? After what you learned, do you think it might be something else? Just elemental magic?"

He smirked. "Ah, you want to be *even more* special, huh?"

"No!" I swatted at him. Stars, it felt so good for us to be back here, to tease and banter about. "I only meant that, if you're not an Aaberg, would you have it?"

"Before the Unification, the Vagles were winter monarchs in their own right, so they have that power. Also, they married into the Falk line, the strongest of all the winter families, long, long ago." His eyebrows raised. "Is that a problem for you?"

Of course. All the noble families had intermarried at one point. With the sweeping news Vale had shared the night before, I'd forgotten that.

"How long ago?"

His eyebrows screwed together as he calculated the blood ties between our families. "I'm certain it has been thousands of turns since a union between a Vagle and a Falk. And I don't believe they've ever allied with House Skau through marriage."

"Then we're good." I took his hand. I couldn't be unrealistic, and I wanted him too badly, anyway. And for the first time since we'd met, I might actually keep him—as long as nothing horrible happened.

"Very good." He grinned at me, and the look of happiness stopped my heart.

Thank the Fates I didn't have to pretend like I no longer wanted him, when in truth, I was certain that I was falling for him. I was also thankful that there didn't seem to be lingering awkwardness between us.

"Would you like a lesson?" he asked.

"Definitely. Teach me how to use icicles like your fath—the king did. And can you teach me how to control wind like you do?"

He nodded. "Show me from the beginning."

I replicated what I'd done, the good and the bad, because I wanted him to see it all. He noted that I had trouble controlling the elements with delicacy, which was true. It was much easier to hurl an icicle than it was to hold one steady, hovering in the air. Or target something precisely.

Once I finished, missing the tree that time, I turned. "Tips?"

"I think you'd do well to work inside the forest," he said. "More surrounded by snow. Enveloped in winter."

I narrowed my eyes. "Winter is all around."

"Try it. If your aim doesn't improve, we can try something else."

I had nothing to lose, so we trudged through the drifts into the woods. The moment we stepped into the trees; snow began to fall.

"Working in a storm might help too. Also, I have one more idea." He held out his hand. "I will direct you. I think that's all you need. Then practice controlling more and more power over time."

I took his hand, marveling again at how perfectly we fit.

"I'm going to use those smaller icicles." I gestured to

those dripping from a tree branch. "And hit the tree with the knob that looks like an orc's face. Right on the knob."

Vale laughed. "Very well. First, experience this."

Warmth flooded me. Vale's magic.

If there was any doubt in my mind that I possessed a purer form of winter magic than him, in that moment, it would have vanished. Vale was strong, no doubt about it, but the feel of his magic was warmer, less harsh, and more wieldable. Which he made clear when he used his own power to grab onto mine and control it. I sucked in a breath, made to fight back, and barely stopped myself, but from the way he watched me, Vale understood.

"Let me. I'm showing you."

"I know. Sorry, it's instinctual."

"You're a fighter. I love that about you."

My cheeks warmed, and I gave a single nod. "Show me."

He did, controlling my power and guiding it through me in a more controlled fashion. The sensation was so odd, but I took notes and when the power simmered under my skin, Vale whispered, "Let it fly."

The release rang through me, amazing, and as my magic did as I wished, picking up the small icicles and shooting them at the ugly-knobbed tree, I marveled. Each and every icicle hit.

"Amazing," I exhaled.

"Now you do it with the control you felt. It was different from how you used your power, right?"

He was correct. Before, I'd been more apt to let my power fling about inside me, and when I tired, it overwhelmed me. But Vale had just shown me a new way, a slower, more methodical way.

I tried once, twice, three, four times to mimic Vale's control. I failed each time, though the improvement was noticeable. If minimal.

On the fifth time, though, I did as I wanted to, striking each small icicle against the ugly tree.

"Nice work." Vale wrapped his arms around my middle. "I knew you'd get there."

"I'm sweating." I wiped away the trickle of sweat that had formed around attempt number three. "That doesn't usually happen so soon, but it was worth it."

His lips dipped to my ear. "I know another way to work up a sweat and make it worth it."

I gasped as he nibbled at my lobe, making his intention very clear. "Vale! I need to practice!"

"Rest is as important as practice."

"You're saying that because you're *frustrated*."

"If I have my way, I intend to become even more frustrated."

"Wha—oh!"

He spun me around and threw me over his shoulder.

My heart thundered as a grin spread across my face. This wasn't at all what I'd planned for the day, but I'd smite the stars before I stopped him.

"Where are you going?" My voice came out breathy.

"Deeper into the woods. I don't want the others to be watching when I make you come."

Oh. My. Stars.

He didn't go too far into the forest before Vale set me on my feet and pressed my back into the trunk of a tree that had long since died.

When his head dipped and his hand cupped my face, my heart stuttered. And when he took my lips, my knees buckled. Stars, I'd missed this feeling. Of us. Together.

His hand dropped from my face to my hips, the prince gripping the plump flesh there with a soft groan. I smiled into his kiss, loving that my curvy figure turned him on.

"I can't believe I almost lost you," he whispered, moving to trail kisses down my neck. "Never again."

"Never again," I echoed, my heart thundering with desire as he reached beneath my cloak, cupped a breast, and stroked. A soft whimper left my lips, only to be met by a chuckle.

"I missed that sound. I want to hear more of it. Different types of whimpers and whines and moans from your sweet lips."

"Yes," I breathed, my hand dropping to his pants, landing on his buckle. "I want—wha—oh!"

Like a flash, he had removed my hands from his belt and pinned them over my head to the tree and held them in place with a single large hand. Looking down at me, he shook his head. "I'm in control here."

He took my lips once more as his other hand

roamed from face to breasts to hips. Everywhere he went, he left a trail of fire.

"Vale, this is so unfair," I purred, trying to get him to see sense. To see how much I wanted him too. "Let me touch you."

"Not now," he ground out, the sound pleasing because I could tell how hot and bothered he was.

"I want to taste you," I tried again, my voice deepening to a sultry tone that I knew turned him on.

He stiffened, released my hands, and leaned back. His breathing was deep, his long hair wild from where I'd run my hands in it. I'd never seen a more beautiful male.

I was about to leap at him, to kiss him, when Vale took me by the hips, pressing me hard into the tree for a moment before one hand slid to my belt.

"I told you, I'm in control. Stop trying to tempt me." He licked his lips, eyes dipping from where they locked with mine, to my buckle. "You stand here, little beast."

My mouth fell open as he undid my pants and pulled them and my undergarments to the ground. With his feet, he pushed mine out, exposing the most intimate part of me so much that cold air caressed skin that usually remained covered. Then the warrior prince fell to his knees and grinned as he peered at my sex.

"Blazing moon, that looks delicious."

Heat flooded me, but I barely had time to truly feel the embarrassment before Vale licked his lips. Dark eyes flashed up, stealing the very breath from my lungs.

"Lean back, Neve. *Enjoy.*" For privacy, he spread his black wings as he pulled aside the edges of my cloak. "I'm about to."

He leaned closer, spreading my lips and kissing my nub. Lightning shot through me. I was already so wet, swollen, which Vale likely felt because he didn't stop the kisses but looked up at me through thick, black lashes. He winked.

Unable to believe what was happening, I looked to the sky and thanked the stars, the Fates, and the dead gods for this moment. I wasn't sure what I'd done to deserve it, but whatever it was, I would try to repeat that good deed for the rest of my life.

Vale's tongue parted my slit, and he began licking me up and down. I reached for him, for any way to touch him, found his hair, and ran my hand along the shaved under portion before wrapping my fingers through the longer tresses. A rumble came from his lips, and I tugged, needing a deeper connection.

He gave it to me by slipping his fingers inside my pussy. I gasped, my breaths becoming thinner, my chest tighter and my breasts heavier as he worked me up and down, his tongue playing with my engorged nub.

Where in the world did he learn to do this so well? Never mind, I didn't want to know. I only wanted to be the one to receive this attention. The only one. The last one, though I did not dare say such a thing.

The prince looked up and stopped sucking, but his fingers still plunged in and out, slowly caressing the insides of my tightening channel. My juices gleamed on his lips.

"Neve," he growled. "Let go. And when you do, I want you to say my name. Scream it."

"But I—*oh*, bleeding skies!"

His mouth was back on my clit, his fingers deeper inside me than ever, and my insides quivered. I was close.

"I'm nearly there," I hissed, the back of my head pressing into the rough tree bark. "Vale."

"I need the kingdom to hear you." He began kissing and sucking my clit again.

I looked down at him as his eyes flashed up to meet mine, and in them I saw more than lust. I saw an unspoken promise. I already thought of him as mine, wanted more time with him, more than perhaps I even thought wise. And with that look, I was sure he wanted all the things I did too.

The certainty, the unspoken promise, sent me over the edge. My fingers tightened in his black hair, and I cried out.

"*Vale!*" Stars filled my vision and pleasure overtook me as Vale continued to suck, to lick, to caress.

Suddenly, we were in a whirlwind. Beautiful, glittering snow spun all around us, all the way to the top of the tree. A moan ripped out of my lips as my body went boneless.

My climax dimmed, with many smaller waves following, and Vale was there to drink up each one. When it was over, I leaned into the tree, panting.

"Vale . . . that was amazing."

He rose and kissed me with the same hunger as when he'd kissed my sex. When we parted, he pulled me close, and I buried my face into the furs of his cloak.

"You're amazing Neve. Losing my title is nothing to getting to have you."

CHAPTER 50
VALE

The taste of Neve lingered on my tongue as we strode, hand in hand, back to Riis Tower.

We'd been outside, practicing and reveling in one another for hours. It was time to warm up and eat an early lunch. If Neve were to continue practicing at all, she required strength.

"I want to check on Luccan," she said, her cheeks still red from when we'd taken a second break, and I'd feasted on her yet again. The taste of her, the feel of her body releasing, bending to the pleasure I gave—it was unparalleled. I wanted to feast upon her for the rest of my life.

"We should." I pumped my eyebrows suggestively. "Then we can shower together."

She laughed. "You want to make up for lost time."

"Don't act like you don't."

"I would never. Especially not after the trees witnessed me falling apart."

693

We entered the tower and went straight to the courtyard where Luccan had been working tirelessly. He was there still, concentrating. Anna and Clemencia sat on wooden chairs next to him, chatting, a table of foods and pitchers of drinks, some of them steaming, next to them. I suspected that the ladies were there to make sure Luccan took breaks and ate when he looked too spent. Smart thinking.

In front of him, the air danced in wavy lines. I'd never seen a gateway or portal to the human world being made before, so I took it in with interest as we approached.

That interest vanished, however, when I got a better look at my friend. My brother, in heart. Blood, too, though he did not know that yet.

Luccan appeared to have lost weight overnight. His skin was not only pale but thin in appearance, his eyes sunken into their sockets and red.

"Luccan!" Neve gasped. "You look awful!"

He shot her a glare. "Thanks so much for that uplifting compliment. And good to see you out amongst the people, Vale."

"I can't say the same. Not when you're looking like that."

Luccan snorted and shook his head.

My wife turned to her friends. "Why did you let it get this bad? Did he take breaks?"

"No! He refused to stop! Why do you think we're here?" Anna threw her hands up. She wore far more clothing than Clemencia, so her hands didn't go nearly as high as they should have. Many layers hindered movement, but as a human and not a fae of Winter's Realm, Anna required them. "He won't stop, so we stayed beside him, in case he collapsed."

He looked minutes from doing so. I shook my head. "You have to stop."

"No way. I'm close." Luccan stared at the wavy lines in the air and for a moment, a gleam shone in his eyes —almost manic.

I understood. Not only did Luccan wish to help Neve, but he wanted to succeed. He wanted to be one of the great gatemakers. Pushing himself like this was one way to prove that his power was extraordinary.

"Stubborn arse," I muttered.

Neve shot me a glare.

"He's trying to prove his magic."

"To test it!" Luccan corrected. "As if you haven't done the same."

"Not to this point."

"I'll be fine." Luccan waved a limp, chapped hand. "You two should prepare. I think I'll have this thing ready within the hour, but I won't be able to hold it for more than a few seconds."

All this work for mere seconds of success. No wonder gateways weren't made often.

"Let's go." Neve took me by the hand, a gesture not unnoticed by her friends. Anna and Clemencia shared feline smirks. "We'll be back."

"Don't forget to shower, though," Anna piped up,

the smirk on her face growing. "After all that *hard work* in the woods, you need a good washing down."

"Who are you and what have you done with my best friend?!" Neve barked out a laugh as her cheeks, already slightly red from her pleasure, took on a deeper shade. "How improper!"

"I know. It feels so good not worrying about what I'm about to say!" The human popped a piece of cured meat into her mouth. "I'm so free. And besides, did you think we didn't hear you scream? Multiple times!"

Clemencia's hand flew over her mouth as she smothered a laugh.

Neve shook her head, clearly more amused than upset. "Well, you deserve the freedom, even if I am mortified at the cost."

"I do," Anna replied. "And you need to hurry. I suppose I do too." She stood. "Seeing as I'm coming with you."

Neve's lips parted. "You're sure?"

I didn't know this woman well, but she had a clubbed foot. I hadn't noticed it hindering her to any great degree, but Neve's question made me wonder.

"I want to," Anna said, her chin lifting. "You're fine with it, right?"

"I am if you are," Neve answered sincerely. "But we might be heading into danger. Roar will not be happy to see me."

"After what he did, he should fear your wrath," I said. "Mine too, for putting my wife in harm's way."

"You weren't married at that time," Clemencia said,

pulling the fur cloak she wore tighter around her as a gale swooped into the courtyard, "but that was so romantic, I'll let it slide. And for the record, I'm furious with him too."

Neve took my hand. "We have to get ready."

"Caelo is coming as well." I'd found my best friend before joining Neve in the woods this morning and told him everything. He'd jumped at the chance to leave Riis Tower and seize a bit of action.

"Happy to have another sword." Neve glanced at Luccan, though she said nothing.

I suspected she wished Luccan could come, probably Thantrel too, but the Riis males had to remain at the Tower in case another Courting Festival event was called. There was no use in them earning the king's ire on an errand to confront Lord Roar.

That day might come when they would have to choose between my wife and the demands of the fae who had raised me as his son—but that day was not today.

"No shared shower," Neve said as we left the courtyard. "There's no time."

"Cruel female," I teased.

"I don't like it any more than you do," she assured me as we climbed the steps and then broke apart to go to our separate rooms.

As neither of us had packed anything before a vampire ran us out of my suite in Frostveil Castle, we had only borrowed items. Those Emilia had offered up, and those that the Riis family had to spare—of which there was plenty. Lord Riis had even given the ladies dresses that used to belong to his mother, though I'd seen them wearing trousers and tunics more often. More practical in the ever deepening cold.

I opted for the Riis clothing. It fit me better than Harald Falk's old attire, and I was not ready yet to wear the emblem of the white hawk. No matter how much I loved his daughter.

I sighed, wishing I'd said those words in the woods. They'd been on the tip of my tongue, and though I'd known the moment I'd chosen her over the king that I'd fallen in love, I felt resistance in uttering them.

For I loved the male who had raised me too, but it was a hard kind of love. One born through the turns of wanting to please him, wishing to be loved back. In faint glimmers, I had been.

It was a love born of obligation and fulfilling legacy, two things the king prized.

A hard, cold love that didn't always feel like love.

And yet, I still wanted his love. More than that, I didn't want to betray him.

But in choosing her, I already was.

"There is no right way," I muttered as I gathered *Skelda* and looped her sheath through my belt. "Someone will always get hurt, but it will never again be Neve."

CHAPTER 51

NEVE

Caelo, Anna, Vale, and I stood behind Luccan, dressed warmly and armed to the teeth in case we ran into trouble.

Luccan kept assuring us that 'any second now' the gateway would open, and we'd have to rush through. As he'd been saying that same thing for the last thirty minutes, my nerves had begun to fray.

At least the wait had given us enough time to eat. It also allowed me time to consider what exactly I'd say to Roar if we made it to Guldtown today.

The sheer membrane of my wings tightened. Roar was the Warden of the West, a High Lord in the Winter Court. He lived in a castle and had hundreds of fae at his beck and call. He commanded a large army.

What if he denied seeing me?

For a moment, the question overwhelmed me, but then the weight of my father's sword on my hip reminded me who I was. A daughter of the last Falk king and queen. A survivor of great cruelty and slavery. A fae who had once cowered but could no longer afford such things.

So Roar might think he could tell me what to do, but he'd be wrong. One way or another, I'd confront him.

And if I had to, I'd use Vale's title as Prince of Winter to force my way into Roar's domain. My own would remain a secret for as long as possible, provided that Roar had not already guessed my ancestry, which I deemed about as likely as not.

"It's happening!" Luccan called out, a new level of excitement in his tone. "Prepare yourselves!"

Clemencia gasped and wrung her hands, covered in white bandicota fur gloves. "Best of luck! Oh, I wish I could go west!"

I was glad she hadn't tried to come too. After Sir Qildor's whipping, I worried enough about Anna and Caelo being spotted, though I didn't try to dissuade them either. Anna because, out of everyone who attended my wedding to Vale, she was the least likely to be harmed by the king and queen, for Anna was human. I'd learned from Emilia that Queen Inga didn't really see the humans living amongst her. Why would she have seen Anna in Vale's memory? And if she had, it seemed very unlikely that she'd remember my friend.

Caelo was different. The king wanted to punish Caelo—had already commanded it before the court.

However, the knight was powerful, and Vale agreed that another skilled soldier would be useful.

Though it was selfish, I was happy to have Sir Caelo along.

"Best of luck." Clemencia laid a hand on my shoulder. "I'll miss you."

"We'll be back," I assured her because where else were we going to go when this was done? We had no plans to return to Avaldenn and no other place to go.

"Get ready!" Luccan yelled. "It's really opening!"

My gaze snapped to where the air had been shimmering with wavy lines, and my breath hitched. A gateway, circular and beaming with light, was opening and growing wider by the second. He had done it. With my nerves trickling through me, I patted the side of my cloak, assuring myself that I still had the pouch containing the jewelry I'd taken from Queen Revna's rooms. From this point forward, there was no telling what would happen, but we would no longer be able to rely on the generosity of friends.

"Once you can step through, do not delay," Luccan instructed.

I stepped forward, but Vale put a hand on my shoulder. "Let me go first."

Though I knew he only said it because he cared, I bristled. This was my journey.

"No, Vale, let me go first," I said. "I need this."

For a moment, he looked like he wanted to argue, but then he stepped aside. "You first."

"Like now!" Luccan growled. Sweat dripped down his face at a faster rate and slipped into the collar of his cloak, wetting the fur. "*Go!*"

Though I would have deemed the gateway too small to step through, I did as he said, ducking and entering the tunnel of light. The moment the light inside touched me, I cried out. Unlike the other gateway we'd walked through, this one was hot and prickly. Was that because it was new? Or was it wrong?

"Go!" Luccan screamed. "I can't hold it for long!"

Fighting through the pain stabbing at my legs, my arms—everywhere—I took another step, only one, and before I knew it, cold wind whipped through my hair again. So fast, so short, and I was out.

I exhaled and looked around to be sure I'd landed where I intended. The day was windy but clear and the sun was still high in the sky, so it took only seconds for me to catch the golden towers of Roar's castle glinting in the sunlight.

Luccan had really done it. Not even sure if he'd be able to hear me, I thought to call back to him that he'd succeeded, but at that moment, someone exited the gateway and ran right into me. I fell, but they caught me and pulled me up.

"Step away from the gateway, wife." Vale ushered me a couple of steps away, which turned out to be a very good thing, as Anna had opted to sprint through the gateway.

Caelo followed her, bending low so the quiver full of

arrows and bow he carried on his back didn't catch on the portal. He laughed as he exited. "You are always good for a laugh, Anna!"

"That's *terrifying*! Never again!" My best friend appeared bloodless.

"Painful too," I added, watching the gateway shrink before my eyes.

"It was," Vale agreed. "Probably because it was underdeveloped. But it did the job. I'd recognize Guldtown anywhere. Luccan seems to have deposited us outside the city wall."

"Exactly where I requested," I said.

"The Red Mist Mountains are that way, due west." Caelo pointed to the mountain range that I once thought I could traverse to freedom. Stars, I'd been so delusional.

No, not delusional. Desperate.

"And the main gate is at the south of the city, right, Neve?"

"Yes."

"Then it should be this way." Caelo waved, and he and Vale led the way, which I was all too happy for them to do because their hulking forms cut through the deep snow.

I'd put myself in the front when it mattered, but for the time being, I fell in step with Anna, watching her carefully. Her foot rarely hindered her, but she also did not often walk through drifts this deep either.

"How does it feel to be back?" she asked.

"Like nothing." My admission surprised me.

Guldtown was the first place I'd lived and experienced freedom. More than that, I'd lived in true luxury. For a while, I'd even considered if I might come to love Roar, which would have made this my home.

But when I thought of home, I didn't conjure up thoughts of this place. Rather, I thought of nothing. No place, but people.

Anna, Clemencia, Saga, and Sayyida.

Vale—yes, him most of all.

In a short time, so many had clawed their way into my heart. While I had them, I had everything.

The moment the same gate I'd passed through with Frode came into sight, Anna cast me a sidelong glance.

"Stop worrying about me," she whispered. "I'm here to support you, not the other way around."

"Why can't it be both?"

She smirked. "It can, but I want you to know that I notice."

My heart squeezed. Anna had changed so much since being freed. She was more outspoken, less fearful. I loved this side of her.

"Noted. I need to show my face up front, anyway." She didn't reply as I caught up to Vale and Caelo. "I'll do the talking."

"We're right behind you, little beast."

The soldiers on guard did not fail to see us coming. Nor did they make a move toward us, just waited until we stood right in front of the city wall.

"I'm Princess Neve," I said, trying to ignore the

butterflies that erupted in my belly. "I've come to speak with Warden Roar."

"Our lord said to be careful about who we let into the city," one guard retorted. "No one from Avaldenn."

So, Roar *had* arrived in Guldtown. Either that had happened recently, or Lord Riis's spies were not accurate. I would bet it was the former.

"I outrank your lord. You will let us in." I waved to the others, and in that gesture, the soldiers must have noticed Vale—or realized who he was for the first time.

"The Warrior Bear," one whispered.

"My husband," I added. "Now, move aside."

The gate opened, and we strode into the city and down the long cobblestone road leading through the heart of Guldtown.

That victory had been won easier than I'd imagined. Perhaps most of that was due to the fact that the soldiers were in awe and even scared of Vale, but I took the triumph, no matter how we'd achieved it.

As it had the first time I stepped foot in the city, it struck me as well-kept, the buildings all nice and tidy, the people too. But after living in Avaldenn for a while, I also recognized that Guldtown was a rather small city.

"There's more wealth per fae here than anywhere else." Vale walked by a shop displaying gorgeous gowns and a few lovely dresses for daily wear. Even from a glance, I recognized the craftwork as expert. It wouldn't have surprised me if Roar had gone to this very shop to purchase the gowns he'd gotten for me.

"Because of the mines?" I asked.

"That, and, as much as it pains me to admit this, Roar has opened many new businesses since he took over as the warden."

He often had meetings with the Merchant Guild. I hadn't asked about those gatherings because I'd been having my head filled with matters of court. I'd been focused on what mattered at the time, not Roar's duties.

"The Lisika family has always been cunning in business," Caelo agreed. "Many knights come from this area. They have often benefited from that house's wealth."

"What's that?" Anna asked, not following our conversation at all as she pointed to a shop I'd been inside.

"A store for tea." I smiled as we passed Tvali's tea shop. "I've been there. The tea maker is eccentric."

"It looks calming. Smells good too."

"It's nothing like the weak tea we had growing up. Once I'm done giving Roar a piece of my mind, we can go."

From that point on, much of the conversation became Anna asking what certain shops were and one of us supplying an answer. Often, people did double takes when they recognized either me or Vale, but no one stopped us, either to talk or to detain us. After that happened a half dozen times, I allowed myself to take in the city. It surprised me how many places I recognized, especially as we neared the castle. Each time I found one that struck a memory, I became a touch angrier.

Roar had made me feel safe and like he cared. Then he'd *left*. No explanation. Not even an attempt at contact. He could have sent a letter too, after all, he had sent someone to break the blood vials sealing our magical agreement.

In short, he'd never cared for me at all, no matter how much he'd pretended to.

We turned down the street leading to the castle, and, now properly pissed, I rolled my shoulders back. Another set of gates rose in front of us, but when I strode up to these, I didn't feel nervous. No, I was a female who would be given her due explanation—in the matter of Roar leaving and if he had recognized me as a Falk. About the Ice Scepter too. If anyone should be nervous, it was High Lord Roar Lisika.

Once we got to the soldiers, I lifted my chin. "I'm Princess Neve, here to see Lord Lisika."

"Apologies, Lady Neve." The soldier ignored my title. "You are not to be let in."

"Me specifically?"

"Yes."

"*Why?*"

"You betrayed our lord by marrying the prince."

I scoffed. "Is that how he's spinning it? Well, let me—"

Vale stepped forward. "You *will* let her in. Else, you will find yourselves in a fight with me and Sir Caelo of the Clawsguard."

I wanted to be annoyed that he wasn't letting me handle the issue, but truth be told, he looked so handsome, so righteous that I couldn't muster any negative emotions.

"Do you wish to face us?" Vale asked, hand on *Skelda's* hilt.

These guards did not fold like the ones on the city wall. However, they also didn't seem too keen on the idea of fighting the prince and a Clawsguard either.

So I took back the upper hand and called upon my winter magic, then directed it at the two guards. Though I didn't possess the king's finesse yet, I was naturally powerful and my morning of lessons with Vale had proved fruitful. Frost covered the pair, then a thin sheen of ice. The effort was draining, but it needed to be done. This city required a show of my power, so I would give it.

"Stop!" one of the guards called out before he could no longer use his lips. "Please!"

"Will you open it?" I bore down on my power.

"Yes, just s-s-stop!"

A wave of my hand and the magic ceased. They were still frozen, but I didn't need them to open the door. I'd only wanted to hear the words. Two strides forward and I stood before the one who'd begged. I ripped the keys from where they were latched to his hip and opened the gate.

"Thanks for that." I dropped the keys on the ice and strode onto Roar's property.

Servants and other soldiers strolled the grounds, but though they all looked twice when they recognized me —or Vale—no one stopped us. Just like in the city.

Apparently, Roar had only seen fit to warn the gate-keepers that we were not permitted on site. His mistake.

Walking in a line of four, we marched up to the front door of the castle, and when we arrived, a faerie was already coming outside to meet us. One I recognized.

"High Staret Celi." I took in the older male fae. Like last time, he wore a robe that glittered like the night sky. "Are you here to welcome us?"

"I'm afraid not, Lady Neve. I—"

"Princess Neve," I corrected him.

The old male's wrinkled face tightened, and his blue eyes widened for a moment before he recovered. "Ah, yes, so I've heard. Apologies, Princess Neve." The staret looked at the others, and upon recognizing Vale, bowed. "It is good to see you, my prince."

"You don't *seem* too excited," Vale replied, surprising the staret again.

"I'm assuming that is because Lord Roar did not expect to see me?" My arms crossed over my chest.

The staret's mouth opened, then closed, and opened again before he answered. "No. I believe he didn't expect to see you, though, of course, he took precautions for that—precautions which you seem to have sidestepped. And I assume you are here to see him?"

"I am. Show us to him."

"I'm afraid I cannot."

Stars give me strength.

I exhaled. "Why not, Staret Celi? Because if you're about to tell me that Lord Roar ordered you not to, that is not good enough. By title, I outrank your lord. As does my husband. It is *our* demands that you will follow."

Much of the blood leached from Staret Celi's face.

"Princess Neve, I cannot take you to him because he is not here."

"The guards told us he has returned to Guldtown," Vale said, his tone low and threatening.

"He did. And he left again. So you see, I cannot take you to him. I—"

"*Where did he go?*" I demanded.

Staret Celi swallowed, prompting me to exchange glances with Vale. Where in all the nine kingdoms would Roar have gone? Guldtown was the safest place in Winter's Realm for him to hide. Here he held every advantage, and while the king could still threaten to have him hauled back to Avaldenn to face punishment, Roar could ignore it. In this city, Roar commanded an entire army, one rivaling that of the royals, which lived in the far east. It would be impossible for a few of the king's soldiers to face off with an army.

"You would do well to remember, High Staret," Vale spoke when Celi remained quiet, "that it is within our power to *detain* you. Should you fail to answer my wife, I will make that detainment . . . uncomfortable."

"This is *my* home."

"For now."

Staret Celi reared back. "You'd let him do that, Princess Neve?"

"I believe that you, out of anyone in this castle,

might have heard about what happened between Lord Roar and me," I replied, eyes narrowed. "He owes me an explanation, so yes, I would keep you detained until you told me what I needed to know." I paused for dramatic effect. "*Or* you can tell us where Lord Roar is, and we'll be on our way. You won't have to suffer."

The old fae stared at us, as if unable to believe that his word and his title weren't good enough, and when I thought he'd deny us again, he exhaled. "He's at one of his mines. He only returned to the castle long enough to set his affairs in order and then he rode for the mountains."

Which made no sense at all.

"Which mine?" I pressed.

"Gersemi Mine."

"Do you know it, Vale?" I looked up at him.

My husband shrugged. "It's one of the oldest in the kingdom, but I've never been. No one in my circle has. All the Lisika mines are on this side of the Red Mist Mountains."

Of course they were. If they were on the other side, the mines would belong to the vampires. The western territory bordered the Blood Kingdom.

"Staret, how far away is it?" I pressed.

"With the latest snows? A half day by horse."

"Thank you." I nodded to the holy fae. "With this information, we'll be going. Staret Celi, have servants pack skins of water and food and bring them to the stables for our journey. Also send a guide to show us the way. Do not delay."

Staret Celi's eyebrows shot up in surprise that we'd kept our word. That expression was the last I saw of him before I turned.

"I remember where the stables are," I said to my companions. "Let's saddle up. If we leave now, we can get there by nightfall."

CHAPTER 52

VALE

Thanks to the punishing pace Neve set for the mountains, dusk neared as we closed in on Gersemi Mine. We had only needed to slow when we entered the mountains and the roads narrowed to allow for single-file travel, but if my little beast had it her way, we would have galloped for ten straight hours.

I'd never been more enamored with my wife.

"How far now?" Neve called out to the guide riding in front of her.

I tossed a smile over my shoulder at Caelo, who returned my grin with an amused shake of his head. He, too, enjoyed seeing my wife take the reins.

"Around this corner coming up, Princess Neve," said the guide, a male dwarf of around my wife's age.

I took the guide's race and the vast quantities of food and water we'd been sent off with as a sign of

Staret Celi's goodwill. Or intense fear. Either way, it worked in our favor.

Dwarves hailed from one of the two mountain ranges that bordered Winter's Realm. And though, over time, many of those dwarven mountain kingdoms had fallen, the dwarves understood the mountains and the pathways cutting through the great rocks better than most other races of fae.

"Thank goodness we're close," Anna piped up from the back. "My legs are exhausted."

"Riding all day will do that," Caelo agreed, shifting the quiver full of arrows on his back. Mine wasn't rubbing, but his motion was a good reminder to move, so I did the same. If you did not adjust your quiver every so often, you might wind up with a rash you didn't even feel coming. "You did well."

"I learn from the best." Pride laced Anna's voice.

While I was not used to being around a human in this way, during our journey west, Anna had grown on me. When we were not so rushed, I looked forward to getting to know my wife's best friend better. Perhaps even becoming friends with her myself.

"Slow!" The guide pulled back on his horse's reins. "Take this corner with great care. Parts of the road have eroded, and it's even narrower than what we've been riding on. In this spot, it's easy to fall off the side of the mountain."

The path we'd taken was already quite narrow. How did they get wagons up here to transport the gold and minerals?

"Should we risk it?" Neve stared over the edge of the mountain, into the wooded area below.

The guide replied, "Follow me and you will be fine."

"No," I said, recognizing an option that the dwarf did not, perhaps because it was not available to him. "Those who can fly will do so, leading the horses by the reins."

The dwarf frowned. "I will manage on my own."

Stubborn arse didn't want to be picked up. Fine, it was his life. "Do what you will. Anna, we'll come back for you and your horse."

The guide rode ahead, proving he could manage, while Neve, Caelo, and I teased our wings out of the slits in our cloaks. It might cost us a few minutes of daylight, but I did not regret my caution. The dwarf could gamble with his life. I would not do so with those under my protection. Especially not the one I loved.

Neve shivered and took her horse's reins. "It's colder with your wings out."

"They're sensitive," I agreed, already feeling winter's bite on the tender membranes, though my wings had only been exposed for a minute. "The sooner we get around the bend, the sooner we can tuck them away."

Neve slowly began guiding her horse around the corner. I breathed a sigh of relief when, from the other side, she called out that she'd made it.

I went next, leading my horse along. Thankfully, the horses were all well-trained and though I sensed the steed's anxiety rising, we made it around the bend where the path widened before the fear could catch. Caelo's crossing was even easier. He possessed elven blood and was undoubtedly using those powers to calm his animal.

Only Anna remained.

"I'll carry her," Neve offered.

"You're sure?" I asked.

"She wouldn't like you doing it. She barely knows you."

"Hopefully, that will change soon."

Neve beamed at me. "I hope so too."

Caelo followed, in charge of Anna's horse, and it took only a moment before Neve fluttered around the corner with Anna wrapped around her body. Caelo followed in short order.

"That was a production," the dwarf muttered.

"We didn't grow up on the side of a mountain, so shut it," Caelo barked.

The dwarf shrugged and waited for the rest of us to mount our horses before we carried on.

For the first time, the scene below was not overtaken by trees but rather a pocket of land that had been forested and dug out. The mine spread before us, just down the mountainside.

Neve leaned over her horses' neck and studied the area. "Looks like they've already shut down for the day, though." She squinted below. "Where are the houses? The people?"

According to the guide, the mine workers lived

outside of Guldtown, closer to the mines in which they worked.

"I don't know, Princess Neve," the guide said. "I've never come this far."

"What?" My wife's eyes flared. "Then why were you given to guide us?"

"My father, afterworld bless him, used to come with the lord. For much of the journey, it is the same as going to visit an old dwarf village where my family is from. I've been there to pay respects, and one visit, Father told me the way to the mines. In great detail too, hence why I knew about the eroded portion. Father liked to be detailed when it came to the mountains. Anyway, as you've seen, once you are on this road, there are no others until you reach the mine."

"Yes, I wonder at that," I said. "How do the wagons take the gold to the city?"

The dwarf shrugged.

My eyebrows pinched together. I knew little about the Lisika mines, but I would expect a person from the west to know more.

Then again, he does live in the city—on castle grounds, at that.

"There has to be another road," Caelo offered. "Perhaps one farther west."

"Must be," I agreed.

Again, the dwarf shrugged. "Down?"

"Down," Neve agreed.

Progress was slow, but that gave us the opportunity to take in the mine and any activity that might arise. On the last count, I remained confused. As my wife had observed, no one was outside. Nor any homes.

How could there be an active mine if there were no people to work it?

The guide twisted. "I'm not sure where to go from he—"

An arrow bolted through his gut and the dwarf fell forward, off his horse and onto the trail. The horse skittered a few paces down the path, her eyes wide and rolling.

"Neve!" I barked, my heart rate spiking. "Move!"

In an instant, the bow I'd taken from Roar's castle and attached to my saddle was in one hand, an arrow from my quiver in another. I knew without checking that Caelo had mirrored me, and I scanned the area down the path. Movement behind a tree that dangled from the side of the mountain gave away our attacker.

"Come out. Do not shoot, and you'll live." I nocked.

The attacker did not appear.

I pulled back my arrow. "One more chance."

A person leapt out from behind the tree, landing on the path, his arrow drawn and ready to fly. But they were too slow. The instant I'd seen the weapon, my own arrow was steaming through the air.

It sunk into the attacker's heart, and they fell to the snow, staining the white red.

"Bleeding skies," Neve whispered.

Something wasn't right. Why were we being shot at?

"Sentries," I motioned to Caelo. "The road widens

considerably from here on out. If it's easier to travel for us, it is for them too. There might be more."

"What about the dwarf?" Neve asked.

I gazed down at the guide. There was nowhere to put his body, but she was right. We couldn't leave him.

I dismounted and went to the dwarf. Hefting his body was easy. Easier than coaxing his horse to me, which necessitated Caelo's assistance. Finally, I slumped the body over the horse. It was the best I could do.

"Caelo, go first. This horse is trained to follow."

Wordlessly, Caelo readied his weapon again and took the lead. My wife rode after Caelo. I ushered Anna behind her and fell in line, my weapon at the ready. I spared only a glance to find that the horse carrying the body had indeed followed before I focused on the trail again and on the threats that might be lurking.

And thank the stars we were prepared, for as we descended the mountainside, three more archers, none of them particularly skilled, attacked. One by one, Caelo and I felled them.

When the last met the snow, Neve's horse stopped. She dismounted.

I stiffened. "Get back on your horse!"

"They're dead, Vale," she called back as she approached the body.

"Look out," I said to Caelo because I wasn't about to take my eyes off my wife.

Neve knelt next to the body and turned it over. Blood stained the male's chest, already seeping into the cloak he wore. It took only a moment for Neve to stand, her face pale.

"He's *human*."

"Excuse me?" Surely, I'd misheard.

"This is a human. Rounded ears, no lingering magical imprint whatsoever. And he hasn't been dead long enough for it to be completely gone."

"That makes no sense."

In this kingdom, humans were only slaves. Or in rare cases like Emilia, servants. They were allowed to work only in the Tower, the House of Wisdom, and noble homes, for there they would always have shelter, food, and protection. Out on the free market, it was not guaranteed that a human would ever be hired for work when many fae looked down on their kind.

Neve mounted her horse again. "I have a bad feeling. Let's get down there."

Still alert, we rode down into the carved-out portion of the mine. In the crater, I looked at the mountains surrounding us, their sharp peaks towering above.

There was nowhere for people to live. There had to be another road out of here, probably the same one for the wagons carrying gold to Guldtown.

"I would say let's look around"—Neve turned her horse on the spot—"but as far as I can see, there's nowhere to go. I—oh!" She pointed.

A female, dressed in thin clothing, walked out of the entrance into the mountainside. She was running quickly and did not see us.

"What is she doing?" Anna whispered.

Her question was answered a moment later when the female scurried up the crater that dipped into the dug-out mine and darted inside the trees. The human pulled down her pants and fell into a squat. I averted my eyes, as did Caelo. My wife and Anna, however, did not.

"Once she's done, we need to speak with her," Neve said.

"I think there may be a problem with that." Anna pointed. "She's spotted us."

"She's running!" Neve hissed. "Come on!"

She was about to run her horse, but galloping up the steep crater was risky for them.

"Fly," I said, and Neve didn't miss a beat.

She pulled her feet from the stirrups and soared. I followed behind her. We caught up with the female, and I flew up behind, ripping the female off her feet. That allowed me a first look.

A dirt-covered, thin face. Furious eyes. Rounded ears.

"Let me go!" the female—no, the woman—howled and kicked wildly. "Let me go!"

"We want to ask you a question," Neve said, landing and trying to appear calm, despite the fact that we'd chased the woman down. "Please. We don't want to harm you."

"Then let me go! I need to get back to work!"

"Work?" Neve sucked in a breath. "In the mines?"

"No, at one of the lovely shops just round the corner." The woman ceased her kicking and flailing

725

long enough to scowl at me. "What else is there around here?"

"Seemingly not much," I said. "But you're human."

"Well spotted."

I blew out a frustrated breath. "Why would you be working the mines and not fae?"

The woman stilled again, and this time, a dry laugh rang out of her. "The only fae I see are the lord and the few he brings with him. Fae don't work, mines. Humans do."

"That—is not what the rest of the kingdom thinks."

"Where is the village?" Neve asked.

"Village?" The woman's eyebrows pinched together. "Days away? I don't know. Everyone stays in the mines."

Neve stared at the woman for a moment before her gaze lifted to meet mine. "This makes no sense."

"Agreed." I murmured. "Lord Roar is supposed to be here. Where is he?"

For the first time, her scowl fell from her face. "My lord is where everyone else is—inside the mine."

CHAPTER 53

NEVE

The door to the mine creaked open, sending the scent of dirt and dust up my nose and a shiver down my spine.

Humans toiled down there, mining gold. And from the looks of her ragged, dirty clothing and gaunt face, she worked hard and didn't get out of the mines much.

My mother told me to come west. I'd assumed that she wanted me to journey west to confront Roar and obtain closure. Perhaps also to gather information on the Hallow too, though I was fairly certain that House Lisika had lost that.

But could she have sent me here for something else entirely?

Why would he use humans? Because they're free labor?

While that made a bit of sense, dwarves would still be far more effective and knowledgable when it came to the mountains. Stars, even faeries would be a better choice. All races of fae were stronger than humans and got more done in less time. And as much as I despised Roar, he was not stupid.

He had a reason for breaking the rules and running his mine as he did and something told me it wasn't all about gold.

The moment I stepped into the mine tunnel, motion-activated faelights flared to life. Good. Excellent vision aside, I didn't want to fall down a mineshaft. And though I hadn't let on, I worried about Anna's mobility in a place with such an uneven ground.

Gagged, the woman eyed me sidelong. We'd debated leaving her outside, tied to a rock, but Caelo had brought up the fact that these mines were very old and likely very maze-like. The human knew where to go, so we'd gagged her and told her to lead the way to Roar.

"Take us to your High Lord." I patted the sword at my side—the one I'd taken from my father's room. I had no intention of using it on the human. She was too helpless, but I would threaten to get her to do as I wished.

She reached to the side, patting the rope attached to the wall that miners used as a guide if the faelights went out. The motion said *follow me*.

And we did. Down a wider entry tunnel that progressively narrowed until we walked two by two. The human remained at the front, Vale beside me and Anna and Caelo at the rear. Though my best friend had not trained in weaponry, I'd given her one of my daggers. Better to be safe than sorry.

Faelights continued to ignite as we approached, but somehow the tunnels grew darker and darker. I shuddered. How could anyone work in these conditions? Let alone live down here as the woman had confessed before we'd gagged her . . .

The human stopped, and I nearly bowled her over. She twisted and glared at me.

"Sorry," I whispered.

With a sharp thumb, she gestured right.

Ah, she'd told us about this. The mines spun outward like a spiderweb, but it all began with a T, an initial breaking off point.

"Closer and single file," I said to the others. Vale slipped behind me, and I waited until the other two got into position before facing the human again. "We're ready."

The woman grabbed the rope and continued on.

Within minutes, another split occurred. The woman reached back and took my hand. Vale gripped my hip, saving his hand for Caelo, and Anna hung on to Caelo's cloak. Just as discussed. Three more splits in the tunnels later, and we remained connected, though I was feeling far less confident.

What if the woman is tricking us? What if—

The tunnel we'd been trekking down opened into a great cavern. I exhaled.

"Bleeding skies," Vale whispered right after me as we stared down into the bowl below. On the edges, homes had been carved into the rock, and in the middle, larger buildings of stone dominated the space. "It's as if a city built by dwarves crumbled."

I could see how this would resemble the ruins of dwarven cities. Though there were stark differences. A great lacking in this place that made me shudder.

Greenery grew in the dwarves' cities because dwarves, like fae, could have earth magic. Though most of them used it to shape metals, a few would be trained to work with plants to grow food. If there were enough of them, and a few limiters, fae with the power of sunlight, people might survive within the rock and never see the surface.

Humans, however, didn't have magic to help them survive under mountains, and I did not see healthy cascades of green. Just black and gray stone and the odd faelight or torch. Most of the buildings were in desperate need of repair too.

The woman waved us forward, and we descended steps cut into the stone. At the bottom, I took a moment to scan the surroundings. Carved into the walls of the mountains with open doors and open windows that allowed us to peek inside the homes was evidence of lives being lived. Blankets spread out on the floor and basic cookware littered their stone tables.

Though I was appalled by the conditions, the woman remained unaffected. She kept walking through the city, passing two larger, nicer homes built of stones. Through the windows, which were made of real glass, I spied a bed and other amenities that the other homes could not boast.

I pointed. "Are those overseer's places?"

She twisted to take in what I referred to and nodded. So at least two fae remained down here to keep track of the humans working the mines. How could they live with themselves? Slavery was permitted in the kingdom, but these conditions . . . well, they were exactly the reason the law stated that slaves had to be kept in noble homes, the House of Wisdom, or the Tower of the Living and the Dead. No one should have to live like this.

My fists clenched, but I said nothing more, just followed the human. Finally, we reached the end of the little city and approached another circular tunnel, delved deeper into the mountain.

"How much longer?" I asked.

She held up a finger, which I took to mean one minute. Soon I'd see Roar, and this would be over. I'd have the answers I needed.

"Don't let him manipulate you," Vale whispered.

"Never again," I agreed.

We entered the tunnel, and voices drifted over from the other end. The woman was correct in that wherever she was taking us had people, hopefully, Roar was still there too.

Faelights flickered on in waves as we walked. I both appreciated their illumination and wished they were not there. I'd much rather surprise Roar. That way, he had less of a chance to get his story straight and figure out ways to twist the truth, as he was so adept at doing.

The end of the tunnel came into sight. The sound

of people speaking intensified, but there was no echo of hammers. Wherever we were going, the miners must not be working.

When the tunnel opened, a stench assaulted me. It smelled like piss and shit. Before I inquired about the stench, the woman stopped and pointed down.

The scene before me froze my blood.

Near a hundred humans languished in cages. Some stood there, quiet. Others pleaded with some unseen figure; their palms pressed together. Faelights were not used here, but rather flickering torch lights illuminated their faces, dirty and miserable.

"What in the nine kingdoms?" I whispered, pulse quickening as I took in cage after cage after cage. "Is *this* where you live? I thought . . . the homes we passed . . ." I trailed off at a loss. The homes were still awful, but this was worse. Far, far worse.

The woman twisted, eyes wide, and shook her head. I wanted answers, so I reached out and extracted her gag.

"*I* don't live here. I work the mines and earn my keep!"

"Does he pay you?"

"My lord feeds and clothes us."

So that was a no. Just as I'd suspected. Roar was blatantly breaking the law for his own gain.

But that still didn't explain the caged people. My eyebrows pulled together. "Why the difference in their treatment?"

"*They* came in through the portal recently. Within

the last moon or two." She pointed to the far end of the rooms. Far away and beyond the masses of bodies, a faint light glowed. "Fae who work for the lord take them and cage them until the vampires come."

I stiffened. "Vampires?"

The woman nodded. "They buy them." She paused, fear flickering across her face momentarily before she donned a mask of steel once more. "I suppose that could be me. One day. If we don't mine enough gold, the vampires buy us too. But that hasn't happened in many turns. We always try to mine enough gold to keep our lord happy."

My vision dimmed. The mine disappeared, and I was transported back in Frostveil, the vampire prince cornering me, taunting me.

Prince Gervais had been so smug when he'd told me Roar had been duplicitous. What exactly had he said? I thought back, ripping at my memory until I reached that day and that terrible moment. He had said the Lisika mines produced gold for centuries and that one would think they'd need to diversify.

Diversify . . . My stomach dropped.

Can you think of nothing as valuable as gold, wildcat?

People. Human life. *Any life.* That was more valuable than gold.

Roar didn't just use humans to dig and labor in his mines. He sold lives, *human slaves*, to the Vampire Kingdom for gold. I swallowed. Did he really even need the mines? Or were they simply a cover for more nefarious purposes?

"Burning moon!" Vale hissed, putting things together, even without the thinly veiled hint I'd received from Prince Gervais. "He sells slaves!"

My body tightened as the horrible truth washed through me again, colder, harder this time. Roar, the male I'd once put my faith in, was a true monster.

I had been a slave. Roar had known it too—from the very moment we'd met. Perhaps that was why I hadn't seen slaves in his home. Maybe he'd hidden them. Or maybe he simply kept them all here—working to the bone in horrific conditions. I shook my head, unable to believe how stupid I'd been. How much I'd been able to overlook. Like how Roar had known about the potion the vampires gave slaves to keep them powerless. The Warden of the West knew so bleeding much about the vampire court because he was doing business with them.

My fists formed tight, furious balls and I glared down at the scene below, searching for the male I wanted to rip to pieces.

"I swear to the stars," I growled as frost crackled at my fingertips. "I will kill Roar for this."

CHAPTER 54
NEVE

My heart thundered as I sprinted down the stone steps leading into the basin of the captured. The soon to be enslaved. Behind me, the others raced to keep up.

To find Roar.

To demand an explanation and then . . . my fists bunched up as one caged human caught my eye and pleaded for help. Bleeding skies, the Warden of the West was a veritable monster.

At the bottom of the staircase, I whirled and stared at the female miner, still ten steps from the bottom. "Where is the high lord?"

She swallowed, unnerved by how I was acting. "He never delves far into the active mines, so I expect he's at the portal, waiting for more humans to arrive." She joined me and gestured through the line of cages.

More humans. How many did the vampires of the Blood Court purchase at one time?

I pushed the questions from my mind. The only ones that mattered were the ones that Roar would soon answer. "Show me."

The miner strode through the cages, illuminated by torches attached to the sides of their cages. Shockingly, the woman did not seem bothered by her own kind being locked up. I supposed that if one knew this happened, and they could do nothing about it, becoming hardened would not be so unthinkable. Perhaps her indifference was how she protected herself. After all, these humans were so close to the place she slept—where she raised her family, if she had one. A single wrong move, if she and the other miners didn't produce enough gold, then she would become like those in the cages. Sold for their blood. To be food.

Food . . .

My breath hitched as a memory of one conversation with Roar came rushing back. He'd told me of the local merchants who wished to import more from the Autumn Court for some reason I could not recall. But practically in the same breath he'd mentioned bringing in goods from the human world too.

When I'd asked what, he'd given a single answer.

"Foodstuffs."

The bastard! Was this what he'd meant? Food for vampires and not the fae of Guldtown?

"Neve, you must collect yourself." Vale came up beside me. "You're dropping the temperature, and these people aren't properly dressed."

I cut a glance to where he pointed at the cages, and

my heart stuttered. Frost covered the bars closest to me. Inside, humans shivered and huddled together, all of them clearly baffled by how the elements from outside were accosting them when we were deep within the mountain mines.

"How?" My voice wobbled as I whispered, not wanting anyone to hear despite them being powerless. That I could already use my magic was a source of pride, but I did not have complete control, and that scared me.

"Your power is responding to your emotions," Vale replied in a soft voice. "It's normal for new magic users. As you become more experienced, it'll happen less, but you have more raw power than most, so you must be careful."

I breathed in and out, steady and slow. Should I need to call my power when faced with Lord Roar, then fine. I'd unleash it to the fullest extent. Not here, though. Not around the blameless humans.

"Better," Vale assured me. "It's already warmed a bit."

I swallowed. "You remember the portal outside of Guldtown? The one you mentioned for supplies?"

He nodded.

"This isn't it, is it?" I had to be certain.

"No. The Guldtown portal is barely ten minutes from the city wall."

Again, anger flared. The bastard.

"This way," the miner said, not paying attention to

us as she cut hard around the final cages and led us to a circular tunnel similar to the ones we'd traveled through thus far, though flickering torches lined this one, not faelights. Just like the ones on the human cages. I wondered about that. Did Roar keep the circle of those who knew about this part of the mines small? So perhaps he did not trust a fae with the power of sunlight, a limiter, to come down here.

I found it unfathomable how one person could hide so much, twist the truth or omit it so well that no one in the wider kingdom learned of all this, but I felt certain that was what had happened. Whether through curated conversation or some magical means, Roar, and maybe even his predecessor, had spun a web of deceit that baffled the mind.

"Close now," the human said.

"Stay quiet then," I hissed.

"I will not say a word, my lady." For the first time, the human's voice trembled.

I felt bad for scaring her, and yet, I did not apologize. Later, perhaps. For now, I needed only to remain focused. The others seemed to sense that because Caelo and Anna had not said a word since we'd seen the soon-to-be slaves.

Then again, Anna might be in shock. Was this how her mother had arrived in Isila? My heart clenched and despite my seconds-old resolve to remain focused, I twisted to find my best friend at the end of our line, her gaze downcast, tears streaking down her cheeks.

I hadn't even thought to comfort her. What a terrible friend I was.

"Anna," I called out softly.

She looked up, sniffled.

"I'm so sorry."

She huffed a breath. "Make him pay, Neve. Make him *pay*."

"I will."

A large but gentle hand pressed into the small of my back. Vale's. "We're all with you."

"I know." I faced forward in time to see light flare up ahead.

"The portal is being used," the miner breathed.

"Right now? That's what the light was?"

"Yes."

"Slow down then," I ordered. "I don't want Roar to hear us approach. And let me go in front."

We were being quiet, but between the miner's heavy steps and Anna's uneven gait, there was some noise and Roar was fae. We had excellent hearing.

The miner fell back between Vale and Caelo, and I took the lead. When we reached the end of the tunnel, I held up a hand and peeked around the corner. A cavern about half the size of Frostveil's impressive throne room opened before me. Immediately, I located a flash of long, copper red hair.

Roar, Warden of the West, and all-around arsehole, stood to the side of a portal as one by one, humans stumbled through to join a group of five. He grasped the young human woman's hand, gave her a charming smile. She let out a laugh and the other humans, all female, tittered. They seemed to be a group of friends, and as I'd grown up with humans, I could guess that they were around my age.

Five other fae stood with Roar—four of them faerie guards donning the crimson and gold of House Lisika, and one unarmed, handsome faerie stood with Roar. The unarmed fae male wore casual clothing that had to be from the human world. The humans appeared excited to be in the mine, and content to look around. One young woman peered down a shaft that led who-knew-how-deep into the mountain. I would bet the jewelry I'd taken from Queen Revna's trove that he had lured these lovely human females here under false pretenses.

Humans did not simply stumble through portals into Isila. They had to come through either with a fae, or soon after a fae traversed the worlds. In the second case, it was usually a curious human following a fae through.

However, in this instance, I was sure they'd been baited.

I scanned the area. Torches illuminated parts of the cavern but left the vast majority in darkness. My eyes caught on a table and the basket of bread atop it. Rage simmered inside me, hot and fluid, making my blood pound in my ears. The table of food was probably lulling any sense of fear inside them, though it should do the opposite. If a human ate fae food, it meant that they'd be forever trapped in Isila.

I waved the human miner forward and pointed to where the woman still peered down the shaft. "How many of those shafts are there? And where are they located?"

"I don't come back here much," she whispered. "It's far from the active parts of the mines—a remnant of when the dwarves claimed this part of the mountain."

"Any help is useful." I sensed she held something back.

"That one that the woman is looking down," she said. "And there's another shaft in the darkness, along this wall and far, far back. Or so I've been told. They say it's large and goes the deepest. Some say to an unstable system too. We miners steer clear."

I kept that in mind and stepped out into the cavern. "You have some explaining to do, Roar."

Fast as a snake, he twisted away from the human he'd been flirting with and found me. Emerald green eyes became as round as saucers, but Roar recovered, and his lips curled up in an oily smile.

"Neve. You escaped Avaldenn, I see."

"E—escaped? Does that mean you've heard about what's been happening in the city?"

"Not since I left, but Prince Gervais was after you. It's why I had to leave. He threatened me."

I believed that. Prince Gervais had called Roar duplicitous, and he certainly had not wanted me under the lord's protection.

"Threatened to tell the king of your illegal endeavors too, I take it?" Vale stepped out of the tunnel behind me and from the corner of my eye, I saw Caelo waiting, sword in hand. Anna and the miner remained a few steps away from the opening of the tunnel. Out of Roar's line of sight. On Caelo's suggestion, no doubt.

"Vale." Roar's false pleasantness faded. "Why are you here?"

"I wouldn't let my wife travel west without me."

"Oh, right. Your wife." Roar drawled as if he didn't care at all. I suspected it was all one great farce.

"What are you doing with those humans?" I wanted to see if he'd admit it. Or if he'd talk in circles.

"Don't play stupid, Neve. You're too intelligent for such things."

No games then. Good. We were so far beyond them.

"How could you?" I stalked forward, frost forming at my fingertips.

Roar caught the magic, his eyebrow raising practically to his hairline. "Your potion wore off."

One guard pulled a sword and ushered the human females to huddle behind Roar, as if I were the dangerous one. As if I were the one who wanted to hurt them.

"Surprised at what power I wield?" I flicked my fingers above. Snow fluttered down, earning me a few *ooohs* and *ahhs* from the human women. Roar, however, smirked.

"You've known who I was since the moment Frode

dropped me on the ground in your throne room and you saw my scar, didn't you? You knew I was one of the Falk twins?"

For a moment, Roar didn't answer, but it was all the response I needed. He'd known.

"Don't try to twist the truth," I pressed. "I found Brogan's last note. In it, he spoke of a baby with a crescent scar, right where mine is."

This close, I caught the flicker of surprise ripple across his face before he hid it. The male was a master at hiding things.

"He spoke of something else too, Roar. An item long lost. One you told me about. One that might change the fate of this kingdom. Do you know where it is?"

"Brogan," Roar's voice resonated both with longing and annoyance. "The golden child. The heir. My brother—and a pain in my arse. To this day, it seems." He shook his head. "And of course I don't have it. My brother probably attracted attention on the road, bandying about the Scepter, and they were all killed for it."

For the first time, I got the sense that Roar blamed his brother for many of his woes.

"It's not your brother's fault all your family's secrets came to light. You shouldn't have loaned me the book."

"It seemed an easy enough ploy. Give a female who loves to read a library, give her all that she ever wanted, and a purpose. Tell her you need her, and most would fall in an instant."

"Fall?"

"In love. I wished for you to love me."

"We had a contract binding a false engagement, but you were really trying to force me into loving you!?"

"And I failed." Roar's green eyes narrowed. "You had to fall for the prince, the stupidest Aaberg."

My blood thrummed. "Don't speak about Vale that way."

"I'll speak of him however I want," Roar snorted. "You and him, you make no sense. But I told you, Neve. Together, we would have been *unstoppable*. A Falk heir, Princess Isolde, with the lord of the wealthiest house in the kingdom? One with an army to rival the royal army. We could have reshaped Winter's Realm! Do you have any idea how powerful the last Lisika and Falk marriage was? It unified the realm!"

My heart clenched. He'd even known which twin I was.

"*We* were never a true couple, Roar. Only on paper, but never in my heart, no matter how many times you tried to force yourself on to me." The number of times he'd tried to kiss me, to keep me close and cloistered, came back to me. I'd missed so many warning signs— taken them as acts of protectiveness for a female who held no power of her own.

Well, I was no longer that fae.

"Force himself on to you?" Vale growled. He came to stand next to me and a whine rang through the cavern as he unsheathed *Skelda*.

Roar laughed. "Are we to fight, then? In here?" His

cloak, the red color of House Lisika, fluttered as he gesticulated to the mine cavern.

"You act as though you don't deserve to die," I growled, prompting the women to take a few hurried steps back. "As though you didn't put me in so much danger. As if you didn't keep things from me and then left me to the wolves. And as if you're not, at this very moment, luring humans over and selling them into slavery!"

"*What?!*" one woman screamed and looked at the bait faerie. "You said we would go to a faerie ball!"

"Everyone's got to earn a living, love," the bait faerie replied, his accent odd, from the human world. Though I'd taken him as a full fae before, that he'd lied told me he had to be a half-blood, half human, most likely.

Still a cretin.

"Don't eat the food." I spoke directly to the humans. If they didn't eat, then they could return home. That was, as long as Roar did not close the portal.

Did he have that ability? Or had this one been left open since his father's passing?

Roar chuckled, ripping my attention back on to him, where it should have been. My eyes bulged. His soldiers had drawn their swords, but not Roar. No, he had nothing but a dagger on him. No bow and arrow, Roar's favored weapon, and nothing else large and powerful enough to best *Skelda*. Nor the sword I carried —the one I'd taken from King Harald's suite.

However, the Warden of the West didn't need steel.

Not when he possessed the deadly power of tooth and claw, each growing at a profound rate as he shifted. For the first time, I'd see Roar's shapeshifting ability.

And as his magic changed his body and another form took shape, I realized it might also be the last time I witnessed such a thing.

CHAPTER 55

NEVE

I blinked, taking in Roar's animal form, the glowing white fur patterned with brownish-red spots, his long tail flicking behind him. As lovely as he was deadly and so incredibly large. *Much* larger than I'd imagined. Or perhaps it was just Roar's shifted form, and the regular felines were smaller. Blindingly white and lovely, in this form, Roar had to be as large as the golden snow leopard statues flanking his throne room. Twice, maybe three times, Roar's already impressive size.

How to defeat such a creature?

"Caelo, out here." Vale rushed forward.

I suspected he was intending to go for Roar, but two of the faerie guards sprinted ahead of their lord to meet Vale. The others came at Sir Caelo, who raced past me a second later. Their swords clanged, the sound of metal-on-metal echoing in the chamber. Near the portal, the human women shrieked.

I risked taking my eyes off Roar and found that the faerie who'd lured the humans to this world was nowhere in sight. No doubt he'd escaped—slipped back through the portal to safety. The coward.

"Neve!" Vale shouted above the din of swords. "Arm yourself!"

I swallowed and called my powers. Roar had slipped around the fighting and had had his sights set on me, his pace slow, his gait as graceful as a true feline. Though his expression should have been unreadable, I thought I caught a smirk there.

We'll see who is smirking at the end. I unsheathed my sword.

Roar faltered, almost as if he'd recognized the blade. I took that opportunity to seize the upper hand, rushing forward, my free hand outstretched and magic flowing through me. A blast of frost momentarily blinded Roar and a hiss sang through the mine when my blade met fur. Blood sprayed across my face as I retreated before he lashed out with claws and teeth.

Would he kill me? I wasn't sure. Knowing my secret opened up many avenues of possibility for him. But one thing I was sure of was that the others weren't safe.

My throat burned to warn Anna and the miner to run, but I swallowed my words. Roar did not know they were there, and Anna could not feel the cold of shackles of slavery around her again. It might break her. If Vale, Caelo, and I did not survive this, I hoped they ran far, far away.

With protecting my best friend in mind, I sized up

Roar. He was not approaching, and I detected a familiar curious look in his eyes.

I realized that he wanted to see my magic in all its glory.

It was time I showed him.

Vale and Caelo were still fighting, both with magic and steel. Positioned behind Roar, it would be easy for me to strike them on accident. I could not risk it.

I cut a quick glance into the dark part of the cavern, the place where no torchlight reached. Where no one else could get hurt. Somewhere in there, along the wall we'd entered by, lurked a shaft. A large, deep one.

And Roar's wings are non-functional.

Was the shaft large enough for an oversized shapeshifter to tumble down? Did Roar know about it?

Before I questioned my own sanity, I raced into the darkness, banking sharply for the wall. A roar sounded, followed by the soft, padded footsteps.

My vision adjusted quickly, though the darkness was so complete, I couldn't see too far ahead of me. Just far enough that I didn't slam right into the wall when it suddenly appeared out of nowhere. Pivoting directions, I stuck my sword-less hand out, allowing it to graze the wall every few seconds, so as not to lose my way.

Keep going, I told myself when the darkness seemed to shrink in, raising the hair on my arms. Stars, it was terrifying back here. *Eventually, you'll find the mine shaft.*

In the darkness, Roar growled, and I realized that leaving my back unattended might soon spell disaster. So I whirled, listening for the direction that Roar followed, which turned out to be right behind me. He'd likely been scenting me. I called upon my powers and sent a storm of snow his way.

A hiss told me I'd struck true, and my heart leapt as his emerald eyes flashed in the darkness. My mouth went parchment dry. He was so much closer than I'd imagined. Leaping forward, I closed the distance between us, swiped my sword, and struck the snow leopard in the cheek.

He loosed a mighty roar, and lashed out with his claws, each one as long as my fingers. Before I moved out of the way, one caught on my shoulder and tore it open. Shrieking, my wings lifted me into the air as I struck again, this time right where his front limb met his torso.

Hot blood spurted across my neck, and before Roar so much as spun, I flipped in the air and sliced across his massive back quarter. More blood sprayed, invisible in the darkness, though I was sure that by now I was covered in it. Still, I'd won an advantage. Those injuries should slow him. They—

Roar reared back and a giant paw batted me out of the air against the stone wall. I groaned and slid to the floor. My skin burned from the scrapes and my heart raced, but fear was a greater motivator and somehow, with the help of the stars, I'd managed to keep hold of my sword. I shoved myself off the ground and took to the air again and delved deeper into the unnerving darkness.

"Neve!" Roar growled, telling me that he'd shifted.

In true shifters, that act would speed his healing. I wasn't sure it worked that way with fae shapeshifters but suspected that might be why he'd done so. "I would have spared you. But now . . ."

"You'll have to catch me to do anything to me," I shot back, hoping to enrage him, to blind him in his fury. "And a snow leopard can't fly as fast or far as a hawk!"

Furious, fast footsteps hit the stone as the shifter-fae raced after me, and for the first time, I allowed myself to feel my shoulder. The cut wasn't large, only about as long and wide as my finger. The scrapes from the wall felt worse, though I supposed that with how hard I'd hit the stone, I should have been thankful I could see straight.

"Someone's been training," Roar growled into the darkness.

I ignored him and focused on the darkness. Where in the world was the shaft? How far back did this cavern go?

I scanned the ground, safe knowing that Roar would not touch me, even if he caught up with me, for I could fly away.

I was still searching for the cavern when his next attack came, a surge of frost. I shuddered as it struck, and dropped a bit in the air, which Roar must have expected, for he sent another shower of icicles my way.

I gasped as one ripped across the top border of my wing, and I fell from the air, my sword dropping from my hands and skittering across the stone. I rolled as I hit the ground, crying out from the pain in my shoulder.

And stopped right at the edge of a mine shaft. My heart thundered. I'd almost fallen right into that vast darkness. Almost gave away my plan. Trembling, I pushed myself up.

A low rumble of a laugh rang out. "There you are."

He sounded conceited, but also tired. Vale claimed that Roar did not have much winter magic. Had he already spent that talent?

"Here I am," I retorted, smothering any fear I might feel in my voice.

"You've always had a feisty heart, haven't you?" Roar replied, his tone softer, taunting. "Even when dropped at the floor of my throne room, you scowled up at me like you might scare me away. Broken slave that you were."

My blood boiled. "I was not broken. Nor am I now."

"For now," he replied, his voice distorted. Vibrations filled the air. I guessed that Roar was shifting again.

When emerald eyes gleamed at me through the darkness, they were larger than normal. More feral too. Yes, he'd returned to his feline form, the more deadly form.

And still, I stood firm on the edge of the massive hole in the ground, waiting. Using myself as bait.

"Do I terrify you, Roar? A female who knows her true worth? One who sees you for what you are too?"

A hiss sounded and then those green eyes moved up, up, up. Roar was pouncing.

Though I envisioned sharp extended claws, I waited. Waited until those gleaming eyes got terrifyingly close, before dropping and flattening myself to the cold stone.

The snow leopard hit the side of the gaping shaft. Rocks tumbled, and claws scraped against stone, fumbling for a grip, before a feline wail shook me in my soul.

The seconds ticked on, and the sound grew fainter and fainter. My heart skipped a beat, barely daring to believe that my plan had worked. Roar had taken the bait and was now descending into the deepest pits of the mountain. I rose and stood at the edge of the shaft in time to hear a distant crunch.

Then nothing.

CHAPTER 56
NEVE

"Neve!" Vale's voice called out and torchlight flared in the darkness. "Where are you?!"

"Here!" I shouted back and began running toward him. "I'm safe and coming your way!"

He stopped, and I was at his side a minute later. Blood covered my prince, my husband, and my breath hitched.

"You're hurt," I breathed.

"Strike to the leg," Vale acknowledged. "It's superficial, though. Most of the blood isn't mine." His hand extended to hover over my shoulder. "What's this?"

"Claws."

He swallowed and his gaze then went to the scrapes marring one side of my face, my arm. "And I was batted into the wall, but I'm fine too. Much of this blood is Roar's from when I struck with my sword." I assured him when a feral expression came over his blood-spattered features. "Actually, I need your help to find my sword. It fell out of my hands."

"After you slew Roar?" Vale asked, eyes scanning the darkness. Understandable. Roar was a great warrior in his own right. But he hadn't been appropriately armed, because why would he be? He hadn't been expecting a fight. No one stepped foot in these mines unless he wished it.

"I didn't kill him. Not directly anyway." I grabbed Vale's hand and guided him back to where I thought I lost my sword. "He shifted and chased me. At least he chased me until the moment we came across a mine shaft large enough for him to fall into."

Vale blew out a breath. "Clever little beast."

My heart warmed. "I need to be sure the shaft is deep enough that he won't survive."

"I'll check for you," Vale said.

I nodded; glad he understood that I did not wish to do so. "Thank you."

As much as I'd wanted to kill Roar for what he was, for selling so many into a life of misery, I didn't want to see the body. I was not so bloodthirsty.

We searched for a few minutes before the torchlight cast upon my sword. I retrieved the weapon, sheathed it and then nodded in the wall's direction.

The shaft gaped open wide, far more intimidating with the firelight flickering on its edges.

"I can smell his blood." Vale's nose wrinkled. "And it's large enough to have devoured him whole. All that's left is to see how deep it goes."

"Careful." I took the torch from his hand.

He spread his black wings. "I will be. You never know what lurks in the depths of the mountains."

Before I could so much as wonder at what he might mean, Vale dropped into the abyss. The faint beat of his wings assured me of his controlled descent, but it didn't take long before I no longer saw him. In his absence, a cavern opened in my stomach that did not fill until an age later, when Vale reappeared, dust in his long dark hair.

"I didn't reach the bottom but went far enough to know that Roar would not survive the fall." He cleared his throat. "Stars save his soul."

The phrase was meant to comfort, to honor, and I suspected that even though Vale disliked Roar, it was a knee-jerk reaction. Polite or not, no such words would leave my lips. If Roar had earned eternal damnation in the afterworld, that was because of the choices he'd made.

"Vale!" Caelo called out, his voice far, far away. "Is there trouble?"

"None!" Vale replied. "We'll be right there." He looked at me. "Once we defeated the Lisika soldiers, Caelo set to helping those human women through the portal."

I exhaled a long breath as we hugged the wall and began walking back toward the illuminated portion of the cavern. "Thank the stars they didn't have time to eat."

"Agreed," he said, face wincing at his limp.

"Though I'm sure they're traumatized from what little they saw."

Still, those women had been lucky. So very lucky. The same could not be said for those in the cages not so far away.

My throat tightened. What were we going to do with those humans?

I did not voice the question as we made our way through the darkness and into the light. When I saw Anna, she let out a sob and rushed forward, throwing herself upon me.

"I'm covered in blood," I protested, trying not to see the guards Vale and Caelo had killed, their bodies already pushed up against a wall.

"I don't care!" Anna wailed. "I thought that monster was going to eat you, Neve!"

I patted her back. "I'm fine."

"Injured, though," Caelo said, coming closer, his nostrils flaring. "Some of that blood is yours."

"I only got a scrape," I replied.

"Only, huh? A warrior at heart already."

I smiled at him, and as Anna drew back, I caught sight of the female miner watching us warily. She hadn't left the relative safety of the tunnel that brought us into this cavern. Perhaps she could not. She was shaking so badly.

"Vale," I whispered and nodded to the miner. "What are we to do with them?"

He swallowed. "I don't know."

I was sure there were hundreds of miners working

the mines right now, in addition to the caged humans. Those who had been fated to be food for vampires.

No, that would never happen. Though I was not so optimistic as to think that the caged humans had not eaten the food of Isila, and therefore could go right home, they would not be slaves. Not to the vampires. Not to anyone.

"We need to take them somewhere safe," I said.

Anna nodded vehemently.

"Neve, we're quite far from . . . well, *anywhere*." Vale turned to me. "And it's not like we can take them to Guldtown and announce what we've done."

"Is there a nearby village that they might go to?" Even as I asked, I realized how silly it sounded. Fae thought humans, with their weak senses and no magic, were so very far beneath them. The prejudice ran deep, and it was unlikely that the humans could work anywhere as free people. Anywhere other than in this deep, dark mine, that was.

"No villages," Vale said and then cocked his head. "However, there is an abandoned dwarf stronghold where the Ice Tooth and the Red Mist Ranges meet. It's not ideal, and quite far on foot, but they might live there undetected."

"What are the chances of survival, though?" Caelo asked. "The mountains are harsh."

"Not great," Vale admitted. "It depends on the food stores they have here. And the condition of the stronghold when the dwarves left it."

Slim, but that was still something. I'd had a slim

chance of surviving when I'd escaped the Blood Court and I'd done it. I was still here. Perhaps the humans could survive too.

My chin lifted. "They deserve to have the choice of whether to stay here or move. Though staying will eventually mean slavery—still, they need to hear that. And be given an educated choice."

Vale nodded. "Agreed."

"Let's speak with them."

I turned, found the miner still standing there, listening to everything we'd said. She waved a hand, as if to escort us back, though this tunnel had no offshoots. We fell in line, Anna coming to walk by me, tears still glittering in her dark, slanted eyes.

"Are you well?" I whispered, knowing that all of this had to be a lot for her. Who knew if maybe her own mother had entered Isila through this very mine? If Roar had sold her to the Blood Court. I was no mind reader, but I felt certain Anna had considered these things too.

"Well?" Anna turned to look at me. "Neve, I'm so proud of you."

"Oh?"

"You're about to change so many fates."

Did she miss the part where the journey would be long? Brutal even. Or that when we got there, the humans, with their fragile bodies, might die anyway?

"It's dangerous," Anna said and kicked at a stray rock in the tunnel. "But giving them a choice—that's what matters."

"Yes," I agreed, understanding her words deep in my bones. "It does."

She reached out, took my hand, and we walked the rest of the way down the tunnel in silence.

The moment I heard voices, I steeled myself. And yet, seeing so many humans caged, still managed to suck all the breath from my lungs.

How could Roar have done such a thing? Had his father been a slaver too? Was selling bodies and souls to the vampires really how House Lisika had amassed so much wealth?

The answers lie at the bottom of a mine shaft. Splattered against the rocks. It had taken no time at all for me to end a family line and, though I wished for answers, I did not regret it.

The humans closest to the opening of the tunnel noticed us and fell silent. One by one, others quieted too. Odd, that. Before they'd cried for help, sobbed at their plight.

Then I remembered we were covered in blood. Ah, yes, that might bring up some questions.

The miner turned to me, eyes still wary, and stepped aside, as if to say *well, are you going to get on with it?*

A kernel of doubt seeped in, and I couldn't help myself as I glanced back at Vale.

He nodded. "You can do this."

He was the reassurance I needed. I exhaled, turned back to the humans, and released Anna's hand to raise both of my own.

"We're not here to harm you. Rather, the opposite."

I cleared my throat. "The fae who would have sold you to vampires is dead, and I'm going to release you and present you with options." I paused. "I assume you have been told that since you've eaten the food in Isila, you cannot return home?"

A single sob cut through the quiet, but no one looked surprised. Roar, or one of his soldiers, had told them. Probably mocked their pathetic fates.

"I'm truly sorry for that," I said, my voice a touch softer. "But you will not be sold to anyone. And we have a place for you to live, if you wish to go with us."

"Let us out!" a male voice bellowed. "Let us out and then talk!"

I nodded, already knowing what I'd do to free them. "Stand back from the doors of your cages."

In each cage, the humans backed away from the doors, and as I walked by every cage, I froze the locks. Vale and Caelo passed behind me, shattering the metal with vicious swipes of their swords.

In our wake, humans spilled out from behind the bars. Though I'd worried that some would try to flee and likely get lost in the mines, no one did. They huddled together, whispering.

When we were done and the last humans bolted for the safety of their own kind, I exhaled. I'd put all that I had into freezing those locks so that they could be shattered, and exhaustion settled into my bones.

But we were so far from done. I turned to find Caelo and Vale waiting for me, their swords now sheathed. Where was Anna?

I craned my neck around the warriors and a lump rose in my throat. My friend was standing with the other humans, talking to them. Was she telling them of our plan? Reassuring them?

Whatever she said, it had a visible effect on the humans. Though some wore sorrow, defeat, and a million other emotions on their faces, many looked looser. Not so terrified.

Vale shifted, so that there was a little space between him and Caelo. "We're with you Neve. Moral support and, if you'll have us, a queensguard."

All my breath left me at that word. *Queensguard.*

I looked to Caelo, who dipped his chin, agreeing with his friend—the prince he'd sworn his own sword to. Now that sword was mine, if I wanted it.

Do I?

The question froze me inside, and though I wasn't quite ready to answer it, I stepped between the two males, my guards. My friends. Together we approached the humans, all of whom fell silent.

Anna beamed when we stopped before the crowd of a hundred or so. Encouragingly, she nodded, and I assumed that whatever she'd told these people, they'd be receptive to our plan.

"You're now free," I said. "And while I have a place in mind where you might live, it's not ideal. It's far away, and we'll have to walk through the mountains of our kingdom."

"Which is where?"

Right. All that they'd seen was the inside of a mine.

"The Winter Kingdom of the fae," I replied. "It's always winter outside, in some form or another. Lately it has been very cold. And it will probably storm as we travel."

Many exchanged nervous looks.

"But I think it's the best shot you have at survival," I added. "You cannot stay here because, one day, vampires *will* come. They will be looking for blood slaves to fill their bellies." My voice hitched. "And if they take you to their kingdom, you will never again be free."

Silence rang, until one human, a woman with a few streaks of gray in her long brown hair, stepped forward. "Anna told us you're a noble, like the fae who caged us?"

"I am."

"But you were also once a blood slave?"

"Since I was young." I swallowed. "I do not wish that fate on any of you."

The woman nodded, as if that was all I needed to say to convince her, though Anna must have said far more. "I know nothing about these kingdoms, but freedom is better than being beneath a master. And I'm willing to risk the journey for mine. I'm coming with you, no matter the dangers."

One by one, others agreed until the entire group had chosen a chance at freedom. I exhaled, relieved, but only for a moment before the human miner stepped out of the group, a frown on her dirty face.

"And what of those who mine these mountains?"

She'd seen the dangers too. When the vampires journeyed here to pick up more slaves and found none in cages, they would still have options. The miners.

"I intended to ask you to join," I said. "We'll need you to help."

Her eyebrows screwed together.

"We'll need to pack food and warm clothing," I explained, gesturing to some people who wore pants cut off at their knees. Wherever they'd been taken from, it wasn't a land of eternal winter. "I'm assuming that the mining community has food and supplies?"

The female miner nodded. "We receive supplies— food, clothing . . . seeds, even."

I arched an eyebrow.

"One of the overseers has earth magic. He set up something that helps us grow underground. It's in a section of the mountain that we didn't walk through." She shrugged as if she didn't know how the magic worked, which she probably didn't.

"A fresh wagon filled with supplies came one moon back. I can't say if it'll be enough for so many." She turned and assessed the crowd. "But we have practice in stretching things. We have to do it all the time."

"Then come," I said, hoping that they all would.

The more the better. These miners, being so secluded in the west, might even know how to hunt or trap animals. In the new location, that could be the difference between life and death. Growing things without a fae gifted in earth magic would be difficult, but that was an issue for later.

"Fine," the miner said, and then, as if at a loss for what to say next, she broke from the group and headed to the stairs. "I'll go rally the rest of the miners. Tell them what happened."

"What of the overseers? And any guards?" From what I'd seen passing through the little city, there were at least two overseers, but the mines were vast. There could be more.

"You took care of the few guards who stay here. And the overseers are both probably dead drunk by now. We'll take care of them."

I swallowed and nodded as she left to climb the steps that led to the active mines. When I could no longer see her, I twisted back to the other humans, still standing there, most looking so lost, but some defiant— as if a spark had been brought to life in them.

I hoped they kept that spark and spread it into an inferno that consumed them. For that fire was what we'd all need to survive the journey to come.

THE NINE KINGDOMS OF ISILA

The Blood Kingdom - vampire
The Elven Kingdom - elves
The Winter Kingdom - fae of various races
The Autumn Kingdom - fae of various races
The Spring Kingdom - fae of various races
The Summer Kingdom - fae of various races
The Wolvea Kingdom - wolvea shifters
The Dragon Kingdom - dragon shifters

*** Each kingdom is colloquially described as a court, though technically, the court is a specific place or places in the larger kingdom.

Some kingdoms have additional names, such as the Winter Kingdom being called Winter's Realm or the Dragon Kingdom being called the Kingdom of Flame.

THE HIGH NOBILITY OF THE KINGDOM OF WINTER

HOUSE AABERG - ROYAL HOUSE
King Magnus Aaberg
Queen Inga Aaberg née Vagle

Children
Prince Rhistel Aaberg
Prince Vale Aaberg
Princess Saga Aaberg

The royal house is not a part of the Sacred Eight.[1] They do rely heavily on the families of the Sacred Eight but the royal house is distinct from all others.

Before the White Bear's Rebellion, House Aaberg was a member of the Sacred Eight. Since the rebellion House Riis took their place as a reward for loyalty to House Aaberg.

❄

THE SACRED EIGHT FAMILIES OF WINTER'S REALM

* Lord Sten Armenil - Warden of the North - Head of House
* Lady Orla Armenil née Balik
Children
* Marit Armenil - female
* Connan Armenil - male
* Rune Armenil - male
* Tiril Armenil - female
* Jorunn Armenil - female
* Raemar Armenil - male

* Lady Vaeri Ithamai - Warden of the East - Head of House
* Lord Tiarsus Itamai née Skau - deceased
Children
* Hadia Ithamai - female
* Adila Ithamai - female

* Lord Tadgh Balik - Warden of the South - Head of House
* Lady Kilyn Balik née Armenil
Children
* Sian Balik - male
* Baenna Balik - female
* Eireann Balik - female
* Saoirse Balik - female
* Fionn Balik - male
* Garbhan Balik - male - deceased

* Carai Balik - female
* Filip Balik - squire to Prince Vale of House Aaberg - male
* Colm Balik - male

* Lord Roar Lisika - Warden of the West - Head of House

Unmarried

No children

* Lord Leyv Riis - Head of House

Unmarried

Children (only the children at court are included)

* Luccan Riis - male
* Arie Riis - male
* Thantrel Riis - non-binary

* Lord Airen Vagle - Lord of Coin - Head of House
* Lady Eliana Vagle - deceased
Children

* Queen Inga - married to King Magnus Aaberg
* Captain of the Royal Guard Eirwen Vagle - Father to Lady Calpurnia Vagle - his wife has passed to the afterworld
* Fival Vagle - acting lord in their family seat in the midlands - male
* Selah Vagle - married to a wealthy Jarl in the midlands - female

* Lady Nalaea Qiren - Lady of Silks - Head of House

* Lord Virion Qiren née Ithamai - deceased Children

* Aenesa Qiren - female

* Thalia Qiren - female

* Iro Qiren - female

* Lady Fayeth Virtoris - Lady of Ships - Head of House

* Lord Kailu Virtoris née Oridan, from the Summer Court

Children

* Vidar Virtoris - betrothed to Princess Saga of House Aaberg - male

* Sayyida Virtoris - female

* Njal Virtoris - male

* Amine Virtoris - female

EXTINCT GREATER HOUSES - ALL MEMBERS OF THESE NOBLE HOUSES WERE KILLED DURING THE WHITE BEAR'S REBELLION

House Falk

King Harald's royal house

House Skau

Queen Revna's birth house. She married into House Falk and had six children with King Harald.

Beneath the Sacred Eight there are hundreds of lesser houses. These are led by jarls of various territories.

---

1. Prior to the White Bear's Rebellion, the Sacred Eight were actually the Sacred Nine, with House Skau being the ninth member, and House Falk being the royal house.

ACKNOWLEDGMENTS

This book was such a joy to write, and I can't wait to continue the story of Neve and Vale and Winter's Realm.

First and foremost, thank you to my husband, my biggest cheerleader and best friend. I can't believe I get to do this life with you.

To my local writer friends, another thank you. Many of you won't even read this book (not your genre, I get that!) but you've made such a difference in my life. This career is a solitary one, but having local writing friends to talk with makes all the difference.

I'd be remiss if I didn't thank Booktok and all those reader who have shared, reviewed, and loved on The Winter Court Series. To say that app has changed my career is an understatement.

A huge thank you to my ARC team, especially the members who spotted and sent me those last pesky typos prior to publication. Lacey Mullins, Sadie Nickles, Shaelynne Marshall, Carlie Taylor, Bobbie Jo Schultze, Debbie Turk, Natalie Baker, Donna Daigle, Lauren Searcy, Megan O'Lena, Francesca Knowles, Katie Lewis, Mortisha Johnson, Alexis Almanzar, Erica Keating, Gijzette Strickland, Teighlor Dantzler, April Stacey,

Barbara Zukowski, Marie Reed, and Saundra Wright, thank you so very much for your help.

To all my readers, thanks for picking up Neve's story. I hope you'll continue it in A Hallow of Storm and Ruin.

All the magic,
Ashley McLeo

ALSO BY ASHLEY MCLEO

The Winter Court (Crowns of Magic Universe)

A Kingdom of Frost and Malice

A Lord of Snow and Greed

A Hallow of Storm and Ruin

A Crown of Ice and Fury

Coven of Shadows and Secrets (Crowns of Magic Universe)

Seeker of Secrets

Hunted by Darkness

History of Witches

Marked by Fate

Kingdoms of Sin

Bound by Destiny

Standalone Novels

Curse of the Fae Prince (The Spring Court: Crowns of Magic Universe)

Spellcasters Spy Academy Series (Magic of Arcana Universe)

A Legacy Witch: Year One

A Marked Witch: Internship

A Rebel Witch: Year Two

A Crucible Witch: Year Three

The Spellcasters Spy Academy Boxset

The Wonderland Court Series (Magic of Arcana Universe)

Alice the Dagger

Alice the Torch

The Bonegate Series - A Fanged Fae sister series

Hawk Witch

Assassin Witch

Traitor Witch

Illuminator Witch

The Bonegates Series Boxset

The Royal Quest Series

Dragon Prince

Dragon Magic

Dragon Mate

Dragon Betrayal

Dragon Crown

Dragon War

About the Author

Ashley lives in the lush and green Pacific Northwest with her husband, their dog, and the house ghost that sometimes makes appearances in her charming, old home.

When she's not writing fantasy novels she enjoys traveling the world, reading, kicking butt at board games, and frequenting taquerias.

For all the latest releases and updates, subscribe to Ashley's newsletter, The Coven. You can also find her Facebook group, Ashley's Reader Coven.